SALTSWEPT

SALTSWEPT

KATALINA WATT

First published in Great Britain in 2025 by Hodderscape
An imprint of Hodder & Stoughton Limited
An Hachette UK company

The authorised representative in the EEA is Hachette Ireland,
8 Castlecourt Centre, Dublin 15, D15 XTP3, Ireland (email: info@hbgi.ie)

1

Copyright © Katalina Watt 2025
Map illustration © Charis Loke 2026
Katalina Watt photograph © Magdalena Kaminska 2024

The right of Katalina Watt to be identified as the Author of the Work has been asserted by them in accordance with the Copyright, Designs and Patents Act 1988.

All rights reserved. No part of this publication may be reproduced, stored in a retrieval system, or transmitted, in any form or by any means without the prior written permission of the publisher, nor be otherwise circulated in any form of binding or cover other than that in which it is published and without a similar condition being imposed on the subsequent purchaser.

All characters in this publication are fictitious and any resemblance to real persons, living or dead, is purely coincidental.

A CIP catalogue record for this title is available from the British Library

Hardback ISBN 978 1 399 73504 9
Trade Paperback ISBN 978 1 399 73505 6
ebook ISBN 978 1 399 73507 0

Typeset in Adobe Garamond Pro by Manipal Technologies Limited

Printed and bound in Great Britain by Clays Ltd, Elcograf S.p.A.

Hodder & Stoughton policy is to use papers that are natural, renewable and recyclable products and made from wood grown in sustainable forests. The logging and manufacturing processes are expected to conform to the environmental regulations of the country of origin.

Hodder & Stoughton Limited
Carmelite House
50 Victoria Embankment
London EC4Y 0DZ

www.hodderscape.co.uk

For Craig

Part One

Getting the Crew Together

CHAPTER ONE

FINLYR

IT'S A HOMECOMING that feels more like being kicked in the belly than being greeted with warm, open arms.

'State your business,' the Seaguardian asks with bored indifference as we dock.

'Returning home.'

They look me up and down and sniff. 'Name and origin?'

'Larkin, Spring Isle.'

'There's a tithe to dock a ship. Are you the captain?'

'Aye,' I say through gritted teeth, indicating a crate of assorted goods. 'Collected from my passengers. Some returners, some visitors.'

The Seaguardian inspects it for a moment before nodding and letting me pass through. My duty to my passengers ends here. When the news of Paranish opening reached Lassair, mine was one of the only seaworthy vessels ready to set sail. Most of the others were tethered to the floating market and chose guaranteed trade rather than take a chance on Paranish. It was unknown to the locals and after it had been closed off to trade for centuries, folk were wary of sailing all the way out there. But I was Paranishian and still had my native tongue, although it had been a few years. My ship – *Saltswept* – was barely finished with repairs, but I jumped at the chance to go home. No, more than that: the chance to leave Lassair and the memories of my latest voyage. What should have been my last. As we hauled to Paranish, my passengers dreamed of beds warmed by lovers or hearths stoked by family. I have nothing but cold cider and strangers waiting for me in the capital.

I sling my pack over my shoulder and feel the solid ground beneath my feet. I've a thirst to quench.

Meandering the streets of Umasa is akin to finding your way to your bed drunk and in the dark. Desperate and nauseating. The streets are narrow and the buildings close, pressing down on you. It's just as I remembered. The same salt-washed grime in the alleys, dirt beneath my fingernails I never quite got out.

I've arrived on market day, with strange stalls put up faster than I'd have thought. Foreign smoky herbs waft over from a wooden structure furnished with colourful silks. Bright birds perch on a table with gleaming gems in their beaks, the sunlight catching their feathers and the sparkle of their wares.

We're all creatures of comfort, no matter how far we crawl from home. I creep through the crowds, unfamiliar voices thundering in my ears. I catch traces of Lassren on the wind and cock my head like a dog.

'How much is this?' a Lassairian trader asks.

'Value in the eye of the beholder, dear heart,' replies a Nishian merchant in a clipped, serious tone.

'What does she mean?' the Lassairian trader asks, turning to their companion.

'You mark its worth,' their companion explains in Lassren. 'Offer her something.'

How simple when folk say what they want. None of this circling each other like beasts before the fight. You want; I have. You give; I take.

Holy Aistra, I need a drink. No, not just a drink. I need a piyata cider.

I slink away from the noise, down the wynds and closes that newcomers to Umasa avoid. They're dark and narrow and only lead you somewhere if you know what you're looking for.

This is my old haunt, but I keep my hand close to my hilt. Many fools get soft and comfortable after years away from home. I'm no fool.

The tavern is nearly empty, which suits my purposes. I mark a table in the back nook and signal the keep. The wooden table is sticky with decades of spilled cider, and the fabric of the chair has darkened and worn where elbows and shoulders have rubbed against it. I survey the other patrons sitting in the cosy glow of the candlelight. The day outside is bright and bustling, whereas we have sought the solace of dark and quiet corners.

'You one of those returned wanderers?' the barkeep asks as they take my order.

I squint to focus on their face dancing in the candlelight.

'Aye, back on Paranish soil.'

'You'll have plenty of goods to barter then,' they say with a tight smile.

This motherland courtesy hiding sharp teeth again.

'Oh, I'm good for it,' I wink, and they head off with a nod and grunt.

I wrap my hands around the cold mug and sip slowly, feeling the tart and sweet flavouring burning my tongue. Soon I'm pleasantly light-headed and the drink goes down quicker. My thirst might be quenched at the bottom of this cup.

After a few rounds, I catch the man at the next table dipping into my bag, fiddling with the sliders and latches, trying to unlock its secrets. Thinks I'm cider-soaked, the cheek. The place is louder now, drinkers swimming at the edges of my vision. I swing at the man's face and miss, my body crashing into him hard instead. His knee meets my belly and then we're brawling, the bright, sharp pain of flesh on flesh. Of everything being on the table, teeth bared, nails on skin. He catches me in my bad leg, and I go sprawling.

When I wake, I'm on the ground, but not the tavern floor. It's the packed earth of the alley. My entire body hurts. The stone wall is cold and rough, and this is as good a place as any to close my eyes again.

'You all right, stranger?' A gentle voice wakes me from my momentary slumber.

I peel open my sticky eyes and some dirty-faced waif peers down at me.

'Aye,' I say, beginning to stand. 'Gathering my bearings, is all.'

The waif helps me up, surprisingly strong under that wiry frame. 'Are you sure?' they ask.

'My thanks, but I know my way from here,' I reply, leaning against the wall for support.

Their face is swimming in and out of focus as they say: 'There's an inn at the corner of that street. The keeper's named Narra. She'll see you right.'

My mother tongue of Nishian is too dulled by the cider to say more. I simply nod and grunt assent.

'Make sure you get yourself to bed, all right?' they say.

I stare at the stonework of the alleyway, listening to the revellers inside the tavern. The ground smells like cider and piss. When I can finally turn my head without wanting to be sick, the stranger is gone. I crawl away from the stench towards the next building.

The darkness creeps at the edges of my vision and I could just sit right here and close my eyes. Even with my eyes closed the world is spinning. The best cure for that is sleep, and I pass into the unquiet slumber of the drunk.

The soft light of the dawn wakes me gently. When I open my eyes I jerk up at the sight of a Seaguardian. Fuck.

'Up you get, pal,' he says, voice gently mocking as he hauls me to my feet. I let out a breath and lean into him, moving my scabbard behind my cloak. Better he thinks I'm some helpless sailor. 'You have lodgings?'

I stare at him. He's clean-shaven and younger than I first presumed, with hair cropped close to his head. His crooked nose is the only thing that breaks the symmetry of his face, but it makes him more intriguing to look at.

'Somewhere to call home for the day?' he elaborates, eyes roving over me.

'This is my home,' I croak, and he laughs.

'Oh, a returner. Welcome back to Paranish. Are you from Umasa?'

'That I am.' I make a show of eyeing his pristine white uniform, the embroidered blue wave and sunrise sigil. 'And you're a Seaguardian.'

He stands a little taller, jutting out his chin. 'Indeed.'

'My mother was of your noble profession.' I make my voice a low, soft growl.

I follow the Seaguardian's eye to the shopfront I was unwittingly using as a bed. Wooden stands and drapes of cloth protect its wares, but I clearly see the rectangle of books beneath. The painted sign hangs from the awning: *Good Morna's Victuals and Volumes*. Not something you see every day. Books were the worst thing to barter. Heavy, perishable, and useless unless you could read. No wonder the shop's main goods were food and drink.

'In need of a bedtime story?' I ask, quirking my brow. I finger the Seaguardian emblem, and his eyes turn hungry.

'If I remember correctly, there are some barracks not far from here.'

Nestor liked to fuck completely naked. Most of my trysts involved only getting as much clothing off as needed to do the deed.

'I want to feel all your skin on mine,' he says, unlacing the front of my shirt.

I stop his hand. 'What if we play a game?' I ask, unbuttoning his breeches. 'I can be the Seaguardian—'

'And I'll be the queen,' he says, words tumbling out. The blood rushes to his face.

I take off my belt, not missing a beat. We all have authority complexes, parental issues – name your poison. Nestor has already commanded the bunkmates out. Not that I'm against an audience, but now I understand why he wanted to keep this between us. The Seaguardians are supposed to worship the queen. Role-playing as her is a particularly perverse form of treason. Lower-ranking officers have been hanged for less.

He fashions a dress out of the bedsheet, and I slip into his uniform, pulling the jacket closed when his eyes are averted. Nestor grabs me, planting kisses on my collarbone. By Paranish, his lips are inches from the brand. If he sees that mark, it's all over. I won't be some nameless sailor. He won't be able to overlook the cutlass. He'll have to ask questions about where I've been for the last decade. Getting a good, no-strings fuck after months of a drought is never as simple as it seems. I push him against the wall and trace kisses down his body, dropping to my knees. I need to distract him and so I take him in my mouth. He moans, his fingers in my hair. And then he pulls my head back and the moans die in his throat.

His jacket has fallen open, revealing the brand on my chest: a line tattoo of a cresting wave and a sword. Nestor pushes me onto the bed, and I fall back, breeches round my ankles. He's out into the main barracks before I can hide the mark and then there are hard hands all over my half-dressed form. By Paranish, I'm done for now. I swallow, trying to find my honeyed tongue.

'Save your spittle, pirate. We'll find out your true name and deeds soon enough.'

CHAPTER TWO

RIS

BIBA IS TRYING to help again. She's a small figure in her dark dress among the white sheep, the scant streaks of golden wool catching the light. I watch her from the open door of the barn, pausing my work at the loom. There's a warm sun today, but a tickling breeze moves through the trees, bringing salt spray up from the coast.

'Fetch, this way,' Biba tells the dog, running after him as he does the real work of getting the sheep to their pen.

She runs up to me, panting, dog at her heels. 'Look, this one has gold in it.' She shows me a scrap of wool, which one of the sheep has shed. 'Only the finest Spring Isle wool,' she says in such a serious tone that I can't help but laugh.

'Even if it is to wipe that mewling maw.'

Her eyes go wide.

'Aistra bless their birth,' I mumble quickly.

There's to be a baby at the Bastion, the only possible heir now that the king has passed. That will be my task for later: weaving this wool into a pattern fit for a royal blanket.

Biba stares at the wool, holding it up to the weak sunlight. She frowns. 'Why is there so little?'

I sigh. 'I don't know, my love. But we must make do with what we have.'

I take a deep breath and survey the farm: the cottage at the top of the hill and the shed where we shelter the vegetable garden, and at the bottom of the hill the hardy orchard firmly away from the sheep's pen. My ancestors built the farmstead from two robust golden sheep, impressing the royals with the lustre and quality of the work we produce. We've kept the home fires burning for generations. But some kind of sickness is taking hold, and everything I've tried has failed.

We switch positions, with Biba in the barn and me in the fields. The hours pass quickly as Biba cards the wool, brushing out the clumps and knots to create a soft, flat layer for the spinning wheel. I keep an eye on her from the field as I shear the sheep, the rhythm of my work lulling me into a focused trance. Fetch disturbs me every once in a while, for belly rubs. My body knows the way, years of daily toil. Biba's about the age I was when I took on the trade. It took time to remember my father's words, to find my own way of teaching her hands to hold steady. But I was nothing like her, nothing extraordinary.

I make my way back to the barn with the meagre basket, my mind already on the loom in the corner and the next months of labour. The queen is still early in her pregnancy, but a babe arrives whenever it sees fit. Hopefully we'll be done before Magliyab festival. Biba is catching on fast, but teaching an apprentice means half the work gets done in double the time.

Fetch slinks in behind me, whining at Biba and sniffing at her pockets.

'I've nothing for you,' she says. He knows treats have been off the menu for months now, but I suppose he's a hopeful dog. We all have a hunger in our eyes these days.

Biba is holding something small and furry in her arms. Fetch jumps onto his hind legs, trying to lick it.

'Down, Fetch. Bad dog.'

He huffs and whines but gets back down on all fours.

I approach Biba and feel the marbled tufts under my fingers. An otter-cat. Stiff but still warm.

'Where did you get this?'

'In the field.'

I look over at the basket of carded wool. It's not as thorough as if I had done it, but I can't reprimand her for shirking her duties. There is so little of my time for her, and the guilt weighs heavy on me.

I examine the creature again – it's not much more than fur and bones. 'It probably starved. There's not much food. Even the fisherfolk are bringing in smaller catches.'

Her shoes and dress are muddy, a tear where the hem has caught on something. I sigh and add it to my mental task list.

'You must leave the dead in peace.'

She scrunches her face. 'I don't think it is dead.'

I smooth her hair down. 'It is – just look at it, my love. I'm sorry.'

'No, I can feel warmth. There's part of it still in here.'

She strokes the dead thing tenderly, petting its smooth head and whispering incoherent soothing sounds. It's a grotesque spectacle. I reach out to stop her hand. The otter-cat thrashes suddenly in her arms, desperate to get out of her grasp. It yowls and jumps down, landing feet first on the floor. After a moment's hesitation, it bolts out of the house and into the trees at the edge of the field. Fetch gives chase, barking in alarm.

'Fetch, heel boy!'

The dog stops in his tracks but keeps an eye on the marble blur, now halfway to Alev.

'See!' Biba claps her hands in triumph.

I glance around, but only the sheep are watching. The otter-cat was dead; it was definitely dead.

I watch Biba sleep that night. She runs warm, cheeks red as apple blush, sweat plastering her dark hair to her face as she swipes at invisible enemies in her dreams. When she was a baby, I told myself this was for her, that it was safer for me to keep her close in case anything happened in the night. I'm still unmoored by the emptiness in the bed, where he used to lie. Sometimes I think I feel him, hear his laughter rippling across the fields. I hope he is as unmoored as I am, drifting forever between worlds. The guilt stabs at me but it isn't as sharp as my rage towards him, even after all this time.

Biba is so much bigger now and I can barely fathom that six harvests have passed since she was born. She strives towards independence every day. It was no comfort when she started to walk. Now I can barely keep track of her, coaxing her out of her hiding places in the woods. One day she will carry herself clear off the Spring Isle.

I've returned to the warmth of my bed when a tapping penetrates my uneasy slumber. There's a dark mass outside the window and I grab the wooden rod for the shutters, bracing. Once my eyes adjust, I see it's the otter-cat, yellow eyes catching the moonlight. It meows gently and I hesitate. It rolls over onto its belly. An invitation for pets. I open the window and rub the soft fur until it purrs blissfully, eyes rolled back in pleasure. The purring gets louder and faster, an intense vibration as though the creature's belly is full of bees. I snatch my hand back. The otter-cat writhes, yowling, its belly spurting blood. It falls off the windowsill and onto the rug with a sickening thud, no longer moving.

I clap my hand over my mouth and try to contain my shock. The blood pooling on the rug smells sweet, like sheep's milk left in the sun. I turn to see if I've woken Biba. She's sat up in her bed in the corner of the room, staring wide-eyed at the gruesome scene. I leap back when I see her.

'Did I do that?'

Her tone is strange, a combination of remorse and morbid curiosity.

'No, my darling. The otter-cat was sick.'

I will not linger on it, lest I make it true. This is an unspeakable power. Holy Aistra, I cannot let them take her from me.

CHAPTER THREE

HANAN

I CAN TASTE the winds whipping across from the mainland, turning to ice as they reach us. The waters of the Winter Isle are swimming with restless souls. Death extends her fingers towards me, and I pull my thick cloak closer, clutching the dark stone talisman around my neck. A carved triangle to represent the strength of the collective of the Temple Sisters and Mothers.

'Do you feel it?' I ask Malostra, closing our bedroom window.

I breathe in the lingering scent of sea salt, sweat, and fraying rope.

Malostra gets up with a sigh. 'Save it for the Mothers, Hanan.'

I stiffen at her words but follow silently as we make our way into the hall. Many of the other Temple Sisters are already gathered, pools of dark dresses and cloaks in the glowing candlelight, and we join them. Above us, there is a large painted glass that depicts the Bastion, beyond which the real Bastion is visible, and we hold our dark faces aloft towards it. The clouds that blanket the Winter Isle part for a moment and sunlight penetrates the cold glass, reflecting a dozen colours onto the stonework floor. I've looked at this every morning and night since I was a child at prayers, ever-present and reassuring. I smile reassuringly at Sister Hoss, who bites her lip and holds the trailing hem of her gown. I remember the overwhelming awe of my first ritual: a feeling of finally being among people like me, of being part of something bigger.

'Sisters of Aistra,' Mother Joca intones. 'Death has come to us today, as it does every day. There is a disturbance in the waters. Some of the strongest amongst you may have felt it.'

I can feel Malostra's eyes on the back of my neck, but I focus intently on Mother Joca.

'We feel the hurt of the dead, their confusion. Let us guide them to the Tree of Life.'

We fan out into the triangle formation, and I take my place beside Mother Lin and Sister Hoss. We hold hands with our neighbours, feeling the warmth of their skin on our own. Hoss's skin is clammy, and she fidgets, trying to loosen my grip.

'Touch is a strong bond,' I whisper to her. 'Do not fight the connection.'

We chant together: *Blood feeds the Roots. Salt feeds the Sea. Song feeds the Sky,* our voices starting low and controlled and rising, first like furious birdsong, then like the waves crashing against the isle. The heat between our hands becomes too much. It feels as if all my skin is on fire. At last, we let go, and I open my eyes, bringing my palms in front of my face. A bright green vine springs forth, pushing its way through my skin and unfurling upwards. I watch as it stretches languidly, and a flower grows from a bud to full bloom in an instant. It blossoms and pulses, a shimmering, vivid ocean blue.

Mother Lin laughs, and I look around as the other women display their floral offerings.

Hoss cries out in alarm at the small bud writhing on her skin.

'You must worship it,' I tell her, placing my hands gently on her shoulders. They lower slightly and she observes the plant, like it's a beast that might bite unbidden.

I grab Hoss and Malostra's hands and we form another, smaller triangle.

'It's the strongest shape,' Malostra explains at Hoss's wide-eyed expression.

The Sisters and I walk in a silent, reverent row to the temple courtyard. The wind has died down and snow falls softly, settling on our cloaks as the Tree of Life stands proud and gnarled. It spans the width of our wingspan several times over and is taller than the temple itself. It's branches and vines reach up towards the clouds, the streaks of colour running vertically up the bark. At its base, hardy flowers such as thrift, lavender, and buckthorn vie for sunlight and resist the salt-laden breezes.

We gather in a crescent moon around the roots, placing our hands on the Tree's petrified bark. It pulls and sucks on my skin as I make contact, thirsty for the nutrients of the plant I've created. I try to resist the maelstrom of my thoughts and focus on the background humming of the Tree, the power of my Sisters.

A man is close to death. The breath is being forced from him. He is choking, regretting a half-life lived well but lived grasping, guzzling the small joys as they came. He is grieving, haunted by a past from which he hasn't moved on. Then he becomes distant, less potent. Now I feel others: human, plant, animal, their terror and confusion like iron on my tongue and stones clashing in my ears.

'Do you have a hold on them, Sisters?' Mother Joca asks.

I struggle to grip their souls, each as slippery as a fish.

As we grip each other's hands, our minds begin to coalesce, our flesh and souls entwining. At first it is an echo, and then all the Sisters' voices come together. In my mind's eye we are standing in a deep well, the roots of the Tree of Life a spiral staircase leading to the bottom. Every Sister stands on a step, their hand on the shoulder of the Sister in front of them in an unbroken chain. The souls are the wind in our hair, passing down through the tunnel of the staircase. At the bottom there is an endless void, and the souls shriek out in fear. We tell the lost souls to move forwards, to pass to the other side. A bitter tang of a thought worms into my mind: we're told they sleep in eternal silence in the Tree of Life, but I don't know what's beyond. Why should they listen to me? What reassurance is there in the honeyed words of an ignorant?

One of the reluctant souls falls into the void. As they descend, they pull my hand, and it's no longer wind against my skin but cold water. I gasp and snatch back my hand to find bright yellow hair wound round my fingers. No, not hair – thread. Golden thread. The rushing torrent of the lost souls is sharp like calamansi.

'Sister Hanan!' Mother Lin cries out, her arms around me.

As I come back into my body, I realise I'm on my knees, gripping the Tree of Life. I feel the other spirits of the dead, distant and calm. They've passed, stepped into the void at the bottom of the well.

'I'm all right. I just felt so—'

'You ventured too close to the Beyond,' Mother Joca snaps.

Mother Lin gives me a gentle look as she helps me to my feet. 'Your empathy is a wonder, Sister, but be careful.'

It wasn't my empathy that almost caused me to fall into the void. When that reluctant soul grabbed me, I felt their fear and then an absence, like the void itself had swallowed every feeling.

Sometimes I think the peace of death would be so delicious. It is a dark thought, which I try to quiet. We are supposed to lust for Life, but I can't help but be tempted by the oblivion of the dead.

CHAPTER FOUR

FINLYR

THE LAST THING I want is to get hard in front of all these people. Although I've heard that it's more common than you think. Auto-asphyxiation. Not something I've ever tried, and there's not much I'm not up for trying. Well, it's too late now. The rope's digging into my wrists and neck. You know, I'm not actually sure I would get off on this.

The Seaguardian turns towards me, his mouth pressed into a thin line as starched and white as his uniform. The clouds part and the sun catches the blue wave and sunrise sigil.

There's nothing more noble than sailing the waters of Paranish and protecting the Bastion.

My mother said that so often it was almost a prayer. Maybe all men think of their mothers on their death days. This wasn't how I hoped my homecoming would end, but I did suspect it would be painful.

'Finlyr Pane,' the Seaguardian begins. 'You are accused of the crimes of piracy, treason, theft, smuggling, and impersonating a Seaguardian of Umasa – and fervent lasciviousness.'

'Didn't realise that last one was a crime.'

Some laughter escapes from the crowd and I turn and smile. They can't help themselves; they love the spectacle.

'Sir, I don't think you understand the gravity of the situation.'

I look down at the gallows' drop beneath me and give the Seaguardian a bemused smile. 'I think I do, my man.' I wink at someone at the front of the crowd, and they redden.

I try to take in the faces of everyone gathered here to watch me die. Hangings are a crowd favourite; it's more packed than a market or feast day. The smuggling lifestyle commandeers a certain air of theatrics, or perhaps dramatic types are drawn to the vocation. I'm certainly the latter. My pirating career was fairly lucrative, and I had no misapprehensions about the lifespan of a criminal – we rarely make it to our thirties. I've been a bit down and out lately, but the majority of my life on the sea was glorious and bloody. Until the Maelstrom. I won't think of that now. What's done is done; my roster of deeds looks like it's finally catching up with me.

I feel the rope cutting into my neck, and I stand a little straighter. It's difficult to maintain proper posture – not that it will make much difference in a few minutes.

'Do you have anything to say at this, the end of your life?' the Seaguardian clasps his hands behind his back with the air of someone congratulating himself on a job well done.

Nestor's at the front of the crowd with his line of Seaguardian comrades. That gold-trimmed jacket looks so proper now. It looked better draped around my shoulders.

I make sure I catch his eye as I say it: 'I wish I'd fucked more.'

The crowd undulates, a barely perceptible shift as someone bobs and weaves between bodies. At first, I think it's someone angling for a better view in the front row. Then I see that the person making their way to the front, right behind the line of Seaguardians, is a kid. They're close to the scaffold now, dressed in a dirty white shirt and loose britches, a hat pulled down low over their face. I squint in the sunlight and watch them creep a hand inside Nestor's jacket and palm something shiny. My compass. All in the space of releasing a breath. Who the skies are they?

'I have many regrets,' I begin to say, conscious that the Seaguardian and the crowd are staring at me expectantly. 'I have done many things throughout my time as a pirate that the law considers improper. But, my dear Paranishians, who decides the difference between a Seaguardian and a pirate? Don't they both sail the open waters?'

The Seaguardian's mouth turns down as if pulled by string, and his eyes flash.

'The Bastion. Correct, my good friend,' I continue, despite my stony audience. 'And who resides in the Bastion?'

'You dare to add treason to your roster of sins?' the Seaguardian splutters.

I cock my head to the side. 'I thought that was already on my docket, no?'

Laughter finally breaks out again among the crowd, and I incline my head, casting my eyes down. They're right by the gallows, face peering out from the gap between Seaguardians. I give them a questioning look, and they flash me a fiendish grin and slide a dagger down their sleeve. I narrow my eyes.

'Finlyr Pane, if you have nothing to say for yourself—' The Seaguardian raises a hand to the executioner, who stands ready to release the trapdoor.

'Wait!'

The crowd lean forward with bated breath.

'I would like to apologise to anyone who has been hurt by my crimes. Nestor, I'm sorry you weren't man enough to keep up with my swordplay—'

'Cease this nonsense!' the Seaguardian snaps. He brings a hand down sharply by his side.

The executioner pulls the lever, and I find myself choking on my words.

I'm crashing down from a large swell on a ship's deck. That gut lurch, where your body anticipates the drop before your mind can even process what's happening. I feel the centre of my being is no longer my core, but my throat. I don't know if you've ever thought about how delicate a neck is, but images of tender flesh are seared in my mind in that moment. I consider all the throats I've slit. Grab them by the hair and expose that soft, bare skin and throbbing veins. It's not an honourable death, but it's a fast one. You bleed out fairly quickly.

This is not an honourable death. Neither is it elegant. I don't know if it's a blessing my neck hasn't snapped, because now I have to wait to suffocate to death. If I could have de-gloved my entire body to get out of that noose, I would have. It feels like hours, my brain flooding my body with a punch-drunk cocktail of chaotic drugs, and my vision darkens. Then there's a white blur, something shiny and silver spinning through the air and catching the light. I fall hard onto my side, gasping for air. Then the screaming starts.

It is absolute chaos in Umasa's town square, people running wild, surging in all directions. People trip on the weight of their skirts. Others are crushed under trampling feet. I can see this from where I'm lying, panting, on the ground.

'Don't panic,' a honeyed voice says close to my ear, and someone helps me up. The stranger. I try to focus on them, staggering sideways before I double over and retch.

'We don't have time for that, Fin,' they say impatiently. 'Let's go.'

CHAPTER FIVE

RIS

BIBA LIES IN OUR bed, clutching her old wooden doll Dodi as she returns to sleep. She's getting too old for childish things, but it's her father's handiwork and she won't let it out of her sight. I understand; he didn't leave her much. It's an ugly thing, roughly carved with baffling features, with scraps of gold thread I held back to give it hair. When she was little, she loved to say, 'sunshine hair' as she stroked it and then patted her own dark strands and declare 'midnight hair'. I miss those days when she was smaller, her words softer. Mine were softer then, too – before the grief and rage had begun to devour me.

I head out of the door and the wind whips up my cloak, tugging at the ends as if to dissuade me from going. From the stoop, I gingerly pick up the otter-cat corpse by its tail. I've been swithering on what to do with it, but I can't leave it here, a horrific reminder of what happened. I could bury it, but the idea of it rotting slowly on my land makes me shudder. I imagine the decay seeping in, infecting everything. Infecting everything even more, I think. The sheep bleat pathetically in the field, and I can't deny it any longer: there's something wrong with them. I've tried changing their diets, isolating the sick, but always the wool continues to thin. The batches are smaller and of poorer quality, requiring more hours and creative ways to weave the fine gold thread and garments, which are our bread and butter.

'What will you do with it?' Biba asks.

It takes me a moment to come back to myself, to the dank blight of the otter-cat held by the tips of my fingers, to my daughter's words. She has pushed the door ajar.

'Give it back to the earth,' I say.

'Why?' Her face is open, her eyes wide.

I hate the why game. It carries on forever, until my answers are either satisfactory or I tire, her questions left unanswered.

'All living things must be respected. We come from the ground and return to it.'

'But what about the Tree of Life?'

All I can think about is how disgusting the corpse feels in my hand.

'Our souls live on and pass through there.'

'Where do we end up?'

I shrug. 'That is a question for the Temple of Aistra.'

'The otter-cat was warm,' she says thoughtfully. 'It hadn't gone into the Tree yet.'

I smell the death in the house and think; *my sweet girl did this*. What else can she do?

'I'll be back later. Sleep now.'

I shut the door harder than I need to and don't look back. I take the long path down by the shore, holding the corpse far enough that it won't stain me, close enough that it will blend into my outline if someone spots me across the Spring Isle. Why did this happen on the night I'm to showcase my new dress? I know I sound like a petulant child, but I've been working on it for months and they're all expecting it. In Alev, we're in each other's pockets – secrets are a luxury. There was no hiding my pregnancy with Biba.

She's carrying high, Larkin. That means a girl.

My husband had chided: 'Low for a boy, and right in the middle for whatever they feel like being.'

That had been seven years ago. After our dreams of adventure had been halted; his temporarily, mine forever.

The sky clears, revealing the mist-coated shoreline of the Winter Isle in the distance as I squish my way across the sand dunes. The tide is frustratingly low, and I have to wade out across the pebbles and shells to reach the water. I toss the dead otter-cat into the ocean and say a silent prayer for its passing. The Temple Sisters will ease the otter-cat's spirit into the Tree of Life. Do they feel a disturbance in nature? I bite my lip and try not think of it. Surely they can't trace anything back to us. The waters spit out the corpse several times before the waves finally bear it out of sight. I wash my hands in the surf and unsteadily clamber back up the hill to the dirt path towards the tavern. I turn to look back at the sea and cringe to see I crushed some bluebells on my ascent. Years to regrow, destroyed in a moment. Aistra, what a mess we make of our land.

It's only when I make it to Alev and the lamplight of Vullis's inn that I notice the bloodstains on my dress. Not large – you'd have to squint to see them. I doubt anyone will notice, but I will know that it's not the crimson dye of the linen. No one can ever know what Biba did, but I'll think on it whenever I wear this dress.

CHAPTER SIX

HANAN

SILENCE IS SUPPOSED to make us pensive, at one with the world. But I don't want to hear my body, and the other Sisters' shaky, reverent breaths as we turn the pages and dip our bone quills into ink. From my desk in the temple library, I'm almost eye level with the Tree of Life, and I follow the winding ropes of the branches as they punch through the stonework of our temple. When I was a novice, one of the older Sisters had lied to me and told me that this was how Aistra was formed. Imagine my gasp of incredulity when I first apprenticed with Mother Lin and saw illuminations of the truth: we built this place on holy ground around the sacred tree.

I watch Mother Lin now as she bends over her parchment, lips in silent incantation as she reads. She blinks in the candlelight, bringing the lamp closer to peer at the scrawls and then gently setting it down on the edge of her desk, careful not to upend or cause any sheaves to catch alight.

'Shall I fetch you more supplies, Mother?' I ask in a hushed whisper, standing gratefully and uncurling my spine from the stiff wooden stool.

Mother Lin startles from her reverie. She examines her desk and gives me a curt nod, before returning to her musings.

I gather my skirts and quicken down the tower stairs to the courtyard, where the Tree looms above me, stretching like a majestic haribon into the sky. The clouds part, and my eyes try to remember daylight. The mosaic tiles of our sun altar glisten and I touch my talisman to my lips. The queen must be smiling at us today. I catch my own image reflected in the glass casement protecting the skull of Priestess Anossa and stare for a moment. Then I pinch the soft skin of my inner wrist, glancing at the white, raised scars. *Do not compare yourself to those honoured ones. We are the waters that only reflect the shimmer.*

I hurry on my way, flashing the woven belt that indicates I am on scholarly duties, but the Sisters all keep to themselves as I pass by. My footsteps echo off the vaulted cloisters and I swing myself round a stone pillar, nearly colliding with a pair of Sisters coming from the refectory. The smell of food, something pungent with garlic, wafts from the kitchens. The chapel and its coloured glass entices me near the exit from the main temple building, and I follow the courtyard around towards the outbuildings.

The rookery is beyond them all, at the edge of the cliff, tall and narrow with tiny slits for windows and a shuttered roof to release the birds. I almost bump into Mother Ossin as I head up the narrow stone staircase.

'Sister Hanan, you're not on duty here today.'

'I know, Mother. I'm on an errand for Mother Lin.'

She nods and I retreat to let her pass.

'You're wild today!' I greet the birds, refilling their bags of feed, seeds and berries scattering as they excitedly hurry to their treats. I let out a loud whooping laugh. Here is my sanctuary, one of the few places I can speak freely, shout when compelled, or sing above a hush.

'Wait your turn,' I try to no avail, moving a large kestrel so a sunbird can dip its curved beak into the feeder. She tries to claw into the handling gloves as I usher her back to her perch, checking the damage to the linen lining.

I press my nose into the drying flowers that hang around the upper level, warding off the stench as best we can. They sway in the cold breeze that blows in through the aperture with its casement hinged back, the unbroken ocean visible beyond. The vellum sheets are on the wooden racks, bound in place with twine, ready to be turned into parchment. I take the lid off one of the barrels, releasing the trapped steam and foul smell of cleaning bones. Bird bones are perfect for quills because they are hollow; it allows them to fly and allows us to write. It makes sense that creating something so rare and beautiful would require so much death and decay.

I take some of the prepared parchments from a drawer and fold the sheets carefully, so they fit in my satchel. When I return to the library, Mother Lin is fastening her travelling cloak, preparing to leave. 'Parcel up these tomes, Hanan. I'm taking them to the mainland.'

The Mothers make the trip regularly. They never say why, but I've caught glimpses of strange parcels, scraps of errant missives with someone named Morna in Umasa. There is no boat to the mainland. All I know is that Mother Lin's cloak is always damp when she hands it to me after her return voyage. It's a mystery, one that eats away at me.

Most of the books here are documents for posterity, at least for those who read: other Sisters and Mothers who will come after us, the stewards of the towns, the priestesses and the royal family in the Bastion. They are ancient, remnants of crushed insects and dried flowers in between the crumbling pages. As I package up the volumes for Mother Lin, I see a letter has been left open as the ink dries. I read surreptitiously: *The king is dead. Long live the queen.*

I compose my face. If the king is dead, then the last priestess must have failed. One in a long line of recent acolytes to serve the king and queen. And if she has failed, she will have followed in the footsteps of her fallen monarch. Traditionally one monarch pair would be served by one priestess. The king is dead; a new priestess will be appointed.

We haven't been told this yet, and with this secret knowledge, I have an advantage over the other Sisters.

CHAPTER SEVEN

FINLYR

'Do you at least have a name, kid?'

They look me up and down before giving me a barely perceptible nod, and somehow, I know I've passed their test. With street urchins like this, secrets are power. They only give it away when they need to, but apparently a scrap of information is my reward for cooperating in my escape.

'Today, you can call me Isagani.'

It takes all my concentration to follow Isagani through the throng. They're made of liquid. They barely look back as I stumble over the rope of the noose and my own bad leg. The sun beats down, hard, and I'm sweating like a spit-roasting pig. Bodies press themselves hard against me and the air tastes like arse. Of course, the weather shifts just at the wrong moment. A classic mainland problem: one moment you're soaked through with rain, the next the water's evaporating off you as the sun bakes you dark and tanned.

I can barely breathe and Isagani's moving fast, almost out of view. There is a commotion, and Nestor barrels towards me in his glittering uniform, surprisingly pristine after rubbing shoulders with the great unwashed masses.

'Seize him!' he yells, fire burning in his eyes. He seems to have taken our encounter rather personally.

I dive towards the ground, grabbing the sword from his scabbard. I hit him in the face with the hilt, breaking his nose – again. I roll gracelessly beneath strangers, cutting my hitches free. I've nicked my skin, but the blood lets me slip my bonds. Isagani hauls me to my feet and snatches a hat from a woman's head. We struggle, me limping badly, towards the sanctuary of a darkened alley.

'Still alive?' Isagani asks, plonking the hat on my head as I catch my breath.

'Barely,' I gasp.

'This way,' Isagani urges, opening a hatch and beckoning me in.

My eyes adjust to the gloom of the basement, the smell of damp. I jostle a crate and hear the clink of empty palm wine bottles. 'Where are we?'

'The cellar of The Painted Tankard.'

I look around furtively in the cobwebbed darkness. 'Won't the owner come down?'

Isagani turns to me. 'They couldn't pay their tithes. This belongs to the Bastion now.'

How much had changed in a few weeks as I waited for death.

'Let's get out of here, sharpish.'

They rummage inside a wooden crate, practically falling into the box, their skinny legs dangling over the edge. They emerge, struggling to hold an assortment of items. Isagani throws me some garments, and I'm hit by the pungent smell of sweat, must, and old perfume.

'What are these?' I choke out.

'You never played dress-up?' Isagani smiles, appraising a purple jacket with brass buckles.

I quirk an eyebrow at them.

'Look, Finlyr Pane the pirate is dead,' they explain.

'I'd say more of a smuggler than a pirate,' I demur.

Isagani snorts. 'Whatever.' They sort through more of the garments. 'Let's become someone the authorities aren't looking for.'

'Such as?'

They indicate the hat. 'A widow with no taste.'

I clutch the hat defensively. 'That old lady was very fashionable.'

Isagani gives me a sour look, and I examine the pile of clothes as I rub my sore leg. I extract a forest green shirt and dark britches.

'You'll need to shave,' Isagani says.

When I look up, I'm surprised to find an entirely different child in front of me. They're wearing the purple jacket with tucked layers of skirts. They've discarded their hat, and their hair falls in loose curls to their shoulders. They've even rouged their face. Instead of the little scamp, a delicate, feminine child stands before me.

I wrinkle my nose. 'What are you supposed to be?'

'No one will be looking for an honest merchant and his daughter while we lay low at an inn.' Isagani's voice is higher, younger. 'People underestimate teenage girls.'

I look at them askance. 'A merchant and his daughter?'

'I'll go by Isa, that way you're less likely to slip up. What about you?'

'Fin doesn't work?'

They shrug. 'You're the outlaw here.'

I had used the name at the Umasa port when I'd arrived. It comes back to me now, unbidden; perhaps because Isagani had used the word 'honest'. When I think of aspiring to that, I think of him. A sailor, one of my old crew.

'Call me Larkin.'

Isagani throws me a closed shaving knife. 'Cut your hair too, while you're at it.'

'Does it make that much of a difference?'

'Darling, hair is everything.'

I use a bucket of water and a candle and hack at my long hair until it's at chin-length. I make a right mess of it, scruffier than most merchants, but it will do. With a sigh, I gaze down and take one last, long look at my luscious beard. I've been growing it out for years. Most people don't realise how much work it is to maintain, especially on the high seas. There's a beard balm I swear by, but my supplies are all on *Saltswept*. I'll pop a vein if the Seaguardians threw that overboard after commandeering my ship upon my arrest.

'Come here,' Isagani insists, taking the razor and cleaning up my sorry job. A well-placed slash and that would be the end of me. But I don't think they'd save me just to kill me.

'Why did you help me?'

'I want to get off this island. Heard you were the smuggler to do it.'

I stare at them. 'I don't do that anymore. Besides, didn't you hear, ports are open to outsiders now.'

'I'm not looking for passage,' they clarify. 'I want an adventure.'

I shake my head and can't help but laugh. 'They all say that, at first – the lost kids who think things are better out there. Trust me, they aren't.'

'Well, you're a dead man walking. What else are you planning to do?'

'Live a quiet life and die old in my bed.'

'Well, you can't do that in Paranish now. So how are we getting off these islands?'

'You're persistent – I'll give you that. But in case you hadn't noticed, my ship's been commandeered by the Seaguardians, thanks to that traitor Nestor.'

'Where are your crew?'

I focus intensely on rubbing my smooth chin as they try to read my face. Eventually, I say: 'Back in Lassair.' *What's left of them.*

'Then who did you arrive with?'

'Returners, like myself. Not many of my crew wanted to go to Paranish.'

They sniff and then slap the side of the crate. 'Well, looks like we've got to get your ship back from those cursed Seaguardians.'

'What makes you think you'll be tagging along?'

'For one thing, you owe me a life debt.' Their voice had been pitched high, soft as silk, but now the edge comes back. 'There's always a place for a good pickpocket.'

They take a compass from their pocket. My eyes follow it hungrily for a second, then I snatch at it.

'So, this *is* yours.' They smile, stepping back to keep it out of reach.

'That was my mother's. It's from Lassair. Irreplaceable.' I try not to sound like I'm begging.

'Why did that Seaguardian – Nestor, isn't that what you called him? – have it?'

'I was . . . I was wearing his jacket when I was caught.'

Isagani finally throws me the compass. 'So you *do* have a penchant for disguises.'

'You're very relaxed about associating with outlaws.'

They look at me. 'You don't remember me, do you?'

I furrow my brows. 'Why would I remember you?'

Their composure slips for a moment, and I see the hurt in their eyes. Hurt, and something else – maybe rage. 'No. Exactly. I'm a street urchin, a gutter snipe with no one and nothing to my name. No one cares if I disappear. Only the Temple Sisters will mourn me when they guide my soul into the Tree of Life.' The speech rolls off their tongue with a combative air, and I sense they've had to defend themselves often, scrapping for a fight. 'I'd rather the rush of danger than waiting for a slow death here.'

Waiting for death. I know that feeling.

'I can already tell you're as stubborn as a tamaraw,' I concede. 'I'm surprised you haven't tried to stow away.'

'I did,' they say, with a self-satisfied smile. 'But few ships used to leave Paranish entirely.'

Very few ships, save those carrying Seaguardians and skeleton crews. I've been the latter before and seen where that leads.

I shake my head. 'Exactly – "used to" – but you have more options now. Why me and my ship? The ship I no longer have.'

Isagani is silent for a moment, before saying, 'I'm not exactly on the right side of the Seaguardians myself.'

I nod. 'Fine. Well, we can't plan our commandeering from here, so what do you suggest?'

'I know the perfect place to hole up. Everything and everyone passes through there. We can plan our attack, sniff out a crew. We're sure to find someone with a taste for adventure.'

CHAPTER EIGHT

RIS

THE GOLDEN HOUR is upon us, the rays breaking through the clouds, heralding twilight. Night is descending fast, and I hurry. The cold comes quick here. Once the sun is gone, it's like the empty side of your bed after your lover has left.

When you live on the Spring Isle, Alev is the only place you can go. It sits at the southern shore, the small harbour a ley line between us and the port of Umasa, on the mainland. The tavern stands hunched against the elements, built of coarse beige stone amidst the dark, earthy brown of bricks. Each roughly cut square, from our own quarries and those of the Autumn Isle, comes together to create a hodgepodge building that has withstood the centuries. Time moves slowly here. Sometimes I look around the Spring Isle and think of how many generations have lived on this land, cradle to grave.

I approach Vullis's Tap, trying not to let fear show on my face. I catch my reflection in one of the smudgy windows and smooth the ends of my hair, which have been tugged free from my braid, noting the flush in my cheeks from the long walk. I've rouged my lips and eyes tonight. I'm more used to muddy breeches and sweaty smocks, and I feel like a sheep dressed as a queen. I take a moment to admire the fabric of the dress as it clings to my biceps. These are rare moments when I think of myself as pleasing to the eye. Larkin once thought so, told me often when we were happy.

I enter the tavern, slipping off my cloak.

'Thought I was seeing the ghost of your pa, Ris,' old Griyo makes the usual joke from his corner booth. A few other folk give a deep, rumbling laugh. I can't help but wonder if they are making a mockery of my attempts at femininity.

'Which one, Griyo?'

'Spitting image of Jon,' Griyo goes on. 'Your girl's going to look just like you.'

'Another round?' Vullis gathers their empty tankards, and I'm grateful for the distraction.

I make my way across the tavern, bending my head from the knick-knacks and tankards hanging from the ceiling. It's not particularly low, but my parents had the same issue. *Long-legged sort, your family.* I'd left the Spring Isle with Larkin and when we came back pregnant with Biba, we only had a few months together. My fathers had gotten word to us on the Autumn Isle. Times had been tough on the farm, and their health was failing. I had been away, on the Autumn Isle and on voyage work all that time, so close and yet so far, sheltered from the rest of Paranish in our little love nest. We had been foolish then – dreamers, the both of us.

I rest my arm on the bar, its wooden surface worn away from decades of elbows and palms, oil and cider staining the grain deep to the root.

'New dress, Ris?' Vullis asks, setting to work pouring a mug of piyata cider from the bottle. It's thick and cloudy and coral pink. I can almost taste the heady sweetness.

I swish the linen playfully, watching the maroon folds catch the candlelight. 'Do you like it?'

Ryla and Kopiro whistle jocularly from their table in the corner. They have their Soklan cards and wares for bartering set out already, going through their benevolent rituals. I grab the mug of cider from the bar and stroll over, sliding onto the bench.

'Is this your big project at last?' Ryla asks, eyes fluttering from my cleavage back down to their cards. I quirk my eyebrows; they've never been particularly flirtatious in all the years we've played.

'She's finally finished. What do you think?' I ask.

'You look lovely, Ris,' Kopiro says, squeezing my hand. 'It's good to see you happy.'

Ryla gives him a smirk. Placing my deck on the table, I shuffle through the cards and recite the old words, familiar like rubbing my thumb over a smooth pebble. *Warmth of my palms. Aligning stars. Bonds of us gathered here tonight. Let me read them, let me know their cards like they are my own.*

'Are you in tonight, Vullis?' Kopiro asks as the barkeep comes over to hand us our drinks.

Vullis grins, watching Kopiro cleansing his cards over the candle flame. 'After you smiled as you drank my twenty-year emerald vine liquor? Twenty years fermenting.'

Ryla laughs. 'If you didn't want to lose it, you shouldn't have bet it.'

'Didn't even give me the courtesy of a dram,' Vullis complains.

'You gambled the whole bottle,' Kopiro says with a shrug. 'Tell you what, I'm experimenting with a new blend with the piyata cider. I'll set aside some for you, if it'll stop you being salty.'

I look up to find Vullis appraising me. 'You're very focused tonight, Ris.'

I smile playfully. 'I hope you're bringing all your wits.'

'If he's any to spare,' Ryla jokes, grinning at Vullis.

'I've got a bar to keep. Focus on your cards, Ryla.' Vullis laughs.

I warm the cards, feeling them pliant beneath my fingers. 'You ready for a good time?'

Time glides like water as slippery as a fish after a few drinks and several rounds of Soklan. Night turns into a dark void outside the windows of the tavern as the room empties, and then we're the last people left. Vullis was hovering around the edges but as the evening wore on, he finally asked to be dealt in. After feeling everyone out in the opening rounds, I've not been able to catch a break. The game's downstream and I'm watching it wash away. I drain my seventh piyata cider, grimacing at the dregs, mingled sweet and tart. I'm grateful Kopiro followed Ryla to Alev and set up his cidery here. I never got used to the Autumn Isle cider, even though it's the original source and traded all across Paranish. I like what I know. I steady my gaze, trying to discern my cards in the candlelight. I look at my bundles of golden thread, now part of Kopiro and Ryla's stacks, and wince. I don't have anything left after badly misreading Ryla's face last round.

The tavern door slams open and three tall, cloaked figures slink in from the rain. They trail a muddy stain across the flagstones, ripping off their sodden cloaks and practically throwing them at Vullis. Underneath there are the distinctive white uniforms of the Seaguardians. But I see that they're not just any common Seaguardians: it's the captain of the royal guard and her lackeys. My heart drops to the floor: Salvacion.

Vullis ducks behind the bar, all shining smiles. 'How can I help you, my fine folk?'

'Piyata cider, naturally,' Salvacion orders, with the low growl of a woman who has shouted orders all day.

Vullis nods and gets to work filling their mugs. The Seaguardians ignore the chill their presence has brought, warming themselves by the fire, the blue wave and sunrise of their sigils catching the light.

'Quite a way to sail on a night like this,' Vullis says, trying to keep the knife-edge of nerves from his voice.

The Seaguardians take their tankards without thanks, eyes still on the flames, Salvacion with a shit-eating grin on her face. 'The cider's not *that* good,' she says. After an agonising pause, she adds: 'I'm here to see my favourite sister-in-law. Our mistress of the loom.'

Ryla and Kopiro shrink in their seats. Everyone looks at me then, and I'm a mouse with my tail under their paws. Nothing can save me now.

'Ris,' Salvacion says, drawing it out serpent-like, savouring the sound. The Seaguardians move across the bar and slide into the seats next to us, movements so languid it's torture. Ryla and Kopiro study their cards furiously, and the silence is choking.

'Nice dress, Ris.'

'Good to see you too, Salvacion,' I say, not meeting her eyes.

'It looks like you've been spending your time well,' she says. She takes a slow sip of her drink and sets it down, smacking her lips together. 'You know why we're here.'

'I told the steward last time. I can't pay yet,' I mumble, staring down at my cards.

Salvacion knocks them from my hand, and they scatter across the table. She barks a laugh. 'Look at me when we talk – it's only polite,' she says. 'You have to settle your debt, Ris.'

I swallow hard, my tongue thick in my mouth.

Her lackeys touch the hilts of their swords. The manner is offhand, as you would adjust a sleeve.

'The sheep are sick,' I explain. 'I've tried finding out what's wrong with them. They can't produce more—'

Salvacion slams her drink across the side of my head. The room swings and it feels as though bells are clanging inside my brain.

Vullis lurches forward to steady me. 'Are you all right, Ris?'

Something wet trickles out of my ear, and I wonder how it can be warm and cold at the same time. Ryla proffers a handkerchief, and it comes away covered in a sickly cocktail of blood and cider.

'Take a walk, lads,' Salvacion tells her Seaguardians, and they get up, moving as if they are patrolling the tavern.

She leans forward, face set in grim determination, and whispers, 'You're out of options, Ris. They know about Biba.'

'What?' I hold the kerchief to my bloodied face, unable to think straight.

Salvacion brings her mug back to her lips, alcohol and blood sloshing together down the sides. 'For the love we both bore my brother,' she says.

Salvacion reaches towards her hilt, and I feel my friends tense beside me – but her fingers brush past to reach into a pocket. She removes a waxed, yellowed piece of paper, the edges frayed where it's been folded over the years. She unfolds it like undressing a lover. Salvacion swipes the contents of the table onto the floor – drinks, cards, and tokens go flying, unheeded. She lays the paper on the table, glancing momentarily at her lackeys who are now at the bar, liberally helping themselves to Vullis's supplies.

'Do you trust these fools?' Salvacion asks, and I nod. She indicates for us all to come closer.

I ignore the stabbing behind my eyes and the dripping of my blood and focus on scrawls of spidery ink. They are meaningless to me, so I desperately try to understand the images. I spot the mainland, the Bastion atop the hill, the other isles like fingers disjointed from a palm. I remember the tale of Paranish's founding, the great otter-cat who jumped across the waters and left an imprint of his paw. Our islands, our home. There we are: the Spring Isle.

'This is a map of Paranish,' Vullis says.

'Glad you'd recognise your own arse, barkeep,' Salvacion says. She hovers a finger near the corner of the map, where a dark void fills the emptiness of the ocean. 'Look here.'

'Looks like a tea stain to me,' Kopiro blurts. Salvacion wags a mischievous finger.

'The Lahon Maelstrom,' I say grimly, staring at the map.

Salvacion nods.

I touch the map gently. 'How did you get this?' I ask.

'The same way I got Larkin's,' she says, crossing her arms.

My stomach drops. We've all heard the stories: tales of unspeakable treasure and, inevitably, the dangers that guard it. If you survive the Lahon Maelstrom, you might just be able to steal it. That's what Larkin tried to do. It had been our dream, until I became pregnant, and my parents fell ill. Those everyday anchors that hold you back. Or at least, they had held me back. Larkin had gone anyway, like a thief in the night. And Salvacion had helped him.

'This is a death sentence!' Vullis protests. 'No one has ever come back from there.'

'Then where do the stories come from?' Salvacion asks, sourly. 'Look, this is your last chance. Unless you want to give up Biba to the Temple. They'll come for her, Ris, and you'll never see her again.'

I stare at Salvacion and see Larkin's stubbornness in her eyes. She wouldn't have risen through the Seaguardian ranks without it.

'I've seen several priestesses in my time,' Salvacion says, meaningfully.

One royal and one priestess was tradition, but our queen has gone through as many priestesses in almost as many years.

Her words are ice in my bones. We all know the horrors, spoken in whispers: families screaming as their children are snatched in the night. As soon as that power shines bright enough, the Bastion knows it.

No one knows how. We live in fear that someone we know may disappear next.

Biba's past miracles have been embers compared to the otter-cat. This has been enough to get their attention. Biba will be taken from me and raised on the Winter Isle and serve them until she dies.

The map lies there, quietly biding its time. The pursuit of a promise. A phantom treasure. My husband knew the folly of adventure.

Eventually, I ask: 'What is the queen looking for?'

'I don't know. But you'll know it when you find it,' Salvacion says. 'And you'll certainly be in the queen's good graces. I'm sure everything could be forgotten.' She stands and adjusts her jacket. 'It may just be fisherfolk talk, but there's an old woman, touched, on the mainland in Umasa. She might be able to help you understand what's happening to Biba. Good luck, Ris.' She claps me on the shoulder, hard.

The lackeys abandon their drinking and throw open the door for her exit. I stare at my blood on the soles of their shoes until they leave.

'I need air,' I tell my friends in the silence of the abandoned tavern.

Ryla helps me outside while Kopiro and Vullis begin to clean up.

It's raining hard, the wind and rain lashing at my face. It slaps me hard as I lean against the stone wall, doubling over, my head between my knees. I retch, but nothing comes up. The bile is stuck in my throat. I can see the fabric of my dress torn asunder, underskirts flashing through the tears. Most likely caught on a nail or splinter when I was on the floor. Ruined, like so much of what I make.

My knees buckle and I fall to the ground. Ryla pushes their short hair behind their ears and crouches next to me, helping me up to lean against the wall. They rub my back. When they go to wipe the blood from my mouth, I tear a scrap of material from my hem and wad it against the bleeding gums.

CHAPTER NINE

HANAN

MALOSTRA IS SOUND asleep next to me. I slowly untangle our limbs and crawl out of bed, narrowly avoiding the crack between the twin beds where we have pushed them together. We always move them to their original spots in the mornings, but over the years we've worn grooves in the flagstones. We've gradually added our own touches of personality to the sparsely furnished room. Dried flowers pressed under the mattress and feathers that have landed on the mantel adorn the simple chest that holds our belongings. The window casement never fully shuts, always bringing the cold sea air straight to my face while I sleep. It's a sacrifice I make for feeling like I could escape out the window at any time. I check Malostra is fully asleep before I tiptoe across the cold floor and out into the hallway. The sconces are lit and throw strange shadows on the walls. The temple is still at this time of night, the other women asleep in their beds. Who knows how many of them sleep soundly in the arms of other Sisters.

Creeping around the corner, I nearly shout as I bump into someone.

'Sister Hanan?' Mother Lin asks, holding a candle up to my face.

'Beg your pardon, Mother.'

She appraises me, silently waiting for me to give my reason to be out of my room at night. We aren't locked in our rooms, not expressly forbidden from roaming the halls when we please. However, there is no reasonable explanation for me to be here save one.

'Night water,' I say sheepishly.

Mother Lin sighs and waves me away. 'Be quick. You'll catch a chill.'

I smile at her concern, rubbing the gooseflesh of my arms under my nightdress. Fire lights our way in wall-mounted sconces, but we only get candles in our rooms and those are rationed. Only the Bastion has the luxury of roaring fireplaces when the mainland's seasons shift. Suffering strengthens us.

I slip into the bathroom and listen for Mother Lin's footsteps to retreat. When I'm certain I'm alone, I heave the stone out of place under the sink. Within the nook is my collection of papers and assorted materials gathered over the past years while scribing for the library. These are little treasures I have rescued from the fire, or mildewing where they have been stuck down the backs of bookshelves, forgotten and faded from time. My studies have intensified since I learned of the king's death and the appointment of a new priestess; there isn't any time to waste. Our abilities are the only things that set us apart from one another, and the queen must have the best. I still haven't fully decoded the language on my latest acquisition, the swirling symbols with tiny serifs and images that look to me like hearts or diamonds, but who can say. Alongside my stash is a small kitchen knife, stolen and hidden away in my cloak during a herb-lore lesson.

I take the knife now and hold it against my skin, where hours earlier the flower had burst forth. I cut slowly and precisely, biting my lip from the pain. I'd hoped I'd get used to it by now. My palm tears, the blood welling quickly to the surface. I look at my dictated symbols and then close my eyes, picturing the cut in my hand with an invisible thread knitting the skin back together. I go over the movements several times and open my eyes, studying at my hand. The skin is puckered, and I watch, a smile quirking my lips, as the skin closes up. It's not as neat as last time, but to anyone else it would look like a lifeline on my palm. I place a finger over the line and rub, as though buffing a jewel. I keep watching intently, my eyes straining in the dim light. Until, eventually, the line is thin, barely visible. I clench my jaw. I must be able to protect and heal a queen, not simply myself.

No one sees me return to the room. Malostra stirs a little as I clamber back into bed and pull her warm body close to mine. She lets out an involuntary snuffle in her sleep at my cold feet.

'Are you sneaking around again?' she asks, her words slurring together sleepily.

You can't share a room with someone for years and not expect them to notice your strange ways. Malostra likes to burn her skin. I don't comment on it, and she ignores the cuts on my hands and arms. We all have our ways of trying to feel something, little war badges of our dedication to the craft. If you're not suffering, you're not succeeding.

'Some experiments,' I say, stroking her hair.

She rolls over and kisses me. 'You've been studying so hard recently. I wish you'd spend half as much time here as in the library.'

I say nothing for a moment and then ask: 'Do you want to practise an exchange?'

Malostra and I have been exchanging for years. At first, we were novices simply trying to hone our skills. We sat on the stone floor, palms touching, transferring energy back and forth. Then we held flowers and passed the life around. Girls make up strange games when cloistered together. We saw each other's bodies through the awkward years of growing pains, first bloods, everything. Then something shifted as we grew. Our experiments became less playful, more earnest, and suddenly there was a desire we couldn't name but recognised as mutual.

Malostra kisses me and it's delicious. I want to crawl under her skin as I feel her body under mine. Her dark hair falls away and I watch the pulse jump in her neck. I kiss her, warm her, make her burn bright. When she's hot enough to burst, I look at her pulse again. I imagine it stopping, her neck cold and still. I reach into her mind, soothing the desperate fluttering thing inside. My fingers are cool, a soothing balm, a healing poultice. I place my hands on the supple skin of her neck and think of the symbols on my tattered pieces of paper under the flagstones in the bathroom. I make the skin dance under my touch, sucking the heat of her into my flesh. I press down and she cries out, shuddering beneath me.

'Stop! Hanan, you're choking me.'

When I look at her face she's crying, her baby hairs slick against her hairline, damp with sweat. There are scratches on my hands, her fingernails bloody as if she had tried to claw me off. I barely felt a thing.

Her hands leap to her throat, to the imprints of my fingers and the broken blood vessels. 'Holy Aistra, what did you do?' she chokes.

'A little death,' I whisper, rolling off her. She lies there, prone, breathing hard.

I know what I should say but I can't; there's a beast stopping my voice. Malostra looks at me like I'm a stranger or a feral animal on the attack, eyes wide and terrified like a bushaella. Her breathing is shallow, and an unholy wheezing pours out of her throat.

'That was intense,' I say quietly, turning to face her.

'Intense?' she repeats, her voice a croak.

I reach for her, and she shrinks away. We both say nothing for a moment.

Eventually her breathing slows, and I hear her swallow hard. 'I wasn't sure you would stop.'

'I'm sorry, Malostra. I got carried away.'

'Carried away?' She sits up and gets off the bed. 'There's something wrong with you, Hanan. I want you to stay away from now on.'

CHAPTER TEN

FINLYR

WHEN ISAGANI SAID they knew a place to hole up, I didn't expect an inn at the heart of Umasa. We stand awkwardly at the wooden desk and watch the guests filter in from the day. It's bustling, unlikely they'll have any space for us, especially with the little we have to our names. I can smell the oniony stench of my own pits, the fearful sweat rolling down the back of my exposed neck. So many folk in close proximity.

'Everyone passes through here,' Isagani says. 'I imagine more so now, now that Paranish's ports are open.'

'And how do you know of this place?' I ask.

'Narra's always got trimmings going. She's been kind to me,' they say, growing red.

I ignore their embarrassment. No shame in helping each other out.

'You're both new.' A woman appears behind the desk and hands us two tankards. Her countenance is bright and open, with dark attentive eyes and an unruly mane of dark curls. 'I'm Ligaya. What brings you to Narra's inn?'

Now I hear it, the lilt of Lassren.

'I'm Larkin. My daughter Isa and I are passing through Umasa,' I say, giving her a small, polite smile.

'Please help yourself to jellied zoa.'

'Jellied zoa?' Isagani asks, with genuine curiosity.

I look at the swirling purple liquid inside the cup.

'A popular beverage in Lassair. I've fashioned my own version, something more like your piyata cider, I think,' Ligaya says.

The liquid fizzes on my tongue. It's only lightly fermented but the thick globules of jellyfish burst with spice and earthiness on my tongue. It pales in comparison to the real stuff from Lassair, but it's not half bad.

'You're merchants, you said?' Ligaya asks.

'From Nila on the Summer Isle,' Isagani chimes in quickly.

'Oh, I'm a fiend for ube,' Ligaya says, excitedly. 'Can't get enough of it when the Summer Isle merchants come through. That's not your trade, is it?' she adds, hopefully.

'Unfortunately not,' I say, warily.

'We're in the business of sourcing crews,' Isagani adds with a smile. 'And what brought you to Paranish?'

'I'm a kitchen witch, apprenticing with Narra for a spell.' Ligaya nods at an older woman making her way slowly down the stairs into the hallway. Weaving between her legs is an otter-cat, black as midnight with steely eyes.

I choke down my drink. Holy Aistra, I thought all the touched were at the temple or the Bastion.

'New guests,' Narra says, coming to stand beside Ligaya behind the desk. Her expression is stern, but her large eyes are warm. 'In the evenings we put on a spread and then guests are free to share drinks and tales by the fire. After you've refreshed yourselves, of course.'

Ligaya leads us up the narrow staircase behind the front desk. I follow in Isagani's wake, watching them deftly hoist their skirts on the steep incline. The wooden stairs are rickety and uneven, but the room itself is cosy. A round window looks out to the town square below and the slanted roof's cedar beams fill the room with a pleasant fragrance. Two short beds line the walls, and they're softer on the buttocks than expected.

'How long must we bide our time here?' I whisper through gritted teeth, as soon as we're alone.

'I'll put word out around town,' says Isagani. 'Get some of my old filchers to listen for any skeleton crews taking off.'

I shoot them an incredulous look. 'And my ship?'

'Didn't you see it in the harbour well enough from the gallows?'

I deliberately let my bag swing around and hit them on the back of the legs. 'Won't be long until it's repurposed as a Seaguardian vessel. Everything I've got left is on that hunk of wood.'

Isagani plumps the pillow and muses. 'We need a time when Umasa will be swarming, when the Seaguardians will be distracted.'

'No easier place to hide than blending into a crowd.'

'Let's go down and gather some gossip.'

The evening brings thoughts of warm dinners in bellies and soft beds. The chaos of the town square has long dissipated, and the stones of these walls feel like a sturdy sanctuary – at least for now.

'Are you expecting a lot of guests now that the Nishian borders are open?' Isagani asks politely, taking a sip of a cup of tea Narra has put in our hands.

'We've seen a lot of ships pass through Umasa in the past few weeks,' Narra answers. 'Not just returners but many visitors for the birth.'

We don't respond quickly enough, and an awkward silence hangs between us all.

'Blessed be their arrival,' Ligaya eventually jumps in, raising her cup.

I make a grumbling noise of assent. 'No use visitors planning; a child arrives whenever they like.'

I'm dizzy, my tongue swollen in my mouth and sticking to the insides of my cheeks. I stare at Isagani. They look pale and green about the gills as they stare back at me.

I hear a sound under the table and look down to find the black otter-cat looking up at me. It wraps itself around my legs, but I spot the sharp glisten of its claws too late. I yelp, hitting my knee hard against the wood, sending the tea service flying and Isagani jumping into the air. My limbs spasm, as if caught in a cramp.

'My good Larkin, are you quite well?' Narra asks, standing suddenly. Her face is the picture of concern, but I notice a subtle glint in her eyes.

'That abominable otter-cat,' I shout, although it's incoherent, because my tongue has become a rubbery nuisance in my mouth.

The black mass jumps onto my lap and gives me a self-satisfied smile.

'Sinigang's a vicious beast sometimes,' Narra scolds.

'It's the otter in him, you see,' Ligaya adds, half-apologetic.

'Get off, you fiend,' Narra insists.

The otter-cat reluctantly jumps down to the floor and sits, looking like a smirking loaf of bread. A voice, deep and vibrating, says, 'You're a dead man walking, aren't you?'

I look down at the otter-cat and its fish-eating grin. 'You can talk?' I slur in a feeble whisper.

Sinigang flicks their ears. 'And I hear pretty well too.'

Isagani glowers at me from the other side of the parlour, glued to the armchair by the force of Narra's stare and what we now recognise as magic. There's no one except Ligaya to save us from whatever fate the innkeeper has in store for us. The room spins and my body barely feels like it's mine. It's not unlike being drunk on palm liquor.

'Hedge witch,' I mutter, succumbing to the heavy feeling in my limbs. I sink as though a blanket weighs down my body.

'Mind your manners, you're still Narra's guests,' Ligaya tuts.

'Falsehoods never last long under my roof,' Narra insisted. 'Who are you, truly?'

'Finlyr Pane,' Sinigang addresses me, whipping his tail across my face as he treads across my lap, ensuring he sinks his claws into my gonads.

'You *are* a dead man walking then,' Narra says, stroking her chin. She's an ample woman, short and stout, with a coronet braid of thick silver hair crowning her head. Her eyes are penetrating, as if she can read my thoughts.

'And your companion?' Ligaya asks, intrigued. 'Who is it really, under all this? Is Isa your true name?'

Isagani blushes deeply, and I remember that there is still a scared kid under the dirt and bravado. 'Isagani. Nobody really.'

Narra touches the top of their head. 'No. I know you. I've seen you here before.'

Isagani's face is a mixture of terror and shame.

Narra continues, her voice nothing but warmth. 'You're everyone and anyone. A skill few of us can truly master.' She stirs her piyata tea thoughtfully.

I don't know whether to laugh or cry. 'Look, are you turning us into the Seaguardians or what? I don't want to do this dance all over again for their benefit.'

Narra smiles, patting her hair with hands that are dark and wrinkled, like worn leather. 'Your bravado hides a hurt, Finlyr.' She reaches down to stroke the otter-cat.

I take deep breaths and count to three in my head. Then I wrench myself up from the chair and throw a punch at the innkeeper.

My fist moves as though the air is thick syrup. Narra sighs and brings the cup to her lips. I fall to the floor, all the wind knocked out of me.

'What have you done to him?' Isagani asks, a hint of concern – but mostly fascination – in their voice.

'A simple binding spell against violence.'

I lie on the floor, unable to move, and decide now's as good a time as any to ask what's been on my mind since we arrived. 'If you're both witches, why aren't you at the Temple of Aistra?'

Narra's eyebrows rise so quickly it's as if I've just asked to rummage through her knickers. 'I was around long before that edict on gifted children. They didn't bother with older self-taught witches like me.' She sniffs. 'We're of little use to the Bastion.'

'And you?' I ask, turning to Ligaya.

She bristles. 'Visitors to Paranish aren't subject to that edict. And Lassair doesn't have such practises.' Her tone is measured but she can't fully hide the disgust on her face. I remember the same reactions from other Lassairians; our fear of the arcane seems downright narrow-minded.

I sigh. 'How long until I can move my body again?'

'Give it an hour,' Ligaya snips. 'And you might want to stretch later. It'll be painful.'

'You'll be staying here until we figure out what to do with you,' Narra says firmly. 'It won't be a royal suite, but we've got room, despite the influx of visitors.'

'So you're not turning us in to the Bastion?' Isagani asks, hopefully.

'Not yet,' Narra says, glaring at me. 'Depends if I have a use for you. Now I think it's time for bed. I'd like footfall as light as Sini's, please.'

CHAPTER ELEVEN

RIS

I'M HALF CARRIED back to the farm by Kopiro, Ryla, and Vullis. We nearly go tumbling over the sea cliffs several times trying to make our way by starlight alone. The world is still spinning, and I'm not sure if it's the piyata cider or the smash to the head.

'I've never met a half-decent Seaguardian, have you?' I ask bitterly.

'I hope they all step in sheep shite,' Ryla curses through gritted teeth.

'Ah but rotten apples, Ris,' Kopiro replies.

I wince. 'Spoil the whole barrel. That's what they always forget to add.'

'I'd rather a fist in the face than the mind games of some of them,' Ryla adds. At least you know where you stand.'

'Speaking of—' I stumble, leaning on Ryla's arm as they help me steady my feet. I let out a groan like an elder.

'Did they break anything?' Vullis asks.

'Just my spirit.'

Ryla barks out a gruff laugh. 'How can you quip at a time like this?'

'It's that or lie in a puddle and wait for death.'

'Grim.'

'You did ask.'

We're not as quiet as we hoped to be. Biba wakes up, frightened by the noise, and then by the blood. Fetch bounds up to me, trying to lick my wounds. My friends try to keep everyone away as they clean me up on the sofa.

'She's all right, little one,' Kopiro says soothingly to Biba.

'Her face is hurt.' I can hear from Biba's warbling voice that she's close to tears.

'Nothing serious. Go back to sleep, Biba,' he tries again.

'She's clearly upset,' Ryla argues, picking up Biba and patting her on the back.

'Let her come,' I sigh, holding my arms out for her. Ryla brings her over, setting her down carefully on the sofa.

Biba reaches for my face with her small hands, and I flinch. I can't bear that I do, but that's the truth of it. Her hands are a weapon.

'Be careful, it's delicate,' Vullis warns gently.

Biba touches my temple and ear, her fingers cold and smooth. Warmth spreads across the side of my head. The room stops swaying and my vision steadies. The throbbing across my head eases, turning from a vomit-inducing migraine to a dull headache behind my eyes. The world narrows, dark edges creeping into my periphery so I can only see Biba's face. She is still on the verge of tears, but she hiccups a joyous laugh.

And now I understand. I snatch her hand away and everyone startles.

'She meant no harm, Ris,' Kopiro says, alarmed.

'I know. I just don't want her to have to deal with me like this.' I bite back what I desperately want to tell her: that her kin did this to me, in some twisted form of protection. Why are we cursed to hurt the ones we love? 'Thank you, Biba. Let the adults talk now; go back to sleep.'

She reluctantly follows Vullis as he beckons her back to bed with the doll Dodi. Her face is full of confusion, as if she's questioning what she did. She didn't look like that after the otter-cat; then it was a detached curiosity. But this stabs at the heart of me. Am I cruel to distance myself?

Ryla takes out that infernal map and unfurls it on the table. We all stare at it like it's a cursed object. No one wants to speak first, and we wait until Vullis has returned from putting Biba to bed. They leave me to break the silence.

'I have to do it,' I say eventually.

'You can't,' Ryla hisses, slapping their hand on the table.

'Ryla,' Kopiro snaps, placing a hand on their shoulder.

'It's the only way.' I direct my stare at each of them in turn: Ryla's raw anger, then Vullis, who bites his thumbnail; and finally, to Kopiro, whose face is the softest among them. They scan each other's faces, too, trying to gauge the group. They are scared and angry on my behalf. I feel their love radiating throughout the room. But this is something I have to do.

'Those waters are infested with Seaguardians and pirates,' Ryla protests.

'And cryptids, if you believe those fisherfolk tales,' Vullis chimes in.

'And no one has ever returned, at the queen's behest or otherwise,' says Kopiro with finality.

The breath catches in my throat at the truth of that.

'You're not a sailor, Ris,' Kopiro pleads. 'How will you get there? You don't even know what you're looking for.'

'Something rare and valuable. It must be,' Ris insists.

'You remember the first edicts, right?' Vullis asks, rubbing his chin. 'Before the edict on gifted children, when the queen's quest was an honour.'

'Promises of titles and cosy little seats up in the Bastion for anyone who could succeed,' Ryla curls their slip.

'Nothing like that anymore,' I reflect, bitterly. 'Now it's a cursed quest, for the foolhardy. A reprieve from a death sentence.'

Vullis places a hand on my arm, warm and reassuring, knowing that Larkin is on my mind. 'He wouldn't want to be remembered that way.'

I jerk my arm away. 'He forfeited that right when he abandoned his family!'

The room is silent, the echo of my shout hanging in the air. Have I woken Biba? Is she really asleep, or feigning it so she can listen to the adults?

'And Salvacion has the gall to ask me to follow his footsteps.'

'She's trying to help you, in her own way,' Kopiro says quietly.

My voice is thick in my throat. 'I know,' I say.

Her form of aid sits heavy on my skin: an impossible choice to remain and live in fear of the day they come for Biba – or to pursue a fool's errand and live to hope.

Over the past few weeks, I have felt trapped here with my daughter. Afraid her joy or sorrow may explode. Unpredictable power in soft, untrained hands. I sneak a look at the door.

'It seems I have become one of those desperate folk. It's the only way to protect Biba. Her powers are stronger now. She . . . scares me sometimes.' How can a mother be scared of her own child?

Kopiro places a hand over mine, as if trying to smother my confession. 'Something is amiss in the world – that's for sure. You're not the only one to feel it, Ris.'

'What do you mean: stronger?' Ryla asks, tentatively.

'She is more than touched,' I whisper through parched lips. 'I've seen her do impossible things. Unholy things.'

'What kind of things?' Ryla presses.

'She can undo death,' I whisper.

It is as if all the air has left the room. Ryla straightens up; Kopiro grips my hand tighter.

Vullis clears his throat. 'In that case, maybe the temple is the right place for her.'

I glare at him. 'How can a place that snatches children from their families be right?'

'She could learn to control her powers,' Vullis pleads. 'I know you're trying your best to teach her, Ris – but you don't have the gift.'

'Are they happy there?' I ask desperately. 'We have no idea what goes on there because we never hear from them. No one does. The best I could hope for is that one day I would see her standing on some balcony at the Bastion, next to the royals. Is that what you want?'

Ryla sighs and opens their hands in submission. 'That's the thing, Ris. We don't know. And we don't know what would happen if she stayed here without guidance.' After a beat they add, 'Have you asked Biba what she wants?'

'Biba is a child,' I snap. 'She has no idea what she wants.'

The silence is thick until it becomes so stifling I must crack it. 'It's only a matter of time until they come for her. If I had any doubts, tonight has taken them away.'

I look over to the map, to the Winter Isle flung out furthest from the mainland. They say you can't see it until you're practically on land because of the mist that surrounds it, an unsettling haar, which gathers around the temple like a shroud. They commune with the dead there, living a life detached from the rest of Paranish – one devoid of bonds and community in the traditional way. They are the Bastion's obedient servants. In theory, it is a great honour to be gifted, but try telling this to grieving parents whose child is being stolen in the middle of the night. Visitors are forbidden at the temple. Once they take them, they are no longer yours. They are theirs.

I swallow hard. 'Do I have any other choice but to do as the queen asks?'

'You'll need to find someone who can read that,' Vullis begins tentatively.

I can understand a map's shapes, but it means nothing beyond that.

'You could try Umasa.'

I blow out air from my cheeks and then cry out as the pain becomes too great. Ryla pats me on the back as I weep. The broken skin on my face stings, and I examine it through puffy eyes, gently touching my swollen jaw. I've never been a dainty beauty, but it will be a few weeks before I can see what kind of permanent damage Salvacion has done.

'Salvacion really fucked up my face.' I try to laugh, then sob again.

'You look like the wrong end of a sheep,' Ryla teases, eliciting another painful laugh.

Vullis, ever the host, begins to build a fire. 'We'll stay here tonight, Ris. Whatever you need.'

'Tomorrow, we can make a plan. Tonight, you rest,' Kopiro gives me a sympathetic look, his eyes gentle and brimming with tears.

'Thank you,' I say, holding each of their gazes.

A glint of light in the corner catches my eye. It's a sliver flash, shining for a moment and then gone. The softest creak of wood I recognise as the bedroom door closing. Another thing to deal with in the morning.

Fuck it, let Biba see. The world is full of violence and broken things, some of them at her own hand. She's not some frightened little bird I must protect. She is growing up faster than I ever dared to believe.

CHAPTER TWELVE

HANAN

MALOSTRA'S BEEN COLD with me, wearing scarves to prayers until the bruises fade and acting like nothing happened until we're in our room. Then it's a silence, hanging thick and loaded. Our beds are pushed against their separate walls, the distance between them an ocean of space. I don't think she knows how to articulate what happened, but something snapped inside Malostra. I have tried to apologise but she says she doesn't believe me. I don't know what to say to that, what I can do to show her it was simply a step too far.

At least having Malostra ignore me makes it easier to focus in classes.

I make my way out of the temple and into field, clutching my woollen cloak close to me. The field is flat and barren of trees, with the wind too wild for anything other than the mighty Tree of Life to withstand, and it is partly sheltered by the temple's courtyard. The plant life out here grows close to the ground, and I take the worn path around the rows of hardy vegetables and admire the brief clearing that shows me the silhouette of the mainland in the distance. A cluster of buildings that make up Umasa, our nearest port town. It looks so close and yet the waters churn ice cold and inhospitable, with nowhere to safely dock lest you get splintered on the rocks. I shiver and hurry to the stone shelter where I can see the rows of Sisters in their long dark cloaks, huddled around the dirt plots of the more delicate herbs and vegetables. Even once inside there is little respite from the wind. It may do a decent job protecting the crops from the elements, but it does little to shelter us.

'Today, we focus on plant lore,' Mother Lin announces. 'We will be dissecting and studying the properties of our garden and meadow.' Her eyes roam over us. 'What are the main crops that thrive in our climate?'

'Leeks, parsnips, kale.' Nusi's face is young and eager. She keeps her hair shorn so she can commune better with nature. She's really taken the suffering-as-strength edict to heart. She beams at Mother Lin's nod.

'And who can name three uses for this herb?' Mother Lin holds up a sprig of lavender, crushing it gently and sniffing it.

'Sleep, fertility, and pain,' Malostra says.

'Elaborate,' Mother Lin encourages.

'Tinctures and tonics – you could create a salve—' Malostra stumbles, trying to get her thoughts in order. The wind whips up our cloaks and dresses, and we break out in audible gasps at the cold.

Mother Lin gives a tight smile; clearly, she, too, is ready to get back inside. 'That is correct. Your task, Sisters, is to create a remedy for abdominal pain. It must be effective, but gentle. Mother Joca and I will judge your efforts and decide the most satisfactory remedy. You have three hours.'

Our cloaks billow around us as we stream into the field and scatter across the isle. Malostra and I eye each other, veering as far away as we can. She goes off in the same direction as Sister Nusi and her friends, and now everyone knows that something is amiss. The women sneak glances at me, heads tilted close as they whisper against the wind. No matter. I will forge my own way, as I always do.

I find my favourite cove on the south side of the isle, my own private sanctuary where I go to hide. It is a great unburdening, when the waves drown out my screams. I've been here more often recently, sitting on a piece of driftwood I dragged here years ago, staring out at the ocean. Strange things have washed up on shore: cargo from foreign trading ships, translucent fish, and most recently a dead otter-cat. Today I'm not here to clean up the debris or rest in quiet contemplation. My place has its useful secrets.

On the edge of a cave, I find the sad, almost bare branches of a sea buckthorn. I grasp the prickly stems firmly and pluck the last orange berries, placing them gently in my pocket.

Next, I seek out the tufts of beach wave, or thrift, which use rocks to shelter from the buffeting winds and salt-laden tides. I pick the flowers and bundle the pink petals into my pocket, ensuring the needles aren't digging into my skin. I scramble up the cliff, following the grooves I've worn into my route over the years. I used to think of inviting Malostra down here, but it was beautiful to have something just mine. We are so rarely alone here; to stand and watch the waves come for me, to slowly take me away, is a secret pleasure.

The other Sisters are running frantically, their focused murmuring just audible on the wind. Everyone has split off now; there are no alliances anymore. I spot Nusi with an armful of lavender, clumps of soil trailing her as she rushes back to the temple. The fool has pulled up whole plants by the root. Has she no respect?

I head to the garden and hide in the now empty stone shelter as the chaos unfolds. It's easy to blend in when you're not drawing attention to yourself. Animals have learned this, as have plants; I mimic them, my movements slow and deliberate as I kneel on the ground, the wet mud soaking through my dress. Parsnips cure stomach ailments. The dirt nests under my fingernails as I gently extract a plant from the soil. The leaves are full and verdant green, and the tuber is fat and a deep burnished orange.

Malostra is right about lavender: it is good for sleep, fertility, and pain, among other things. I gather that last, once the other women have foraged the best from the coastal meadow. I'm left with the meadow's scraps, but I think that it is enough. Through the gaps in the stones, I spy women darting back and forth from the kitchens, their faces red from the heat of their experiments. I slink inside and make to grab a pot. A sharp elbow digs into my side. It's Malostra.

'All the burners are occupied,' she says coldly.

I look around and see that it's true. There are women waiting eagerly, glaring over their neighbour's shoulders as they finish up, as if their eyes could make their Sisters' remedies fail.

I take the pot from the fixture and dash outside; afraid someone will take it from me. It's the ill-favoured vessel, one prone to sticking, misshapen from being dropped too many times. It will have to do, for I have no other.

I return to the cove, finding driftwood and piling it to create a small fire. If the burners are occupied, I suppose I'll make my own. I know how. It is not a skill we use frequently but when I read about it in the temple library, it kindled a memory. It was before I was taken to Aistra, so I must have been very young. It's a smudgy remembrance of woodsmoke and a warm voice. Two big strong hands with dirt under the nails, sparking two stones together, showing me the best shape and texture. The stones catch and the spark jumps into a fireplace. A deep laugh.

I look for suitable stones and copy the motions in my head. I spark two stones, and the fire smokes the kindling. I put my face on the rocks and blow to encourage the embers. Eventually it catches, but not until after I've a lungful of smoke and soot on my cheeks. I hang my pot from a branch over the fire and slowly add all the ingredients, stirring frequently lest it stick to the bottom of the pot and burn. My hands are covered in the sticky residue of my ingredients. I hold beach stones, rubbing my fingers across the whorls and patterns, listening to the soothing clink of them against each other.

I can hear the voices of the dead above me. I'm directly below the Tree of Life, and when I touch the walls of the cave, I can feel the roots reaching out, twitching inside the soil. The murmuring whispers are white noise, mingling with the sweet shush of the waves. I fall into a reverie as I stir, watching everything melt together into a salve.

Give of yourself to the remedy.

The voices coalesce to a command. I listen again to the instruction and feel a sting on my thumb. I've caught it on the sharp corner of one of my stones. How hard had I been pressing down? A bead of blood wells to the surface and I make to put my thumb in my mouth, to suck away the dark liquid.

Give of yourself.

I hold my hand over the pot and watch the bead of blood fall into the mixture. I stir it in, the streak of crimson disappearing into the mixture. It takes me a moment to recognise the bell above the waves. The temple bell, which usually calls us in for prayers. I look out across the water. The sun is much lower on the horizon now, peeking from the clouds that seem to hang permanently around the Winter Isle. Nearly three hours must have elapsed.

I gather my things quickly, ensuring I pour seawater over the remnants of the fire. I would not burn down the temple. I hold the pot steady as I scramble back up the slope. By Paranish, were we supposed to decant it for presentation?

I rush to the temple, pushing open the doors to the main hall. The other Sisters are gathered by the benches, holding vials neatly stoppered.

I must look a sight; hair whipped in the wind and cheeks ruddy. The remedy has almost sloshed out of the battered pot, and I try to compose myself. Malostra looks me up and down and I notice the dried flecks of mud and sand on the hem of my dress.

'Sister Hanan. We had almost given up on you.'

A few of the Sisters snicker and I blush.

'Apologies, Mother Joca. I did not have time to decant my remedy.'

'Well, let's study it before it goes cold.'

Mother Joca crooks a finger, beckoning me to the front of the group. Mother Lin goes first, stirring the mixture and letting it slop off her spoon.

'Consistency is not bad, although it could have done with a little longer to infuse.'

Mother Lin takes a tentative spoonful and makes a sound I can't decipher. Mother Joca follows suit but does not share her opinions with the class.

It is excruciating, waiting for them to sample everyone's remedies. The fire in the main hall needs to be stoked and I am numb from the cold by the time all the Sisters have been assessed.

'Go and ready yourselves for supper. We must discuss.'

Malostra doesn't speak to me when we're back in our room and flounces out after freshening herself at the washbasin. I take a damp cloth and try to scrub the dirt from my gown, but it requires hours of scouring I don't have. I clean up as best I can and change into my spare clean dress.

I hurry down the narrow circular staircase from the top floor, where the oldest Sisters reside, nearly tripping over myself. The smell from the refectory is somewhat enticing today and my stomach growls, but I ignore it and turn into the main hall. I'm almost the last there. I suppose everyone is eager to receive their assessment. We stand by the benches, waiting for the Temple Mothers to take their place at the top end.

'Mother Lin and I would like to commend several Sisters on their efforts. Nev, your tonic was well conceived but a little thin for the requirement.'

Nev looks crestfallen and several of her neighbours pat her on the shoulder.

'Dany, similarly, a solid attempt at a salve.'

Then they look at me. 'Although a little unconventional, Hanan's remedy was one of the more notable ones.'

Rows of faces turn towards me, and their jealousy burns my skin.

'I dare say you've earned your supper tonight. You may join the lower Sisters in the refectory now.'

We file out, the other girls chattering in excitement and frustration. The voices bounce off the vaulted ceilings as we cross the corridor to the refectory.

'She didn't even have a burner,' Nusi whispers to Malostra, incredulous. 'How did she do it?' Malostra shrugs, looking disgusted.

'Well, that was a waste of an afternoon,' Nusi complains loudly, but not so loud the Temple Mothers can hear. 'They're probably not even going to do anything with them, don't you think?'

Malostra sighs. 'I hope they don't make us dump them in the sea after dinner. Someone could use them to help with their moon's blood, surely?'

They still think this is child's play. An Aistra exercise. The Temple Mothers wouldn't waste our time and resources on something abstract. Not at this stage. The remedy is for abdominal pain. I imagine the queen, alone in her bedchamber, no husband, only a child in her belly who writhes and won't quiet.

The king is dead, and the queen is desperate.

My attention is diverted as we enter the refectory. The room is divided by long benches and tables, with a raised platform for the Temple Mothers. They sit in order of age, with the oldest girls closest to the Temple Mothers' table to represent the near-completion of their training. But tonight, my peers spread themselves out so there's not enough room for me. Once the younger classes see this, they also ignore me when I ask to join their benches. Eventually Sister Hoss moves down, and I sit with the youngest Sisters, who barely take up the bench on their table. I try to hunch and keep my arms close after I almost send a pitcher of water flying.

We often eat stews or soups to stave off the cold, and it is easy to feed a group from one large cauldron. It also makes the preparation straightforward, with every class assigned a meal to dish up. Once, when I was younger, we ate a creamy fish soup with the freshest bread. That was the first time I remember a priestess being appointed – such fine things were only given on celebration days like that.

Today we're served a sour red soup made of beetroot and cabbage and little else. I slop half of it down my dress in my rush to eat and curse myself at staining the freshly cleaned fabric.

The Mothers clap their hands, and we quickly fall to silence.

'We are now at liberty to share some grave news with you all,' Mother Joca intones. 'The king has passed, and his spirit was laid to rest by myself and Mother Lin in the Tree of Life.'

'Blessed be his rest,' we all murmur.

'Her Royal Highness will appoint her next priestess in due course,' Mother Joca announces, the unspoken connection understood by all.

Murmurings break out among the Sisters but are quickly silenced by Mother Lin rapping on the table with her knuckles.

I try to remember the last time a girl was selected. It first happened during my second year at Aistra, and I didn't fully understand. I thought she was being sent to her death. How I wailed, until the Temple Mothers explained. The next time was during my first blood. The last one had been Freya, not five years ago. She had slept in the room next to me and Malostra, and had been replaced by a young girl who wet herself and cried for home.

'We have been watching your efforts closely.' Mother Lin adds, 'And will continue to do so. Consider this a time for each Sister to conduct herself with absolute perfection.'

I'd studied the archives in the library, learned the names and dates of priestesses past, hoping to join their historical ranks. I am almost complete in my training and ready for the next step in my path. A fourth priestess in such short succession was a rare opportunity and I would take it. I would do better than the others. I would not fail to please her.

CHAPTER THIRTEEN

FINLYR

NARRA PUTS US to work as soon as dawn breaks the next day. Everyone else is asleep, save Ligaya, who we meet returning with an armful of paper bags. The smell of fresh baking wafts from the bags and she sees the hungry look in our eyes, but Narra promptly ushers us out to the garden.

'Breakfast must be earned,' she says flatly.

The garden is only a small patch of dirt behind the inn, but there's a peace in the smell of freshly turned earth and the sun only just breaking the horizon. She patiently explains her system, getting us to repeat her instructions back to her when she thinks our concentration is wandering.

'Medicinal herbs are in this planter here,' Isagani repeats, hiking up their skirts to point their muddy boots at the spot.

'Now it's nothing compared to Alev or Gretabel,' Narra says, looking around proudly, 'but it's helpful to have fresh supplies of anything we can grow here.'

'We can handle it,' I say, grabbing the shovel and basket. 'Everything that's ready to harvest, correct?'

'Indeed.' Narra nods. 'We're full to the rafters at the moment.'

Outdoor work is harder than I expected. Not that sailing is a lark, you understand; I didn't get this strapping barrel of a chest without hard graft. Gardening is a pleasurable change of pace.

They might be lean and wiry, but they're surprisingly strong. I watch them surreptitiously. There's not much muscle there, but clearly determination.

'Do you think Narra's setting all the guests to work?' I ask, when there's a lull in the rhythm of our bending and gathering.

'Those without goods to barter,' Isagani replies, wiping sweat off their face. 'It's not unusual.'

I quirk an eyebrow, leaning on my shovel.

Isagani's face turns red, and not just from the exertion.

'You've stayed here before.'

Isagani returns to their tasks with spirit.

'Not under this guise, I wager, but you have.'

'Better than in an alleyway marinating in piyata cider,' they say through gritted teeth, just low enough that I can hear them.

My head begins to swim as if I were back there. Oh yes, I've spent many unforgettable nights at The Painted Tankard. Or rather, memorable if I'd not obliterated myself on palm liquor and ciders of all varieties. When I came back to Paranish I saw no reason to break with tradition. It comes back to me, the strong wiry frame on the dirty-faced waif. *You all right, stranger?*

That numb hazy sensation when you feel a bit distant from it all. Like your experiences belong to you but don't affect you. So drunk I can't piss straight? Not my problem. At least, that's future me's problem. Waking up in a stranger's bed? Better than sleeping alone. Too many bitter ends to a game of Soklan to count. A hat to keep the sun and wind off. A cutlass to slice my enemies in twain. Even the scabbard can do some damage if absolutely necessary. And then, of course, a dagger in my boot, although you've got to watch your step lest you slice off a toe. None of that now – everything was taken off me when I was arrested. I've grown used to them always being on my person for years and I feel naked without them. These merchant adornments don't sit right.

'Hey,' I say gently. 'There's no shame in it. We all need a warm bed and a fully belly; those without the means to pay, as much as those who do.'

'I have the means to pay,' Isagani says, defiance in their eyes. A flock of birds is startled from a nearby tree, and they lower their voice. 'I make my way honestly, when I can. I don't like to have to steal, you know?'

'I know,' I say. 'We all do what we can.'

A moment rests between us as the sun peeks over the inn's roof and lights up the garden. Isagani wipes some dirt from a bunch of leafy greens. 'What have you done – to get by?'

'It's what I've done to other people,' I say after a moment. 'Stealing mementos, stealing lives. Everyone has their price; smuggling taught me that.'

Isagani stares at me. 'And how much is a life worth?'

'How much is it worth to you?' I counter. 'You were fairly willing to put your neck out for some random pirate on the gallows.'

The air is thick between us, and we toil again, neither of us wanting to push for more, lest we push each other away. Alliances between outlaws often dance on a knife's edge.

'I didn't realise you were the same man I found in the alleyway. I was there plain as everyone else to watch a good hanging.' I snort a laugh, and they crack a smile. 'But then they said your name. I'd heard stories about that man, a smuggler who could take people away from Paranish. Before the ports were open, that's what you did, wasn't it?'

I sigh. 'Aye, everyone has their price.'

'We thought about leaving, but it was never the right time,' Isagani says. 'There is no right time,' they add. Their eyes are shiny and they quickly wipe at their face again.

They once had someone to dream with, to weave a future with. A hope powerful enough that their memory was the catalyst. I fiddle with my mother's compass in my pocket, and I suppose I know a little about the power of a person's memory to shape a life.

'I fucked up,' I confess. 'My last voyage cost the lives of several sailors. I didn't do my duty. My crew couldn't forgive me for that, and I don't blame them.'

They only held off a mutiny so we could make it back to Lassair in one piece. Left me with my wreck of a ship to seek better fortunes. *Saltswept* wasn't the only patched-up shadow of its former self that sailed back to Paranish when news arrived of the ports opening.

Isagani nods, their face set with grim determination. 'I'm sorry that happened,' they say, their words so diplomatic it's almost amusing.

I go to stroke my beard and then falter at the smooth cheeks of my merchant disguise. 'Why are you so Aistra-bent on leaving Paranish?' I ask eventually.

There's a desperate hope in their eyes. It gnaws at my insides. 'Nothing worth staying for,' Isagani confesses after a long pause. 'I've heard stories about other places, better places. Fancied a change. The world's big, and I intend to see it.'

CHAPTER FOURTEEN

HANAN

THE GROUND HUMS with the voices of the dead, the buckthorn shivering with the vibrations, reminding me of our evening prayers and chants: the cacophony of a choir of desperate voices. I sit beneath the Tree of Life listening to the thoughts and memories of souls suspended in time. These are the ones who have yet to cross the threshold into the void, and so their confusion and agony is the loudest and most potent. The Tree is bent heavy with the weight of the souls it has absorbed, its branches reaching out to the sea and sky year on year. The Tree is bent so far it looks to topple over and crash into the sea, which roils and smashes against the island as if aching to pull us into it. I crawl on my knees to the cliff edge and stare at the roots that have burst forth as if gasping for air.

As a child I measured my growth by the Tree's great trunk: a myriad network of long, snaking branches of all colours and textures, knitting together different species in a tight braid. I once believed I would grow enough to reach around the trunk and touch my fingertips together, and this felt like a significant milestone. As if encompassing the Tree meant I could hold all those souls in my arms. As the years went on, I realised the Tree grew with me – it looks anywhere it can to find nourishment and will cut off or strangle branches when they no longer serve. I would never be able to encircle the Tree.

Malostra says she doesn't hear anything from the temple, that we're too far away. But I do. I hear the voices everywhere on the isle, despite my best efforts. Voices of all living things. It's relentless, the confusion and regret. They are absorbed into the beating heart of the Tree. I can feel how old and weary it is when I touch its bark, both the old, mottled parts that are sloughing and chipping away from the elements, and the emerging bark that peeks through like new soft skin.

I hear voices all the time. When I make night water, when I pray, when I fuck Malostra. Sometimes then the voices stop, for a moment. Then the blood rushes back to my head and with them the heartaches and regrets of Paranish.

I'm too young to die.
Not like this, anything but this.
Will it hurt?
What will happen now?
Will they be there, waiting for me?
I didn't have enough time.
Peace is a lie.

When the voices are quieter, the Tree itself sounds like an old woman sighing. Not in pain exactly, but with the weight of lifetimes on her boughs.

'Sister Hanan?'

A voice cuts through the whispering in my skull. I look up and Mother Joca stands before me, her white cloak clasped around her. Her hair is coming loose from its updo, and she wrings her thickly gloved hands. I have no idea how long she's been there, and she gives me a sympathetic smile. Such an expression is so unusual for her that I stand.

'Solitude is very much your way, isn't it?' she says, beginning to walk around the cliff edge. She surveys the flakes of snow that drift around us. 'Still, it is easy for jealousy to quicken among girls of your age. Emotions flare hot, like a fever.'

I say nothing, knowing silence is the best option. If Mother Joca wants to find a flattering excuse for the other Sisters shunning me, I won't protest.

We make our way across the fields and eventually find the coastal path. It is worn from centuries of Sisters and Mothers promenading close to the cliffs. We must save what little fertile land we have. We circle the temple, giving it a wide berth. I see the main hall illuminated by candlelight and hear voices coming from a casement on the second floor where the youngest girls reside.

We promenade in silence for so long, I wonder if it is some kind of test where I am to hold out for as long as possible. The snow isn't settling but the hoar frost crunches underfoot. It makes a pleasant accompaniment, mingling with the sea to make the voices a white noise in the back of my mind. Eventually we reach the rookery and Mother Joca's voice cuts through.

'Have you given much thought to the latest summons?'

I try to keep my face blank. Every Temple Sister thinks of little else but the summons. Each failure another opportunity for one of us. 'I'm happy to serve the Bastion and Paranish in any way necessary.'

We complete our walk, and she stops us by the temple entrance and the large arched wooden doors. They creak on their hinges as the wind howls through the gaps beneath and the wicket gate clatters persistently. Mother Joca indicates the stained-glass and I glance at the familiar depiction of the Bastion with sun and moon twins in the sky, shining down on it. I turn my back on the temple and look out to the sea beyond. The sun breaks through the mist and there's the mainland, with the true Bastion sitting atop the hill. A ringing fills my ears.

'You're one of the most talented Temple Sisters we've seen in recent years. Your comparative success with the remedy assignment demonstrated that. Your dedication to the rookery, your craftsmanship with quills, and your leather-working are well regarded. And we have noted you are the strongest Sister during the rituals.'

The blood rushes to my head. The Temple Mothers do not give out compliments. My mouth is parched, tongue a rough lump of flesh in my mouth.

I wet my lips and try to speak. I must be humble but not stupid. 'Thank you. I hope Her Majesty is feeling better?'

Mother Joca allows the flicker of a smile. It's a hint, a shadow, but it's enough. 'The successful remedies were gratefully received, yes.'

'I am so glad to hear it and so sorry for the loss of the king. It must be such a hardship for Her Grace, as it is us all.'

Mother Joca examines my face. 'The queen needs all her true allies at her side.'

'Of course, Mother.'

'Mother Lin has spoken warmly of your assistance in the library. I understand you have a keen interest in the written word?'

I nod vigorously and Mother Joca laughs.

'The entire process is an immense learning opportunity,' I say, not hiding my enthusiasm. 'I find creating the tools and equipment as satisfying as cataloguing.'

'You do like to see things from start to finish, don't you? Yes, your efforts in the workshop have not gone unnoticed.'

We walk again and Mother Joca clears her throat. 'Do you have any questions on any of that work?'

I hold my tongue as my mind turns over her question. This is the quandary, the test. I desperately desire to know more about the strange symbols I've transcribed. I know I'm scratching the surface on something powerful, but there's danger in this kind of knowledge. I don't know how Mother Joca will react and I can't let the Bastion out of my reach when it's so close. I let my true question sit on the tip of my tongue, tasting it for a moment, before I swallow it back down.

'I've noticed Mother Lin frequenting the mainland,' I begin. 'I've gathered she is trading with parties there, and I imagine they are books or written materials.' Mother Joca nods and I breathe more deeply. 'With whom does she trade and for what purpose?'

Mother Joca hums thoughtfully and beckons us to make our way back to the shelter of the temple.

'Your observations are astute. The temple helps the flow of information. It's our duty to know when gifted children should come to study with us, for example.'

She makes another thoughtful noise, this time deeper in her throat. 'I am always glad when my instincts are proven correct.' Then she adds, shrewdly, 'You cannot be so naive as to not understand my meaning in seeking you out like this.'

'Your attentions are gratefully received, Mother. The Temple of Aistra has given me so much.'

Mother Joca places a gloved hand on the top of my head, and I bow accordingly, looking down at her sturdy shoes and cloak hem flecked with snow.

'You were nothing when you came to us, Sister Hanan.'

I think about crafting my remedy and the memory of being full encircled by warm arms. The blurry edges of the hands sparking stones. The deep laugh. When I opened up myself, I was granted access to those memories, almost lost to time like feathers on a sea breeze. I had a history before they took me here and made me what I am. My life before the temple is a shadow, but it's not nothing.

CHAPTER FIFTEEN

RIS

Given enough time, objects become sacred. Generations were born and died on this farmstead and the house is full of things they crafted with their hands and touched daily: the wooden highchair carved by my great-grandparents, where Biba sat years ago, rubbing the paste of her food into the grain.

Packing up the entirety of almost forty years is one of the saddest tasks in life. I'm a sentimental sop, and amongst the history is a hoard of useless trinkets that leave me wondering why I do it to myself. But I've always found clean, uncluttered spaces frightening. My father Jon used to call it empty horror, the fear of that yawning space; the echo of a hollow or an abyss. Some people fear being enclosed, but I think of it as being ensconced.

I didn't used to feel this way.

I can pinpoint the moment the hoarding began: the morning I discovered he'd left. The shirt he'd worn the day before was draped over the bed frame. It smelled of him: musky and spicy. I slept with that shirt until it disintegrated to rags. His absence compelled me to keep every fragment of him and our lives together, to remind myself I hadn't imagined our time together; that the promises, now broken, had meant something.

'Why must we leave?' Biba asks, lifting her head from the box where she is organising her things. She is treating the task with great solemnity, as she has for the past week.

'I told you, we must go on a journey.'

'Why us?' she asks, half-churlish.

I exhale sharply. 'I told you to hide this.' I take her small hands in my own and she pulls away, flexing her fingers. Her look is accusatory.

'I've been careful,' she says petulantly. 'I'm doing my best.'

'Not careful enough. Do you want them to take you away to Aistra?'

She shrugs and huffs to the window. 'At least there are people like me at the temple.'

'You might think things will be better there, but you don't know that. I'm just trying to keep you safe.'

'Home is safe.'

I follow her to the window and look out at the farm. 'Not anymore,' I sigh.

I worry the talisman around my neck with my thumb and forefinger. The edge of the crescent moon is thinner, paler, from the years of this habit.

'Why do you rub that?' Biba asks, turning to me.

I look at the talisman for the first time in what feels like forever. I remember the cold of the stone as Larkin slipped the pendant over my head, where it rests in the groove of my clavicle, warmed by my skin. A symbol to the world that we belonged to each other. Twin crescents on our necks.

'It reminds me of your father.'

I see the quiver of the lip, the angry tears welling in her eyes. Soon she's sobbing and clutching at my waist. She's still a child. She conducts herself in such strange, otherworldly ways that I forget this sometimes.

'I'm sorry, I know this is hard. But listen, when we get to the mainland, I need to find someone who can help me. Maybe we can find someone who can help you too?'

She stares up at me and then lets go. 'Others like me? Not at the temple?'

I bind the loose strands of my hair as I consider. 'Most of them are there. I don't know if it's true, but I've heard of others who have – powers like you.'

A glimpse of her hopeful sunshine smile parting through the grief clouds. She's showing me her soft underbelly.

Fetch whines and scratches at the door to the cottage. I reluctantly open it and he comes bounding it, covered in dirt and happier than anyone on the farmstead.

'Couldn't keep him away for long. He knows something's happening,' Vullis says patting the dog on his head. Biba kneels, wrapping her arms around Fetch's neck. I've tried to discourage coddling the working dog but even I can't grudge her this.

I see Ryla and Kopiro crest a nearby hill laden with bags. They set them down near the barn and come over to greet us.

'Are you sure you can manage?' I ask, looking at their weather-worn faces.

Ryla smiles and looks to Kopiro. 'We separated but we can still stand the idea of sharing a home.'

'It's a lot of work on top of your own businesses,' I insist.

'We'll make arrangements,' Kopiro says, giving me a reassuring look. 'You've got other things to worry over.'

They're right. I can't put this off any longer. I'm touched they've all come to see me off. Truly, I underestimated how the years can bind you for life. We have been witnesses to each other's loves, heartbreaks, and losses. Small flames of hope extinguished and reignited. Family legacies weighing like anchors around our necks. They held me when Larkin abandoned us. I wailed in the night as I cried and exorcised everything from my body. They would fight for what is mine, would protect Biba with their lives.

The farmstead looks so small from the Alev port. I can't believe I've spent the majority of my life, on this same patch of land. When I was a child the stone buildings always looked so imposing, the sheep such beasts. It didn't seem that way when I came back, Biba growing inside me. A little wrinkle by my father Jon's eye, a slackening of the skin under Father Nimu's chin. When Larkin and I came here, I had thought Biba would run wild in the fields as I did, sitting on my knee at the loom as I did with my parents, small fingers slowly becoming strong and nimble over the years. It's what I dreamed of when she was still inside me, with her father pressing his ear softly to my belly, to hear her little heartbeat. Quiet and consistent. We dreamed up the fantasies of people deeply in love and untouched by grief. I didn't realise how many dreams would be dashed.

The tattered map lies next to my skin inside my dress as I take one last look at the farmstead in the distance. The sun is peeking over the horizon, the dawn of a new day. I wanted to creep away in the small hours, unable to bear the idea of the whole Spring Isle coming to watch, with their questions and concerned looks.

'We will keep home safe for you,' Vullis says, setting down our bags on the boat's deck with a grunt.

'Is that home?' I ask, nodding towards the farmstead. 'Or is it packed here?' I look over at the bags.

'Not much in the way of worldly possessions,' Ryla says with a wry smile.

I look down at my hands, fingers callused and red from years at the loom. 'I worked my fingers to the bone for their pleasure, and now I get to die for their cause.'

'Hush,' Kopiro insists. 'You won't die out there.'

'You're too stubborn for that,' Ryla agrees, trying to lighten the mood. Their quips are always used as shields.

'What do you think you'll find out there?' Vullis asks. 'Other than death and destruction?'

I swallow hard. I might find fortune. A whisper in the back of my skull tells me I may even find Larkin. I grab the taffrail. 'I can't stay here and wait for them to take everything from me. My only hope is finding whatever the queen wants beyond the Maelstrom.'

'She could stay with us,' Vullis says quietly, looking over at Biba.

He's turned her attention to Kopiro and Ryla now, a serious look on her face as she points to Biba and across the farmstead.

I close the distance between myself and Vullis. 'She could,' I agree gently. 'But I'd never forgive myself if something happened to her.'

'Is she any safer out there with you?'

There's a storm of feeling inside me. The fierceness of my desire to protect Biba. The urge to run. The broken pieces of this quest before me. I can't answer Vullis's question but that is the risk I have to take.

I look from each isle, from the lush greens of Summer, through to the golds and reds of Autumn, and in the distant mist I know hides the Winter Isle. I shiver and wrap my cloak tighter around myself.

CHAPTER SIXTEEN

HANAN

THE BIRD'S NECK is twisted at a horrible angle. I cock my head to the side, peering at the entrails and feathers matted with blood. When I bend down to touch it, it's still warm. It must have crashed into the temple only minutes ago. The wind is ripping at me today, and the huge swells blast sea spray. My skin dances with the pain of the lashing and I crouch low and close to the temple wall for shelter. The bird is a beautiful little thing with bright blue feathers and a gold-tipped beak, and I encircle it with my cloak. So small and so fragile. Hollow bones that allow them to fly but make them vulnerable.

A shiver runs down my spine and the Tree's energy pulsates through me. The sighting of a mokon is a rare and precious thing and the death of one is a terrible omen. I cast a protective circle around myself and touch the talisman at my neck. Even though it's a moment for reverence, my eyes are thirsty to examine its form. My gaze flits across its delicate feathers, its unreal unearthly colours. Such a thing feels shot through with magic, with power. But not anymore. It lies there still, but not restful.

'I'm sorry my sweet,' I say, placing my hand gently on its body. A scream pierces my head, and I pull away. It stops. I breathe, closing my eyes and tentatively stretching out my hand again. Once I make contact, the cacophony begins again. I focus on that awful, frantic noise. The bird is screaming, not on the ground on the Winter Isle but in my head, inside my flesh. I hold on to the bird's body. Pain shoots through my arm and into the bird. It's heart jolts, then beats. It increases rapidly, a murmuration, then a frenzied fury. I open my eyes and see the mokon, moving and flapping wildly. It squawks and I remove my hand, letting it into the sky. It takes flight, a bewildered and ugly movement. It screams again, its eyes red and weeping. Even though we're no longer touching, I feel the wild hastening of its heart.

'Wait!' I shout.

The bird's heart explodes, ripping it from the inside out. It bursts into a nothingness of feathers and blood. What remains of the mokon splatters on my face.

At first, I think the screaming is coming from me. Then I turn around and see Malostra standing at the temple door.

I run after her, so fast my muscles burn and the breath in my lungs is fire. My eyes adjust to the gloom inside the temple, listening for the rhythmic slap of her shoes on the stone floor. Her breathing is ragged and she's crying, gasping for air. The hem of her skirt is just within reach, and I grab at it. We both tumble to the ground and there's a sharp, blinding-white pain.

'Let go of me!' she shouts, stumbling to her feet. Her skirt is torn, her knees bruised. I've caught my teeth on my lip and bring my hands up to my face as blood pools in my palms. Something sharp penetrates my skin, jagged little knives. There are thorns sticking out of my skin and then I see Malostra's hands. She's grown a sunburst of gorse in her palms, and the plant retreats now that it's done its damage. She stands there numbly, not running, no longer trying to escape me.

'What are you going to do?' I ask slowly.

She bites her lip and looks at my bleeding hands.

'What did you do to that bird?'

'Malostra—' I begin, my voice honeyed.

'Answer me!' she cuts me off, salt-sharp.

I hold her gaze. 'What did you see?'

'You . . . fixed it,' she says, and I think there is a tiny sliver of wonder and admiration in her voice. 'But then – something went wrong. The bird became . . . something else.' Her brow furrows as she tries to find her way, to remember and understand what I did. 'You killed it. It died, again.'

The temple's quiet has been broken by Malostra's shouts and I feel the stirring of the Sisters in corridors, moving closer towards us. The rustle of skirts rounds the corner and there's Mothers Joca and Lin striding purposefully towards us, followed by an orderly line of Temple Sisters. We have disturbed the start of afternoon study.

'Are you going to tell them?' I whisper, desperately trying to hold Malostra with my gaze.

'What in the name of Aistra is happening here?' Mother Joca asks, as I dust off my skirts and stand.

Mother Lin eyes the tear in Malostra's gown, the blood on my face.

'In so many generations, we have never seen fighting in these halls,' Mother Joca continues, berating us loudly in front of the silent sisters. I don't believe that in the centuries of the Temple of Aistra's existence there hasn't been a single bout of violence.

The Sisters keep their heads down, peering curiously through their eyelashes at us. Malostra has adopted this pose as well: head down, hands clasped.

I feel bile rise in my throat and am filled with a poisonous disdain for her meekness. I stand arms akimbo and stare directly at the Sisters. They hold the whip of priestess-hood above us, but I'm under no illusions now. I've failed, lost any chance of that. Fuck it, may as well be defiant. Aistra knows I've craved it all these years.

'Explain yourselves, Hanan and Malostra,' Mother Joca commands.

'A lovers' quarrel, I'm sure,' Mother Lin says lightly.

An involuntarily sneer creeps onto my face and the smile drops from hers. The relationships between Temple Sisters are commonplace but to speak of one so publicly, so off-handedly, is absolutely tasteless. I had thought Lin had more decency.

'That's not what it is,' Malostra snaps. There's a wine-stained blush on her face and her mouth is pursed, as if she might cry. 'The bird was dead. And then it was alive again. Hanan, she—' Malostra scrambles to find the words. 'She brought it back to life.'

'Necromancy?' Mother Joca breathes.

Mother Lin's hand goes to her mouth.

'To the sanctuary, immediately – both of you,' she orders.

Mother Lin flutters her hands and the Temple Sisters scatter. Malostra and I are bound by Mother Joca's force of will and follow her up the spiral stairs to the quarters where the Mothers reside. The sanctuary looked much larger the last time I was here, but everything does when you're a child. It was my initiation as a Temple Sister, the first place you are brought, where you say your vows to the Bastion. All I remember is being deathly cold, sure I would never be warm again. I was salt-sprayed and disorientated, wondering where home had gone. The pen had shaken in my hand as I had tried to cross out my name. I'd never held a pen before, didn't even know what my name looked like in written Nishian. I've seen tomes of such lists now in the archive, thousands of girls with the same strikes through their names.

Malostra and I stand side by side, not looking at one another. She has made her choice as I have made mine. If our situations were reversed, I believe I would have made her choice. After all, it means one less Temple Sister in consideration for the position of priestess.

'Necromancy.' Mother Joca spits the word as filth. She stands behind her desk and stares down at the neatly stacked papers and then back at us. 'Where did you hear of this?'

Malostra looks at me. I stay silent.

'She has papers,' Malostra blurts out.

I snap my head round and glare.

'Papers?' Mother Lin asks, stepping forward.

Malostra nods. 'She keeps them in the west bathroom on our floor. Under the flagstones.'

'You followed me?' I can't keep the bitterness out of my voice.

'You didn't hide it very well, Hanan,' she says, voice cold and smooth. 'I didn't see what they were, but she told me she was doing experiments. I only realised what she meant today. The bird was dead. Then it was alive. She did that. It was – . . . unholy, unnatural.'

'Of course, Malostra,' Mother Joca soothed.

'What is your truth, Hanan?' Mother Lin asks, her gaze soft and level.

I release a full breath and close my eyes.

'I have been . . . studying. Experimenting. This is true. But everything I found was in the temple library. I wanted to push myself, to prove myself worthy to your attentions Mother Joca.'

Mother Lin takes Malostra by the arm and guides her out of the sanctuary. 'Go back to your room.'

The last I see of her is that frightened moon face and a flash of her dark curls.

Mother Joca steps forward, her eyes roving over me. 'Did you ever succeed with such experiments?'

Her question surprises the answer out of my throat. 'Almost.'

Mother Joca bites her thumbnail, standing motionless as she watches me. The tension is broken by Mother Lin returning to the sanctuary.

'Show us,' Mother Joca insists.

I furrow my brows. 'What do you mean?'

Mother Lin points to a cobweb on the table leg. At its centre lies a dead spider, curled in on itself.

I move towards it and stare back at their expectant faces. 'What do you want me to do?'

'One of your *experiments*,' Mother Joca commands. Her emphasis on the final word makes my skin prickle.

I crouch down and focus on the creature. This isn't like the mokon. This is a quotidian creature, its energy small and distant, far from the shell of this body. It's like peering through a mist at a shadow.

'It's gone,' I whisper.

'Try harder,' Mother Lin encourages.

I gently hover my fingers near the web, feeling the hum of the strings. A pulsing at the base of my skull begins to radiate and then it's like a candle flame at my fingertips. Here it is. I open my eyes, and the spider is uncurling its legs, like a flower in bloom. It's a stretch in the late morning. The hum of the web increases. Then I hear Mother Joca's voice, and I lose it. The creature sinks back in on itself.

'She did it. She almost did it!' Mother Joca repeats.

'Are you sure that's what it was?' Mother Lin asks, hand over her mouth.

'Do you know what this means, Lin?' Mother Joca grabs the other woman's shoulders and shakes them.

'Surely not?' Mother Lin says. 'We knew she was talented but—'

'She is wanted immediately,' Mother Joca says, hurrying about the sanctuary.

'What is going on?' I ask, hesitant to draw their attention back to me.

'Pack your things, Hanan,' Mother Lin instructs. 'You're going to the Bastion.'

CHAPTER SEVENTEEN

RIS

THE MAINLAND IS everything I expected: raucous, pungent, and barely room to swing an otter-cat. It starts to rain once we dock in Umasa, a kind of dreich mizzle that soaks through everything. The air is filled with the stench of blood mingled with salt water.

Our disembarkation is blocked by a Seaguardian stalking the dock. He eyes us coldly, gaze landing on our bags. 'Name and origin.'

'Ris, from Alev on the Spring Isle,' I say, looking down. It's impossible to make myself small and pretty, so I try meek.

'And what's this?' he asks, pointing to the swelling and bruises on my face.

'An accident,' I say.

He laughs, deep from the belly. 'Oh, aye. And I'm the queen's priestess. And who's this then, another accident?' he asks, laughing harder as he points at Biba.

'Something like that.' I try to smile, to ride this camaraderie.

His expression changes like a mainland wind. 'State your business.'

'We're visiting Umasa,' I say, holding Biba's hand more tightly.

'I can see that,' he says churlishly. 'For how long?'

I blanch. Like a fool, I haven't prepared thorough answers. He watches me struggle. 'A week or so.'

'We're here to see the baby,' Biba interjects.

We both stare down at her and I remember that stupid unfinished blanket.

'Yes, we're taking in the sights, hoping to witness the royal birth.'

He seems to soften at this. I can see it writ plain on his face: he thinks we're country fools on a jolly. I slacken my face into overwhelmed bemusement.

'Keep your wits about you. Umasa's crawling with unscrupulous types. Especially since they opened the docks to foreigners and returners.'

I notice the town square and the empty gallows and dare a question. 'What happened here?'

The Seaguardian follows my gaze. 'Long drop and a short stop.'

The breeze picks up and I shudder.

'On your way,' he dismisses, and we squeeze past him, hurrying onto solid ground.

'Are all mainlanders like that?' Biba asks.

'I certainly hope not,' I answer, leading us down the seafront. I pause, looking at Biba. 'That was very clever and brave of you to think of that. Hopefully you won't have to do something like that again. Do you understand?'

She nods, her expression serious. 'Only help a little.'

Windswept shopfronts line the boardwalk, and someone sweeps sand from their stoop. Biba drags on me, slowing her pace to take in the stream of folk in the streets. I struggle to focus as voices float past on the wind, accented Nishian and strange song-like tongues I don't recognise. At last, I hear Nishian proper, someone arguing with an outsider.

'How can I best make myself understood—' and then the voice shifts into another language, and the outsider laughs, responding in kind.

I stare, trying to find the source through the crowd. Eventually I find them: a person tall and plainly dressed, but the quality of the material is obviously good even at this distance. They are standing in their doorway, pointing to something in the shopfront to the outsider, a potential customer. I can't read the sign above the door, but as we pass by the smell of fresh baking overwhelms me. It is at odds with the shape in the shopfront, square and under a thin silk cloth. By Paranish, do they sell books?

The shop owner can no longer ignore our idle stares. No doubt they think us outer isle folk too gormless to know better. I'm sure my black eye and busted lip don't help.

'May I help you?' they ask.

Biba is looking past them to find the source of the smell.

The stranger softens when they see Biba.

'After your breakfast, aye?' And then adds: 'Take a seat while I settle up here, would you?'

Their warmth and candour is disarming, and I can't help but do what they say.

The front of the shop is lined with shelves, all stacked high with books. The smell of wood mingles with the baking, and we linger, trying not to touch anything. Biba seems reverent, her eyes drinking everything in. She reaches out to a plant wilting in the front window. The stems dance at her presence, as if her touch were water reviving them. I grab her hand and urge her towards a corner near the back. Here I'm on more familiar ground: a wooden table in a nook near a warm stove and display cabinets where rows of fresh cakes, pastries, and pies sit steaming in the morning sun.

'Business concluded, on to breakfast.' The shopkeeper claps their hands as they join us in the back. They smile kindly at Biba, who is stealing a glance at the cabinets. 'Do you know what you'd like?'

'She's a bit tuckered out,' I admit. 'It's been a long journey.'

'Where did you come from?'

'The Spring Isle.'

'Oh, I've heard it's lovely there,' they say politely. I'm not sure what is particularly lovely about the Spring Isle, perhaps simply the novelty of it. 'Welcome to Umasa. I'm Morna.' Morna makes the corresponding hand sign to indicate she. She pushes her hair behind her ear, and I finally catch the small blue ribbon braided into her hair.

'Ris and Biba,' I respond.

'How about I plate you up a few of my favourites?' She smiles.

Biba nods and Morna disappears behind a counter, talking cheerfully as she gathers up an assortment from the display.

'Careful, it's hot,' I say, as Biba takes a seeded bun from the plate as soon as it's set down.

'Open it like this to let out the steam,' Morna says, putting her hands around Biba's and gently tearing the bun in half. She licks the golden filling from her fingers as she waits. 'Salt and sweet,' she informs me.

'What brings you to the mainland?' Morna asks conversationally, tidying the kitchen area.

'To celebrate the royal birth,' I say, feigning excitement.

'You're a bit early.' Morna laughs. 'Although I suppose babes come when they like. But not before Magliyab, I imagine.'

Biba is tugging on my sleeve, and I see half the plate of treats is little more than crumbs and sauce. 'Mama, is this who you're looking for?'

I shush Biba and take a flat cake and nibble at the edges.

Morna busies herself and I can tell she's trying not to eavesdrop, but my cheeks burn. I look at the books in the other alcove of the shop. 'That person you were speaking with, I hope we weren't disturbing?'

Morna takes the opening. 'No, it's a pleasure to have more folk interested in the book trade now our docks are open.'

'You seemed to know their language.'

'Only a smattering,' they demur. 'My partner is Lassairian.'

Morna speaks freely, warmly. I look at her face, pinched with concentration as she moves towards the book alcove, straightening stacks. As I suspected, her clothes are finer than they first suggested. Books are not commonplace in Paranish, but the docks haven't been open so long that trade would be flourishing so soon. I wonder if she has other more established clientèle.

'Are these all stories, these books?'

'Not at all,' Morna says. 'See here.' She takes a volume down from a shelf and beckons us over, lowering the book so Biba can see the pages.

'Look, but don't touch,' she says, not unkindly.

She shows us an illustration, which goes across both pages, diagrams of plants with arrows and scribbles. 'Herb lore,' she explains, pointing to various elements. 'See, this is the stamen and these are the petals,' she points at the diagram and shows Biba. 'Ah, and see here, we have a living example.'

Morna takes down a shrivelled rosemary plant, its leaves curling and brown.

'Look, but don't touch,' I remind Biba sternly.

The plant undulates towards Biba, its leaves stretching out as if reaching for her.

Morna glances between the book and the empty gap on the shelf. 'What was this doing on that shelf? Oh no, this is completely miscategorised.'

I can't risk Morna seeing the plant moving.

'Do you ever see maps?' I ask suddenly.

'Of course,' she says, closing the book and putting it back on the shelf. The rosemary plant is forgotten.

Biba tugs on Morna's arm. 'We have one.'

Morna looks at me, expectantly. We're here now, and we've had the good fortune to stumble upon someone who knows letters. Understanding the map is just the first step.

'Yes, we do,' I say, deciding to show my hand. There will be questions, but I have no choice. 'A fair exchange, of course. Is your advice for sale?'

The bell above the shop door chimes and I turn to see two women enter. The first is drowning in soft light colours, more fabric than woman. She pushes a strand of hair behind her ear and deftly sidesteps all obstacles as she enters the shop and makes her way over to us. She's followed by an older woman, short and stout with a lined round face.

'Who are they?' I ask, standing.

Biba is staring at the women, who smile and approach slowly.

'These are friends of mine,' Morna reassures us, pulling up chairs for the newcomers.

'I'm Ligaya, Morna's partner,' the younger woman says, her voice heavily accented.

'And I'm Narra,' the older woman adds. 'I own an inn not far from here.'

Morna sets about brewing a pot of tea and Ligaya begins to make polite conversation in stilted Nishian. Meanwhile, Narra is staring at Biba, who is beaming back at her.

'Lookit,' she says, uncurling her fist. Inside are some tiny seeds from the breakfast bun she was eating, retrieved from the plate still on the table.

I struggle to divide my attention between Ligaya's chatter and Biba, half standing in my chair to grab her. She cries out, startled by my interruption.

'Excuse me,' I say, holding her to me and moving to an alcove to soothe her. I hide between the shelves as I hear them murmuring.

'Did we do something?' Ligaya asks.

'What happened?' asks Morna, over the whistling of the kettle.

Eventually I hear slow and steady footsteps and see Narra at the edge of the nook.

'I saw what your girl can do,' she begins, her voice gentle. I flinch but she continues. 'She's not the first gifted one we've encountered. In fact, I myself am a hedge witch and Ligaya is my apprentice – a kitchen witch.'

I tentatively come back to the table, staring at Ligaya and Narra in turn.

'We mean you no harm,' Ligaya says, giving Biba a smile.

'You're both – touched?' I ask, setting Biba down on my lap.

'We prefer gifted, but yes,' Narra confirms.

'Like me?' Biba turns to the others, her tears mostly over.

'Can we see what you have?' Morna asks, coaxing Biba to open her hand.

Biba looks to me for approval and I nod. She opens her palm and the seeds are there, sprouted, the little seedlings squashed but alive.

'Now that's lovely,' Ligaya says.

There's something in the gentle wonder of Ligaya's voice that sets me off. I start crying, despite the fact it hurts like something unholy with my injuries.

Narra pats my back, making circles with her hand. 'Oh, bless you. It's been a lot to carry, hasn't it?'

I nod, sobbing and heaving, almost unable to breathe, only to let everything out.

'Mama, maybe they can help us,' Biba says, trying to reassure me.

I bring her into my chest and hold her until the tears cease.

CHAPTER EIGHTEEN

FINLYR

As I break open the savoury bun and let the steam pour out, I grudgingly admit that the day's garden work was worth the exchange. Isagani and I sit at the communal dining bench, rubbing the smalls of our backs, occasionally sighing contentedly. As the day has gone on, more of the guests have risen from their beds, some grabbing a bun on their way out for later, others sipping tea and easing silently into their days. The pastries and tea had been laid out but there was no sign of the innkeeper or her apprentice.

The door opens and we're distracted by the wall of noise and smells that waft in from Umasa. Already I have gotten used to feeling as if the inn is sealed against the outside world. Our hosts have returned, along with new arrivals: two women and a child. One of them is clearly at ease with Narra and Ligaya, leaning into the later, pushing back her hair and revealing the blue ribbon woven near the nape of her neck. The other looks apprehensive and is a little older than me, with a hardy face and full figure. A working woman, some sort of labourer. She has dressed tastefully, with clothes that aren't showy, but well made, and she's tied her ribbon into a bow to keep her hair from her face. Her outfit fits her with little flourishes, as though tailored for her rather than handmade by another and traded for. The child is about six or seven, glittering keen eyes, with a cascade of dark wavy hair, similarly adorned like her mother's, and red cheeks.

Isagani and I share a look, and they raise their eyebrows.

Narra and Ligaya usher them into the kitchen but the latch doesn't quite catch, and it creaks ajar.

I stand, stretching and yawning. 'Come on, squirt.' I pat Isagani on the back and we make our way across the dining room. The other few guests' glance at us languidly, as they had when the new arrivals were ushered in. Lots of coming and going at the moment.

I head towards the staircase to the rooms, swerving at the last minute to an alcove behind them, right beside the kitchen. Isagani crouches by me and we listen to the scrape of furniture, watching through the sliver in the door frame. A scrape of furniture and the women sit down.

'Parched?' Ligaya asks and I recognise a pitcher of that ghastly purple liquid: her truth binder.

The woman and girl take a mug each and sip.

'This is your inn?' the woman asks, eyes dark and wild as they rove over every surface.

'Yes, and you and Biba are welcome to stay here,' Narra says, her voice low and gentle. 'Bed and board for whatever errands you can help with.'

I furrow my brow. Where are they going to put them: the attic? That, or we're doubling up on bunks because we're fully occupied here from what Narra said.

'Got any mending?' The woman laughs, something deep that quickly turns to hiccuping sobs.

'Oh, Ris,' Ligaya says, moving the pitcher away and taking the woman's hand.

'Things have been hard for you. But you're among friends now, and like-minded folk,' the other visitor, the one familiar with Ligaya, pipes up.

'Thank you, Morna,' Ris says, smiling at the child, Biba.

But the child isn't looking at her mother. She's looking at us.

'People,' she says, pointing at the door.

Narra hisses, making her way to the door and staring at us with a face like thunder. 'Speaking of trouble.'

'We didn't mean to eavesdrop,' Isagani says, sheepishly.

Ligaya rolls her eyes. 'You two love getting into mischief.'

'Who are they?' Ris asks, eyeing us warily.

'Other guests at this inn: merchant Larkin and his daughter Isa.'

Ris stands, her body braced.

'What's the matter?' Narra asks, observing the change in her demeanour.

The child is staring at me. 'You're not him!' she yells suddenly, lashing out at me. 'Why would you say that?' she screams and the fireplace roars to life, the whoosh of the heat sending Ris stumbling backwards. The hem of her travelling cloak is aflame, and I run forward, smothering it with the soles of my boots.

'What in fucking Aistra was that?' Isagani asks, scrambling up from the floor.

'She's touched,' Ligaya says.

'Touched?' I echo. 'You gave them the drink, the spell! They shouldn't be able to cause harm.'

'I know,' Ligaya says helplessly.

'That's no petty magic,' Narra says, hand on her chest, breathing laboured. 'Have you done that before, child?'

Biba awakens from her shock, and nods slowly. 'I can do things. Sometimes it's an accident. Mama told me not to show anyone, but they found out anyway. That's why we had to run.'

The atmosphere in the room shifts and a horrific sound like an animal dying comes from Ris. At first, I'm not sure what it is, and then I realise she's crying, smoke gently still rising from the smouldered hem of her cloak.

CHAPTER NINETEEN

RIS

WHEN I WAKE, I feel as though I could sleep for another year. It takes me a moment to understand my surroundings. Dark wooden beams and a lumpy bed. I throw open the curtains and window, letting the weak light into the dusty room. Biba laughs high and bright, waking from her peaceful dreams. I smell the air, sharp and briny, and listen to the voices on the wind: Nishian, Lassren, and other urgent tongues.

Voices from below, shuffling of furniture, heavy footfall on the stairs. We follow our noses to the dining room and could almost cry at the sight of the breakfast spread. Bowls overflowing with rice, fried fish, eggs, wheels of cheese, and fresh greens.

Among the inn's guests I recognise the eavesdroppers: the man and his daughter. His awareness of his broad frame as he moves, trying not to knock his dining companions. He proffers a plate of soft-boiled eggs at the kid. They're wiry, all limbs inside their loose-fitting overalls. Three thin ribbons are clumsily tied into their fringe: blue, purple, and green. She, they, any. They don't look much like a merchant and daughter.

'Hungry?' Ligaya asks Biba and she nods enthusiastically. I hover awkwardly by the bench until the merchant moves down to make space.

We sit, and I surreptitiously eye him as I spoon some rice into my bowl. His face is handsome, a small scar on his right eyebrow, which enhances the dark, strong features. I can tell from his tan lines he recently got rid of a beard. There's something reassuring in the heft of him.

'I'm sorry you had to see that last night,' I say awkwardly. 'Not the most pleasant of introductions. I'm Ris, and this is Biba.'

'Not at all,' he replies. 'I'm sorry we were so rude. Larkin. And Isa.'

I stare at him and then Isa, remembering the names they gave last night. It wasn't a common name; one I hadn't heard in years. 'I would appreciate if you kept what you saw to yourselves.'

The merchant Larkin winks.

'And I'd be glad of some honesty too,' I add and his expression shifts.

'Excuse me?' he asks.

'Those aren't your true names,' I say.

The colour drains from his face, and he turns defensive. 'Are you a Bastion spy?' he asks through gritted teeth.

'Of course not,' I glower. 'But I know you're lying.'

'I'm Isagani,' they say, trying to ease the tension at the table. 'So, not too far off.'

The man looks at me stubbornly. 'Nothing personal, love. We've lied to a lot of folk.'

'I'll keep your cover,' I say, trying to even my voice. 'You've seen what my girl can do. We're in the same boat, friend. A little honesty builds trust.'

'Finlyr,' the man mumbles, relenting.

'Are you really father and daughter?'

'They're my kin,' Finlyr says firmly, and I steal a glance at Isagani, who ducks their head to hide their blush.

A large, black otter-cat prowls into the dining room, and Biba stares at it. She grabs a fish from her plate and holds it out to the creature.

'Biba, that's impolite!' I admonish, but the otter-cat grabs the proffered fish by the tail and lays it down on the rug. 'My thanks, little one,' he says, his voice low and guttural.

'He can talk!' Biba says, clapping her hands together.

'That wee bastard is Sinigang,' the merchant explains. 'He comes with the inn. Unfortunately. Soon you'll want to strangle him with his own tail.'

'He's an otter-cat,' I say.

'Yes,' Finlyr replies. 'You outer island folk never seen a hybrid before?'

'They don't usually talk, do they?' I ask, observing Sinigang tearing into his breakfast, ripping the silver head off the fish and meticulously gnawing at the delicate bones.

'You'll have to ask him yourself,' Finlyr says with a laugh.

I snort. 'What sort of place have we come to?'

'Narra seems to collect trouble.'

'What about those two?' I nod at Ligaya and Morna, who are bringing in plates of bread and pastries and more of those moreish buns.

'Narra's pretty apprentice and her culinary supplier? When they aren't staring at books or plants they're making eyes at each other.'

Some of the inn's other guests are standing around the cauldron, which hangs above the fireplace. They have wooden bowls in their hands and scoop ladlefuls from the pot, one person standing at the cauldron and serving while the others pass filled bowls back. Eventually one makes its way to us and Isagani passes it to Biba.

'Careful, it's hot,' they say, and she grabs it gently but firmly and sets it down on the bench in front of her.

'What is that?' I ask.

'Perpetual stew,' Finlyr says. 'Surely you have that on the outer isles?'

'Aye,' I say indignantly, rootling in my mind for any such thing at Vullis's tavern.

He smiles and shakes his head. 'You're suspicious of everything.'

'If I don't know it, how can I trust it?' I counter.

'Oh, for Paranish's sake,' he mutters under his breath. 'It's magic, that's all.'

Biba looks up from her plate and stares at Finlyr, blinking. We've never heard anyone speak so openly of the touched and their powers. She's never heard such free talk of her power. It must be a relief to find others like you, and to not be feared by those who aren't.

He smiles at her. 'I bet you haven't seen many witches, eh?'

She colours. I look around until I'm satisfied none of the other guests have heard us over the hubbub of breakfast.

'Ligaya told me about the emerald vine,' Biba says slowly.

'Oh, you've heard the love story too, eh?' Finlyr asks.

'She came from Lassair to find an emerald vine,' Isagani adds, seeing my raised eyebrow.

'It was her mama's last wish,' Biba chimes in. I watch as the words come tumbling out. Is she afraid a pause for breath will have her story silenced? 'It only blossoms ever so rarely. And it doesn't grow on Lassair because that's on the water. Ligaya said when she sleeps, she still feels the boat rocking. Makes her feel like her mama's still holding her . . .' She trails off, twisting the hem of her pinafore. She's travel-worn, knees scraped and dirt under her fingernails. She adds, in a whisper: 'Sometimes I feel like that too.'

I blink back tears and try to smile at her. 'I'm glad you've had a chance to talk with Ligaya and Narra,' I tell Biba. 'We don't know many like-folk,' I add for Finlyr and Isagani's benefit.

Biba reaches for my hand, and I feel a jolt, like your heart in your mouth when you miss the final step.

Then the inquisitive chirrup of the otter-cat. He's found his way back into Biba's lap and has probably been observing for who knows how long, so silent he's practically a shadow.

'You're the map-holder,' Sinigang says quietly, just for us.

I nod. 'And you're magic-touched.'

'Not so much touched, as simply . . . am,' he says. 'A strange concept to you, I think. But not to her.' He purrs as Biba strokes his head.

'He's not a pet, Biba,' I say, harsher than I mean to.

She looks at me. 'He's wild, not bad.'

'I don't think you're talking about the same otter-cat,' Isagani says under their breath.

'Narra's cauldron brings together many strange ingredients,' Sinigang says, winking at me. 'You're already beginning to find what you're looking for.'

Finlyr stands up, slapping his knees with those massive hands. 'Right, time to get on.'

A shiver runs up my spine as he moves away, singing a work song I recognise from sailors in taverns. His deep voice is surprisingly warm, low and rumbling as he carries a tune:

> 'Haul away from shore to shore
> The lover of the ocean
> Never could they love me more
> Than sailing the horizon'

Not a merchant, but a sailor. An invisible golden thread pulling us along first from Morna's to Narra's . . . and now to this strange man with secrets I must unearth.

CHAPTER TWENTY

HANAN

I HAD ALWAYS suspected there was a secret passage between the mainland and the Winter Isle; now I know I was correct. The damp on Mother Lin's cloak, the packages of books and writing instruments I bundled up for her, the fact she was always returning with different volumes. I had kept silent and watched, until I was a shadow and they forgot I was there. It had been easier then, to take liberties: letting my glance stray overlong at a scroll, Mother Lin letting me lock up the library after she had gone to supper. Ample chances to copy things out, steal away those symbols and learnings in the hopes that, with enough time, I could unlock its secrets. I feel vindicated by the discovery of the aqueduct, which is what Mother Joca calls it.

'Get in the boat and row,' she commands, untying the dock line and throwing the sodden rope at me.

I stare at the weathered planks, unsure if the thing will even hold my weight.

'The guards will meet you at the other side of the aqueduct,' Mother Lin adds.

Now that it's untethered, the small rowboat begins following the current down the tunnel. I have no choice but to half-jump, half-fall into the vessel with an almighty splash. I grab for the oars and row, feeling the pressure of the wood against my hands as I attempt the strange movement. When I turn to look back, the Mothers are gone.

My breath becomes deeper and less laboured as I fall into a rhythm, muscles no longer screaming though still protesting against the hauling weight. I pause, wiping the sweat from my brow. I can hear my heartbeat and the blood pumping in my veins, but everything else is silent. There is absolutely nothing here. Barely any life in the waters; or if there is, it is so small that it is undetectable. No sky, no vegetation. Only the distant life on the isles either side of the tunnel walls.

When I arrive at the Bastion, the dock is an unassuming stone platform and a door in the recess of the wall. Sconces light my way and cast the Seaguardians' shadows as large and misshapen. I'm secretly relieved to find anything here at all after countless hours rowing through the gloaming. At first, I revelled in the quiet. The absence of the voices of the dead, and the peace of being alone. Eventually, the silence became suffocating. I never thought I'd need that familiar soundscape. I kept looking for it, like a part of myself I'd misplaced.

I'm drenched with sweat and queasy from the motion of the sea. The guards help me dock and we make our way through darkened passages, our footsteps ricocheting around the tunnels. It's a labyrinth down here, with barely lit passages and winding switchbacks. Eventually the guards stop, and I nearly bash into the tall, imposing woman leading our procession.

She indicates a small, wooden door, concealed behind a tapestry. It's the softest thing my fingers have ever felt. The walls here are thick stone and warm from the sunshine that filters through the large, clear windows. Now that we're inside the fortress, light hits the tapestry, which depicts the wedding day of the queen and our late king. I gasp and the sound echoes around the room.

'This way.'

The dazzling white of the Seaguardians' uniforms are clearer in the light. The tall, imposing woman continues to lead the way. As we make our way into the inner parts of the building, the air becomes warmer and the furnishings more luxurious. This must be the inner sanctum where the royals reside. It's difficult to tear my eyes away from the finery. I didn't know such colours existed in the world, and my fingers twitch to caress every material I see. I surreptitiously trace the edge of a lacquered wooden end table, and the imposing Seaguardian catches my eye. I snatch my hand back, but I think I catch the trace of a smile as she turns away.

As we pass by open doors into rooms, I see nobles dressed in finery. They eat and chat and drink with abandon. It feels as though everyone is shouting to be heard, and I don't understand how they can think and talk and listen all at the same time. Living at the Temple of Aistra has taught me that the walls hear everything. Our voices were barely raised above a low murmur at the temple.

The queen sits on her throne in the great hall. I cast my eyes down; flicking looks at my surroundings when I dare. The stained glass of the round window throws dappled light on a man knelt before her in supplication.

'The problems continue, Your Highness. The harvest—'

'Have you discovered the cause?' the queen asks.

Her voice is rich honey. I steal a glance at her. She's younger than I expected, with dark waves of hair pinned back from her face and adorned with flowers, jewels, perhaps even feathers. I can't quite tell from here, but they glint in the light. She looks like something holy. She is the sun. She is more than anything I've seen before.

The farmer wrings the cap in his hands. 'Not yet, Your Highness. No one understands why—'

She sighs, her mouth turning down a fraction. 'Collect rainwater. Send your boats to the other isles for resources. Protect what's left of the harvest.'

'With respect, Your Highness, there is not enough to continue our . . . contributions . . . and feed ourselves.'

The queen lets his words hang in the air, letting him stew in the silence. I venture a look. She places an elegant hand under her chin and stares off in the distance, her gaze detached from the scene in front of her. 'Then you must make do.'

The farmer opens his mouth to speak again but closes it after a fleeting glance at the queen. He bows his head, and I follow his lead.

The imposing Seaguardian steps forward and grabs the farmer's arm. 'Your concerns have been heard, and your contribution is appreciated.'

The farmer's shoulders sag and he allows the Seaguardian to lead him out of the throne room. The leader kneels and forces me to do the same. I drop my gaze to the floor, trying to sink into it.

'What have you brought me, Salvacion?'

'The new offering for priestess from the temple, Your Grace,' Salvacion says.

'Come here.'

Salvacion hauls me to my feet. The queen makes her way out to the balcony, and I follow. She places a hand to her belly, which I now see is swollen with child. The fabric is pulled taut against her skin to accentuate it, and she looks almost ready to deliver. The queen peers over the balcony down the steep hill. My eyes follow hers to a magnificent sun mosaic in the courtyard below us. It spirals out from a jewel in the centre, moving in a meticulous arrangement through shades of yellow, orange, and red. Further down the hill is the sprawl of Umasa port and beyond I make out the four isles, set under various shades of relentless blue sky. Everywhere save the Winter Isle, where dark clouds and fog hang over the Temple of Aistra.

'Everyone is waiting for the birth of this child,' the queen says after some time.

'Blessed be the day,' I murmur, unsure what else to say.

'This is the future,' the queen says, cradling her stomach. 'You must protect it at all costs, do you understand?'

'Of course, Your Grace. I am at your disposal.'

'Indeed,' she says, examining me liberally. Her eyes rover over my entire body from temple to toe and I feel naked despite the layers of robes between my skin and her gaze. 'The Temple Mothers trust in your healing hands. We'd hate to disappoint them.'

I nod. I realise I'm holding my breath, not daring to make a sound in front of the queen.

'You will be my sword and the heir's shield,' she says, and I see her turn away in my periphery. 'A shadow waiting to destroy our enemies.'

'I will serve the Bastion with my life,' I say, bowing.

I cannot believe she is real. She is the sun, and I must not look directly at her.

CHAPTER TWENTY-ONE

FINLYR

I WALK BESIDE Ligaya, and it is a relief to be out of the inn. Despite my years at sea, I still hate being cooped up. The houses and shops in Umasa's town square cosy together like old friends. Earthen tiles glitter in the sun and handmade bunting and streamers cascade from shop awnings and balcony gardens. There's a frenetic energy, the air full of shouts of harried vendors preparing their wares in the town square, and it is even more intense than when I arrived a few weeks ago.

'What if we haven't shipped in enough piyata cider?'

'Is Dally around to help with the market stall?'

'Feels like there won't be any more room in Paranish soon,' I whisper to Ligaya.

'And to think we're giving away beds to you lot,' she returns, a pert smile dancing on her lips.

I catch my reflection in a shop window. A plume in my hat and finer clothes than I've ever had before. My cheeks are fuller, as are my muscles. Turns out it's easier to do garden labour on a full belly. I'm not sure my own father would recognise me now, but the hangman's seen me more recently. Best keep a low profile.

Sea brine sweeps across us as we approach the promenade. We turn a corner and spot a small mound with a large tree, bare branches stretching languidly beneath the sun. Ligaya stops in her tracks and her grip on the satchel tightens.

'What is that?' I ask.

'An emerald vine,' Ligaya says, voice full of wonder.

'Is that worth something then?' I ask, cocking my head at the tree.

Ligaya laughs. 'I don't really know. It still makes my heart skip a beat – that's why I came here, you know. To Paranish. To finish my mother's recipe.'

'Your mother's recipe?'

Ligaya nods. 'She was Paranishian. Always broke her heart that she could never properly make her family recipe: kare, a nut stew with vine. You see, emerald vines only grow here. I met Morna researching the vine; she has many books on herb lore in her collection.'

'You shouldn't trust books,' I sigh. 'They can say all manner of things. Even outright falsehoods.'

'I'm sure Morna wouldn't like to hear you say that,' Ligaya jibes. 'Don't you read?'

'I can, but not many learn,' I say, fingering my cuffs. 'Especially as most of the juicy stuff is locked up tight in the Bastion or the temple.'

Ligaya frowns. 'I hate to think of them all caged up like that.'

The bell chimes happily as we enter Morna's shop, and the relative peace is a relief from the bustle outside. The bookshop is bright and smells like old paper and calamansi frosting. The shelves are meticulous, every spine shining with embossed gold and silver lettering. Behind the counter stands Morna. She pushes her sleek bob behind her ear and reluctantly closes her book.

'We brought you some tea. Narra said your supplies were running low?' Ligaya asks, placing her hand on top of the other woman's.

'Thank goodness – I was beside myself. Bring it into the kitchen, would you?'

Ligaya lays out the pouch of tea leaves. 'Now one teaspoon should be plenty for a book hangover.'

'A book hangover?' Isagani asks, scratching their head.

Morna nods. 'You know when you fall into a book and then finishing it is like crawling out of the sea. Your body feels heavy, and you're dazed for a moment, completely unaware of how much time has passed.'

'And you're hungry,' I chime in. Everyone looks at me. No one says anything for a beat. 'Swimming makes you hungry,' I clarify. I don't know about this book hangover malarkey, but it sounds like the morning after some particularly memorable nights.

I turn away to stare out the window at the crowded streets. So many bodies. So many curious eyes. 'Do you really think a party is good idea while we're in our current predicament?' I ask.

'It's a wedding.' Morna laughs.

'Exactly. You already know you're in love, why the big to-do?'

Ligaya and Morna share a look. Not the kind of look I shared with Nestor, or hundreds of other bedfellows before him. It's like sharing thoughts with only your eyes, its own kind of magic. It's always mystified me.

'Everyone's celebrating something: the Magliyab festival, the upcoming royal birth, the ports opening at long last,' Morna says.

'So, the Seaguardians will have their hands full,' Ligaya says, trying to reassure me.

'I know there's some tenderness left in that broken heart of yours,' Morna teases.

'Whatever happened to small weddings?' I groan. 'Or simply saying your vows to each other, witness only to the powers of Life and Death under a full moon?'

Weddings are not low-key affairs. I usually enjoy the merriment, the booze, the opportunities for a romantic fumble. But not when I'm trying to act respectable and keep my head down. Narra keeps insisting it'll be a small gathering, before reminding me of the hundred spring rolls that need to be rolled and fried, and the fact that we are still earning our keep. She says it in the same tone with which she threatens to haul us in to the Seaguardians.

We roll up our sleeves and wash our hands, setting ourselves at the counter. Grumbling aside, I relish the energy of a communal space. The same energy of a ship, although on board it can't really be any other way.

'Many hands make light work,' Morna says, bringing out the mixing bowl of filling and the thin sheets of pastry.

'Lumpia is easy but requires patience,' Ligaya explains, in the sweet way a parent might explain to a child. 'First you heat the oil until it sizzles, and then you place each roll in the pan, rotating it so the outside crisps evenly and the filling is piping hot all the way through.'

I didn't think this would require so much dexterity. The women have got five done in the time it takes me to wrap one. And even then, mine looks like an overstuffed sausage bursting out of its casing.

'You've overfilled it.' Morna laughs, though not unkindly. 'Here, let me show you.'

I don't quite get the knack but there's something satisfying in picking out which rustic-looking rolls are mine as we drop them into the oil. Mostly because they come apart straight away, the filling falling out and swimming around the oil. By the end of our work, I have oil burns across both my forearms and a sweat breaking out on my top lip. In time we've got rolls aplenty. Let's just hope the palm liquor is as forthcoming as the food.

CHAPTER TWENTY-TWO

RIS

'Oh, that's beautiful Ris. I'm sure they'll love it,' Narra says, surveying my handiwork with a smile.

It's about as much as I could do without my loom and with only scant notice: a patchwork quilt hand-sewn from scraps of fabric Narra had lying around. We've enjoyed meals and nights of hospitality over the past few weeks, nominally earning our keep through caring for the inn and the other guests. No choice but to spend time with this motley crew, and in truth a fondness has grown since our arrival. There's been a loosening of sorts, a comfort in letting go, in slackening my grip just a little.

'For the brides,' Biba says, handing me scraps of golden thread. Then I see the now-bald Dodi doll in her hand.

'Are you sure?' I ask, searching her face.

She nods. 'It's a special day.'

'Oh, isn't that kind,' Narra says, patting Biba's cheek.

'But you love Dodi,' I say quietly, looking at the bits of thread in my hand.

'It's all right, Mama,' Biba reassures me.

The tears come then. At first, Biba looks pleased, but quickly I realise I can't stop sobbing. Biba's face crumples. Narra holds me, stroking my hair. 'What's the matter, Ris? She did well.'

'Her father carved her that doll,' I manage through heaving breaths.

Narra gently pats my back, making circles the same way I soothe Biba.

'It's mine to give,' Biba says. 'Dodi is still all right; she just has no hair.'

'See, there's no harm done,' Narra says. 'And what a thoughtful gesture.'

Narra opens her embrace and puts the other arm around Biba. 'You poor girls don't realise you're looking in a mirror. Look at each other now, really look.'

She's the likeness of Larkin, the strong chin and tufts of thick hair. But her eyes are like mine, wide and wet. Oh, my girl, to hold us all in your small hands. If only they were always this gentle.

'What do *you* see in her?' I ask Narra quietly when my daughter moves away, now gently playing with the bald Dodi doll.

'Something that exists in all of us, Ris: potential. If only we had the power and the opportunity to wield it.'

'Do you think she'd be better on the Winter Isle?'

Narra sighs. 'I can't tell her what she should do. Nor can I tell you. Everything worth its salt has a cost; you just have to decide if it's worth it for you.'

I shake my head. 'I don't know. There's not much for us to go back to. I love my town, but I've seen the land is dying. How can we make a living?'

Narra swears, and it takes me aback. 'The royals try to make the land yield under their strength, reshape it to serve them. That's what's got us into this mess.'

Biba furrows her brow. 'Like my otter-cat. I wanted to play with it.'

Narra looks at me. 'What does she mean?'

I feel my stomach lurch and pull away. 'It was nothing.'

'It was dead,' Biba insists. 'You said so, Mama. It came back, but it wasn't all right. Better not to mess with it.'

'Necromancy?' Narra asks quietly. Her face is all curiosity, no fear there, more an academic study of my daughter's words. 'You know that we are not to make those decisions about Life and Death?'

Biba nods. 'But *they* do. They are in charge of everything.'

Narra stares hard at Biba, taking her shoulders gently. 'No. No one is above nature's order. Not even the Bastion. We must respect the balance.'

'It is a curse,' I say, running my fingers through my hair.

'Blessings, curses, smuggler, sailor – all a matter of perspective.'

Biba twists her skirts, and Narra smiles at her. 'You did well, my love. Your mother is very proud of you.'

She looks at me, and I smile hesitantly. 'Yes, you did well. My reaction – that wasn't about you.'

'Is it about Papa?' she asks.

Narra shoots me a look. 'Should I leave you?'

'No,' I say, beckoning her to stay. 'She needs to hear this, and so do you.'

Narra nods and moves to light a candle, wafting a sweet-smelling herb above the flame. 'To soothe everyone,' she says in a low murmur.

I explain as best I can, but my head is full and my heart is sore. The words are so scant and incomparable.

'There was so much love,' I tell Biba, and she smiles. 'And so much hope.'

When I had first courted my husband, he weaved stories with a fool's golden glint. An honest sailor, but he could never shake the notion that one event, one adventure, could change a fortune. We chased it, but it was ever out of reach, like the sun on the horizon. So many Bastion quests, small gains slowly mounting. We would buy our way out of our futures.

I had mistaken it for seasickness, despite never suffering before. We had spoken of our mutual desire to start a family, but not yet. Once we were back on land, we festered in the revelation, arguing until we went back to Alev, and I saw the joy in my fathers' eyes when we told them. We were buoyed by the idea of stability, of home, of someone to anchor our little family and give us a line to venture further out.

'You were the best surprise, Biba. We all loved you so much and I've never seen my fathers so happy.' I smile, and she beams back at me. 'But then the farm began to fail, and my fathers got sick. Time ran away from us, like so much sand between the fingers. They were buried before they could barely know you, my girl.'

'I wish grandpapas were here.'

'As do I. You would have been their sun and stars.' I squeeze Biba's cheeks, and she squeals away.

Then it was only the three of us, and Larkin was my anchor. The steward blamed us for the decrease in our tithes, and we got desperate. I would catch Larkin looking at the golden wool I sheared and spun, eking out what we could. He would take on any commissions that came our way, sailing out to Umasa more and more as the work dried up. It was a gleam in his eye, his heart longing for the Bastion in the distance. I began to feel like coming home was a moment of reckoning for us both, each looking at the meagre offerings in our hands and our hearts. We wanted to believe things would get better. I never believed he would sacrifice everything to climb higher, no matter the cost.

'I never thought he would leave us,' I tell her. 'I have to believe he thought he was doing the right thing – that he thought he would be able to come back with something to help the farm.'

He went to pursue the quest we'd had to abandon. The same map and quest that haunt me now. When I look at my marriage talisman,

I can only think of how he left in the night with no explanation. He owed us that much. But to disappear, a shadow under cover of darkness, leaving us with rotting land and mountains of debt . . .

'There's no other choice for us,' I tell her, holding her face in my hands. 'We have to find what the queen wants.'

Biba puts her hand on my chest, her fingers cool on my skin. I feel a gentle warmth spread across my heart and lungs and see the talisman glow.

'You rub it when you worry,' she says.

I instinctively rub the charm and feel that soothing feeling spread across my skin, like the warmth of a hearth.

'Words spoken freely like this are a gift,' Narra says gently, and I feel the tension leaving my body. 'We have all shared this space and let out our fears and our anger. Grudges are the heaviest of burdens to carry. She turns to look at me. 'With the snuffing of this candle, let the past rest.' She blows on the flame, and a plume of smoke dances around the room.

I find Morna waiting for me in the parlour a few mornings later, with an air of readiness and an eager expression on her face.

'You've done it?'

She nods and leads me out of the inn.

We walk in silent trepidation through the narrow lanes and across the town square. Even in daylight, I'm not sure I would find my way through these passages without Morna. The streets are swarming, visitors sitting by the harbour, turning their faces to the sun like flowers. The aroma of spiced teas and roasting meat distracts me as we pass the traders, enjoying the influx of new visitors to these shores.

'Not long now,' Morna says, steering me past the seafront and towards her shop.

I step through the door, the tinkling of the bell an airy announcement as we make our way to the stacks of books. Morna has laid out several volumes on a table I hadn't seen before, tucked into a nook behind the shelves. In the centre lies the map, surrounded by strange metal tools.

Morna invites me to sit and picks up the tools, examining them like a farmer her wares. 'This is a quadrant.' She handles something that looks to me like an instrument of torture. All curves and appendages, glinting in the sunlight that streams through the windows. 'You can measure between the horizon and a celestial body.' She pauses. 'Like the sun or the moon.'

I have had this lesson before. Years ago, from my husband, the only other time I'd been to Umasa. His tools had been bartered for, worn from years of use. My memory of that lesson is as rusted as his old tools, so I watch carefully as she indicates each part of the quadrant.

She hovers her finger above the map, tracing the shape of Umasa and its isles, and then out to the blank nothingness of the sea. At the edge is the blot, the Lahon Maelstrom.

'It's not necessarily to scale,' she says. 'More an artist's rendition, which is thoroughly unhelpful. But it's the best we can do. One thing I did find fascinating—'

She breaks off, bringing a candle over to the table and holding the map over the flame.

'Be careful!' I surge forward, sure the paper will catch alight.

'Trust me,' she says, stilling my hands. 'I found it accidentally. Quite miraculous, really.'

It takes a breathless moment for the light to glow through the paper and show the hidden symbol.

'The royal sun,' I whisper.

She quirks an eyebrow at me. 'You've seen this symbol before?'

I avert my gaze. Only official quests and missives have such markings, and without the skill of reading, there's not many reasons I would know this. It was the first thing Larkin would look for when negotiating our passage, the declaration that such quests were sanctioned by the crown. After all, that was the only way anyone would get paid.

She turns away and places the tools into a leather kit. She rolls it up and hands it to me, smiling.

'You would give these to me?' I ask, incredulous.

'Of course. You'll need them once you set sail. I'm afraid I don't have everything you need, but hopefully someone else in your crew will have the other pieces.'

'My crew?'

'Well, you'll need someone else to crew a ship, right?'

Holy Aistra, I haven't thought about this at all. With Larkin it had been simpler. Commissions were going like morning rolls: small jobs for the crown, so many boats, so many eager crews. Most of them were eventually turned into Seaguardian vessels, commandeered for the crown. The queen wanted a strong navy, a defensive line across our seas. Then there were no more commissions. Except the big one, the evermore: the Lahon Maelstrom. First went the brave, then the reckless, and then the desperate. I suppose that's what I am now.

I pause, chewing over my words before I speak them. 'The sailor, Finlyr,' I begin.

Her eyes sparkle. 'You know about his past?'

'A little.'

'If you trust him, then he would be a great asset.'

I bark a laugh. 'Who can I trust?'

'Trust us,' she says, with earnestness so fierce it makes me shudder.

They could have left us to our own devices, our business our own, but since we arrived on Umasa, Morna, Ligaya, and Narra have shown us nothing but warmth and generosity.

I sigh. 'Why are you doing any of this? You owe us nothing; we're strangers.'

She laughs. 'That is why the ports have been closed for centuries.'

'What do you mean?' I ask.

'You have no love of the Bastion, but you run on fear – just the same as them. Ris, you are a startled animal sometimes,' she says, with a fondness and familiarity I find alarming and disarming in turn.

'What do you know about fear?' I snip.

She settles into her chair, waiting for me to calm like a kettle off the boil. 'Where do you think these books come from?'

I look around at the shelves lined with books and for the first time see the craft and care it takes to scribe and to bind. She must do this all herself: a labour of love.

'You don't see many books, not even on the mainland,' she sighs, adding quietly, 'What I wouldn't give to see the library at the Bastion or the Temple of Aistra.'

I bite my lip, not knowing what to say. When something doesn't concern you day to day, it doesn't necessarily occur to you to think beyond. My time has been spent with the loom, worrying about the animals. I had no thoughts for books – who wrote them, where they came from, what use the written word could be.

The shop bell rings, and Morna gestures for me to stay in the back room as she goes to the counter. 'How may I help you? Ah, it's you. Good to see you again.'

I peer between the bookshelves and see a woman dressed in a travelling cloak with a heavy bag, which she places on the counter.

'More transcriptions,' the traveller says, setting out a pile of books for Morna to examine. The traveller leans closer and whispers, 'And what word on the wing?'

Morna glances back to where I am and I look away, pretending to be fixated on the map.

'I am with company,' she tells the traveller, meaningfully. 'But there is an Umasan maya looking for a new home.'

The traveller nods and bundles the now-empty bag into her cloak. 'Until next time, Morna.'

Morna carries the books over to the back room and looks at me.

'That was no ordinary customer, was it?' I ask.

She looks at me and then at the books, deliberating. 'Actually, prior to the ports opening, that was my main customer.'

'Who was she?'

'I don't need to tell you everything about my business,' she says.

I glance at the books she's acquired. Although I can't read them, I recognise the Bastion symbol, the same royal sun we saw materialise on the map.

'You're working for them!'

Morna shakes her head. 'No, not exactly.'

'I knew there was more to your motive than kindness,' I hiss, starting to make my way out of the shop.

'Ris, please, let me explain.' Morna grabs my sleeve and looks at me imploringly. 'We all work for the Bastion, whether we like it or not. That was one of the Temple Mothers. She brings me books and I give her information.'

'What kind of information?'

'About the children.'

I pull away, disgusted. A filthy little snitch. The Bastion always knows when touched children exhibit their first signs of magic. And now I know why: because people in their own communities sell them out.

'I'm not proud of what I do, but I do what I must,' Morna says, voice hoarse and desperate. 'They make better lives for so many of those girls. They give them power and opportunity they never would have had otherwise.'

'Do Ligaya and Narra know?'

Morna turns pale.

'No, you would never tell them you're betraying their kind. Were you going to do the same to Biba?'

Morna is on the verge of tears. 'I swear, I would never do that to you. I only tell the Temple if the kids would have a better life there. It's what's best for them.'

I shake my head at her. 'Who gave you the right to decide? You need to tell Ligaya and Narra everything, or I will.'

CHAPTER TWENTY-THREE

FINLYR

I'VE HAD TOO MUCH palm liquor already. It's not helped by the fact I've barely eaten anything. It's like a feast day, where all the fancy dishes are laid out, but you can't touch them 'til the family's gathered. Aistra, that was my first temptation, and I failed every single time, sneaking a sticky sweet treat when my parents' backs were turned.

A spread of pies, rolls, and sweetmeats diverts my attention. Cakes piped with violent purples, petal crimsons, blush pinks, sunshine yellows, deep blues. Narra reminds me of my father, an exact location for every dish.

'Let me guess, you only like weddings for the food,' Ris says, batting my hands away.

'You've already branded me a cynic. In my experience, the more expensive the wedding, the shorter the marriage.' I smile.

The happy couple descend from the upstairs rooms, dressed in their finery. Ligaya is wearing a patterned robe with long bell-shaped sleeves, the material bedecked with embroidered vines. Morna is wearing a fitted blouse with capped sleeves and a flowing skirt. There's a glimmer where they've woven golden thread into their hair. Doubtless Ris gave it to them as a gift. Despite myself, I get a bit misty-eyed.

The couple gasp at the decorations and beam at the guests, admire the food. It's sort of nice being part of this collective project, despite there being only a few well-kent faces. The women take each other's hands and stand under the banner of flowers I tattered my fingers to assemble. It does look very nice; you can barely see the bloodstains on the thorns.

Narra stands, holding a weave of white linen.

'We have a couple. We have cake. We have guests. A few words and seal it with a kiss.'

'Ligaya,' Morna says, looking into her partner's eyes. 'I didn't think love could hit me as suddenly as an Umasan season change, but life can surprise you.'

A ripple of laughter dashed with sobs and lumps in throats.

'Whatever happens next, there's no one I'd rather be with than you.'

Ligaya's voice wobbles. 'You're such a wordsmith. It's partly why I fell in love with you, Morna. Through the salt and the sweet, I would be yours and by your side.'

Cheers and applause roar through the room as the newly-weds kiss and embrace. They exchange the Paranishian token of union: moon talismans. They hold the talismans as Narra wraps the weave around their joined hands. A sealed bond. They hope for life. We throw flower petals, and everyone comes forward to them, enveloping Ligaya and Morna in warm hugs. And finally, there's food.

'I'm happy for them,' I say, as we sit and eat.

'I think it's beautiful,' Isagani says, rearranging some wildflowers in a vase, 'they're making a vow to each other. A promise that they won't ever leave.' The kid's voice shakes, and I look at them, blinking away their tears.

I nudge them gently with my shoulder. 'I'm not going anywhere without you.'

'You better not,' they say, shaking it off with a joke.

Ris thrusts a mug at me, a sparkle in her eyes. 'Quench my thirst?' she asks.

I fill our glasses and pass the wine around. The room is warm, and the hum of voices reaches a new wave of intensity.

'My body is begging for a nice soft chair,' I say, finally setting down my cutlery and patting my full belly.

In the corner a revelry of song has started, with empty cups tapped as accompaniment.

'All right then, let's get sentimental. Are you old enough to drink?'

'You know I'm not,' they say.

'Let's get you a tankard anyway.'

'Do you think that's a responsible thing to do?' Ris asks with a hiccup.

I shrug. 'Well, let's get me one, then. I want to feel my age tomorrow.'

'Well, you've fewer turns of the sun than I do.' Ris laughs.

'Surely not.' I squint at her.

She playfully punches me on the arm. I'll admit it hurt worse than I would've expected.

'All right, that's a game I can't win. How about Soklan?' I suggest, taking my cards out of their cloth pouch.

Ris's shoulders loosen and her eyes sparkle. 'I've heard your shanties; I know you're a sailor. Most honest sailors don't dabble in Soklan.'

'Is that so?' I ask. 'And how many dishonest sailors do you know, farmer?'

'Wasn't Soklan invented by the royals?' Isagani chimes in. 'That's what my grandmother always told me.'

'I wouldn't be surprised,' I say, shuffling the deck. 'The game's about reading your opponent. Using their own secret weaknesses against them. So, I propose a wager.' Ris raises her eyebrows as

I continue: 'If I win, you show me that map you've got Morna deciphering.'

Ris considers this. 'And if I win?' she asks.

A discordant thudding interrupts our conversation, and we abandon the game setup.

'Is that knocking?' Ris asks.

I weave my way through the crowd, leaving her and Isagani in my wake.

As I approach Narra, she is deep in conversation with Morna and Ligaya, and looks perturbed by the disturbance. Ligaya looks grave, the most serious I've ever seen her, and Narra chews her bottom lip, mulling something over. Morna turns, wiping away tears. This feels like something more than newly-wed emotions.

'I'm sorry to interrupt,' I begin, warily. 'But there's someone at the door.'

'We'll continue this discussion later,' Narra tells Morna, sternly.

'Something amiss?' I ask.

'Nothing to concern you,' she says, moving through the guests like water on her way to the door.

She opens it casually and, I can't see who's she talking to, but her expression remains placid. Then she looks back inside and catches my eye. Her expression remains unchanged, but she brings her hand up to her face, as if brushing away a stray hair. Her fingers are splayed across her eye like a child playing a game of hide-and-seek. I follow her silent instructions, twisting through the guests and looking around for Isagani. They aren't anywhere in the downstairs common areas, and I dash up the narrow stairs to our room. Isagani is deep in thought looking out the window.

'Hide,' I command, grabbing their hand and pulling them back into the corridor.

'Where?' they whisper, following fleet-footed in my wake.

We make our way to the top of the inn, and I look around frantically. Then there's nowhere left to run. We hear people stomping up the stairs, their gait slow and heavy. Doors slam below us, and the sound of furniture scraping. Seaguardians. They're checking all the rooms.

Isagani struggles with a window, and I join them, hoisting the stiff wooden casement open. It's awkward and narrow, but we wriggle through, perching on the sill. The brickwork is firm and luckily it hasn't rained in Umasa today, so the stone is rough against our fingers and easy to grip. Isagani goes first, smearing against the wall and using their feet for purchase to scramble up to the roof. I see their small face peering over the ledge at me.

'Hurry!'

The Seaguardians are closer now, and I quickly shut the window, following Isagani's steps. I'm too broad and tall to copy their movements.

Then the door bursts open, and a huge figure strides into the room.

CHAPTER TWENTY-FOUR

RIS

For an outlaw, Finlyr is surprisingly easy to sneak up on. He almost soils his britches when I find him in the room at the top of the inn, half out the window.

'By Aistra, I could kiss you,' he says, leaning against the wall.

'Well, don't,' I whisper, closing the door. 'What's going on? There's Seaguardians downstairs.'

'They're here for us. Well, mostly me,' he says, catching his breath. 'I'm supposed to be dead.'

'Fin!' I hear Isagani from above. 'I can see *Saltswept* from up here.'

'*Saltswept*?' I ask, joining Finlyr at the window. We can see the whole town from this vantage point, peering into open windows where other folk are caught up in their revelries, unaware of what's going on the other side of the alleys from them. We're sea-facing, the port stretching out with the vessels small blots on the moonlit ocean.

'You have a ship,' I say.

'Can we talk about this later?' Fin pleads, starting to crawl out of the window.

'Not so fast,' I say, grabbing his shirt. 'How do I know you won't disappear and never come back?'

'I can make no promises. Right now it's life or death, Ris.'

'You know about my map. Do you know where it leads?'

'The Lahon Maelstrom,' he says.

'How do you know that?'

'Ris, the Seaguardians—' he begs, tugging to free his shirt.

'How do you know?'

A moment's silence. 'I've sailed there before,' he finally admits.

'Take me there.' It's not a question.

'Ris, there's nothing there but death.'

'Yes, well, death is coming for us all.'

'Quicker for some if you don't let me go. The Seaguardians will be here any minute.'

'I'll help you get your ship back. Just promise you'll take us to the Maelstrom.'

'Anything to get off Paranish. It's been nothing but trouble since I came back.'

'Do we have a deal?'

'Aye!' He agrees.

'Haul arse, then,' I say, helping him out the window.

I give him a boost, and he uses brute force to smash his way up, scraping against the stonework and barely biting down a yell. I have my two arms on the flat of the roof and am trying to hoist myself up. Isagani grabs at my shirt and tries to haul me over.

'Get your legs up higher!' Isagani calls desperately.

I grab Finlyr's flailing legs and help him get his arms anchored on the ledge so he can raise himself up. He wriggles like a tamaraw wrestling in mud.

He's just out of my arms when the Seaguardians burst through the door.

'Found ourselves a warm body,' one of them says, and I turn around.

'Any reason you're alone in the dark, my pet?' says another.

'Stargazing.'

'Beautiful,' the first one snarls, shoving me out of the way. He looks out of the window, surveying the area.

One of the other Seaguardians staggers towards me, the smell of palm liquor on his breath. 'Want to join us for a round, sweetheart?'

I shake my head, and he pushes me against the wall.

'That's not very comely of you.'

I whip out my dagger and place it under his jaw. 'Get your hands off me.'

'I'd love to know where you were hiding that,' he croaks, trying not to bob his apple too close to the blade.

I bring the blade closer, nicking his skin.

The other Seaguardians turn now, hands on their hilts. 'Drop the knife, lass.'

I drop the knife and catch it in my other hand, close to the guard's nether regions. 'Would you rather lose these or your life?'

He backs off at last. 'Wouldn't fuck an ugly broodmare like you anyway.' He scowls and throws the near-empty bottle on the floor, sending glass smashing and liquor flying. I turn and cover my face as tiny pieces bury themselves in my skin.

'Let's get the rest of the liquor and head.'

The drunken one makes a lewd gesture, but they leave, laughing and spitting as they stagger down the stairs.

'Bunch of bastards,' Isagani says, once they're out of earshot.

'Ris, are you all right?' Finlyr asks, descending the wall.

'I think so,' I say, examining the shards. 'Didn't expect I'd have a blade.'

'I hope they choke on their own sick.' Finlyr sneers. 'Let me get those out.'

His touch is careful as he extracts the fragments of glass. They're mostly in my forearms, the rest of me covered by my clothing.

'I'm so sorry, Ris,' he says quietly as he dabs the wounds with a clean linen.

CHAPTER TWENTY-FIVE

FINLYR

I WAKE EARLY FROM a restless sleep, feeling sore and tender, but the inn is peaceful and still. Isagani is nowhere to be found, so I wander into the town square, cloak tied close around me and my hood up. The weather is bright but chill as I make my way to the harbour. I drink piyata tea from a flask, sweet and earthy, with the leaves steeping gently at the surface.

I see a figure peel away from an alley, emerging into the light of the main streets. It's only then I glimpse the others loitering against a wall, barely moving. The person strolls across the street, moving towards the harbour. They survey the seafront, breathing in the briny air.

'Nice view and all that,' they say.

Isagani is dressed similarly to when I first met them: plain, baggy clothes specked with mud, and an unassuming, dirty face. The blue ribbon is gone.

'Have you been scheming?' I ask. 'Heard anything from your filching friends in the streets?'

They sigh. 'Whisperings, but the Seaguardians are crawling Umasa with the influx of visitors. And there will be more for the Magliyab festival, not to mention the royal birth. It's all about finding the right time to commandeer. We need a distraction.'

It's still early, and the docks are fairly empty, with only a few merchants setting up their market stalls. At this time of day it's mostly bakers and tea brewers, as well as the fishmongers and greengrocers. I stare across the harbour at *Saltswept*. It's the first chance I've had to properly look at my ship since they took her from me. She's collected more barnacles in the time she's been docked, but there's no obvious damage. Except I know every inch of that ship, and there's something wrong, something new. What is that by her prow?

I start across the seafront to get a closer look.

'What's wrong?' Isagani asks, following me.

By Paranish, they haven't! They've desecrated her with the royal sigil. I let out a moan and smack the rail of the promenade.

'What is it?' Isagani asks again, voice full of concern.

'Do you see that unholy royal sigil? They're nearly done preparing her to become a Seaguardian vessel. It's an abomination. Oh, my girl, you were made for greater things.'

Isagani nods in sympathy, but they don't understand. Only a captain would truly know what a violation this is. I examine her further.

'From the way she's listing slightly, the hold isn't empty – thank Paranish.'

'Aye, that's good,' they agree.

'You have no idea what that means, do you?' I ask, and Isagani gives me a vague smile, their cheeks round apples in the biting wind. 'Means it's got food and water on board.'

For a moment I truly feel that we're a merchant father and his churlish daughter. Isagani grabs my flask of tea and takes a sip, staring at my ship again. A couple of Seaguardians pace the dock, clapping their gloved hands together.

The clouds part and the sun beats down on us, sparkling in Umasa's waters.

Isagani watches me. 'Why do you look like a tamaraw in a hot spring?'

'I'm thinking about Ris.'

'Oh, are you now?' they ask, waggling their eyebrows.

'Not like that. Her map. The Lahon Maelstrom.'

'Oh,' they say, expression suddenly serious. 'I still don't understand why in Aistra anyone would go there.'

'When you're starving because your harvests have failed again, wouldn't you give anything for even a bowl of rice? Hunger drives us to desperation.'

Isagani is quiet for a moment, and I think of their wiry limbs, the way they move in the shadows. Suddenly their face brightens with a memory. 'I *have* heard of this place. From my grandmother – I thought it was just a story.'

'Stories come from somewhere.'

'Says the man who doesn't trust books. Has anyone ever survived?'

'Not without going a bit salt-mad.'

Isagani looks at me properly then. 'So that's what happened to you.'

I grab the steaming flask and turn away.

'Why would you go back there?' They push, moving to my other side and forcing me to look at them.

'I owe it to my crew. They believed in this quest, in me, and I failed them. Sailors are dead because of me.' I shake my head and sigh. 'I really fucked up out there, Isagani.'

'And you think martyring yourself is an answer? I need you—' Their voice grows louder, breaking.

The patrolling Seaguardians look up at the noise. I place a callused hand on Isagani's shoulder.

'Gently, now. That ship is only going to stay in the harbour for so long before the Seaguardians have fully repurposed her and then she's lost to us. It's an insult. She deserves to go down properly, the way she should have. The way I should have.'

'How many times do I have to save your arse before you value your life?' They hiss through gritted teeth.

'I'm doing that now,' I counter, voice hushed. 'I want to take Ris to the Maelstrom. She's going there whether I help her or not. She doesn't stand a chance without me. I want to get her there and back if I can. She needs a sailor, and we need a navigator.'

'And what makes you sure she's up to the task?'

'I'm not entirely. But I know she can read maps, at least according to Morna. And now she's got some navigational tools. It's better than naught.'

Isagani is silent for a moment, then they laugh. 'It's a miracle.'

'What is?'

'How you can be so self-serving and self-sacrificing all at once?'

I can't help but laugh, too.

'Stubborn as a royal.' They sigh.

Not the first time I've heard that. 'Look – I can understand if you don't want to come. It would be wild of me to involve a kid—'

'Biba's half my age!'

'Biba's gifted.'

Isagani glares. 'I'm not a child; I'm almost fully grown. I can hold my own. I need to get away from Paranish.'

I study them. 'You said you tried before. Why?'

'I owe it to her to actually leave this time, to find something better.'

'Who?'

There is a brief silence. 'My grandmother,' they finally say. 'She's the only one who ever cared about me. If we could've left before she'd still be alive.'

There's nothing I can say to that. I let the moment pass, and then gently pull them into my side. 'Even if leaving might kill you? There's no glory here.'

'My grandmother knew of a smuggler in Umasa named Finlyr Pane. She never found him. We didn't know he'd fucked off to Lassair by then. She wanted to get off this island, but the Bastion took its tithes despite the harvest shrinking. They practically starved us, then blamed us for not producing enough food. The Bastion killed her, plain as if they had put her on the gallows.'

Fuck. I hug my kid closer, and we stand there for a long time, the wind whipping at our cloaks. Some sellers battle to pin bunting to their stall, all bright orange flames and stars.

'The Magliyab festival,' I say into the top of their head. 'It's next week.'

'What?' they ask, pulling away.

'You said it's all about timing. Well, Magliyab is the perfect distraction. The Seaguardians will have their hands full with travellers. And the queen's expected any day now. Last night was too close a call. It's time for us to get away from Paranish.'

CHAPTER TWENTY-SIX

HANAN

I STARE OUT THE large windows of the queen's chambers, which overlook the mainland towns. Each one is beginning to light up as the sun sets, like stars scattered across the night sky. My breath catches as I'm reminded of lighting candles in the temple at dusk. I didn't think I'd miss the rhythms of Aistra.

'Do you know what we celebrate tonight?' the queen asks, and I'm brought back to my task, the loose strands of her hair beneath my fingers. Attendants usually flutter around her like birds: maids, attendants, envoys, courtiers. For novelty, she sometimes dismisses her lady's maids, and we are almost alone this way. Although she is never really alone, accompanied by the child in her belly. And Salvacion, the Queen's Royal Guardian, the Captain of the Seaguardians. Salvacion is always here.

I shake my head, and the queen turns towards the window, looking down at Umasa. 'Your naivety is a breath of fresh air. Magliyab: the festival of flames.' She stands and appraises herself in the mirror.

The dress is midnight blue, such as I've only seen in the glass of the temple. She has only worn gowns that mask her pregnancy, and now she is standing I gasp to see it fully. Around her waist is a large, embroidered sun, swirling dizzyingly until it reaches her navel. The swell of the child fills it perfectly.

'Is it not a pretty thing?' the queen says, and I realise I must be staring.

'Yes, Your Grace.'

I hurry to secure the braid into a crown around her head. Dazzling golden thread shaped like stars glitters her hair, woven between the locks. I cast my eyes down, away from her face now rouged and painted. I sense her appraising my formless black gown, which must appear so similar to temple robes in her eyes; my plain, unadorned features. We continue in silence.

Preparations finished, I trail behind her as we enter the banquet hall, followed by a procession of lady's maids. I see one of them scowling at the braided crown. From this angle, it is slant.

'Pet,' she says, so quietly it may have been a cough.

I shoot her a cutting look, and she colours, making the warding sign of the circle at her heart. Fool girl, doesn't she know the symbol of life's cycle is the same one we worship at the temple? Later I touch the bare skin of the lady's maid's throat, on the pretence of moving a loose strand of hair. The lady's maid starts, shrinking back from my touch. The patch of skin reddens into a sore rash, eventually splitting open. A slight harm, payment in kind.

The queen takes her place at the head of the table, and I kneel behind her chair. The tall gilt frame conceals much of the room, but I can hear the amiable laughter and smell the steam of something rich and succulent. I shift my weight back onto my heels. The stone beneath my knees is as hard as the temple pews, but never has worship been as tantalising as this feast. From my vantage point, I can make out a great pit in the centre of the room, burning white-hot with stones. Flesh is skewered on a spit, spinning slowly like a dance, above the fire. Whatever it is, it is huge: with limbs and no head. An attendant hacks at the meat with a cleaver, and I chance another glance. By Paranish, it is a massive bird. I see the limbs now for wings, strung close to its body. I can't tell what type of bird.

'We feast tonight in honour of Magliyab, the festival of flames,' the queen says. I angle to catch her profile as she raises a steaming bowl of broth. The smell of the meat mixed with the oil, herbs, and smoke makes my mouth water. I haven't eaten all day. 'We nourish ourselves from the land and sea and sky so that we may nourish it in return. And the next stewards will spring forth from our bodies like Paranish's own crops.'

The queen raises the bowl to her lips, and I see the nobles mirror her. I almost drop the bowl that is thrust at me; the server barely breaks stride. The broth is tangy and sour at first, then mellows to a salty umami flavour. Small sharp onions float on its surface alongside the fat of the meat. I stare at the meat, red and tender in the middle, surrounded by crispy skin. I take a morsel in my next mouthful, and it bursts on my tongue. I've never tasted the like. I have been eating dirt until now.

The feast goes on for hours, and my legs are numb from kneeling. Eventually the queen stands, and we all follow.

'Please, my friends, continue your festivities. Enjoy, enjoy!' The queen raises her hands in elegant deference, the long sleeves of her dress billowing out. She reaches for me, and I help her descend her dais, shadowing her as she leaves the banquet hall. Salvacion dogs our steps, always just behind.

'I have a frightful headache,' the queen says, bringing her fingers to her temple.

My hand is twitching before she even tilts her head. I brush her hair back, placing a light cooling hand on her neck until her breathing slows, and she lets out a sigh of pleasure, her skin gooseflesh.

We look at each other in surprise. I step back and flush, wondering if I have done ill. The queen breathes heavily for a moment.

'Do you know why you were sent to me?'

I shake my head and cast my eyes down.

'The last priestesses were all grave disappointments. None of them could save my husband from the wasting sickness,' she says. Her voice is steady, but I catch the cloud in her expression.

I've heard whispers of the wasting sickness, one that only strikes down royalty. Malostra once confessed she thought it was nature's punishment for keeping their marriage circles so small, only marrying into nobility every once in a while.

'This child is a symbol of hope for Paranish. I will not let anything happen to them.'

I must be her herbalist, her midwife. That is the realm of the priestess: to keep the royal family happy and healthy, by any means necessary. That is the danger from which I must shield her.

She walks down the corridor, and I follow in her wake. She moves slowly, observing everything in the Bastion. Her fingers move across the fine candlesticks, the golden embroidered tapestries. Eventually she stops outside a great wooden door. I feel a humming from within the room, and I'm transported back to Aistra, to the temple library.

'Midnight is an hour for absolute secrecy,' she says, touching her finger gently to my lips.

I repress a shiver as the queen reaches for her waist and retrieves her chatelaine. I have seen her fondle this absent-mindedly. She is never without it. Even when she goes to sleep, it rests under her pillow.

She fingers a key from the collection and places it in my hand. The metal is cool to the touch, as is her skin. I flinch at the contact, as though some unspeakable threshold has been crossed again. She indicates the door, and I slip the key in the lock. It turns reluctantly and I push the heavy door open with my full weight.

'You may wait out here, Salvacion.'

Salvacion hesitates, eyeing me for a moment. 'As you wish, Your Grace.'

As we step inside, I'm hit by the familiar musty smell of old books, the hint of paper and ink and the promise of secret knowledge. My heart flutters.

The library is huge in comparison to the temple's and the queen leads me round the maze of shelves and drawers. The domed ceiling has been painted with all the seasons merging into each other, with a sun and crown at the centre. I cannot imagine the thousands of hours of painstaking detail and labour going into something that hardly anyone would ever see.

'I am very particular about who has access to this place. But I understand the Temple of Aistra has similar rare collections. I trust you know how to behave around such artefacts.'

I stare at her, mouth agape. 'You would grant me access to this?'

She smiles, all polish and teeth. 'It is your duty to refine your skill as my priestess. I expect you to study, to practise, to experiment. The library has many secrets to uncover. You are already skilled at herb lore, and treating ailments. My husband suffered greatly; his body slowly devouring itself after it would no longer be satisfied by the food it could get. Nothing was ever enough to satiate him. I want this child to be strong and healthy and full. It must be able to heal itself quickly should anything happen.'

She lingers, and a shiver runs down my spine. How much did Mothers Joca and Lin relay to Her Majesty?

I explore, a child again. I run first my eyes and then my hands over the tomes, barely believing I have access to this wealth of knowledge. I follow the labyrinth, finding staircases that lead to walls, and alcoves with no purpose.

'It is a strange and wondrous thing, this place. Thank you, Your Majesty.'

The queen rests her hand on her belly again, giving me a look of satisfaction. She appraises me, like a newly commissioned garment. She nods once, approving the Temple Mothers' choice. I must succeed where the others have failed.

CHAPTER TWENTY-SEVEN

FINLYR

'Magliyab, the day of fire,' I say, with a dramatic flourish. 'Perfect for blending into the shadows. Time for a drink and some revelry.'

Isagani fidgets with a mask, trying to attach it to their face. 'Why do they make the eyeholes so small? I can barely see out of this thing.'

Ris tuts and helps them before turning to me. 'There will be no chaos or drinking tonight. Now help me with this, won't you?'

She hands me a cloak of midnight blue, and I can smell oranges and embers as I brush against her skin.

'You look like a fine lady,' Isagani tells her.

She colours, and I laugh at everyone's earnestness, something we've seen more of in the days after the wedding.

'You're in for a spectacle,' Narra says, patting my hand.

She's not wrong; as we leave the inn and make our way through the streets to Umasa town square, I'm sure I've never seen so many people in one place. We melt into the crowds, the energy vibrating between bodies. Everyone is dressed in costumes of light: stars, moons, candles, and flames bejewel garments, headpieces, and handmade masks. We've all favoured masks and cloaks, our laden bags not an uncommon sight among the throng of travellers. In the town square, where mere weeks ago I stood facing down death itself, is a bonfire. Nothing to fear from a little fire. If all goes off without a hitch, Magliyab might become my favourite festival.

Market stalls are assembled, packed with wares from every corner of Paranish. Traders with coloured glass beads that catch the firelight, stone weights, and hollowed-out bones for spindle shafts. Ris comes up beside me and eyes the offerings. She points to the boxes of pickled fish and vegetables, some hardy ube root vegetables, which will survive the bumps of the journey. There are dried hard flatbreads and pies and most importantly the palm liquor and home brew. Finally, she indicates a bright pink flower, handling it gently when the vendor gives it to her.

'Lotus. You can use every part.'

I give her a quizzical look.

'Aistra, what do they teach you on the seas?' She pulls me closer, pointing to each part. 'Roast the seeds. The flower makes tea. Wrap the leaves. The roots have a great crunch.'

'You've been spending time with Ligaya.'

'You could learn a thing or two from women's labour. Who do you think puts those clothes on your back?'

Ris turns to the trader and pulls out a skein of golden wool. They do the Nishian dance of haggling: the vendor tries to barter for double what our haul is worth.

'That doesn't even cover the time and labour bringing this wool over from Alev,' she insists. 'Work with me here.'

The vendor demurs, insisting the vegetables are of the finest quality, before Ris points to a bottle of palm liquor. 'Throw in another of those, and we're satisfied.'

The vendor looks at the dusty bottle and then shrugs, packing it into our haul.

Our cargo is modest compared to what I'd like to be sailing off with, but we're putting to sea under unusual circumstances. And from my recent trip to the dock with Isagani. From the way she sat lower in the waterline, I assume *Saltswept*'s already loaded with some basic provisions. Or at least I hope it is.

'That was impressive,' I say as we walk away from the stall. 'Who would've thought you'd be bargaining for more liquor?'

'I'm partial to a drink,' she says, smiling. 'Although I suppose you're more used to stealing than negotiating.'

'Stealing is negotiating,' I insist. 'How much your life is worth.'

She gives me a look, part incredulous, part scathing.

'I'm just more upfront about my methods than the royals. How is a tithe any different?'

She clucks her tongue. 'Your loose lips. No wonder you got caught.'

'That wasn't why I got caught,' I correct, hiding a grin. She sees it anyway.

'What did you do?' she asks with mock exasperation.

'More a question of whom.'

'Who was she?'

'*He* was a Seaguardian. And we were role-playing.' I pause. 'I was wearing his uniform.'

'Loose tongue and loose britches.' She laughs.

I shrug, smiling. 'I'd been sailing close to the wind for a while. Nice to feel alive sometimes.'

There are stalls everywhere, and I eye the victuals and libations for later. The group in front of us are sneaking flasks of home brew between them. Good thinking. But none of that tonight; got to keep a clear head. We keep to the back of the growing crowd, the Seaguardians standing in a circle by the bonfire to ensure no one gets too close. A cheer goes up from the crowd as one of the Seaguardian takes a torch to the bonfire. It catches quickly with an alarming whoomph that we can hear even back here. A wooden emblem in the shape of a woman sits atop the bonfire, tall and proud. She has one arm bent as a perch for a bird, wings outstretched to their full span. Some poor sod has to craft that effigy every year just for it to be burned. Seems like a very expensive party.

I do a quick survey of my crew, making sure we're all accounted for. Ris is directly in front of me, Biba next to her, squirming to get a closer look at the hubbub. Isagani stands with Narra, Ligaya, and Morna. Narra's bag is open just enough to expose a small, dark head with big, yellow eyes and pointy ears. Sinigang was adamant that being stuck in a small space surrounded by open water was his nightmare. But being stuck in a small space with that otter-cat is mine. I don't care how lucky they're supposed to be in a storm. But Narra insisted that his skills would be useful on the voyage, and he didn't disagree.

Now that it's come down to it, I've got sickness in my stomach. We did some scouting a few days earlier; the docks are in absolute chaos with all the ships full of visitors coming into the harbour. *Saltswept* was lightly guarded with only a couple of patrollers, but any Seaguardian not engaged with water traffic control had a flagon in their hands. There might be no better night to commandeer my vessel.

'What's the burning figure all about?' Biba asks.

'They say she was an enemy of the Bastion,' says Narra.

'What did she do?' The young girl can't take her eyes from the pyre. She watches the figure blacken in the flames, eyes wide. 'It must have been bad.'

'Intimidation tactics,' I say. 'Let this be a warning to the others.'

Our group falls silent, and I realise the treachery of my words. I've never been good at pretending to love the royals, although I suppose that's not really expected of an outlaw.

'Low tolerance for criminals shows strong leadership,' Ris says in a flat tone, for the benefit of anyone eavesdropping.

The wooden emblem collapses on top of the bonfire, and the crowd cheers louder. Some folk pick up instruments and the fluid dancing of drunken merriment begins. A song is taken up, first by a few voices, and then by others. A traditional Magliyab tune, with a rolling beat, which begs for dancing feet:

> '*She was a trickster and a thief.*
> *She was a traitor to the crown.*
> *She was corrupt beyond belief.*
> *Follow her way and you will drown.*'

Even the nearby Seaguardians are compelled to watch the revelry, succumbing to the glow of the fire and the warm press of bodies.

'It's time,' Narra says, squeezing my arm.

'What are you going to do?' I ask as we slowly extricate ourselves from the crowd.

'Pockets of mischief,' she replies with a wink, disappearing into the fray with Ligaya and Morna.

We hide in the shadows of the buildings, eyeing my ship. She's not looking too weather-worn, and she's only anchored and tethered by one rope. The Seaguardians on duty are loosely patrolling, which mostly involves walking up and down the dock as they talk. Why would anyone want to patrol the cold dark docks when nothing's happening there?

CHAPTER TWENTY-EIGHT

HANAN

Once I have been given unfettered access to the library, for weeks I barely go elsewhere in the Bastion. The queen encourages me to spend my time there, and I'm happy hiding away while she throws parties and hosts feasts, filling the palace with people as if she fears being alone.

She promotes my studious nature, and I wonder if she can tell how content I feel there. There is little light in the room, so I must make do with candles and lamps, which are all very well and good except the words are like the footprints of ants, if they are legible at all. It is different from written Nishian, patterns of symbols indicating letters. Painstakingly slow work. Impossible without a key. However, I have been able to find duplicates of some texts I had gathered from the temple library. Thank Aistra for our transcriptions. I have found similar symbols and begun to decode them. I am astonished at how much more I can get done here; those small snatches of time at Aistra were so fleeting.

I stare at myself in the mirror, squinting hard until my face is a soft blur. I imagine my eye in minute detail, looking at the blown-out pupil and the bloodshot whites. I think of my iris like a forest, turning from the hazel of wood bark to the lush green of the leaves. I blink and come back into myself. I look at my eyes again and catch the hints of green seeping away back into hazel. I try again, this time imagining a huge wave crashing over that forest, engulfing it in dark blue. This time I catch my eyes before they fully turn back. It's a small, useless glamour, more like a game for me. Something less volatile than necromancy.

I go to the window and open the shutters to the day. It's windy and overcast in Umasa, which will help my flight. I place my hands on the stone of the windowsill, feeling the pattern beneath my fingers. I lean out as far as I dare and let the wind whip my hair as I fix my gaze on a window below. I envision an insect crawling out of my ear and taking flight, down to the window. It slips through the crack between the shutters and finds an on-duty Seaguardian. They swipe at the bug as it passes by their face, and I can hear their heartbeat, their breath. Their hands cause a gust, which throws me against the wall. I'm knocked back from the windowsill and out of my vision.

When I come back to myself, I find the queen standing in the library drinking from a goblet. Her belly is larger, her face round, and her lips full and dark from the drink. She's dressed in a soft purple gown that hugs her chest and flows loosely from the waist. It reminds me of illustrations I've seen of a flower shaped like a bell, which is toxic if it makes contact with the skin.

'Your Majesty!' I exclaim, standing and dusting off my dress. 'What a pleasant surprise.'

She seems amused at my alarm and comes closer, removing some debris from my hair.

'You are making yourself at home, I see.' She smiles, only teeth. The gesture doesn't reach her eyes.

She meanders around the room, fingering open volumes and my scraps of notes as she approaches. She holds out the goblet and I take it, confused.

As I'm about to drink, she puts her hand to the rim, inches between my lips and her skin. 'Turn this water into palm liquor.'

I hesitate a moment before she lets go. We both stare at the goblet and I think about lambanog, as the common folk call it. The Temple Mothers would drink the imported stuff on occasion and also called it thus. I imagine the water turning cloudy and sweet, trying to anchor the transmutation to an image of the natural world. I think of drawings of coconuts cracking open, the fermented juices pouring out. The liquid changes, and my hand shakes as I return it to the queen. She keeps her eyes on me as she imbibes, licking her lips.

'You look grave,' she says, tipping the goblet to my lips. 'Drink, revive yourself.'

I sip slowly and feel the heat of her gaze on me.

'Your progress pleases me, Hanan.'

'Thank you, Your Grace.' I bow my head. 'It is my honour to please you.'

She gives an amused laugh and brushes my lips with her finger, wiping away a drop of liquor.

'Come.'

We walk through the corridors to a part of the Bastion I have never seen, sequestered in the lower passages. We stop before a large room, and she pushes back a wooden screen. Dark green marble tiles cover the walls, the floor, the ceiling, and everything feels close, the atmosphere thick with an aromatic steam of fresh herbs and spices. The queen removes her shoes, and I follow. We proceed barefoot into the tiled room where servants hurry back and forth with jugs of steaming water, filling a tub set in the floor. Sampaguita petals and apple slices float in the water, imports from the Spring and Autumn isles. The water has the same sheen as the queen's saltwater pearls.

She stands like a doll, arms stiff and away from her sides, and it takes me a moment to realise she is waiting to be undressed. A servant puts down their jug of water and bends down alongside me. We unlace the layers of fabric, and the queen dutifully moves and steps when asked. Eventually she is dressed only in her skin. She does not colour nor try to hide herself, and I realise the queen has lived her whole life being looked at. She has been bathed and dressed since she herself was a baby. Her skin is smooth and dark, and I grow hot at the sight of her breasts and the hair between her legs. The swell of the baby is less pronounced without the sea of fabric. She has mere weeks to go. The queen stretches out a hand, and I lead her to the bath. She steps down slowly, as if descending her dais, then sinks into the water with a moan. Only her eyes and the top of her head remain, and she looks directly at me. She bobs up, her dark hair slick against her head.

'Enter, Hanan,' she commands.

I look around and try to conceal the blush on my cheeks. Near the doorway stands Salvacion, the queen's tall and brawny Seaguardian. She adjusts her stance, folding her hands in front of her and pointedly not looking at me.

The servant strides over to help me disrobe, and I baulk.

'Your Grace, surely you would rather bathe alone?'

The queen laughs, the sound echoing off the marble walls.

'It will do me a world of good to have you bathe with me and use your charms. Besides, they say hot water soothes the body and soul, and you are looking very ill these days. You must not wear yourself out for my sake.'

I wave off the servant and undress quickly, fumbling with the hooks and clasps of my dark gown. I try to fold the clothes neatly in a wooden bench on the corner, but I can feel the queen's eyes on me. I hurry to the pool and slide in, looking everywhere but her.

'You have not been eating,' she observes. I cover my breasts and feel the ribs close to the surface of my skin. Perhaps I have lost track of time occasionally in the library. 'I will not have you weak, Hanan. You must maintain your power.'

'Yes, Your Grace.'

'Come here.' She finds my hand in the water and interlaces our fingers. I gasp at the touch. I feel something humming and tugging within me, a dull ache in my chest. I close my eyes and touch the talisman at my neck. I feel the queen like a gentle push on a door, the pull on a lock of loose hair. I drop my hand to the water and begin to carve a circle around me. Her nails dig into my other hand.

'No barriers.'

The scents of the bathwater are replaced by sea salt, woodsmoke, and petrichor. A sharp stabbing pain in my fingers, like the cut of a blade, and the tart taste of calamansi fruit on my tongue. I hear an animal cry, desperate and shrill. Then the sound of wings beating, the air around me full of the rustle of feathers.

I open my eyes and look to the queen. She is breathing heavily and shaking. Her face is so close to mine I can smell the sweet leaves she chews to clean her mouth. We are cheek to cheek, and I can feel her breath in my ear. Then her head moves down towards the flesh of my neck, until her lips are on the soft skin. Her teeth sink in, and I think of a fruit bursting under a blade. She drinks until the room begins to narrow in my vision. The wound pulses under her lips, and the pain begins sharp until it throbs, and then there's a deep pleasure that washes over me, making me light-headed. My skin tingles, and enduring the pain becomes one singular point of focus in my mind. It becomes my holy mission. I hear her swallow and she drops my hand as she backs away, wiping a drop of blood from the corner of her mouth. She is glowing; there is no other way to describe it. It is as though she is a candle, and the light pours out from her eyes and skin.

'Thank you, Hanan. You should rest. You may find your strength depleted.'

My eyes grow heavy as she speaks, her voice a lullaby. I feel hollow and empty, as though I had swum the whole way to the Bastion. I look down at my body. High on my left thigh, almost at the hip, is a mark. It glows, the lines a whorl. A wave and a circle: a sun. I paw at it, but it doesn't come off. It's ridged and deep, a mark on my skin. I'm so weak my vision swims. What did I just let her do to me? I'm inexorably bound to her as though a tether runs from my being straight to hers.

CHAPTER TWENTY-NINE

FINLYR

'SHE WAS A TRICKSTER and a thief,' one of the Seaguardians sings along with the crowd, his back to us as he taps the side of his tankard in time with the beat.

Behind him on the docks, *Saltswept* stands huge and proud. In this light, and at this distance, the prow juts out and the figurehead of a barnacle-encrusted seamaiden greets us.

I take the dagger from my boot and hold it up to the moonlight, close to the Seaguardian's throat. He stills at the cold of the blade.

'Take off your jacket. Quickly now.'

The Seaguardian tries to turn to see his attacker, but I push the blade closer. He wobbles on his feet, out of fear or inebriation. Or both. He's a tangle of limbs as he struggles to take off the white Seaguardian uniform, and I tear it from him. He cries out in pain as I wrench his shoulder. I shrug on the jacket, covered in muck but still the badge of authority we need.

We hoist ourselves up onto the ship's ladder, one by one. Painfully slowly, the shadows our friends. We can only hope the impishness the women on land are spinning will last. Ris stays with me, uncoiling the tether and hauling the rope up with her as she climbs the ladder. I'm the last one down here, and I take a packet of sleep dust Narra gave me. A hedge witch's last defence. I'm sorry she didn't use it when the Seaguardians almost ruined Ligaya and Morna's wedding, although I suppose unconscious Seaguardians at the inn would have raised a few questions.

I open the packet and blow it in the guard's face. He staggers on the dock, and I think he's about to lose his footing when he gives a wild yell, trying to attract attention. I go to grab him when something dark shoots down from the deck above me. The Seaguardian falls into the water with a splash and a yell that is drowned out by the raucous cheering from the town square. Then a mass of wet dark fur is by my feet, and Sinigang is panting. We look at each other and then I pick him up, ignoring the blood on his mouth as I climb the ladder.

'Oh, look at what they did to her,' I say, looking around the main deck.

Close up, I can see the parts that have been replaced: that awful royal sigil, the weapons racks with their shiny cutlasses, their piles of white Seaguardian uniforms in trunks.

My hands and eyes rove over the familiar things that remain: the sculpted taffrail by a carpenter, the sturdy masts, crimson cloth-weave sails from a fabric trader, and the woven reeds that line the wooden planks harvested by my own hand.

'Fin, can we set sail now?'

I look between the taffrail at the hubbub in town. I can't see them but I hear Ligaya, Morna, and Narra on the edges, weaving their spell as they sing and clap. Then I peer into the dark water. Without his pristine jacket, the Seaguardian's body can't be seen.

We scramble up to the quarterdeck, and I grab Ris by the elbow, gesturing at her to cast off. She follows my lead, pushing hard at the helm. Isagani's up in the crow's nest, unfurling the sails so we can steer the boat out of the harbour. They can't catch us now. And by the time they've alerted the rest of the Seaguardians, we'll be out of the bay.

'I do like this game,' Sinigang gives me a wicked grin.

'I can't believe we pulled it off!' Isagani yells down to us.

Ris is slumped against the mast, looking at her shaking hands. Her face is pale, and I call to her gently, placing a hand on her arm. She looks at me, as if I've woken her from a nightmare.

'I saw what he did.'

Sinigang, ears burning, pads over to us. 'Did you think I only had sweet magic, Ris?'

'We had to,' I demur. 'We needed to get out without being seen.'

Ris looks grim and stares at the blood spatter on my shirt from where Sinigang's muzzle rubbed against me.

'What's going on?' Isagani says, starting to descend from the crow's nest. 'Let's go!'

'We have to get out of here first,' I say, and Ris eventually nods. 'Isagani, get back up there!'

'Are you sure she's seaworthy?' Ris asks, grabbing the tiller.

'She'll get us there, don't worry,' I say. 'Gentlefolk, welcome aboard *Saltswept*.'

'Celebrate later, Fin! They're on our tail!' Isagani shouts down.

'Take this,' I tell Ris. 'You're my first mate.'

'Oh, how generous,' she bites, as I leg it down to the captain's quarters.

The familiar smell of cedar and resin. The shelf that homes my collection of tchotchkes from my travels. There are unfamiliar things, too, like velvet cushions and bags of nuts and seeds.

I grab my spyglass, still buried in my clothes chest, and return to the deck.

'Yes, you beauty!' I cry triumphantly, eyeing the shore in the distance.

Isagani wasn't wrong. There are a couple of other vessels following in our wake, bells ringing aboard as a warning.

Sinigang whips his tail, and I feel the breeze increase. I stare at the otter-cat. 'What? Narra told you I'd be useful.' He smirks and spins his tail in circles, causing a wall of air to fill the sails.

'Sinigang, you absolute legend! Do more of that.'

He begins to purr, vibrating violently. First his purrs shake the deck of the ship, then the waters around us jump and dance with the rhythm. It ripples out further, causing huge swells to form. Rogue waves emerge and roll off towards the shore, crashing against the Seaguardians' vessels.

'Holy Aistra, you'll sink them!' Ris shouts between breaths as she works.

'Isn't that the point?' I yell back, bracing against the roiling.

The ships struggle against the waves, changing course and spreading out.

'They're going to pin us!' I call to Isagani. 'How far 'til we're out of the bay?'

Isagani braces against the crow's nest as the mast is blasted with spray. 'Not far. Can we outrun them?'

Sinigang looks exhausted, still bloodied about the mouth, and his pupils blown out. 'Got a little more in you?' I ask.

'Trim those sails and we'll see.'

The otter-cat ceases his purring and whips his tail in slow fluid motions. The waves break, and we catch the wind, and I steer into it as we haul away. The Seaguardians lag, still pursuing us, but we've put some distance between us. There's no chance of them pincering us now. We clear the bay and push into open water just as Sinigang lets out a yowl and collapses from the taffrail.

Part Two

Adventure Awaits

CHAPTER THIRTY

HANAN

THE QUEEN SPENDS the next weeks among company, always filling the place with people since the Magliyab festival. Her spirits are high as she laughs, skin aglow. She drapes a hand across her belly as she drinks, and her eyes meet mine as I hide in the shadows. I catch my reflection in the glass: a tall, gaunt woman, with greasy hair that falls around her shoulders like a shroud. My skin is dull, and my eyes vacant. I don't remember the last time I walked the grounds, felt the air on my skin. Each time she takes from me, I need to recover. I will lie in bed staring at the brand on my thigh until it no longer glows, no longer burns from her draining me. At first, I was bedridden; then I crawled. Now, I stumble.

I stagger away from the queen and her courtiers. The halls are full of noise and the press of warm bodies, and my feet take me to the cold, dark corners, the lonely hallways. By habit I find myself at the library, slipping the key into the lock, the metal warm from my skin as I held it in my pocket.

Once inside, I need to feel something tangible under my hands, to know I'm secure in here. I run my fingers across a tapestry of Paranish, tracing each of the isles in turn. When I brush against Aistra, I feel something behind the fabric. The indentation of a door, but there's no handle on this side. This must be how the queen sneaks up on me. I long to know where it leads but content myself in knowing the library has finally begun to reveal its secrets to me. For now, I place a stack of books just in front of the tapestry, hoping it will act as an alarm the next time she decides to visit. Something falls out of one of the volumes, a thin piece of paper stained with inky fingers. I carefully unfold the page and recognise Mother Lin's handwriting:

> *Sinaya. I am sending a sheaf of mansegrass as you requested. Blessed be His Majesty and we pray for him daily at the temple.*

The faint fragrance of the mansegrass is all that remains, and the messy fingerprints speak to the desperation of its recipient. One of my predecessors, who failed to save the king. I drop the letter, the anxiety seeping from the paper to my skin. My desperation has a new energy, hounding at my heels. I will not be like this priestess. I will not let her leave me so hollow. I must armour myself against draining. I will not extinguish as quickly as the others.

I begin hunting through the stack of tomes, thirsty for knowledge and the power it can bring. My arms ache as I heave the books around and my breathing becomes laboured. I try to ignore the cries of my body, still healing from the binding and now weakened by the drainings. To have such liberal access to the history and secrets of generations of priestesses is a luxury I could not have fathomed as a child at the temple, and I won't squander it.

I am poring over a volume when something hits the window, startling me. The pane is half open, and I see a bird collapse on the sill, its neck broken. It's a small, colourful thing, round and delicate-looking. I am reminded of the bird at the Temple of Aistra, the one that set this ripple across the water of my fate. I wonder at this bird now, prodding the energy field around it to see how much is left of it. Then I cast a protective circle, placing books end to end around me. I would prefer to use something that hasn't been transformed from its original nature and I'm used to using stones to ward off any energy that might interfere with my intention. However, books will have to do. I hold the bird gently in the palm of my hand. I can sense the life ebbing out of it like blood from a gaping wound. In my mind's eye I place my hands on that wound, and the pain ricochets up my arms and into my neck, a violent snapping of bones. I muffle my screams, biting on my sleeve. Once I've cleared my tears, I look back at it. The broken neck has snapped back into place, and its head rotates in one fluid motion. Its little heart starts beating, wings fluttering in confusion, and then it's out of my hand and dashing about the room. Its desperate trilling pierces my ears, and I try to catch and calm it.

My anxiety rises with its pitch, and I remember the exploding heart, the viscera.

'Please, be calm!'

The bird reacts, landing on my pile of books. I see its breathing slow, its eyes less wild. The colour has returned to its feathers. Brilliant violets and sunset pinks, with the oranges of summer adorning its beak and head. It has a comically long beak for such a small thing.

'We both want you to live. You must trust me, though. Can you do that?'

The bird looks at me and cocks its head. I wonder if I have gone mad. It inclines its head, as if in understanding, and I let out a small laugh. It twitters at me in turn, and I do believe I have slipped into an entirely surreal world. Truly, I have lost my mind if I am talking to a bird.

For the rest of the afternoon, it is my research companion. The bird sits at the windowsill, looking out, but seems uninterested in flying away. It is strange and comforting to have another living being in the library. I fashion a perch for it and wonder if I should cage it. I've never found anyone else in the library, and I'm unsure who else save the queen has access. Would it be more suspicious to transfer the bird to my rooms? But the servants clean there, which they never do here, if the dust is anything to go by. No, I think the bird is best kept secret and safe in the library.

I sneak out of the library, slipping past the feasting hall, which is full of music and dancing, and almost lose my footing at the sight of the queen singing:

> 'Highest of halls and tallest of towers
> That's where you sleep, my love.
> Thickest of walls and over each hour
> That's where I'll find you, my love.
> Warmest of sheets and wildest of dreams
> That's where you'll wander, my love.
> Deepest of rivers and darkest of hearts
> That's where you sleep, my love.'

Her voice is high and strong, knifelike through the air. It stops me in my tracks to watch her, the emotion writ on her face, her pale, delicate throat raised in supplication to the sky. I count in my head and force myself to move away, to break the spell that would keep me watching her until she stops.

The kitchen servants are used to my coming and going, fetching dainties for the queen, and I steal away some seeds and nuts. The bird adores them, nipping gently at my fingers, and presses its soft head against my skin. When I lock it up for the evening, it coos mournfully.

'Do not worry, friend. I will be back in the morning.'

As I lock the door I wonder if the bird will be alive when I return. I marvel to see it alive and well but I remember the initial soaring of my heart when the mokon came back. That was a temporary miracle.

When I enter the library the next morning, the bird is still there. It wakens, untucking its head from its wing, and chirps at me. Every time I unlock the library doors I hold my breath, and it is still alive. The bird is still with me the next morning, and the morning after that. I begin to keep a small flame of hope in my heart for it, tallying the days like a lover. Then I make the mistake of naming it, Pocket, on account of its size. It seems content in the library, grateful for the treats and company I bring. I wonder at such a life for a creature, so close to the sun and fresh air and yet closeted here in the dark with me. It is my experiment, to twist life from death, wrestling its essence back from the grave.

CHAPTER THIRTY-ONE

RIS

EVERYONE ON THE ship's deck watches as Sinigang falls from the taffrail. Biba is the first to react, and she lunges, shooting her arm through the rails to grab the otter-cat before he falls into the surf. She pulls him bodily back onto the deck, and I run to them, grabbing Biba.

'Why did you do that?' I shout, crying and holding her close.

She yells out in pain and clutches her shoulder.

'Are you hurt?'

'Worry about Sini,' she says, and Isagani leaps down from the rigging. They gently hold the otter-cat and strokes his fur. 'He's breathing.'

'That was powerful stuff – no wonder he's out cold,' Finlyr says. 'He'll be all right,' he adds, giving Isagani and Biba a reassuring look. It's one I recognise: tamping down the churning in your gut to save face.

We follow Isagani and Biba as they carefully, almost ritualistically, take Sinigang down to the living quarters to rest. I try not to see the shape of the dead otter-cat from the farm, and Biba catches my eye, as if she knows what I'm thinking. I focus instead on the hammocks rocking gently from the ceiling and the dim lanterns flickering overhead.

On the deck I try to breathe a little easier and watch the Paranishian isles slip over the edge of the horizon. We're deep in the nighttime hours. For better or for worse, we have thrown our lot together – and home, whatever that means now, is out of reach. I grip the rail and think of Larkin watching this same view, no anchor in his stomach.

I'm reassured as Finlyr starts to relax, his chest and shoulders expanding. I wasn't sure he would pull it off, but we're here: actually on board *Saltswept*.

'We want to make it as far away as we can, quickly and quietly,' Finlyr tells the assembled crew. 'Usually, a random vessel in the near waters wouldn't raise suspicion, but we left . . . a bit of a mess behind us. Hopefully we have enough time before the entire fleet is on high alert.'

Finlyr catches my eyes, and I feel heat creep up my neck. He's trying to placate me, but I can't forget what I saw, the vicious way Sinigang leapt upon that Seaguardian. At least one Seaguardian dead; Sinigang and Biba hurt. So much blood on our hands.

'I need everyone to follow my command. We're short-handed and these hours are critical.'

He is our captain, and I have to hope he's worth his salt. There are too few of us to work this vessel, and my stomach lurches.

We work ceaselessly, elbow to elbow at the helm. It's bloody heavy: a different heft to holding bucking sheep or lugging baskets of wet wool from the riverbank. My arms burn, and I struggle to find purchase on the planks of the deck. I try to steady my ragged breathing. My mind knows how to engage with this kind of work. It quietens, and I push my whole self into my muscles. Soon Finlyr and I barely need words, our eyes and hands aligning to fit the gaps in each other's work as we toil to the rhythm of the waves. The sweat stings my eyes and I wipe my forehead with the back of my arm.

Isagani is up in the rigging, their sinewy silhouette nimbly crawling among the ropes and woven reed sails. They look frazzled, dropping knots as quickly as they can tie them.

'Hurry up, Isagani, I need that sail catching the wind.'

'I'm going as fast as I can, Fin! There's a lot to remember!'

'We're losing it; get to the topgallant shroud!'

'Where?'

'Oh, for fuck's sake, over there!' Finlyr points, hand coming off the helm.

I try to hold steady as the vessel creaks beneath us. 'None of us know how to sail, Fin. Not like you do.'

As Isagani scuttles over, their foot catches in the line tail. They jostle, righting themselves with a surprisingly vile string of words.

Something shifts in Finlyr's face, like a cloud passing across the sun. Then the wind moves, and the ship is going against it. Even I can see we're being pushed back the way we came.

'We're being taken aback, hoy up!' Finlyr shouts and gives a piercing whistle through his teeth. He begins to sing:

> 'Haul away, you salt-swept urchins
> Heave away the sand of yore
> Ride the waves of navy merchants
> Seeking fortune evermore.'

Finlyr's voice is sure and steady, booming across the deck.

'Get on the capstan,' he directs me to push the great rotating circle of spokes and ropes and begins the song again.

Biba pushes alongside me and joins in the song, keeping time. She doesn't know the words but yells the start of each line, her small body lurching forward against the resistance of the capstan.

'Stay up there, Isagani,' Finlyr encourages. 'And make sure the sails are hoisted aft.'

'What are you talking about?' Isagani shouts.

'We're trying to go into the wind again, so we're turning the ship slightly!' I yell, translating the seafaring lexicon.

We can't rightly help if we don't know what he's saying, but I must admit the repetition of the song is taking the edge off my burning muscles.

When we are finally given leave of our posts, the sun is high in the sky. Isagani and I slump down on the quarterdeck, able at last to survey our surroundings. We lean against the capstan, legs splayed towards the split-level to the helm, where Finlyr stands. The ropes hang like vines from the rigging. We sit in amiable silence awhile, furnishing ourselves with slings of fresh water.

'I hope Narra is all right,' Isagani says, scrubbing a hand through their hair.

'She can hold her own – don't worry,' I try to reassure them, despite my misgivings. Our plan made it difficult for Narra, Ligaya, and Morna to be linked to us, but everyone was at the mercy of the Bastion. I had to hope they would go unremarked as they kept to themselves.

'So this is home now?' Isagani asks, looking around with a lantern. They open a store cupboard, and the spiders scatter to the shadows, revealing a bed of thick mould.

'This ship's certainly seen some things,' I say, jamming the cupboard door shut.

The wood's splintered hard in places on the deck.

'That taffrail was handmade by a Lassairian carpenter,' Finlyr says when I complain. 'And those cupboards just need a bit of a clean. At least we now have hearty supplies thanks to the Seaguardians.'

We've not much more space than in the rooms at the inn, and there was some heated debate around who would sleep where. Everything rocking and roiling, my body is already restless. Biba seems not to mind; perhaps she finds the movement soothing.

'Well, I'm the captain and this is my ship, so it's only natural I should take the captain's quarters,' Finlyr insists. Isagani opens their mouth to protest. 'Sorry, squirt, not sharing.'

'Without me, you'd be dead,' Isagani grumbles, face scrunched in frustration, but it's like wading through mud with Finlyr. The man is as stubborn as a tamaraw.

I silence Finlyr, stepping between him and Isagani. 'There are three chambers and five of us. You can have the largest – the captain's quarters, but you must share with Sinigang.'

Finlyr grimaces. 'You tell the otter-cat when he's woken up.'

'Biba and I can bunk together and Isagani can have their own room for once.'

'A lifetime at sea counts for naught with you, does it?'

'It counts,' I say, begrudgingly. 'Just remember that I'm the one who furnished you with that.' I point to the map, now in his breast pocket.

He considers and then hands me the map. 'You're this voyage's navigator. What do you see?'

I stare at the sky, trying to map the constellations. 'I'd have to consult the tools. What direction are we going in?'

'Exactly.' He smiles, his eyes glittering. He gets out a gold-rimmed pocket compass.

'That's a fine piece of work,' I say.

'It was my mother's,' he says, his voice raw and reverent.

'Was she also a sailor?'

Finlyr nods. 'She was a Seaguardian.'

I baulk. That was not what I was expecting.

'Like the man we left for dead?'

His mouth sets into a hard line. 'Yes. We did what we had to.'

Like Ryla, he had a Seaguardian mother – but what had led him to this path? I stare at him anew, and it feels as if I've really known nothing about him before now.

'Back to business. We're heading north-east.' He clears his throat, and I look again at the map.

I allow him to keep his secrets, for now. 'I think we need to bear further east,' I suggest, looking back south at the distant shapes of the isles. 'There's the Winter Isle, so we're a straight shot too far north.'

Finlyr tilts his head, following my hand and then looking back at the map.

'We don't want to run straight into the Maelstrom; we want to approach it side-on and angle into it. Lest we smash ourselves to smithereens.'

'Wouldn't we prefer to see it coming at the bow?' I counter.

'We won't be getting too close too quick.'

The two of us stop and stare at each other.

'I see your point,' I say slowly. 'However, we don't have an infinite supply of food and crew, so we can't exactly hang around. Either we're going in, or we're not.'

'And I concede that,' Finlyr replies tightly. 'But I'd prefer us all to make it to the other side in one piece.'

'Fine,' I admit. 'But we can't exactly anchor at the Maelstrom. How do you propose we get through safely?'

Finlyr laughs. 'Let's worry about that when we get closer, eh?'

I hear the undertone, something unspoken, a shadow to the lightness of his tone. I've seen the darker side of him, the smuggler he was – the core of him at his sharpest, most ruthless. What is he not telling us? What happened to him out there? And how in Paranish will we avoid the same fate?

CHAPTER THIRTY-TWO

HANAN

POCKET IS JUST over thirteen weeks alive when the baby begins to move within the queen's body.

The door to the library shakes as a fist pounds on the wood and I jolt up from my pile of books and papers.

Salvacion appears at the door, pale-faced with bags under her eyes. 'The queen fares very ill. You must come at once.'

I disentangle myself from my parchments and ink and hurry in her anxious footsteps, with barely a moment to blow out the lamps and lock up. Pocket looks at me dolefully as I leave; Salvacion doesn't even notice the bird.

We weave down corridors, and I have to run to keep up with Salvacion's long and urgent strides.

'What has happened?'

'It's best you come quickly,' she responds.

The curtains are drawn, and the room is bathed in candlelight. Even so, I can see the bloodied sheets and the waxy sheen on the queen's skin. Despite her earlier protestations, there are midwives and herbalists surrounding her now. She seems to have given over to anything in the hopes of relief. The herbalists press tinctures and tonics at her and she takes everything, seizing every bottle and vial with shaking fingers.

'Your Majesty, Priestess Hanan is here,' Salvacion announces, and I rush to the queen's side.

She grips my hand, and I feel the bones crunch together. I collapse into a kneel, and the heat from her palm is excruciating. Perhaps I misjudged her; perhaps she fears being alone rather than craving it. There is no one left except the baby inside her. Marriage tilts the world only for the elites, who use it as a game. But perhaps an accomplice is better than nothing.

'Hanan,' she implores, her voice weak and reedy. The child is partially out of her, its small feet visible. A breech birth.

'Why is no one doing anything?' I demand, surprised at the sharpness of my tongue. Bile rises in my throat as I examine the queen, and the herbalists and attendants finally spring into action.

I turn to Salvacion and whisper, trying not to let the queen hear: 'The child should have been moved within her beforehand.'

'It all happened so quickly,' a herbalist demurs. 'The baby came too soon.'

'Evidently,' I snap, frustrated by their mawkishness. They are despondent, resigned to it all. No wonder the king had fallen into death under such hands.

The queen reaches for me, and I'm stunned by the strength she has left. 'Hanan, don't let me die,' she whispers, tears and sweat dampening her pillow.

I don't know how long it takes. Time passes unknown to us within that room as the queen labours to no end, herbalists and midwives clamouring.

'Ease her passing,' it slips off their tongues. 'Protect the babe.'

They have written her off, and they look towards the heir sliding out from between her legs. I feel anger rising in me at their looks at the queen, a mere chalice, a vessel emptying.

'Get me more towels,' I bark at them as I kneel beside the queen. She's cold now, her skin pale blue like chips of ice.

'What is happening?' she asks, trying to sit up on her elbows.

'Your Grace, please lie down,' Salvacion says, gently but firmly pushing her back onto the pillows.

The queen cries, asking over and over for her child, where is her child? I place my hands on the queen's abdomen. I close the bed curtains around us, creating a protective circle. I stay there, feeling her flesh become warm and pliant beneath my fingers. I won't let her go. She calms and quiets, finally sedate.

The baby is silent as it enters the world. We all know it has passed from this world as quickly as it entered it, a fleeting moment of life. I hold it, so small in my hands. I think of Pocket, of the mokon at the Temple of Aistra. I look at the lifeless lips, bluer than their mother's, the waxy eyelashes, the small, curled fingers.

I move my hands around the baby, placing my thumbs on its torso, on the small ribs. I push. I hear a scream, but I must go on. I push until a rib cracks, a softer sound than it should be. Now I can feel it, the muscle beneath my fingertips. There is some blood, some life left in it. I feel the heat, distant like embers under the remains of a fire. In my mind's eye I toe the remnants, uncovering the embers. I bring my face close and blow, the white coals turning red, then catching. A small flame. A small hope, but it is there. With tending, it will grow large and steady.

Another scream, from the baby in my arms.

The glamour has been smeared away like paint. The queen is not a heavenly body, but one of flesh and blood. It seems so clear to me now, as her breath finally slows and her eyes become less wild. The baby has settled on her chest, cheeks flushed red and face snuffling against her skin. She won't let them separate, as though she is touch-starved. She has dismissed everyone but me, and the aftermath of pain resonates around the chamber like the echo of a scream. It is an energy like I've never felt before.

That's a lie. It is the same energy I felt when I put my hands around Malostra's neck. Pupils blown out in fear of death, of pain in their final moments.

'She looks like her father, don't you think?'

The queen's voice startles me. I thought she had fallen asleep at last. I don't know what to say.

'I never knew the king.'

He lived in stories, in the symbol of the Bastion. In the tapestries and statues and emblems. To know a royal likeness was to know Life and Death themselves. To try and put it into words or images was to look at the sun in the reflection of the water. To protect yourself from blindness. But perhaps the royals didn't want us seeing them directly to look upon their flaws. In still images they could be more than human.

'Or perhaps she looks like her mother. After all, she never even knew her father.'

The queen hands me the princess, and I'm so astonished that she is in my arms before I know what I'm doing.

'I can't—' I begin to protest, and then I peer down at the child's tiny face. Her eyes are open now, wide and roving curiously. She has a slick of fine dark hair, which moves under my breath.

'A princess and her priestess,' the queen says, with satisfaction.

The child is reaching out for me in this world and the other, her tiny arms grasping at the air. Her essence is more insistent than the queen's, reaching out, longing for my energy like a mother's milk. She seeks me out and then I feel rain against my cheek. We're still inside the birthing chamber but yet there it is, the feeling of rainwater and the smell of petrichor. A waft of smoke. Then the sea is caught on the breeze and reaches us. I feel sick with remembering, the world tilting under me and dizziness overwhelming me. The princess is trying to drain me. I try to push it away, to pry the fingers away one by one from my mind. I open my eyes as the baby struggles in my arms, breaking free of the blanket and thrashing.

'What's happening?' The queen asks, alarmed. 'Did she resist?' Her eyebrows are furrowed, and she bites her lip, examining the child in my arms.

'No,' I say, before realising my mistake. I was the one who resisted.

The queen turns back to me, a hunting look in her eyes. It bears no resemblance to the worry I saw etched in her expression moments earlier.

'What is it then?' the queen asks, her voice low.

I am fire-walking here. I match the queen's gaze, pushing down the memory of when we bathed, how I felt after I let her drain me. This is what we were practising for. I am her well from which she draws, over and over again, waiting for the rain to refill me. Rage rises like bile in my throat. I cast it to the back of my mind and breathe, taking her hand. She starts back, surprised at my boldness.

'It is . . . different than with you,' I start, gently making circles with my thumb on her wrist. 'I was surprised. But I know now. Let me try again.'

The queen pauses for a moment, and all I can hear is my breathing, ragged and shallow despite myself. I must be her shadow. I must not fail, not after I have come so far.

'She is your princess; you must let her in.'

The queen reaches forward and touches my clavicle. I gasp at her cool soft fingers. She unlaces the front of my dress, and my skin is gooseflesh.

'Feed her.'

My queen has commanded me, and I cannot deny I'm morbidly fascinated. I bring the princess up to my breast and let her take from me. It's a short, sharp pain, which becomes a dull ache after a time. I feel distant from my body, as though it is happening to someone else and I'm observing. Then a dizzy spell hits, and I lean on the queen for support. The princess drains until I am spent. When I prise her away, the substance isn't milky white but a strange mingling of blood and streaks of forest green. I am a withered husk, and I barely make it back to my chamber before I collapse. As I lie on my bed, I watch the stray droplets dry on my dress. My pulse in my neck is slow, struggling to regenerate the blood I have given. I have saved the princess, and her life will forever be tied to mine. We are bound together, and the queen needs me to sustain them both. After all, is it not the neck that controls the head?

CHAPTER THIRTY-THREE

FINLYR

WE'VE BEEN WHITE-KNUCKLING since setting sail, but I feel my chest expand as we make our way into more open water. My crew are salty and sweat-crusted and I know I have to say something. It's a storm brewing in a confined space, which never ends well. We're short-handed, even with Sinigang now awake. He's still too weak to help, and he sits in Biba's arms and she strokes him as if in a trance.

'I'm just trying to keep you all safe. Look, I've taken a . . . sojourn . . . from sailing. I'm getting my sea legs back under me, as are all of you.'

There's an agonising silence. We're drifting past the Winter Isle, the Temple of Aistra just visible through the mists. Weak sunlight pierces through the fog, and the stonework reaches out to us, tall and imposing like a creature in the shadows waiting to strike. The towers its claws, the stained-glass windows its teeth.

Sinigang hisses, and Biba clutches him tightly to her. Even I shiver in the rapidly cooling air, the unsettling quiet.

'This is the place, isn't it?' Biba asks, staring at Ris.

Her mother nods, grim-faced. 'This is where they train them.'

Biba moves across the deck, barely noticing as Sinigang wriggles in her arms. She is entranced by some silent song.

Something else emerges from the mist. Bleached woven reed sails. Gold trim on the masts. Seamaiden figurehead on the prow. An official Seaguardian patrol.

'What should we do?' Isagani asks, as rocks form in the pit of my stomach.

'Should I bite them?' Sinigang asks, swishing his tail. 'It's venomous if I sink my teeth in far enough.'

'We know,' Ris says, giving the otter-cat a sour look.

He's got some of his fiendish energy back. I can't help but wonder if our proximity to the Winter Isle has something to do with that.

I recoil. 'That won't be necessary. We don't know that they've been alerted to a stolen ship yet. As far as they know we are a legitimate quest vessel. But Biba get below, just to be safe.'

Biba nods and makes her way to the living quarters. We all try to act natural as the Seaguardians approach slowly. The dazzling white of those pristine uniforms makes me sick. They motion for us to steer into the wind and throw lines across to tether our crafts together. Gangway planks slap down as they board, a couple of lackeys setting it down and coming to land on our deck.

I watch the person I deduce must be their captain. They eye the royal sigil on *Saltswept*'s prow. 'What's all this then?'

'We are on a quest for Her Royal Highness,' I say, bowing with a flourish. 'Blessed be.'

'You'll have some proof of that then, won't you?' the captain smirks, picking at their nail beds with a knife.

We all look at one another. Ris has a pallid sheen on her face that tells me this isn't her first run-in with them.

She composes herself and steps forward. 'Certainly,' Ris says, lowering her voice: a deep, honeyed resonance, commanding and broaching no argument.

Ris proffers a hand casually at me, without looking my way. I scrabble in my shirt for the map and hand it to her; she unfolds the yellowed paper with attentive care. The moment stretches out between both crews, and I dare not breathe. Ris hands it carefully to one of the lackeys who unfolds it and holds it up to the sunlight. It takes a moment for the mist and clouds to clear enough for the light to penetrate the paper. Then we can all see it glowing like a fire ember: the royal seal. A sun with whirling beams, shining blindingly in the corner of the map. I avert my eyes and notice the outline of the seal hitting the deck. I try to swallow the gasp slipping from between my lips. A faint rattle emanates from the lodgings below, and I hold my breath. Be quiet, Biba.

The captain nods begrudgingly. 'Another skeleton crew,' they signal to their crew. 'Disembark.'

The flunkeys begin their retreat, tossing the map back at Ris. 'Fair seas,' one of them says, his tone spitting a curse.

Once they are safely out of earshot, we all turn to Ris.

'How did you know it would do that?' Isagani asks, handling the map like it might explode.

'Morna showed me,' Ris says, tentatively.

'Why did they call us a skeleton crew?' Isagani asks.

'It's because they don't expect us to come back,' Ris responds sourly, a grim line set across her face.

The words are barely out of her mouth before the ship judders and groans, a beast awakening from a slumber. A hammering comes from the doors to the living quarters. It's slow and rhythmic, almost drumming.

'What in Paranish is that?' I ask.

We look around, confirming the Seaguardian ship is still leaving us, its silhouette in the distance.

Sinigang's fur stands on end, hackles rising. 'I don't like this,' he says, growling.

'Well, we don't allow stowaways,' I say, cautiously taking the steps down to the doorway. My hand is on my scabbard, and I unsheathe my weapon as I open the door.

At first there's only the dark hallway beyond, and then the putrid smell of death.

'Stop!' Biba yells, emerging from the dark. She runs out onto the deck and tries to shut the door behind her, but I'm blocking it.

'What? What is it?' I try to ask her, but she's frantic.

I see the silhouette of a huge man in the shadows and drive my blade into soft flesh. I meet resistance, and then I'm being pushed back, and as we reach the light, I find what's on the end of my weapon.

They walk out in all their viscera, bloated from their time underwater, bones visible, clothing mottled. I pull my blade from the body I speared, but the thing keeps on walking. This one is tall, with a tattered hat on their head. Another with decaying puckered skin makes their way over to the capstan and gets to work. More swab the deck, gripping the mops with gnarled and swollen fingers. They keep coming until they outnumber us and then some, getting to work as if we aren't there.

Biba screams, backing herself up against the taffrail. Ris and Isagani have their fists up, ready to throw hands. Sinigang hisses, shaking himself like his fur is wet.

'What *are* those things?' Ris asks, veering out of the path of one of them who shuffles by humming.

'They look dead,' I say, staring at them with morbid fascination.

'Why aren't you stabbing them, Fin?' Ris asks, panicked.

'It didn't seem to do much!' I counter, laughing nervously.

'Are they . . . helping us?' Isagani asks, eyes following a corpse ascending the rigging.

'Looks like it,' Sinigang says, bristling.

Isagani follows behind a corpse, and with a deft movement they filch a box from the undead, sliding it right off their belt loop. They quickly work at the puzzle of the box, sliding the pieces into place so the picture on the outside is complete. It clicks open, and out pours seawater and grime. All that's left is a freshwater pearl and a rusted sextant.

'A sailor?' I ask, examining the treasures over Isagani's shoulder. 'They move like they're acting on instinct.'

A great cacophony under the hull, like an explosion beneath the water. It ripples outwards and back towards the Paranishian mainland. *Saltswept* bucks and roils, and we find something to hold, although the skeleton crew are unfazed. Akin to Sinigang whipping us up a breeze, a strange wind catches in our sails, and the undead continue their labour with organisation and fervour.

'This didn't happen to you the last time, did it?' Ris asks.

I shake my head. 'This is new. I would've remembered a crew of undead sailors rising up.'

'What nonsense,' Ris admonishes me. 'Everyone who passes is ushered into the Tree of Life.'

'Tell that to them,' Isagani says warily.

'A temporary waking from their eternal slumber,' Sinigang says, slinking around Biba's feet. 'It reeks of unholy magic.'

Biba slowly unpeels herself from the taffrail and approaches the sailor who swabs the deck. She touches their skeletal hand and jumps back, as though burned. 'Restless souls,' she says, her voice strong and words like an incantation. 'Sailors who died for the crown.'

'Plenty more of them since I last did this voyage,' I say, checking Biba's hand for a wound. She looks fine, if shaken.

'Do you think the royal seal summoned them?' Ris asks, looking pale.

I nod grimly. 'Looks like it. I'm not ungrateful for the help; we need all hands on deck.'

'It's an abomination,' Ris snaps and then claps a hand over her mouth.

'Life and Death must be respected,' Biba echoes, staring at her mother.

The tension is as thick as the fog we just left behind, and I try to suss out what is unspoken between them.

'There is nothing good about this. It's disgusting,' Ris insists, heading towards the balustrade.

'Where are you going?' I ask. 'Aren't you going to help me navigate?'

'Why don't you ask one of your new crewmates?' she snaps, slamming the door to the rooms below.

CHAPTER THIRTY-FOUR

HANAN

I AM SEQUESTERED IN bed until the queen deems me strong enough to leave. I detest being at her will, which sounds foolish, as I have been at her will since I stepped foot in the Bastion. Actually, even before that, though I did not know it. The shadow of her fingers has moved every moment of my life. As a girl I didn't fully understand how I had come to be at the Temple of Aistra. Now that I am at the Bastion, I understand it a little more. Children bought, children snatched. Whispers that may their way to the Bastion like vibrations on a spider's web. Either way, taken from their families as soon as the power they demonstrated was strong enough. Too strong to be controlled, strong enough to be moulded. As a Temple Sister, I had thought commune with the dead was the holiest duty to which I could aspire. Now, I sense a dark shadow to the power being nurtured in me.

One night, when I am restless in bed in the quiet hours before dawn, I feel a strange stirring in my body. It gives me the same thrill I had sneaking texts from the temple library; the first time I saw the word 'necromancy', the first time I could give voice to the sense of something forbidden, something straddling Life and Death. I am too weak to move much, so I examine my body bit by bit. My arms have the same tingly sensation as when they go numb in the night. Cold runs down my neck all the way to my feet, like ice water has been poured over me. My hairs all stand on end as the smell of decay reaches my nose. But I can find nothing that would be its source. Something out there has been disturbed, like turned earth.

I feel a lump at the small of my back as I try to go back to sleep. Within the mattress, I find a little stone figurine of a bird with a hole in its chest. Perhaps a talisman from a previous priestess? I hide it in my gown's pocket and rub the bird's head to soothe my nerves. It's comforting to think of the other priestesses who have come before me. Less so to think of their fate, which befalls us all, of withering into dust after we are spent.

Later that day, the queen visits me, bringing a bowl of sweetened rice porridge.

'Your Grace, you are too kind, but I can manage myself,' I insist as she holds the spoon up to my face like I'm a baby.

She watches me silently as I eat, my hands less shaky today. The fatigue from the draining is like the weather in Umasa, some days overcast and others perfectly sunny. It can turn suddenly, so I try to follow the language of my body.

'How is the princess?' I ask, keen to get her eyes off me.

'She fares very well, thanks to you,' the queen says, a warm and self-satisfied smile dancing on her lips.

'You are too generous, Your Majesty.'

Her praise makes me feel emboldened. I must ask her. It's now or never. I open my mouth.

'I hope to continue my studies, to better be able to serve you, Your Grace,' I say tentatively, avoiding her eyes.

She considers. 'I would not have you tire yourself out, Hanan.'

'Of course, Your Grace. In moderation, I'm sure I could achieve a great amount. It would be a shame to lose momentum on the progress I've made.'

'Say it plainly, Hanan.'

'I wish to return to the library, today.'

She eyes me for a long time. 'Very well. I shall leave you, but listen for the bell summons. I won't have you peering over dusty tomes all day every day. Not now the princess is with us. She is your first priority.'

It takes me longer than I hoped to dress myself and make my way down to the library. I lean against the walls, taking each step slowly, and sliding the key into the lock feels like coming home.

Nothing has been touched in the library, and Pocket's food tray is almost empty. I make my way over to him, and he gives me a gentle nip, followed by a pleased trill.

Once he's settled, I retrieve the volume I was working on the day the queen went into labour. I gather my papers of translation and continue my work at double speed. I didn't understand what I was looking at before, but now there's an inkling of something in my mind. I hold the warm bird figurine as I work. The volume is weathered and mouldy, ill-maintained and forgotten in the back of the stacks. I doubt anyone has catalogued or reviewed the collection for years. Doubtless the other priestesses utilised the resources here, but it seems the last scholarly-minded one was perhaps my predecessor who wrote this volume.

At last I have some semblance of a translation. It makes no sense. It's a jumble of words that don't string together to form sentences of any meaning. Pocket flies over to me and stands on the parchment, obscuring some of the text.

'Thank you, but that's not helpful.'

I listen with bated breath for the summoning bell, but nothing comes. Still, I must work quickly. I've no idea how often the queen will let me back here undisturbed.

The bird figurine has grown slick in my pocket from my fiddling, and I place it on the desk. Out of the corner of my eye I notice a word peeking through the hole in the figurine. I look again. No, that can't be right. I adjust the figurine so it moves slightly across the page, near the top of my transcription. It's a cipher, with the figurine acting as a focus lens. When I look through the hole I can string the meaning together. The words dissolve in my mind's eye, forming the shape of a woman. She hovers above the book, only head and shoulders, with the rest of her like an inky trail dripping back down onto the pages. It is the priestess who authored this account. She appears incorporeal, a shadowy figure of smoke and ink.

'Who are you?'

'Priestess Sinaya. One who came before.'

'Were you one of the—' I catch myself. I wanted to say 'failures', but that feels impolite around a spectre. 'One of the healers for the king?'

Priestess Sinaya gives a wry smile. At least that's what it looks like to me. I remember the letter I found from Mother Lin and the faint remnants of mansegrass.

'Heal and harm are the sun and moon. A gift may also be a curse.'

Of course she speaks in riddles. Did she deliberately do something to the king? Were the failures to cure him intentional?

'Do you mean a literal gift?'

'Kept close and secret,' she responds. 'But they squandered it.'

'What do you mean squandered? What gift?'

'The only gift they ever desire: power. Power over Life and Death.'

A shiver runs down my spine. The apparition seems to stare straight into my being, and her eyes narrow, as though I am something tarnished.

Experimentally, I open my other eye and remove it from the hole in the bird figurine. The Priestess Sinaya of smoke and ink disappears.

I look back through it, and there she is again. Pocket flies over from his perch and lands on the spectre's outstretched hand.

'What happened to you?'

'When I tried to stop them, they expelled me from the Bastion. Before I was banished, I stole the gift, with plans to hide it.'

The spectre freezes, and Pocket flies over to me, startled. It is as though something inside her has broken.

'What happened? Where did you hide it?'

'I sought help from the ones who practise the forbidden gift.'

The priestess crumbles into dust on the page. I take my eye from the bird figurine, back again, squinting to find her. The words on the page are nonsense once more. Nothing I do brings back the spectre of smoke and ink.

The summoning bell rings distantly outside my library. I shake myself and blink in the fading light. Soon there will be footsteps on the flagstones outside my door. Who knows when I'll next get time to try and speak with Sinaya?

I know my predecessor's fate was a grim one. I don't dwell on what I know of priestesses who displease the royals. I am not foolish enough to forget how many women have come before me. How many has the queen burned through and discarded? As she said herself, everything fades.

Malostra was morbidly fascinated by it, but I hated those cautionary tales. I can only hope for the priestess that death was quick, as I hope it will be for me when the queen finds out what I intend to do.

CHAPTER THIRTY-FIVE

FINLYR

IT'S MY HABIT TO wander the deck in the early morning, when the rest of the crew are still asleep. I had forgotten that some of our new crewmates will never need to sleep again. I nearly bash a door in the face of an undead wearing a tattered hat, who is momentarily perplexed by the obstacle, before moving around it.

'Sorry,' I say, reflexively, before shaking my head at my own stupidity. A shudder runs down my spine at the smell, a pervasive rot that has been with us since our additional crew was awoken by the map. Even the salt-brine air up here can't quite rid the stench from my nostrils.

Despite this, I'm pleased to see we're keeping course and the seas remain calm enough that sending everyone down to rest was a decent choice. Still, I don't like to be away from the helm for too long. I breathe in the salt air and look around at the peach-blush skies. It feels good to be back on the open water. I have new eyes looking at this ship and remembering the years spent upon its decks. There's not a section of wood or rope I have not laid hands or eyes upon. I didn't realise how landlocked I'd felt in Umasa, biding my time, not knowing if the next day would be my last. But it didn't feel how it had before the noose. That felt heady and free. The time at Narra's had been more like watching sand fall through an hourglass. The future slipping through your fingers.

To my surprise, I find Isagani standing on the taffrail, leaning precariously over the side of the ship. They lower a net into the water. It's got a homespun quality about it, but I have to admit I'm impressed. After watching them teach Biba Lassairian hitches, I figured Isagani has some nautical knowledge after all. Still waters run deep and all that.

'Catch anything?' I ask, and they startle, nearly going overboard. I catch Isagani by the scruff of the neck, much as I did the night we commandeered this vessel. I pull them back to their feet and grab the edge of the net, fastening it to the taffrail.

'I thought you were Big Red!' they say, clutching their chest.

'Who?'

Isagani points to a tall and broad corpse wearing red britches, currently at the helm.

'Thanks for the flattering comparison. You're not seriously naming them, are you?'

Isagani shrugs. 'Why not? They were people once.'

My stomach squirms as I look at the undead crew. 'Once.' I turn to survey Isagani's net, a welcome distraction. 'Well, you've not got any sinkers on this.' I laugh as the net continues to float like a jellyfish on the water's surface.

'I didn't know that,' Isagani snaps, crossing their arms. They pull their wide-brimmed hat down to cover their reddening face. I whip it off and scruff their hair. They're no longer playing at merchant's daughter and have taken to loose, comfortable garb and tying their hair back from their face. 'I was trying to catch some fish, to make a nice breakfast for everyone.'

I hide my heart-melted smile.

'I'll help you after breakfast and maybe we can have a nice fish lunch or supper – how about that?'

When we go down to the galley, I'm alarmed to see one of the undead cooking. They are clattering about the cramped counters, pots of upended herbs and discarded half-chopped ingredients littering the surfaces. They bounce their head off the pots and pans, which hang from the ceiling rack. They've a fire going on the stovetop, with the flames alarmingly close to their rags. A pot bubbles over with what looks like rice porridge, the undead stirring haphazardly.

'I suppose breakfast is served?' Isagani says, an amused grin on their face. 'I'll wake the others.'

We all sit in bemused silence, bowls of slop in front of us, as the undead chef goes off to find other duties.

'A corpse made this?' Ris says, failing to hide her disgust.

Everyone plays with their food, and I realise we're each waiting for the other to take a spoonful first. I taste the porridge and let it sit on my tongue. It's plenty hot, which is the only thing I feel for a while, until eventually the flavour begins to burn through. It's creamy, a bit gritty, and then there's something sour. At first it's almost pleasant and my mind recognises it as calamansi. I can see the yellow fruit rinds on the counter next to the empty pot. Then an earthy taste, almost damp dirt. I look at the calamansi again and notice dark brown spots on the undersides.

My throat can't bear to swallow. I dribble the foul mess back into the bowl.

'Fin, that's bad manners,' Biba says.

'Rotten,' I try to say.

'What?' Ris asks, sniffing the porridge. She takes a tentative bite, flicking her tongue against the spoon like a lizard. She instantly recoils and pushes the bowl away. 'That's awful! How did it take you that long to notice?'

I shrug, trying to contain my nausea.

'What happened?' Isagani asks.

I suspect I know what happened, but I have to see it with my own eyes. I indicate for everyone to follow and we make our way over to the storeroom. I unlock it and am hit with a musty, foul aroma. My heart sinks. This confirms it.

Everything was stored properly, or so I thought. I had done a cursory check but excuse me for trusting the Seaguardians actually know the first thing about sailing. The queen's finest indeed.

'What are we going to do? Is everything ruined?' Isagani says, voice beginning to take on panic.

'We'll have to ration,' Ris has already begun to strategise.

'I say we mutiny,' Sinigang chimes in.

'Look, can we all just take a breath? Let's take stock of everything first before we start catastrophising, yes?'

They reluctantly agree, and we begin to rootle around in the cupboard, assessing every item for ruin. It is not as bad as I had imagined, but the calamansi has begun to rot, a green fur forming on the underside of some of them and an unpleasant squishiness when I inspect them. My hands feel around the walls. By Paranish, there's damp in here. This wouldn't have happened under my command. Must have been those damned Seaguardians. Don't they know a storeroom's supposed to stay dry? Idiots to the crown. For fuck's sake, there's barely room for one person in here. We bump in the half-light, all elbows and knees.

'I need some fresh air,' Ris says, backing out of the cupboard. She stands on the deck, backlit by sunlight, a proud silhouette, arms akimbo. What she doesn't know is that the sun is also lighting up the shape of her body beneath her linen garments. I avert my eyes. She can probably sense my thoughts and by Paranish this is not the time for it.

'Not everything is lost,' I say, matter-of-factly. 'The water is fine. We should dry everything out here. It's a pleasant day for it.'

I look up and Sinigang is staring sourly at me. 'So, we're all agreed the undead should stay out of the kitchen.'

'You may as well help me fix my net now,' Isagani sighs, watching the scattered food items drying in the sun on the deck. 'So we can at least have something for breakfast.'

I retrieve stone net sinkers from the now-empty store cupboard and attach them to the net one by one.

'You need to spread them out properly to ensure the weight is evenly distributed.'

'And how often do I need to check the nets?'

I stand straight and look at Isagani. Their eagerness would be endearing to anyone with a kind heart. But I can also hear something underneath it. Not just eagerness, but eagerness to please.

'Where did you learn the Lassairian hitch, Isagani?'

They shift uncomfortably, scuffing the toe of their boot against the decking. 'My grandmother.'

My eyebrows shoot up in surprise. 'Was she a sailor?'

Isagani shakes their head. 'Not quite. Fisherfolk on the Summer Isle. Lassairian hitches were better for nets, she said.'

'A noble enterprise, fishing.'

'It was, until the waters got poisoned.'

'What do you mean?'

'It happened slowly, the coral reefs dying, species of smaller fish disappearing. We barely had enough to feed ourselves, never mind pay the royals' tithe. That's when the Bastion took notice.'

This is the most words Isagani has ever strung together, and I find myself holding my breath, afraid to break the spell.

'Blamed my grandmother, insisted she pay her debt. I knew they'd come for me after she passed. Debts don't die with you apparently.'

'So you ran,' I whisper, placing a hand over theirs.

They flinch, then look up at me, pouting proudly. 'What would you have done?'

'The exact same thing,' I say softly. 'You looked out for yourself. And you're not the only one.'

'It was never the right time, she said, to leave Paranish. Our family lived there for generations; she wouldn't abandon our home. For all the good that loyalty did her.'

'She'd be proud of you, kid. And I'll make good on her wish. I'll take you to a fresh start, if we survive this.'

Silence covers us like a blanket. We watch the gentle movement of the waves and listen to the slop of the water hitting the bow.

Slowly the fish enter the net, the stillness making it invisible to them.

'Now?' Isagani asks.

'Wait until it's the right time,' I insist.

Others gather, thinking it must be safe for how many fish are there, chomping on the hull's algae.

'Pull!'

We tug at the net, and the weights move upwards, tightening the net around the fish. They flip-flop as we haul them onto the deck, gasping for air until they are still.

'It worked!' Isagani yells, delighted. 'Should I take these to Ris?'

I examine the fish, making sure they're all dead. There's a surprising variety of species here, including deepwater luminous roughy, tiny dragonfish with deadly teeth, and translucent glass squid shaped more like a bird than a marine creature.

'You've done well, Isagani. I'll take it from here.'

I haul the net across the deck and down to the galley, slapping it down on the floor triumphantly. 'Look what Isagani reeled in.'

Ris turns her attention from the counter, where she's reorganising the food for the store cupboard. At first she seems surprised by the strange marine creatures, and then she smiles.

'We'll have pickled fish for days,' she says, pointing to the myriad jars on the counter.

'Could make a nice fish stew or a pie or a . . . grilled . . . there's plenty of other things you can make with fish.'

'That's true,' she considers, tapping her finger on her lips. 'But let's just say your menu is a tad . . . repetitive.'

'At least it's not mouldy porridge.'

'Fine,' she concedes, clearing the sink. 'Help me prepare these, will you?'

'We'll have to gut them all now,' I say, hauling the net into the sink.

'We can salt what we don't eat now.' She pauses. 'The salt is still dry, isn't it?'

I make a non-committal noise. 'I think so.'

She sighs, raising her eyes to the skies. 'Paranish, just give me a knife.'

I raise my eyebrows. 'You want me to furnish you with a weapon?'

'You want me to *only* gut the fish?' she asks, leaning past me to grab a knife and a slippery candidate from the net.

We work in amiable silence for a while and when Ris next opens her mouth, I'm surprised to hear her tone is sincere.

'Where did you learn to chop like that?'

'Why, are you intimidated?'

'No, you're making a mess of it.'

I look down at my handiwork and then at Ris's neater pile of innards. 'Where does a farmer get off telling a sailor about fish?'

'By Aistra, your pride is a bruised mango.' She laughs. 'Come here.'

She takes my knife and nudges me playfully aside, standing before my work and demonstrating. 'You're too fast; you need to slow down and hold this bit here so it doesn't tear away. Peel it back, layer by layer. Like undressing a lover.'

My face must be an open book; she laughs at my discomfort. 'Are you confessing that Biba's father was a siren?' I jest.

Her body stiffens, and I step back from the heat of her body. I hadn't realised we were so close to one another.

'Try to keep it cleaner with the next one,' she says, but the warmth and levity is gone from her voice.

'Did I do something?' I ask, gently.

'Just realised how hungry I am,' she says, with a tight smile. 'Let's get some of these ready for eating.'

CHAPTER THIRTY-SIX

RIS

I CAN'T HELP BUT laugh when I remember Finlyr's distressed face trying to gulp down that foul porridge. It's what he deserves for his oversight with the storeroom.

'Swabbing the deck is all fine and good but cooking requires human hands,' I insist, sorting through the goods to be stored once the cupboard has been cleaned. 'People who can actually taste if something's going to poison us.'

Finlyr rolls his eyes at me. 'If you're prepared to do it all, that's fine by me.'

'Hey, that's not what I said. We can take it in turns; everyone will pitch in.'

'I'd like to see you try and make Sinigang pitch in.'

I sigh. 'He can be moral support.'

Finlyr raises his eyebrows. 'A real improvement on a skeleton.'

He's finally got the hang of preparing the fish. It's only taken until most of the net was empty.

'Have you heard the kids have named them?'

'Named what?'

'You know, the undead.'

I turn to him. 'By Paranish, they need to amuse themselves, don't they?' I work the bones out of the flesh and set them to one side. 'But I don't like it. Those things should be dead. I don't want Biba and Isagani getting too attached. I'd rather we managed how we did before. They give me a terrible feeling.'

Finlyr laughs, cleaning his knife.

I stop my work and stare at him. 'There is nothing humorous about this – you know that, right?'

'You and I are the same type.'

'And what's that?'

'We have to do everything ourselves.'

I shift uncomfortably, realising we're elbow to elbow again. He looks at me and blows his growing hair out of his face. It was a bit of a mane in Umasa, but now it's growing longer, there's a wave to it. Sometimes he ties it in a knot atop his head. I've seen him teaching Isagani how to rope-braid their hair to keep it out of their face.

'What about your crew? Surely a captain must delegate.'

He shrugs and sighs. 'They were capable enough, but it was my ship, you know? Everything is ultimately my responsibility.'

'Not anymore,' I insist. 'You have to let someone else take on some of it.'

'Hence the undead crew.' He smiles. 'See, I knew you'd come around.'

I bump him with my shoulder, and he mimes being in great pain. The door to the galley swings open, and we jump apart.

'Holy Aistra, you have to come see this!' Isagani shouts down at us.

Finlyr and I share a look. Their tone is one of utter excitement and amazement, but we have that parental instinct to presume trouble. We clean up and head back towards the deck as quick as we can.

The supplies are still drying on the deck, and Isagani and Sinigang peer into the store cupboard. The door is open wide and it's a still a mess of mould and cobwebs. In the shadows sits Biba, right next to the pile of produce we had decided was too spoiled to be saved. She grabs a mango and squeezes. The skin is wrinkled with brown spots.

It looks like mush and the smell of mould permeates the air. When she removes her hands from the mango the fruit is the oranges and pinks of a sunset, and a cloying floral aroma hits my nose.

Finlyr grabs the mango, disbelieving. He stares and then examines his sticky fingers where the juices have leaked. He shoves them into his mouth like a child. He sucks for a moment and his face lights up. 'It's good,' he says, gleefully. 'It's really good. How did she do that?'

By Aistra, I had almost forgotten this problem. The reason we had to flee in the first place.

Isagani stands, mouth agape, as Finlyr continues to make a mess of the mango. 'You'll be sick,' they say. 'The fruit's no good.'

Finlyr shakes his head excitedly. 'Fresh as the day it was picked.'

'How is that possible?' Isagani asks, coming towards Finlyr and peering over his shoulder. They narrow their eyes at Finlyr continues to eat, as if they're waiting for him to explode. They examine another rancid mango, and hand it to Biba.

'Can you do that again?' Isagani asks.

Biba looks at me and shakes her head, returning the fruit. 'I didn't do anything.'

Both Isagani and Finlyr turn to me then. 'Why is she afraid?'

'She has to learn to control it,' I say, quietly.

'Ris, this isn't like the fire at the inn,' Finlyr begins, placing a hand on my shoulder. 'This could help us. It's a blessing—'

'If you'd seen what she's done, you wouldn't call it a blessing.'

The undead carry on, completely unaware of the tension on board. I watch one of them scurrying around, swabbing the deck with a swish of its mop. Another rustles as it moves, the sickening sound of broken ribs knocking together.

'Stop it!' I yell, holding back tears. 'That noise is driving me to the plank.'

'They won't be commanded,' Sinigang says, jumping onto the taffrail. I'm trembling as the otter-cat sidles towards me. His fur under my fingers is calming, his small body so warm. He purrs gently. 'Let's all go below deck and make some tea.'

We gather in the captain's quarters, pot of tea steeping on the table. It's cosy here, with a touch more space than the galley. My eyes wander across Finlyr's glass-fronted cabinet, with an odd assortment of objects he must have gathered on his travels. Shells, sea glass, and curios I can't even name line the shelves. By the velvet-lined couch is an open trunk of miscellaneous bottles and naval equipment, including a sextant and astrolabe. Biba and Isagani bundle up on Finlyr's bed, making cloaks out of his blankets. I look at Biba, trying to find outward signs of it. I have never seen a Temple Sister or Mother, nor a priestess. Are they marked from the beginning, like a birth dark-wine stain or a freckle? Or does it come with time, with deed? Is it the fine white webbing of scar tissue or a bruise that never fades? Perhaps there is no outward sign at all.

Isagani picks up a tome from the bed and begins to flip through it before Finlyr promptly snatches it away.

'Thought you weren't much of a reader?' Isagani asks quizzically.

'Great for propping up wonky tables.' He laughs, setting the book aside.

I tilt my head and catch an image on the fore-edge of the pages: a creature of both dragon and woman curls its tail around an elated-looking man, while seamaidens rise up from the foam to feed him. Not much of a reader indeed.

Finlyr sets out the cups and slowly pours the tea. We all silently watch this ritual. Everyone takes their cup in a ceremony of civility, and Sinigang inclines his head to drink.

'We all know the cautionary tales we were told as children,' I begin, haltingly. 'Don't act strange or they'll take you to Aistra.'

'Where you'll only have the company of the dead,' Finlyr adds.

'You'll never go hungry if you're chosen as priestess to the Bastion,' Isagani says, a longing in their voice.

'They can teach you to control your power,' Biba whispers, looking into the middle distance.

'Are you – afraid of what you can do?' Finlyr asks her.

'Shouldn't I be?' she asks, biting her thumbnail.

'She could hurt someone,' I insist. 'You don't mess with Life and Death; it's a power we don't understand. Doesn't it bother you that those *things* are sailing your ship?'

'It's turned out pretty useful,' Finlyr says, surveying one of the undead trying to right their lopsided head. 'Not all magic is bad, Ris.'

'Yeah, look at Sini,' Isagani says, scritching the otter-cat.

I lean in closer to Finlyr. 'Do I have to remind you what he did? When are you going to tell the children?'

'That was different,' Finlyr insists. 'He did it to help us; he had to.'

'Where will you draw the line? You're fine with skeleton crews and restoring decayed fruit. Not everything will be so harmless.'

'Then why did you bring her here if this quest is so dangerous?'

Biba and Isagani look up. Our hushed argument has broken through to a shout.

I hesitate. 'I didn't have a choice,' I continue, lowering my voice. 'Find whatever it is the queen wants, or don't come back at all.'

'What will you do if you don't find it?' Finlyr asks, voice thick.

'Well, if we make it out alive and empty-handed, we're already running. I made that choice when I left with Biba. Why stop?'

'That's some life for a kid,' Finlyr says.

'What's wrong with that?' Isagani chimes in, combative.

'What would you have done instead?' I retort. 'Left her to the will of the Bastion or have your friends die trying to keep her safe?'

'I don't know, but shouldn't she have some say in it?' Finlyr asks, mussing his hair in frustration. 'What do you think, Biba?'

She considers the question, looking down at her own hands. Finally, she says, thoughtfully, 'I want to know what I can do.'

I study Biba, remembering how I was so excited to know her, to see her grow into a person. She has so much potential; it's up to her to choose what to do with that power.

'We don't understand her power. She can't control it.'

'Yet,' Finlyr insists. 'She can learn with practise.'

'Today she's making mangoes ripe again; tomorrow she might be boiling the ocean beneath our feet,' I continue.

'I see your point, but those are very different extremes,' Finlyr continues, rubbing at his stubble. 'Not all magic is so malignant and destructive.'

'Consider the tea,' Sinigang says, dipping his paw into a cup and licking it.

I sip my tea again and the tingle runs from the top of my scalp down my spine. My jaw pops, finally unclenching. I stare down at the mug and inhale the floral aroma and the oils of the herbs. On the counter is the bag containing the leaves, wrapped with Ligaya's unmistakable bow.

'Power itself is not malicious. It's how it is wielded. Sometimes magic can be delicious,' he says, a glint in his eyes.

We fall into an uneasy silence. After a moment, Finlyr stands, draining his mug. 'I think Ris could do with some alone time right now.' He says, ushering everyone out of the captain's quarters.

When they are gone, I slump back into my chair and let the tears finally come. I try to cry silently, my body heaving, when the door opens again. I abruptly try to fix my face and Finlyr turns heel at the door.

'Sorry, I didn't mean to disturb you,' he says, reluctantly coming closer. His face is flushed, and he holds out a slice of mango, cut and scored ready to eat. 'I thought you might be hungry.'

'Thank you,' I say, as he places it gingerly on the table.

'I'll leave you alone now,' he says, shutting the door again.

I watch the mango until the rich smell of it is too much to bear. I pull a chunk of the scored flesh from the skin. It comes away so easily, so softly. I put it on my tongue and chew, letting the explosion of the juice run down my throat. By Paranish, it really is a good mango. I reluctantly swallow and take another piece. Before I know it, the tears have stopped, and all that remains is the empty shell of the mango skin.

CHAPTER THIRTY-SEVEN

HANAN

THE QUEEN INSISTS ON moving out of the birthing chambers as soon as possible. She clutches my arm with one hand as we ascend in a muted procession to one of the upper bedrooms, where she installs herself. She has my things moved to a connecting bedroom; she wants me kept close at all times. She allows no one else near her or the princess.

For weeks food is brought to us: lavish platters of meats and rice balls, stews and cakes. The queen insists we eat together, and I find the lady's maids glowering at their usurped position as favourite. My mind wanders to Pocket. I haven't seen him in days. I wonder if he's found some food. If he's worried about me. How stupid to be worrying about a bird, but I can't help myself.

'We are fading into nothing.' She sighs melodramatically. 'We must have energy.'

The queen insists on a regular exercise routine. One afternoon we stroll, the child in her arms, cloistered from prying eyes. Salvacion accompanies us even here. There must be very little the queen can conceal from her shield. The arbour sits in the middle of the courtyard next to the sundial. It's position and pendulum mechanism allow the queen to be in the light across the day, gently rocking the princess. Today the air is chill, but the sky is cloudless and we walk the concentric paths lined with flower beds and shrubs, almost labyrinthine in design and breadth.

'I must feel the air on my skin, Hanan,' the queen says, breathing in the flowers of the inner courtyard. They remind me of the perfume the queen dabs on her skin, crushed white flowers trapped in oil in glass bottles. 'A daily turn about the gardens is good for my constitution, is it not?'

I nod, still unused to the way in which she defers to me like this. Even bundled, I can see the princess is looking healthier. She has gotten bigger, her cheeks full and round with large curious eyes. She squirms and fusses, throwing the blankets off. Perhaps wanting to feel the air on her skin, like her mother.

'I am glad to see the babe looking so hale,' I say, filling the silence. The queen seems content with my omnipresence, but I find her attentions stifling, afraid I'll say something ill-considered.

'A great many things are well since your addition to our household.' The queen smiles, and I avert my eyes. Her gaze is like the sun and I cannot stare directly into it.

'I can't take credit for all these successes, Your Grace. It is very generous of you to say so, but the work here is all your own.'

I share a look with Salvacion, who lets a slight smile slip out. We both know that many invisible hands lighten the load of the Bastion, without which the careful order of things would collapse.

The queen gives me a wry look. 'You must stop your pandering, Hanan. Are we not friends?'

I'm not sure how to answer this. We are nothing like friends, but my queen will have whatever she wants.

'Of course, Your Grace. I will do whatever you ask.'

She indicates we sit on a stone bench, and she inches closer to me. I can't help but stare at her. She's so close I can smell the oils and perfumes in her hair and on her skin. She smells sweeter than all the treats that have been ferried up to our rooms of late.

The lustre has returned to her skin, her hair, her eyes. They are shrewd and watchful but with a fervent energy behind them. I feel exhausted looking at her and clutch the cool stone for support. To feel something sturdy and unyielding beneath my fingers.

She clicks her fingers, and Salvacion brings a large box, which they set down in front of me.

'I have brought you an old friend,' the queen says.

'For me?' I ask, unable to hide my surprise.

She nods and I lift the lid of the box, a gasp escaping my lips. Inside is an old and knotted branch, as long as my leg. I reach forward and the air between the piece of wood and my fingertips burn. It's not possible for it to be here, so far removed from its home.

The queen smiles and I feel a twist in my gut. 'The Tree of Life. You know it so well.'

'What is it doing here?'

I ache to touch it; that's how weak I've become. I pine and yearn for it, despite everything. She sees it in my eyes. The queen grabs my hand and encloses it around the wood, too quickly for me to cast a protective circle. A sharp jolting pain shoots up my arm and into my chest. My heart constricts, as though being squeezed by a vice. I gasp and reach out for the queen, but she holds us fast against the wood. I put my entire weight on it and use it like a cane, standing fast and pushing against her.

Then the world tilts under me. I taste that bitter, familiar calamansi. Sea salt and woodsmoke and rainwater in my nose, on my skin. The souls are all so lost, drowning in pain and confusion. Rent asunder from their resting place. The sanctity of peaceful Death, constant sleep in the Tree of Life. She has maimed the tree and violated the souls who rest there.

I feel their memories: the smell of freshly baked bread. The laughter of an old friend. The warm callused, hands of a grandfather.

At Aistra I was part of a group who ferried the souls of the dead to the Tree. We nudged gently, coaxing them. Their fear was like feathers on my skin.

This is something else, a sharp bite.

'Bring them to me,' the queen insists.

I feel her energy tugging at mine and I try to resist. It's unnatural. Is it any more unnatural than my dabbling in dark magic? Necromancy was forbidden at the temple. What I did to Malostra, just as cruel. It's forbidden and tastes rich. Besides, there's so much potential energy in those dead souls. I've seen what it does for her, felt the pleasure run through my body.

I let the energy of the souls pass through me and into her. It's the reverse of ferrying the souls. Instead of guiding them to the tree, I'm yanking them from the wood and pushing them into her body. Their fear is more than feathers this time, it is a sharp beak and talons. The pain is too much to bear, and I tear my hand away from the wood. I collapse on the steps of the dais and the queen breathes in deeply. The princess begins to cry.

'Take her to the nursery; she's quite fatigued.'

In my periphery, I watch Salvacion take the bundle from the queen's arms. On the ground beside me is the branch, the bark withered and scorched.

'Here, Hanan,' the queen says, helping me to my feet. She hands me the branch and I lean on it, resting my weight between her and the wood.

CHAPTER THIRTY-EIGHT

FINLYR

Even Ris is reluctantly grateful for the undead when the weather turns. The ship roils, and we hunker down, buckets at our bedsides sloshing around with every creak and moan.

'What if Birdy falls overboard?' Isagani asks when the storm is particularly bad.

'Birdy?' I echo and then sigh. 'By Aistra, which one is that?'

'My double. The one who climbs the rigging.'

Can a man get no peace? There is little to do but drink, and I hold the palm wine bottle like a babe in arms. We're gathered in my quarters as it's the only space below deck big enough for all of us. Ever since the mango incident we've gathered more often, as if there's something fearful about being alone. Often Isagani or Biba will come wandering by during the day looking for Sinigang or something to amuse themselves. Then Ris will come looking for one of the kids and before I know it, they're all here, making themselves comfortable. Or as comfortable as we can in the current seasickening conditions.

I fiddle with my compass. As I look down at the worn metal, I think about my mother. Her voice, tripping over itself to get the words out fast enough to keep up with the flow of her thoughts. The gap between her teeth when she laughed, head fully thrown back in mirth. The missing little finger she had lost to rope-burn early in her sailing career.

How I wanted to be like her. Maybe if she were home more often I wouldn't have felt that way. Or perhaps that's the cynicism of years like dust settling on my shoulders. She always returned with a far-fetched tale. She once swore she had kissed a seamaiden and kept a charm in her pocket, which she insisted was a rock from the caverns of Orin.

No nobler thing than sailing Paranish and protecting the royals. That's what I thought then. She spoke about the late king, the current queen's father with warmth. She spoke about the royals with reverence and admiration, but also a familiarity of which I could tell she was immensely proud. I wanted that pristine white uniform and the blue wave and sunrise sigil.

'I've spent the best years of my life on this,' my father had said once, smoothing the spare uniform for her next voyage. It always had to be crisp and clean. It was years later I realised that was the point. Bedecking your personal guard in such impractical finery.

There was something in his voice. It wasn't jealousy, but there was an unpleasant bitterness to it. He never told me his secret feelings about my mother's position, but I was thankful it kept a roof over our heads. There was a grim determination on my father's face when the news arrived of my mother's death. Almost an inevitability in the set of his jaw and the dark circles under his eyes.

I take another swig from my palm wine.

'You do know there is a return voyage?' Sinigang's voice comes from the pile of blankets on the bed.

I grumble. 'Not yet guaranteed.'

Sinigang disentangles himself, head popping up to admonish me. 'You're drinking more the closer we get to the Maelstrom.'

'It helps the nausea,' I insist as he eyes the bottle in my hand.

'Returning to old habits?' he asks.

'There are worse ways to cope.'

Sinigang grabs a stone from the loose pocket of skin beneath his armpit, and begins to roll it between his paws, like a toy.

'Eugh, Sini. Not on the bed.'

'This is my favourite stone. Excellent for cracking open seafood.'

'When do you ever do that? You're domesticated.'

Sinigang jumps off the bed and drags something from beneath the bunk. It's pale, almost translucent, and a dead cloudy eye looks back at me. Some sort of marine creature. Like nothing I've seen before. It wasn't designed for sunlight.

'Sini, that is foul,' Ris says, scrunching her nose.

'I've been finding all sorts of strange things floating on the sea. This washed up in Isagani's net.'

My stomach drops, like when your foot misses a step. A momentary lurching. The dream comes back to me. Cold, wet slithering, the smack of skin against wood. The taste of salt and sand in my throat.

'What's wrong?' Ris asks, reaching out to touch my hand. Her fingers are rough and warm against my cold and clammy skin.

Sinigang stares, and I hate the way the otter-cat seems to gaze into my soul. 'I'm going to check on the bone boys.' I excuse myself, grabbing a sealskin jacket and heading up to the deck.

I have to hold on to the railings, slick with rain, as I inspect the sails and ropes. Everything is battened down, in good nick to weather the storm. The undead are nowhere to be seen, likely below deck in the storage hold, which is where we've figured out they go when there's nothing to attend. It's surreal; they stand there, still and blank in the dark.

Nothing is broken, and I'm half impressed. We've been moving in shifts to check on things, and my living crew have been quick learners. They're not work-shy, and it's reassuring to have some conscious heft in addition to the undead. Even when the work is frustrating, laborious, and repetitive – at least we're all mustering, cleaning, and inspecting our rigging and ropes. I lose my footing as the ship crests a wave and get knocked to the floor. The ship moves at an angle, and I scrabble for purchase as the force of a crashing wave pulls me from the deck.

Captain, Maelstrom ahoy!

It had come out of nowhere. The watch, boatswain, and quartermaster were all too focused on the approaching Maelstrom. As was I. At first, we thought it was the storm, a rogue wave, a wall of water. But it was something living. Something from the depths that should never have seen sunlight.

I come back to myself and the current swell. I swing around freely, groping for purchase. My fingers find my sealskin coat, caught on a loose nail. The fabric is slowly ripping under my weight. Below me is the cold surf and one painful drop.

My hands tremble as I claw at the wood, but it's no use. It's slick and smooth beneath my fingers. Panic seizes my throat. I can't breathe. As the sealskin rips, I begin to fall through the coat, choking on the collar as I try to stay inside it.

Then I feel hefty arms around me, cold skin sticking to my own. I'm dragged back on board and bodily hauled onto the deck. We go down with a thud, pain ricocheting across my body. It's Ris, hair pinned atop her head, in another sealskin coat. I try not to put my full weight on her but my knees buckle.

'You're all right, I've got you!' she says, tilting my head to the side. She pounds on my chest, presumably trying to get any seawater out of my lungs.

She fetches a skin of water and sits me up so I can drink. I push it away.

'We have to save the fresh water,' I tell her.

'With a storm like this, rain won't be a problem.' She laughs, giving me the skin again.

We get back below deck, practically bringing a deluge of water with us.

'What happened?' Biba asks.

'We almost had a man overboard,' Ris says stoically.

'I won't let it be like last time,' I tell her.

'Last time?' she asks. Of course, she doesn't know. She wasn't there. 'Fin, what happened at the Maelstrom? Why are you so afraid?'

'We've got to keep moving,' I say, shrugging off her concern.

'We're doing our best, Fin,' Isagani says.

'Our best isn't good enough!' I snap. 'I won't lose anyone else.'

Isagani looks down at their hands, but I can see the hurt in their eyes. Their palms are sore and blistered from rope work.

'You're supposed to be our captain,' they say quietly, almost to themselves.

'I *am* your captain,' I say, staring at each of them.

'I just saved your life up there, and you're pulling rank?' Ris says, incredulous. 'You're still keeping secrets from us – what happened last time you were at the Maelstrom?'

'It doesn't matter. What matters is it won't happen again.'

'These are our lives, Fin. I'm done putting my family at risk for this male pathos fuckery.'

Heat creeps up my neck. I want to tell them everything, to exorcise the memory of that horrific day. But the words die in my throat. I have to put it away. I have to do what I couldn't then and be strong and lead my crew.

'I won't have insubordination on my ship,' I tell Ris as she barges out of the quarters.

'Big words for a pirate,' she cuts back.

'Go choke on a pickle.'

CHAPTER THIRTY-NINE

HANAN

'YOU ARE A TREASURE, Hanan,' the queen says, kissing my forehead.

She helps me back to my room and into bed. Her strength is alarming, when mere weeks ago our roles were reversed. She tucks the blankets around my neck, swaddling me. 'I'll have the servants send up more food. You must gather your strength.'

'What did you make me do?' I croak.

'It's a symbiosis, isn't it, Hanan?'

I feel drunk, like nothing really matters anymore. As though this is all happening to someone else. This is nothing like the drainings from before. Those were like a cup emptying as she gulped me down, time slowly allowing me to refill.

The queen smiles, a sharp and toothy thing. 'Why do you think Paranish's mainland is in a state of flux, while the seasonal isles are steadfast?'

'Because you devour it.' The words slip out, and they are acid on my tongue. I don't know what compels me to talk back. 'The farmer's complaints of a famine. The harvest will never be plentiful because you cut the life in its prime. It's never given time to grow fully. You drain life from everything, like—'

A parasite. I stop my tongue and the queen looms over me, holding the blanket tight against my body.

'Everything must feed. The divine in their time and the salt of the earth in theirs. Speaking of which, I've been feeding Pocket.'

I start and sit up. The queen laughs, forcing me to lie back down. 'You are so charming when you think you are unobserved. But shrouds have no pockets.'

I can feel my face flush, humiliation washing over me. The queen laughs at her own little joke. What has she heard? What has she seen?

'I'm nurturing your talent, furnishing you with everything you could need to fulfil your potential.' She strokes my cheek, and then turns away. 'You have everything you need, right here.'

She opens my window and looks out into the world. I'm supine but I watch her expression as she surveys the rustics at their daily toil. I can hear laughter and chatter from the market below and in the distance, the bells of farmyard animals. Then she faces me again, fingering the woven blanket on my bed. 'You like this?' she asks and I look at the fading golden threading.

I stay still, unsure what to do or say.

'Everything fades eventually. Then it becomes dirt for seeds and the next harvest. That is the cycle of things, is it not?'

I nod, holding the stone bird in my pocket. She will tell me whether I want to hear or no. I would be stupid to do anything but lie there and listen.

'It's a delicate balance, and I take great pride in my duty as steward to Paranish.' She pushes back a strand of hair and looks out the window again. 'Not everyone understands that balance. The sacrifices it takes to maintain order.'

Beneath the potions and powders, even beneath the layer of my energy on her skin, she looks tired. She is beautiful, no doubt, in the austere and elegant way only someone born into privilege can be. She is soft of hand, and hard of look. For the first time I wonder if she loved the king. If she mourned his passing as more than a dutiful widow with a dominion to rule in his stead. But from what I knew about such arrangements, theirs was likely a political match rather than a union of affection.

My power can only sustain her and the princess for so long. She will always need more. This is what it has always been about. Paranishians are the soil underfoot in her garden. Our blood will make the mangoes taste divine.

'I hope you understand that balance, Hanan. I've had such . . . disappointments.' She smiles at me, and her look is one of genuine sadness, a hint of regret about the eyes. Then they are hard as stone again. 'I would hate for you to dash my hopes.'

I sneak into the library as soon as she leaves. My body protests, but I don't know how long I have until she begins to post guards at my door. I'm conscious the queen knows more than I assumed, but either way I'm cursed. I can only arm myself with knowledge.

I summon the Priestess Sinaya's spirit as I did before. She smiles when she sees me. Can a ghost form new memories? Does she recognise me?

'Priestess, I have need of your history.'

'It is impossible to separate mine from the rest. We swim in the same water, all of us.'

'What happened to you after you left the Bastion?'

'I sought knowledge from the ones who practise the forbidden gift.'

I hold my breath, half expecting her to crumble into dust again. But she remains. 'The forbidden gift – do you mean – necromancy?'

She says nothing.

'Who were these people? How did you find them?'

'That knowledge is lost to me.'

'What do you mean?'

'I am a specimen trapped in glass. It is all a cycle: birth, death, rebirth.'

I try to hide my frustration and try a different tack. 'I must know more about this squandered gift. What was it?'

'Energy trapped in a gilded cage. It sustained them all. It was their plaything. They disrespected it.'

'Energy, an object?'

She shakes her head.

'A living vessel, then.'

She says nothing.

'What happened to you?'

'I don't know if my plan succeeded. The rest of my story is lost to me. I can only hope I hid it well.'

'Where did you plan to hide it?'

'Take root where the sea meets the sky.'

She says nothing else of consequence. I still don't understand how we're communicating, how far her consciousness stretches. I feel a flicker of energy when I summon her, but it's inconstant, unstable. The energy of the dead has always felt this way to me, but this temporary resurrection of the dead is bitter, burning.

Eventually I thank the priestess and release her to her rest.

Pocket sits on the windowsill, looking at me with a questioning gaze. He tweets softly, nuzzling into my hand.

'Go on now,' I say, smoothing down his feathers.

He surveys the ground, judging the distance, and shakes his tail experimentally. After a couple of tentative hops, he leaps from the tower, dipping until a breeze catches him. He extends his wings and swoops around to look at me before taking off.

I watch him until he's nothing more than a speck in the distance. The Bastion feels darker for his loss.

'We will both be free of this place soon,' I promise.

I am not alone when I lock up the library.

'Shouldn't you be resting?' Salvacion says, startling me in the hallway.

I study her face as I let my heart rate settle. Her posture is less stiff than usual, and there's a focus in her eyes.

'Shouldn't you be with the queen?' I risk a retort.

She smiles then, coming closer. I lean back against the library door. 'I like you,' she says, towering over me. 'You've got more spirit than the others did.'

'Is that so?' I ask, barely breathing.

'Tread very carefully,' Salvacion whispers. 'It's never a matter of if she's done using you up, but when.'

I stare at her face illuminated by the torchlight. It's weathered and hard, but this is the first time I've really looked at her. There are freckles on her nose.

'Why are you telling me this?'

'I've served the Bastion for many years, seen many priestesses come and go. I know about that thing you have in there. And I've seen you with the princess.'

CHAPTER FORTY

RIS

WE STEW FOR WEEKS, steering clear of each other as much as we can, which is difficult in such close quarters. Finlyr's barbed comments are as prickly as a sea urchin. The bickering is relentless; we blow hot and cold. Which is more than can be said for the wind, which still does not blow at all. The weather is more changeable on the open sea than on the Paranishian mainland. I'm grateful that we gathered rainwater in the barrels during that last storm, the one that almost claimed Finlyr's life. I almost miss the rolling of the ship on those giant waves; now looking out on the horizon is daunting in its nothingness.

There's not much by way of entertainment on *Saltswept*. I think everyone else's main attraction is watching me and Finlyr fight. I can't stand having idle time; it drives me to distraction. There's nowhere to go, so I've made little projects for myself: Isagani and I fish; I watch Biba trying to make the ube sprout.

I'm checking the supplies in the storeroom one evening. Since the porridge blunder, I'm not taking any chances. Then I hear them: Isagani and Sinigang, conspiring on the quarterdeck above me.

'Do you think they'll resolve this soon?' Isagani whines.

'Flames eating each other – that's what it is,' Sinigang says. 'They'll run out of air eventually.'

'Rocks banging together,' Isagani says, and I hear them knocking their closed fists against each other. 'More alike than they think. Both stubborn.'

'Death by a thousand cuts,' Sinigang says, voice smooth and rich.

'I wish Fin would just be honest with her,' Isagani sighs.

'He told you what happened?' Sinigang asks.

'Not entirely. But it was bad. The guilt sent him to the bottle. He was in a right state when I met him.'

'Sometimes there's a peace in the inevitability of oblivion,' Sinigang muses.

I quietly back out of the storeroom and go to sit on the forecastle deck, where Isagani and Sinigang won't see me. As luck would have it, Finlyr is making his way across the deck, passing the brim of his hat through his fingers.

'Oh. I didn't realise you were here.'

'There's not many places to be on *Saltswept*.'

I can see him trying to read my face, feeling out my mood. 'What are you doing?'

'Dancing with tamaraws. What about you?'

'Trying not to piss off my first mate even more,' he says, gently.

'I'd take the tamaraws.'

He tentatively sits down next to me. The silence is stifling for a moment, and then he sighs. 'I wish I could tell you everything.'

'What happened to your crew?'

He looks haunted. There's something buried there, something he's holding back.

'You remember back at the Magliyab festival?' Fin begins, fiddling with the infernal hat again. 'I told you how I got caught?'

Paranish – that seems a lifetime ago. I nod.

'I received a commission – an honest one, for once. A royal one, even. Anyway, that was an ill-fated quest. It's my life's greatest regret.'

He gets up and paces the deck, dropping his hat on the helm spokes.

'Tried to drink myself into the ether, but that didn't work. When I crossed paths with Nestor, it was easy for him to turn me in. Trying to curry favour for a promotion. Delivering me to the Bastion was a nice little sweetener for him.'

'What a bastard.'

His fingers go to his throat, to the scar I know hides beneath his beard. I let the silence stretch for a moment and look up at the sky. It's a perfectly clear evening; the stars pricks of light on a dark canvas.

'You've been an excellent first mate. This isn't your first time on a ship, is it?'

'More than just a farmer.'

He looks shame-faced. 'I'm sorry I said that.'

'We've both said some foul things.'

'Aye, we know how to get under each other's skin,' he says, smiling. We sit in silence for a few moments, listening to the gentle bobbing of the water against the hull.

'I can show you the stars?' I offer, and he grins.

We lie down on the deck side by side, and I point out the constellations.

'My knowledge is limited,' he confesses. 'I've always been blessed with exceptional navigators.'

'He admits a fault!' I turn to Finlyr – Paranish, you're actually very close while lying side by side with someone. Our noses could almost touch.

'I'm waiting for those words, Fin.' He blinks at me. His expression reminds me of my late husband. 'An apology. I'm waiting for you to say sorry.'

The tension has bubbled, and there's nowhere for it to go on this ship. It's exhausting. He cringes but eventually says it. 'I'm sorry. I've been somewhat vile.'

I bask in the moment. Why is it so often up to the wronged party to teach the other how to apologise?

'The way I learned, navigating is to look at the light and swells on the waves. We follow the clouds, bird flight. Measure the dead reckoning by the debris floating in the water.'

'There's a lot more strange debris floating in the water these days,' Finlyr grunts. 'The world's off-kilter.'

I stare at the sky and think of the thinning golden wool. 'Like our farm.'

'There's something wrong and I blame those in their high tower.'

'The shoreline of the Spring Isle is closer than it was when I was a girl,' I say, after a time. 'Warmer waters, stranger things afloat. Nature is ill at ease.'

'Those with power always try to control and exploit.'

I consider this for a moment, looking at my hands. 'Is it like that everywhere?'

Finlyr looks at me, and I feel his breath on my face. He sits up, as if realising how close together we are. 'Things have gotten worse.'

'Why did you come back?'

'Not much business in smuggling once the ports were open.' He smiles, but his body stiffens, and I know this isn't the full truth of it.

'What did you smuggle?'

'People.'

I stare at him.

'We helped them leave Paranish. There are those desperate enough to risk everything for a new life, and they paid us for the privilege.'

'And were they right?' I ask, my voice soft. 'Was it worth it?'

He takes my hand and squeezes it. 'Things aren't better in Orin or Lassair. Same problems, different people.'

'Is that why you stopped smuggling? The guilt?'

'The only ones profiting were the pirate smugglers. I couldn't do that, not after—'

The moment stretches between us, dark thoughts clouding our minds.

'There are those desperate enough to risk everything for a new life,' Finlyr says solemnly. 'And most of them pay for it *with* their lives.'

'You used his name,' I say at last.

He sits up then, as if he were a puppet pulled by string. 'I wondered if you knew him. You seemed so startled when we first met.'

'Because you were using my husband's name.' I struggle to get the words out. 'What happened to him?'

His expression is the most open and vulnerable I've ever seen on him. Eventually, he says, 'Larkin was on my crew. One of the most loyal sailors I ever met.'

The memory of Larkin's voice comes back to me.

This will change everything for us. It's such a small dream, isn't it? To choose for yourself. That's freedom. But to have it, you need power. Now we'll have something of value. Both feet on the shore.

'Tell me what happened,' I insist, grabbing at his shirt.

'I fucked up, Ris,' he confesses, his body crumpling into itself. 'I should have gone in after him, but it all happened too quickly. He was overboard, and then he was gone. The Maelstrom took him.'

I hit him hard in the jaw and he staggers over, palming his bloody mouth. 'Why the fuck did you do that?'

'I don't believe you.'

'It's the truth!'

He stares at me, eyes wild, face bloodied, and the only thing I can hear are my choking sobs.

'Ris, I'm sorry.'

I collapse into him, and we stand there, my knees buckling as he holds me.

'He left us. And now he won't ever come back.'

He strokes my hair gently. 'I know, I'm sorry.'

'He left us behind. This was our dream, and he left me behind.'

I let the rage seethe like poison through my body, crying until I feel spent. Finlyr says nothing, just holds me, and I listen to his steady, calming breaths. I want to hate him, to blame him, to trade him in Larkin's place. But in my heart, I know that's not true. I am tired of being the martyr, the widow. The ruin of fury is eating away at me.

CHAPTER FORTY-ONE

HANAN

THE QUEEN CALLS ME to the throne room. Lately we have been cloistered together in the upper chambers and gardens. I don't think I've seen her hold court since the child was born, although it has only been a few months. There haven't been this many courtiers gathered here since the Magliyab festival, and the Bastion hums with expectation. My chest burns, bile rising up my throat to make me sick. They are here for one purpose, and their eyes crawl over me. I hold on to the withered branch, as wretched as the memory of it is, for balance. I had thought the plain gown I was given upon my arrival the finest thing I would ever feel against my skin, but the queen has bedecked me in one of her cast-off gowns – deep crimson embroidered with golden thread. I feel like a weed moonlighting as a flower.

The sunlight pours through the oval window above her, the coloured glass dappling a rainbow across her face. I'm reminded of the glass in the Temple of Aistra, where I spent so many hours on my knees, looking up at the illusion of the Bastion. Malostra told me she dreamt of being a priestess ever since she could remember. She was one who came willingly, who showed her power proudly.

My footsteps echo off the flagstones as I approach, flanked by Seaguardians, Salvacion leading the procession towards the throne. The queen sips from a goblet, and I can smell the rich alcohol even from here. She taps her fingernails on the side of the cup, metal and precious gems clinking as she waits. Salvacion helps me kneel on the floor, and I bow my head, the cane rattling beside me.

The queen doesn't say anything for a painfully long time. I hear the shuffling of eager steps and the sound of her chalice being refilled before the servant retreats.

'Life is so fleeting, don't you think, Hanan?'

I flick my eyes up to the vague shape of her. Does she really want an answer?

'Most of us spend our lives trying to outrun death. But not you.'

Her voice is the same as the day in the baths. I could slip into the liquid of her voice, let it envelop me in its warmth. Until it would hold me under.

I shift on my knees, and Salvacion notices my struggle. She helps me up, and I lean on my cane, head still bowed.

'You are an inquisitive little otter-cat, aren't you?'

The force of the queen's stare makes the hairs on the back of my neck prickle. I am too tempted; I must look up at her. Her expression is hard, eyes alight, but not quite with anger. It's something else, like a hunter smelling blood. There's rage, but there's also anticipation.

'I'm impressed by you, Hanan. There hasn't been another priestess of your calibre for generations. Your studiousness is a testament, but your raw power – that is not something that can be taught.'

'Your Grace is too kind,' I say softly, the courtesy tripping off my tongue unbidden.

'I do not say this to flatter you, Hanan. I've invested a great deal in your potential. Nurtured it, given it opportunity to grow. Is Pocket not a testament to that? Your little spectral escapades? The hale and hearty princess?'

She lets the words hang, and I consider. Who is to say I would've been able to do those things without the queen? The luxury of time and resources. It took me years of covert study at the temple to resurrect that mokon for just a moment. In a few months I've resurrected Pocket and kept him alive. I've not only spoken with the dead but conjured its likeness from a text. The princess would not be alive if not for me. If the Temple Mothers could see my necromantic progress, their eyes would roll back in their heads. My mind wanders to the fatigue, the empty pit in my stomach, the figurine of the stone bird. A sacrifice worth making.

She puts down her chalice and turns her attention to her courtiers. The queen descends from her throne and places her hand over mine, on top of my cane. The floor beneath me hums gently, as though thousands of bees were underfoot. I startle, listening to the whispers in the walls. Voices distant and indistinct, melting into each other. Voices of the dead.

'They are connecting,' one of the courtiers says in amazement.

The queen grabs my cane before I can protest. Then she raises it high, and I flinch back. She brings it down with a sickening thud, but the pain doesn't come. When I open my eyes, I see that her left arm is at a strange angle, bones crushed and protruding from her skin. She does not yell, does not show any sign or semblance of pain, but continues to stand proudly, resting on my cane. She grabs my hand and places it roughly over her wound. Her skin is warm and supple beneath my grip, but pain radiates across my entire being.

I try to resist, but it is like scratching an itch. I reach for her wound in my mind, let the energy from the Tree flow through me and back into the queen. I feel the wood pushing out of her flesh, the bones knitting themselves back together, the skin smoothing over. My cane falls to the floor with an unceremonious clatter.

The courtiers stand in stunned silence. I collapse to the dais, panting.

'She performs miracles, but she needs more training,' the queen says, examining her arm. It is exactly as it was before. 'And as a gift to my loyal supporters, I will grant you the chance to taste of her powers and let her taste yours.'

The courtiers start forward and I find myself cornered on all sides by those who long to touch me. My body goes rigid. They begin to murmur excitedly and then stop. The queen has her hand outstretched, and they retreat.

'Patience,' she says firmly. 'This is no trinket to be squandered.'

Salvacion helps me stand and returns the cane. When she makes to leave, I grab at her uniform. *Please be my shield,* I try to tell her with my eyes.

She removes my hands but squeezes them twice, holding my gaze.

'This is a gift. You must prove you are worthy of it. Every courtier in Paranish will have the chance to make their case. As stewards your successes must show me you are worthy. The final decision will be mine.'

There are murmurings among the crowd but none of them dares protest. From my time at the Bastion, I've learned the courtiers are the most ravenous of Paranish. I've observed them take the queen's morsels when she grants them, securing a better standard of living in exchange for 'overseeing' the towns. There is no such thing on the Winter Isle, Aistra being governed by the Temple Mothers with a direct line to the Bastion. It hadn't occurred to me to wonder how the other isles and towns within were run.

I try to still the roiling in my belly and stand up straight. I will have my dignity, if nothing else. The queen remembers me then.

'You may retire to your chambers, Hanan.'

How kind, I think bitterly as Salvacion helps me leave. The courtiers barely part as we push and shove between them to the door.

I feel their hands brush across the fabric and my skin. It is a desperate hunger.

'Do you need guiding back to your chambers?' Salvacion asks, concern in her voice.

'No, thank you,' I tell her, brushing the tears from my eyes. I lean on my cane as I walk, determined to do it on my own.

'I had no idea she was going to do that,' Salvacion says, catching up with me.

'What? What did she do? You should have the courage to name it.'

Salvacion exhales in frustration. 'I am doing what I can, Hanan.'

'Do you think all your little treacheries will do anything?' I ask her, emboldened by anger. 'While we eat her food and the rest of Paranish starves?'

'Every drop of water is needed for a flood,' Salvacion insists, grabbing my arm. 'Little rebellions are all some of us have.'

'Well, I'll try to remember that when I'm an empty husk,' I sneer, shaking her off.

She doesn't try to follow me. I make my way to the queen's chambers and through to the nursery, where the princess coos gently in her bassinet. I dismiss the lady's maid.

'The princess needs to feed.'

The maid looks at my fine dress, now dirty and bloody.

'I said leave.'

The maid goes abruptly then.

I scoop up the princess, swaddled in a soft golden fleece blanket. If I bartered this, how far could I get? The princess has grown to know my touch and the promise it brings. She comes to me easily, nuzzling into my chest. I hold her in the crook of my arm and gently brush her cheek. Soft and fluffy as pandesal. She sneezes and then wraps her hand around my finger.

She is sweet milk, cloying and overpowering in her want. I feel it thick and furry on my tongue, the sickly but pleasant smell of sleep. I give in, and calamansi cuts through and mingles with her essence. Our energies flow into each other.

I come away feeling dizzy and nauseous, my mind clouded and body weak. Thoughts slipping like water through my hands. The babe fusses slightly and then settles.

'Hush, Raina,' I murmur, wrapping the blanket back into place. I never use the name the queen has chosen, the one which she will present to the Paranishian public. To me, the princess is Raina. There's a peace in having a secret from the queen.

'What are you doing?'

I turn to find the lady's maid standing in the doorway. Perhaps she thinks my duties are that of an ordinary wet nurse.

'Sating the princess,' I respond.

Her eyes rove over us both and she approaches slowly. 'Shouldn't you return to the queen?'

My mouth twitches into a frown. 'In good time.'

The maid comes forward and takes Raina from my arms. Immediately the child begins to wail, face red and scrunched. I reach out to take her back, but the maid moves away. We stare at each other, and I feel heat creeping up my neck. The princess continues to cry, and the sobs turn to something else, like she can sense my anger.

'She doesn't want you to hold her,' I tell the maid.

'How do you know what she wants?' She looks at me, afraid and disgusted. Her mouth is turned down in revulsion, and she recoils.

A loose strand of hair curls its way down the nape of the maid's neck. I watch Raina scrabble at the air, thrashing in her distress. She finds the hair and yanks, pulling the maid's head taut at an awkward angle. The maid yells out, almost dropping the princess.

'I'm here, darling,' I say, grabbing Raina and prying the chunk of ripped hair from her fingers.

'That little—' the maid begins and stops herself abruptly. She's frozen in shock, and I purse my lips to keep from yelling.

'What were you going to call the royal princess?' I ask the maid.

'I – I won't disturb you again, Priestess Hanan,' the maid says, her lip practically curling as she says my title.

As I hold Raina, I stroke the soft fuzz on her cheek. She will grow to be as cold and hard as her mother. But with a different whisper in her ear, she could be something else. More than a queen. And I would be her right hand. Beyond our little treacheries. What if I could break open the dam and start the flood?

CHAPTER FORTY-TWO

RIS

I SCRAMBLE OUT OF bed when I hear the clashing of metal breaking through the calm of dawn. I hastily dress and follow the sound up to the deck, where Isagani and Finlyr are practising bladework.

'You're light-footed, but your defensive stances need work,' Finlyr says, parrying with his sword.

Isagani has slipped my dagger at some point and wields it now, tossing it and catching it like a spectacle.

'Don't lose a finger,' I say, narrowly avoiding the dagger as it lands blade down in the deck.

Isagani smiles sheepishly and bends to work it out of the wooden boards.

'Joining the swordplay lesson?'

'Why would I need that?' I say, folding my arms. 'I only came up because I heard fighting. I thought we were in trouble.'

'And if we were, what would you do?'

I hold up an arm and flex a bicep.

Finlyr smiles and gives an impressed nod. 'So you'll be great at wielding this,' he says, handing me the sword. 'Swing like you're chopping wood.'

The heft of the metal in my hands feels reassuring, and I sweep in wide arcs. I can feel my own strength, but this is a new way of moving, another method of inhabiting my body.

'You need to raise your elbow, like this,' Isagani mimes, lunging forward and stabbing some imagined enemy.

They have flourish, raising their free arm with panache. They are ever-shifting, always liquid.

'Bend your knees. It will ground you for blocking and dodging,' Finlyr says.

'How?' I ask, voice tired and churlish.

He moves closer, behind me, gripping the pommel of the sword and bending his knees into the crook of mine. It's a strange sensation. At first I buckle a little, and then I sit into it.

'Your movements should be controlled and slow. You only need to use a little bit of force, encourage the blade.'

Isagani moves away as Finlyr adjusts my posture. They stand at the edge of the deck, fiddling with the mounted bows on the aftcastle.

'Don't touch that unless you aim to shoot,' Finlyr insists when he sees what they're doing.

Isagani has been growing tetchy in the last couple of days, unused to being stuck in one place with nowhere to run. The lessons are getting tired, and I doubt they've ever had this much idle time. They prowl around, hating it. We are all itching to get going, but there's still not much to do until the wind picks up.

'Those arrows are finicky to replace, takes a while to fletch and shaft-make,' Finlyr says, his voice warmer. 'I'll teach you sometime.'

Everything is so still, and the humidity presses down on us. The silence of the sea unsettles me, as though she's preparing for something. I can see sweat glistening on Finlyr's skin, the scar around his neck, invisible now that he's growing out his beard. He had taken to wearing high collars and scarves when the ruse was still going, but I had seen the angry red of it, as though a collar of hot metal had choked him.

Sinigang appears on the deck, padding intently across the taffrail. He paces back and forth with a fretful look in his eyes, his ears perked and his fur on end.

'What's wrong, Sini?' I ask, lowering my weapon.

'What is that?' he asks, sniffing the air.

We pause and join him at the balustrade.

'I don't see anything,' Isagani says.

Sinigang loafs, tucking his paws underneath himself. 'Something has changed.'

I look out at the horizon and see ripples on the water – they are in the distance, but gradually making their way towards us. At last, a blessed breeze reaches my skin, and our sails begin to catch the wind. As if awakened, the undead crew come out of their storage room and get to work unfurling the sails and preparing to tack.

Finlyr and I take the helm, weapons forgotten. We can move. We need to move. They approach as we take off excruciatingly slowly. It seems unfair that so much bodily effort means so little on the grand scale. Once we've caught the wind and harnessed it, it's like a deity pushing us forward.

Isagani heads up to the crow's nest with Birdy, and I go to wake Biba. She's already up and turns as I come in.

Biba moves to stare out of the porthole.

'Who are they?' she asks, and I scramble onto the bed to follow her gaze. Approaching swiftly is another vessel, cutting through the water on our port side. They seem to have come out of nowhere, hovering on the water like an illusion: a Fata Morgana.

'I don't know, darling. Let's get up to the deck, quickly now,' I say, trying to keep the panic out of my voice.

'What do you see Isagani?' Finlyr is shouting up to the nest as we emerge on deck.

Isagani shields their face from the weak sun with a hat. They stare and then shout down at us: 'A royal sigil on the flag!'

'Seaguardians?'

'No, the ship doesn't look nice enough. And no uniforms.'

Finlyr and I give each other a puzzled look. Sinigang jumps up onto the taffrail and narrows his eyes.

'They have a map.'

'How in Paranish can you know that?' Finlyr asks sardonically.

'Otter-cats have impeccable eyesight, which you'd know if you'd cared to ask.'

'A mystery wrapped in an enigma,' I mutter. 'No wonder Narra sent you along.'

'Well, the undead crew on their deck somewhat gave it away.'

Finlyr swears in a strange language. I suppose he picked up that colourful Lassairian phrase along with the taffrail.

I take out the folded map, which I've protected with my life. That wretched royal stamp. 'Looks like there are still others as desperate as we are. There were so many copies back before. I didn't think any other crews were still mad enough to do this.'

'What do we do?' Isagani asks from aloft.

Finlyr sets his jaw. 'We'll both be fighting for the same current. We could ride their slipstream, but ideally, we want to outpace them.'

'And is *Saltswept* faster?' I ask.

Finlyr grimaces and calls up. 'You wanted to know how that ballista works right, Isagani?'

CHAPTER FORTY-THREE

HANAN

'Dress warmly,' I am told when I open the door to my chambers.

It's the first time I've spoken with Salvacion since that disgusting display in the throne room, but any honest words die in my throat when I see she's accompanied by other Seaguardians. They wait for me to get ready and then escort me down to the docks.

I try to feel the smooth wood of the bird talisman in my pocket, but it's no good through the thick gloves. Much of the Bastion remains a mystery to me, with only the queen holding the keys and the knowledge to wander the halls freely. It is strangely soothing to be back here, remembering the innocent who arrived at the dock bewildered and hopeful.

A Seaguardian helps me into a boat, and Salvacion assists the queen into another. The queen has the princess in a sling wrapped around her as we are rowed through the aqueduct. I try to still my hands, which itch to hold the baby. Raina's cries echo around the tunnel; we are all ill at ease. Unlike the last time, I take in everything, surveying the tunnel and wondering at its strange workings. Set into one section of the stone wall is a metal door with intricate grooves and a lever for a handle. I survey it discreetly as we row by.

'Mothers Joca and Lin, Your Grace,' the Seaguardian announces, tying the boat to the dock.

I turn to confirm the sight with my own eyes. Mother Lin smiles thinly at me, and Mother Joca nods stiffly. They both look in fine fettle with a giddy energy about them. The royals never visited Aistra in my years at the temple. What are we doing here?

The Seaguardian lands and offers a hand to the queen, who continues to clutch Raina close to her.

'You have done fine work in bringing Hanan to my attention,' the queen says, leading the procession. The Seaguardians stay close and Mothers Lin and Joca trail her. 'She is exactly what I was looking for.'

'Your Majesty is too kind.'

I scramble up to the dock on shaking legs and follow the party to the light at the end of the tunnel, blinking in the winter sun.

'We are so honoured you have chosen to grace us with your presence,' Mother Lin fawns, breathlessly. After a moment she adds, 'To what do we owe such a privilege? Your last missive did not say.'

There is a pregnant pause so long and awful that I watch Mother Lin's cheeks spot pink, as though she had been slapped by the queen. Instead, the queen lets her gaze glance off her like a blade on ice. 'It has been too long since the Bastion set foot on this soil.'

'You look well, Hanan,' Mother Joca says bluntly, staring openly at my fine gown, the fullness of my cheeks. I have been eating better than I ever have here, my outward appearance of health betraying the fatigue in my bones.

'Priestess Hanan,' Salvacion corrects.

Mother Joca looks at Salvacion as though she were a weed that had sprouted a mouth.

'I wish to see the Tree of Life,' the queen says, already proceeding towards the temple.

'But Your Grace, the Sisters are in prayer,' Mother Joca protests, keeping pace. 'We can clear your way if you give us—'

'No need. We shall be efficient.'

Salvacion and the other Seaguardians flank her, opening doors and securing routes as she walks, never breaking stride. I follow in her wake, and we're all swept along and at the great Tree before I can let the sick feeling in my stomach rise.

The queen stands before the Tree, its long branches dancing. There is an outer layer of branches, thick hair-like vines, beyond which I glimpse the inner tree and the vivid colours of the bark. It has grown layers to protect itself, and now the Tree is opening up to us, revealing its heart and core. It pulses and breathes, streaks of colour radiating as if lit from within. A mist emanates from its roots, a hazy blue cloud that forms into figures. Eyes and mouths emerge from the fog, open and hungry. The queen sighs, and the sound echoes around us. The princess wakes then, as if rising from her slumber at her final destination. She stretches in her sling, making those small noises to let us know she is ready to be in the world.

'Look where we are, my love,' the queen whispers to her daughter.

I turn my gaze back to the Tree, unable to witness this tenderness. There is a withered stump where part of the limb has been cleaved, weeping sap. I lean on my cane and it burns beneath my grip.

Mother Lin notices my gaze and then stares at my walking aid. 'I'm glad to see it go to good use.'

The bile rises then. Good use? Our sacred Tree has been butchered, not truly in service of my body, but in service of the queen's greed. Up in the library, faces peer down at us, half concealed behind tomes and stacks. The Tree has never moved so much; it threatens to brush the brickwork of the courtyard built around it. Some of the Temple Sisters have taken note of our interrupter, their faces eager and eyes wide. To look upon royalty is to look upon the sun. This is what I had always believed.

I move forward to the queen's side. 'Your Grace, what are we doing here?'

'Hanan,' she says, her voice strange and distant. 'Now comes the harvest.'

She places my palm onto the Tree, her own hand atop mine. The bark bites and oh, Aistra, it hits me hard like the rush of falling. I can't breathe. The energy vibrates and hums into my bones, ricocheting through my body. I try to absorb it, to filter it, to maintain it. I can't control the power. I've never felt so raw, as though the Tree's entire being flows through me. Blood pools in my mouth and chokes me as I try to scream. My skin feels like it's on fire, flesh melting from my bones.

I can't break the connection. The queen's hand is like an endless weight on top of mine. I try to redirect it. I feel around with my mind, desperate to find anything to ground me. The Seaguardians are untouched and therefore useless. I consider the queen, but she's holding Raina, and I can't risk what might happen. I spark my energy around the Mothers; they are surely powerful enough, but my bond with them isn't strong enough to be sure. There is only one Temple Sister who would be close enough to even have a chance. I feel her then, Malostra's energy in the library amongst the other girls. I disperse the energy, letting it flow in as many places as I can and absorbing what my body will take. Malostra is my grounding point, my anchor.

The others are moving around me, trying to pull me away, but I am rooted in place. I cannot break the chain. I try to gulp down the energy, but it keeps coming from the Tree. It overwhelms me and we're all pulled under.

CHAPTER FORTY-FOUR

FINLYR

Ris and I take the helm, steering portside to face the oncoming vessel. Now that it's closer I can see their ship is smaller than ours, with fewer sails and the length of three trees stump to stem, but it is crewed by more living than dead. They will be nimbler, more reactive. We have heft, that's all. We can't risk another ship getting to the Maelstrom before us. They're right ahead of us, moving into the ideal position to take full advantage of the wind, trying to force us into their wake.

Isagani stands at the ballista, sight-testing the range of the arrow. I fear they might get catapulted into the sea from the weight of the recoil.

'We don't have many arrows,' I counsel. 'So we fire a warning shot first.'

'And if that doesn't work?'

'It would be a great time for Sinigang to show us some more of those particular skills Narra promised.'

Sinigang hisses. 'You'll thank me when the time comes.'

'Aim for the crew. Loose the arrow!'

Isagani strains, trying to pull back the string. They don't have the strength to give it the tension needed. The arrow lands halfway between our deck and the other ship.

Ris curses, jumping to the ballista, and I barely have time to steady the helm alone. She stands behind Isagani, letting them aim again.

Isagani lines it up carefully, tongue poking out of the corner of their mouth. Ris slowly pulls back the string, sitting into the tension with a smooth and mighty squat.

'Now!' Isagani yells, and she lets go.

The arrow finds its mark. It does less damage than I hoped, but it's certainly got the other crew's attention.

'Take cover!' I command as their returning arrow finds its mark. I can hear the sloshing in the brig. I can only hope they are taking on water faster than we are.

'Ris, get down to the bilge pump!'

'The what?'

'Below the keel. Pump the water out, or we'll sink!'

Paranish, they can somewhat make their way around the ship but only just. Ris nods, hurrying down to rid us of some water.

I keep us steady as Isagani climbs back up the rigging. Sinigang and Biba stay on deck, Biba holding the spyglass and both of them relaying what they see happening on the other ship.

'Going again,' Biba yells.

Saltswept gives a low painful moan, a creaking in the hull of wood catching and disliking what it finds.

The ship lurches, and we try to stand. We steady our balance as the vessel rolls one way and then another. A huge spray and the deep otherworldly wail. It hums and vibrates, like someone blowing across an empty glass bottle. I dare not turn around, but I dare not miss it. I glimpse a huge tentacle slithering back beneath the waves, dark, livid purple suckers on mottled orange skin. Across the way, I hear the other crew screaming and cursing. I don't blame them. I felt my spirit leaving my body the first time I saw it.

'What in Paranish is that?' Ris yells from below.

'Is that a—?' Isagani asks, in disbelief.

'It can't be!' Ris counters.

He's much as I remembered. He bobs towards the surface, almost a curious spectator. Translucent save for the streaks of red across his tentacles. Sailors have often mistaken whale penises for kraken, but there's no doubt here. He looks at me with his dark glassy eye, triple the size of a porthole, surveying me like a fish in a bowl. Now that he's here, I feel a strange calm wash over me. Like being in the eye of the storm. Or in the eye of a kraken.

The kraken reaches for us, huge appendages striking the water around us. He catches the edge of the deck. The taffrail splits and tumbles into the water.

'Hey! That taffrail was handcrafted by a Lassairian carpenter!' I shout, clinging to the deck for all I'm worth.

'I don't think it cares, Fin!' Ris shouts, ducking behind a crate.

I unsheathe my sword and take aim at the undulating tentacles, wrapping themselves around the mast. I step forward and come down with a hard overhead strike. An unholy shriek from below and the kraken begins to uncoil. Then another scream, this time from above. Isagani is on the rigging, entangled and frozen in fear.

'Stay still, Isagani!' I insist, running over and scaling the ropes. It's only when I'm halfway up I realise I've dropped my sword.

Isagani is within reach now. I cling to their shirt, and we slowly make our way back down to the deck.

'Birdy fell, I couldn't stop it!' Isagani sobs.

I look around at the chaos on the deck. The undead don't have the reactions for this, trying to continue their duties with no preservation instinct. The deck roils and some of them lose their footing and go over, Knuckles unable to grab anything with their gnarled fingers.

The kraken has retreated from its wounds, but it approaches again, moving swiftly. Its tentacles crash against the hull and we're all thrown off balance. I scramble away from the exposed side of the deck, which now ends in a treacherous drop into the water. The ship tries to right itself and we go flying, living and dead crew alike. Biba screams and I see her small face as she slips from the deck.

I lunge, but she's out of reach. There's a circle of bubbles on the surface of the water where she fell.

'Biba!' Ris yells, rushing to my side. She's peeling off layers, preparing to dive, when something breaks the surface of the water. A crown, the kraken's round head floats near us. And atop it is Biba. She's wet and gasping, but she's alive. She lies down on the kraken, her fingers gently stroking above its eyes. He looks up at her and another deep moan erupts from its body. *Saltswept* vibrates with it, and I feel the resonance in my bones.

'Go now,' Biba commands, with the precocious authority only she could muster.

The kraken's eyes begin to close, and he gives a groan.

I wait for my moment, and then I reach for Biba, grabbing her bodily before the kraken sinks back below the waterline. She yells as I lift her up onto the deck, bruised and scratched, but otherwise unharmed.

'She's trying to protect her babies,' Biba protests as I try to wrap a blanket around her.

'Babies?' I ask. Guess my old pal was an old gal after all. 'But don't they die after they—'

Ris wraps me in a hug, cutting me off. 'Thank you,' she says, giving me a pointed look and shaking her head.

The mothers die after they lay their eggs, giving their final days to protecting their young. Biba will have to learn that sometime, but not now.

Isagani's lips are bloody and I take the kid's face in my hands. I tip their head back, inspecting the gummy gap where their front tooth used to be. 'What happened?'

They garble something, tongue flopping around. I release their head. 'Gone with the taffrail.'

There's a slight lisp on the 'th' and 'eff' sounds, and I pull them close. They squirm, unsure, and I let them go.

'Does it hurt?'

'I've had worse,' they tell me, tugging their shirt collar up and feigning nonchalance.

'I'm sorry about Birdy. And Knuckles. We'll check on all of them, all right?'

'I know they're already dead, but they're part of our crew, you know? He was my rotten boy.'

I nod and clap them on the shoulder.

'There she goes,' Biba points, and we all look across the water.

The kraken has re-emerged by the other ship. They are desperately shooting arrows at her. Fuck, why didn't we think of that? I suppose staying afloat and not having the kids fall to their death was a priority. The kraken cries out when they hit her, blood in the water, deep midnight blue. She thrashes, coiling around the ship. She is immense, pulling the ship off balance. The crew's screams can be heard from here. It takes a sickeningly long time for the ship to finally sink. It disappears beneath the waterline, the kraken's wails still ringing in my ears.

'Holy Aistra, that's awful,' Ris whispers, when we finally break the silence.

'We should patch up the damage we took,' I say, assessing the casualties.

'That entire crew is dead, Fin,' Ris says, staring at me.

I indicate the flotsam of the shipwreck floating in the distance. 'Wake up, Ris – that could have been us.'

'No, it wouldn't,' Biba says, staring at me assuredly.

'What do you mean?' I ask, meeting her gaze.

'I told her to stop the other ship,' she says, a strange smile coming over her face.

'You talked to that thing?' Ris asks.

She nods, looking at me perplexed. 'Did I do something bad?' She turns back to Ris. 'Mama, your edges are sharp again. You are spiky, like a rambutan.'

Ris squats down to Biba's eye level. 'You know you are powerful, right Biba? You have to be careful with that. It can hurt people, including you.'

Biba curls her hands into tight fists then. 'I'm only trying to protect us.'

'Meaning good doesn't always lead to doing good. It can be scary for us sometimes.'

One day she's sprouting ube and making mangoes fresh. The next day she's commanding a kraken. I look at this tiny kid again, and this innocent baleful expression. She genuinely doesn't seem to grasp the complexity of what just happened. A shudder runs down my spine as the wind picks up even more.

CHAPTER FORTY-FIVE

HANAN

WHEN I REGAIN CONSCIOUSNESS, my body feels soft as bruised fruit, as though the insides are scrambled in this sack of skin. I haul myself up onto my side and cry out with every movement. My cane is destroyed, a burned and useless husk. My stomach roils and I blink at my surroundings. I'm on the uneven ground, my back aching from the branches I fell upon. I can't have been out that long. I stagger to my feet, trying not to throw up.

'Mother Joca, come quick!' Nusi runs down the stairs from the library, a wild look in her eyes.

Mother Joca looks bewildered and it's the only time I can remember seeing her unsure what to do.

'It's Malostra!' Nusi insists, grabbing the Temple Mother's arm.

'Malostra?' I echo, trying in vain to follow them.

'What is the meaning of this?' Mother Lin accosts me by the shoulders, and I yell out in pain.

The queen is surrounded by the Seaguardians, leaning heavily against Salvacion.

'Raina,' I say, making my way towards the princess but Salvacion steps forward to shield the queen.

There's a faint dark outline on the Tree where my hand rested. A distant smell of woodsmoke.

A scream comes from above and we all turn our attention to the alcove into the temple library. Mother Joca stands there, ashen and trembling. 'She's dead.'

'What did you do?' the queen asks.

I can hear her words, but they sound distant.

'I didn't do anything! I tried to keep it under control. The energy is unstable; it's dangerous.'

'You are the only danger here, Hanan.' Salvacion draws her blade and points it to me, the others following.

I am a fool. I remember the Autumn Isle farmer. Not only are people dying, but so is the world. The faded gold, the blighted harvest. And still the royal contribution from the commonfolk never ceases. The cup is almost empty.

'Maintaining balance, isn't that what you called it? It's never been enough, has it? Your greed outstrips your resources.'

The queen's face goes cold and hard. 'You are a dangerous traitor. You were nothing, and you return to nothing once more.'

'You can't take back what you taught me,' I say, squaring up against Salvacion. I know I can't take her, but I won't go down without a fight.

'But I can bind you,' the queen says.

Mother Lin gasps. 'Your Majesty—'

'We have no choice,' Mother Joca insists, covering Malostra's body in her cloak. 'She killed Malostra. Think what could have happened to the queen and the princess.'

I can sense the space growing smaller around me until I can feel the Tree against my back.

I arc my arms wide, beginning to cast a protective circle. 'You must listen to me. She means to use the souls of the dead as a source of power!'

'Treason,' Mother Joca yells. 'You leave us no choice.'

'Do it now!' the queen commands.

The Temple Mothers lock arms and begin to chant. 'We bind you from harm. We bind you from power unearned. Everything that lives must die. To the Tree of Life we all return.'

The stones begin to shake under my feet and break apart, flinging me backwards. Great snake-like creatures shoot out of the ground, spraying dirt everywhere. Vines with teeth for thorns bite at my flesh. The smell of turned earth fills the chamber. The roots strike at my body, coiling around me with their brutal touch. I try to fight them off, to finish my protective circle, but they break through. They hold me fast and keep my body rigid. My skin burns under the touch of the roots. My bones crack as I'm pulled from a great height. I'm dragged into the ground and under it, watching the earth close up above me until there is nothing but darkness.

CHAPTER FORTY-SIX

RIS

THE SHIP HASN'T FLOODED, and we're all still here, a little worse for wear. Since the encounter with the kraken and the enemy ship, Finlyr and I have been slowly cataloguing and repairing the damage. I'm clearing the last of the debris when I feel cold steel against my skin. I look up to see my dagger, out of its sheath and aimed squarely at my heart.

'Enough cleaning, time for swordplay.'

Finlyr passes me a sword, and I unsheathe it. 'How gallant of you to offer me the sword this time.'

'I thought you might want the advantage,' he says with a smirk.

'I don't need the advantage,' I retort, parrying his attack.

'At least you know which end is which. You've come on leaps.'

He turns about. It seems almost unfair that he's defending from a sword with a dagger, but I'm sure he likes the challenge. Finlyr's giving good this time. I worried he was being soft on me, trying to build my confidence. I hate that. He moves like water, anticipating my movements before I've even started making them. It's like he's in my head. I must have some tell, some giveaway in my expression. He's not as fast as Isagani, but compared to me, he is like the air. He leads me in a dance around the repaired mast and catches me on the other side, pinning me with his arm and pointing the dagger just above the loose lacing of my shirt and below the moon talisman.

Finlyr follows my gaze and then meets my eyes. 'I've always wondered why the Paranishian symbol of union is the moon. She's inconstant, ever-shifting.'

I'd rather him kiss my steel than pin blame on a witness to my husband's folly. It's not his fault. There are no more secrets between us, and I feel a lightness now.

We're breathing hard, cheeks flushed. My pommel catches his hand, and he drops the dagger, bringing his fingers up to his mouth.

'Are you bleeding?' I ask.

'No, thankfully.'

He bends to grab the dagger, but I kick it with the toe of my boot. It spins across the deck and under a crate.

'Ris!' he says, frustrated.

I wouldn't rile him up if it weren't so entertaining.

'Fine.' He stands, seeing my impish look. 'Then I will simply disarm you.'

'I'd like to see you try.'

Then he's charging at me. He tackles me, a little cautiously, for the blade in my hand. I push Finlyr hard in the chest. He looks taken aback, his hands flying to the place on his skin where his shirt hangs loose, as if my touch has shocked him. He rounds on me, and I stagger back. Finlyr pushes me roughly against the wall. The wood buckles beneath the force of it. I drop the sword, and it clatters to the deck. His hands are still on my shoulders, and we stare at each other, his eyes moving to the rise and fall of my chest. The sword and the fight are forgotten. I watch a bead of sweat roll down his neck and become trapped in his clavicle. It holds there for a moment before travelling down his chest. There's a mark I'd never noticed before, a line tattoo of a cresting wave and a sword. Our eyes meet again, and the moment pulls taut like a rope against a sail. His look is so open and vulnerable, as if he's showing me all of him. His expression teeters on the knife-edge of my decision.

'Come here.' These words undo him.

His arms slacken, and he pulls forward, closing the gap between our bodies. The pressure of him knocks the wind out of me. I gasp for air as he kisses me, his mouth desperate as it comes for my lips, my tongue, my neck. His stubble sends shivers dancing across my skin. And then his hands show no mercy. He holds me fast, pushing me desperately against the wall, pinning me there.

I grab at his shirt and pull, ripping the arm. He stops, snapped out of his frenzy. He looks down at the torn fabric and then gives a wicked grin. He lunges at me and paws at my own shirt, letting out a whimper when my breasts are revealed. He takes my nipple in his mouth, cupping me with his hands. He looks at me, and I buckle. He fumbles with my skirts, his fingers snaking through the fabric to find me. I'm slick and his fingers sink into me smoothly, parting the damp fur between my legs.

Sea spray laps at the boat's edges and drenches us. The boat rocks and Finlyr's arms tense, bracing me against the wall. I hoist my legs up and wrap them around him. Finlyr raises me up and holds my weight, and then I push at him, forcing him to tumble onto his back, taking me with him. I crawl on hands and knees until I'm above him, tugging at his belt and breeches. He reaches for me between my legs again. I slap him away. I grip his arse while I stroke him until he howls. He looks to do something desperate, clutching at me, forcing me close. But I won't give in, not yet. I move up so my knees are either side of his head and lower myself onto him as he squeezes my arse. I would come, or he would die.

He goes to the task with frantic vigour, with an eagerness that makes me wonder how many other cunts he's devoured. I barely have time to think before I come all over the decks, knees shuddering, threatening to crush his skull. I slowly release him, and he tries to sit up, to reach for me. I slam him down again, pinning his arms above his head. I take a loose rope and wrap it around his wrists. My fingers fumble as I unwrap the sheath from my pocket and slide it onto him. He gives out a cry as I mount him. I hold him down as I sway and rock my hips, rolling and bucking slowly at first and then speeding up until he screams and cries out for me.

'Don't you dare give up on me,' I tell him as I hold his gaze, riding him hard.

I fuck him so hard I think he's concussed himself on the wood. I hold him then, rolling my hips back and forth slow and deep. He dives for me, kissing and biting my mouth and breasts. He tastes salt-swept and pushes himself deeper inside me. I let go of the rope then and his hands come loose. We grip each other like weathering a storm. I come hard as he bites down on my nipple. I shudder, muscles seizing up. I feel him inside me as I tighten, and he gives a sound of surprise and pleasure.

There's a moment of stillness where I don't want to dismount him, to feel the emptiness where he's just been. I breathe hard in his ear and then bite the lobe. He gasps, and I get up, letting my skirts fall. Warmth drips down between my thighs. He looks at his shirt, ripped beyond repair.

'Well, that's done for.' Finlyr laughs.

I offer a hand and Finlyr stands. He removes the sheath and cleans up, tucking himself back into his breeches. My heart leaps into my mouth as I hear the crash of a door opening, followed by the unmistakable sound of one of the undead, broken ribs knocking against each other.

Finlyr rushes over to the door, holding up his breeches, and flings his full body weight against it.

'A bit of privacy for the lady, please.'

He takes off his torn shirt, offering it to me as a towel. Suddenly I feel shy and turn around to clean up under my skirts. There's so much of his skin on show. He brings me towards him, placing his lips tenderly on the bare skin of my shoulder.

'Looks like we needed to work it out physically,' Finlyr says with a grin.

I punch him on the arm. 'Is that how you work out all your conflicts?'

'Only with the prettiest opponents,' he says.

I shake my head and try to hide my smile. He takes my hand and interlocks our fingers.

'You like someone who pushes back,' he says, pushing against my palm. I meet him with equal resistance. Eventually he breaks the grip. Something has softened between us.

'Looks like we're both disarmed now.'

CHAPTER FORTY-SEVEN

HANAN

My body tries to heal itself, painfully slowly. For every piece that tries to knit itself back together, I rip again, as though I'm in a storm of glass. It's flaying my skin and dousing my insides with alcohol. It's pulling my body through a jagged hagstone. Like a fist around my lungs and someone holding my head underwater. My eyes and nose and mouth are full of dirt. I am buried at the base of the Tree, the hum of the dead a deafening cacophony.

My body is useless to me right now, so I reach out with my mind. I feel lighter, like I'm crawling out of my bones into the dirt. My mind grasps out for the roots that bind me fast, connecting with everything and everyone that has ever been. I try not to let it overwhelm me this time and I begin to move my fingers, my physical body, within the dirt.

I writhe and stretch until I find something solid. I try to make out its shape with my fingertips: rough and smooth in places, long and narrow. Then another, similar to the first. And then something round, with two holes and a serrated line. By Aistra, my touch tells me what it is, but I want to disbelieve it. Touch is the only sight I have down here. It is a body, a skeleton. My mind is penetrated by another's thoughts, a distant singing:

She was a trickster and a thief.
She was a traitor to the crown.

She was corrupt beyond belief.
Follow her way and you will drown.

The same song the drunken Umasans had sung the night of Magliyab: the festival of flames.

I can feel the roots extending even deeper into the ground, following them like a winding path to another place, distant yet connected. There's an energy there; it burns bright and brilliant, like nothing I've felt before. I ache to go to it. It is like a fire for a lost traveller.

The Magliyab festival is for her. Priestess Sinaya, my ghostly adviser. So the priestess did succeed in stealing the gift before she was expelled. They made an example out of her. Obey or die.

Take root where the sea meets the sky.

Hearing these voices feels the same as during time in the cove, when I created the remedy for the queen. My time as a Temple Sister feels so long ago now, but it has been less than a year. Everything I had worked for was a lie. And when I tried to warn them, they silenced me. As they have so many other priestesses. I thought it was only the Bastion, but the rot goes all the way to the core. Everyone is complicit.

I want to die. I lie there and try to let myself decay. It would be so easy to sink into the roots, to let the Tree reabsorb me as it so desperately wants to do. This is what we were told would be our end, a noble and holy one. But dying would be too easy, and I've suffered too much to let it stop now.

I crawl to the surface, every fingernail's breadth of purchase hard won. My body and my mind are in disarray, and I try to bring them together, to muster any sliver of energy I have left. I push against the dirt, loosening the binds of the roots, until with a final gasp my grave lets me go. The air is ice in my lungs, but it is ecstasy to feel anything.

I pull myself up by the loose stone slabs until I am lying on my back, dirt in my eyes, staring at the night's sky in the temple chamber. The Tree reaches up as if to touch the stars, and I have never hated anything more.

I make my way to my feet and twist and hack at a branch until my hands are bleeding. It finally gives way with a snap. *I'm taking this. I'm taking some of the power back.*

I lean against my roughly made cane, feeling the ambient energy spark up my arm. That's a good start.

I trail blood up the winding spiral staircases until I reach the Mothers' sanctuary. It's the only logical place where they would be. At first, I thought they would have returned to the Bastion, but the queen would want as much gifted energy as possible to protect her. Better to stay here where she can hide behind the Mothers' skirts. They have posted Salvacion and the Seaguardians at her quarters along with casting a protective circle. She must be terrified.

But what they haven't accounted for are shadows. I know this place like my own body, and I use the dark corners to my advantage. Eventually they will sleep, they will change shifts, they will pause. The Mothers are nowhere to be seen. Perhaps they are with the Temple Sisters, reassuring them that today's horrible events are nothing to lose sleep over. I bide my time. As for the protective circle, I have a theory and only one opportunity to test it.

I find my moment when a Seaguardian relieves Salvacion, just enough time for me to slip past unnoticed. I take my new cane and drag it across the threshold of the chambers, only breathing again once I sense the circle has been broken. The energy has been disrupted by the remnant of the Tree, and I'm grateful for it.

The princess is sleeping in a makeshift bassinet next to the queen's bed. She barely protests as I lift her out and place her in the sling I find nearby. She burbles gently.

'You are mine, Raina. You need me.'

The queen sleeps soundly, which disgusts me more than it should. After all the harm she's inflicted, her mind rests peacefully at night. I stare at her, taking one last look. *I gave this child her life back; she is as much mine as she ever was yours.* Everything that lives must die, the queen always tells me. But how can something live without a heart?

As we escape from the temple, I know what the queen will do when she finds Raina is gone. She will scorch the earth, but I won't be there to see the destruction.

I climb back into the wooden boat in the aqueduct and follow the halo of light ahead. I struggle with the oars, the water splashing over me. The aqueduct reverberates my struggles in an eerie echo, and the dim light throws strange shadows off the walls. I have to keep rowing. Finally, I reach the curious metal door I saw when we first arrived at Aistra. I ease the boat to the wall of the tunnel and reach for the grooved handle – some sort of lever. The door slides back to reveal a giant, spiralling screw. Water sloshes through the open door and pulls the boat onto the base. I look up and between the spokes of metal I can see the sky. Now I notice the crank in the chamber. I reach out for it and begin to rotate. The giant metal beast springs to life, groaning and sloshing. Sheets of water fall from the opening at the top. I yell and turn the crank the other way. The mechanism turns, and we're spiralling upwards as it funnels the water from the aqueduct to the top. We're spat out onto the open ocean, between a rocky outcrop. The boat is thrust by the current and we emerge from behind the rocks. I see the Bastion, high on the hilltop in the mainland.

My limbs burn and scream as I row, and I give every lungful of air to getting away. Then the waves are pushing me. The Bastion becomes smaller than the stained-glass window of the temple.

I am not built for physical labour. My body's strength is in its mind, not its muscles. How I wish it were otherwise in this moment. My arms are weak and shaking by the time the Bastion has disappeared from view. I turn into the tide and rest for a moment. There is a satchel containing skins of water and breads and cheeses stowed in the boat, no doubt forgotten by the Seaguardians. I try to eat slowly, to make it last. I give some water to Raina, who takes a little but then begins to search for something else. She whines and wraps her hand around my finger. But nothing happens. I can smell sea salt, but that's too real, too present. No woodsmoke, no calamansi, no petrichor. I can only hear the sloshing of the waves against our rowboat. I look deep into myself and try to find the invisible string that will connect our energies. It is a snuffed candle within me. I can't access my powers.

Part Three

Things Are Not What they Seem

CHAPTER FORTY-EIGHT

HANAN

I HAVE NO CHOICE but to row. The last remnants of Paranish slip across the horizon, and there is nothing but open ocean. Perhaps it has always been this vast blue expanse. When night falls is when the fear sets in. The temperature drops, and a haar rolls across the water, obscuring everything around me. I shiver as I row, almost dropping one of the oars. That's when I call it. Raina and I curl up in my cloak and I set the oars beside us. There is no sleep, only the sloshing of the water against the boat until the cycle continues and the sun brings us warmth.

I stop and portion out how much we can live on for that day. Eventually I give in to Raina's cries. I offer her my breast as I did before, but there is nothing for her there, no food nor energy. I try to keep her warm and dribble fresh water from the skein into her mouth. I protect Raina like an extension of myself. I sense nothing; even if there is life, I don't feel it. I feel nothing now, just hunger and pain and fatigue.

The sun becomes a blessing but also a curse. We shiver in the night and bake in the day, with no shade, no shelter. I become unsure if I'm awake or asleep. The sloshing of my oars in the water begins to sound like fish approaching. I have no way to catch them. Sometimes I reach out with my hands, but they slip through my fingers, if they were even truly there to begin with.

My body has never seemed so fragile and brittle. My skin feels paper-thin, my bones soft as clay. No wonder the royals wanted more than what plain mortality could give. Is this how the others have always felt?

I begin to see things that aren't truly there. I'm following our first waymarker, a formation of rocks in the distance. Out of the fret comes not stone but a human form. A woman. Malostra, hovering over the water, arms outstretched. For a blissful moment I think everything that happened was a night terror. The warmth spreads over my body, and in my hazy euphoria I distantly understand that hypothermia is setting in. Malostra disappears into the fog and I have nowhere left as an anchor. I continue to row blindly until the sun sets in the haze. I am pulling the oars into the boat for the night when fingers crawl over the lip of the vessel.

Malostra emerges from the water. 'Come into the water, my love. Swim with me.'

I turn away from the figure and focus on Raina, trying to cradle and shush her. She has taken water and little else. I keep her little body close to stay warm. She sleeps so much, I worry soon I won't be able to wake her. I feel a cold mist on my skin but I close my eyes until it passes. The sensation of being hollowed out won't leave me. I can't get warm, and my skin is like ice.

The boat rocks and I come to myself, steadying my hands on the centre thwart. Out of the corner of my eye, the oar, wood like bone, slips into the water. I think I'm drowning, but then I realise I'm crying.

I feel my ribs beneath my fingers. More prominent than they ever were at the Bastion. We lie in the boat like fish and stare up at the stars. I must fall asleep under the warm dry blanket as I wake up shivering, my breath like smoke around me. I jerk awake, startling Raina who cries out in alarm. Holy Aistra, she's all right. I blow on her tiny hands and swaddle her tighter. The sun beats down, but it is a distant thing, and I have never been colder. An incessant knocking in the background. I look around for the source. My boat is jutted up against a rock. It hits the side over and over again.

By Paranish, it's land. I mean, it's a desolate pile of rocks in the middle of nowhere, but it's real. The stone is sharp and rough, cutting my fingers when I test it. There is no helpful slope, nor smooth approach to berth. I take the tatty rope and hook it onto a large pillar of a stone. Heaving myself out of the water and onto the rocks is the hardest thing I've ever done. I tentatively feel for the vibrating life inside the stone. There's a sickening silence. It unnerves me and I slip again, my ankle hitting the rock awkwardly. It washes over me far too slowly. I can't feel it. I can feel nothing of the life around me because I was pulled from the living world.

I feel out the wall, for hand and footholds. This is an unknown language to me, despite growing up in a stone temple. My blood marks the places of my endeavours and frustrations. We get there and I'm more broken skin than whole. I sit on the rock and kiss the top of Raina's head. We are on dry land. We are alive. As if a curtain is being drawn back, a glorious holy rain tips down.

I sit there, enveloped in the storm as the leaves and seaweed swirl around me. Everything is so loud, the waves crashing urgently. I cup my hands and drink from the pools of rainwater. I laugh. At least, I think that's what the sound is. It comes from deep within me, an animal mania that consumes me completely.

I feel possessed, the shock of seeing it stilling the anguish in my throat. Through the sheet of rain I see a shape coming towards me. I gulp down rainwater as I stumble across the jagged rock. I blink away the rain and push at my temples, making light spots wink in my periphery. I try to use the pain to gauge if what I'm seeing is real. My senses are foreign to me now. Malostra came to haunt me; perhaps my mind now taunts me with the promise of salvation.

CHAPTER FORTY-NINE

FINLYR

Ris comes up from the mess, and the smell of spices and yeast follows, sweet and nutty with a subtle kick at the back of the throat. 'Grub's up, you miserable lot.'

Paranish, I should let Ris cook all my meals. I'm a man who could eat boiled rice and veggies all day, but she's somehow found herbs at the back of cupboards I didn't even know were on board. I could rustle up something that would keep body and soul together, a touch better than the undead, but not by much. I stroke my stomach, looking on fondly as she sets down the pot of rice stew. While I love to eat, Ris seems to find a delight in preparing meals I don't understand. A calm washes over her the way I do when sailing. A peace in having total control of her surroundings.

We sit around the bolted-down table, elbows tucked close, and pass the serving dish around. Biba takes an overly generous spoonful and slops some of it down the side of her bowl.

Isagani tears a corner of flatbread and dips it into the stew. I follow and, by Aistra, it's crisp and stuffed with dried herbs.

I take a spoonful, and the stew is sour and warming and spicy by turns. 'What is this called?'

'Sinigang,' Biba says.

The otter-cat chirrups, bringing his head up from his bowl on the floor.

'Is that your namesake?' I ask. 'Explains a lot.'

'Here,' Ris says, handing me a mug of palm wine.

I sniff the cup, watching sprinklings swirl on the surface of the drink, catching the light. 'What's this stuff?'

'Just drink it, it's good for you,' Ris says with a wink.

The liquid touches my tongue. A merry dance of spices: cloves, cinnamon, and something familiar I can't quite place mingling with the sweetness of the wine. This woman is something else.

'Like it?' She sees the star struck look on my face and claps me hard on the shoulder. 'You've everything you need right here; you just don't know how to use it.'

Sinigang laps contentedly. 'You should keep her around, Fin.'

I'm almost positive no one saw our deck escapades, but living in close quarters like this, perhaps they have sensed something has changed between us. There's an ease, a familiarity that is hard to conceal.

'Can I try?' Isagani asks, reaching for my mug.

'No,' Ris says, firmly. 'When you're older,' she adds, more gently.

She sips her own drink furtively. Sinigang narrows his eyes at me and then at Ris, sniffing the air, whiskers twitching.

'That wouldn't be crushed silphium I smell?'

Ris colours, half gagging on her drink.

'Not something you'd commonly find in a ship's kitchen.' Sinigang smiles.

Once he says it, I can place the herb. It's something I haven't used since my younger years when I still lived on Paranish. Most people like the reassurance of the sheath's visibility, but I suppose Ris is being extra cautious. Silphium can protect from unwanted pregnancy, but it's no barrier for disease like a sheath. Still, two methods of protection are better than one.

I tip the rest of the stew down my throat before it cools too much. The hot tangy spices slid smoothly down my throat. My skin prickles momentarily, and I'm awful hot. But then the feeling passes. It's like a cool balm is pressed against my skin. The sweat doesn't prickle on my skin. In fact, it feels chill.

Ris gets up for seconds of the stew.

When I stand to leave for the lavvy, I pass behind her at the counter and whisper in her ear: 'Please let me know the next time you put something in my food.'

She starts, beginning to protest. 'I thought you would be used to it, since – you know . . .'

'Since I'm always putting it around?'

She blushes hard. 'That's not what I meant.'

I sigh and slap open the door. 'I'm going for a piss.'

I'm hydrated and then some. I barely make it to the lavvy to untie my troos before I'm pissing like a horse. When I return to the mess, the others are having a little sing-song:

> 'My love sleeps underwater.
> Salt-swept with pearls for her eyes.
> Her hair tangled in seaweed.
> Dreaming eternal, she lies.'

Ris surprises me most of all. Her voice is low and strong, an unwavering alto that rings out across the room. Isagani has some stone pipes on a string around their neck and accompanies Ris's singing. It's the first I've seen of them, but Isagani's full of surprises. The mess takes on the quality of a tavern deep in its cups. But Paranish, this is not the place for it.

'Have you all taken leave of your senses?'

They startle to a stop. Sinigang says nothing.

'No singing. Nothing that could tempt a storm.'

'But we sang before, to haul away,' Ris protests.

'That was different. You don't sing about drowning out on the sea.'

'Sailors are superstitious, the lot of them,' Sinigang says.

'Yes, well, aren't you supposed to be good luck in a storm?' I snap.

The smirk on Isagani's face dies. 'You're serious, aren't you?'

'We are merely visitors to these waters,' I continue. 'And we must pass through with as little disturbance as possible.'

A whistling. A groaning of the wood. Ris bounds up the stairs faster than I can. We're all on deck. I look at her, the shimmer in her eyes.

The skies open and the rain begins to pour headlong on top of us. The rain barrels will be full again. I'm soaked through, not with sweat, but with a heady mix of salt spray and rainwater.

'I hope you're happy now!' I spit pettily as the ship crests another wave.

'You don't really think we caused this?' Ris insists, grabbing at a rope for purchase.

Isagani surfs the deck, trying to grab anything not bolted down and shove it into the chambers below.

'I don't believe in coincidences,' I shout back. We can barely hear each other over the wind whipping like claws. My heart is pounding in my ears. I'm used to the weather turning foul out at sea, but not as fast as this. It's not natural. Lashings of stormwater hit the deck. For a moment I don't recognise our skeleton crew, and it feels like I'm with my old crew, the forms shifting in the rain.

I remember Larkin there, hauling rope. The man whose name tripped so sweetly off my tongue when Isagani and I were shaping our disguises. A name I would never forget. I try to blink away the rain from my eyes.

'Captain, what do we do?' Isagani shouts.

I swallow, throat dry and my tongue sticking awkwardly to the roof of my mouth. A swig from my waterskin. Except it's not water, but palm wine. I choke it down. Better than naught.

I familiarise myself with the situation, taking note of the wind, planning my next instructions.

Ris has the spyglass up to her face, nearly giving herself a black eye as the ship rocks. 'What is that?' she shouts.

'What? What?' I yell, swiping water from my eyes. I can't see a blasted thing.

'Land ho!' she shouts, snapping the spyglass shut. She's smiling like she's possessed.

'We're not trying to find land!'

'But there's someone out there!'

'We're not trying to find anyone!'

'I think we can get closer. We have to help them!'

By Paranish, she's probably hallucinating. Who in Holy Aistra would be on a random rock in the middle of the ocean? In a storm, to boot.

'Gimme that spyglass!'

Ris tosses it, bloody fool. It nearly slips, but I manage to catch it gracelessly.

I slide the spyglass open and wipe away the condensation. My view bobs and bounces but I can see it. There is a blighted rock in the middle of the ocean. It's a steep and jagged stack, no bigger than a tavern long table. It's covered with molluscs and algae but there is someone standing against the elements. Clad in black, arms outstretched to the skies. A creature from the depths. Paranish, we've summoned something.

'Fin, what should we do?'

It's like I've woken up. Like startling awake in my bed after a dream, feeling like I'm falling. The words are out, commands leaving my lips and my hands finding familiar purchase. My head clears, a fog of drunken stupor and terrible decisions sloughing off my skin. Paranish, it's been years since I've felt this raw and alive.

CHAPTER FIFTY

RIS

SURVEYING THE OCEAN WITH my spyglass has become a nervous habit of mine, since the kraken. If I don't have it in my hands I find myself sanding down the edges of the broken taffrail with a rough cloth. It feels like a charm. If I can see everything around us then nothing can hurt us. I know that's illogical, but I suppose this is the petty magic I try to work. When I first see the figure, I have to stare through the spyglass for an eternity before I understand what I'm seeing. Rain creates a waterfall, which obscures my vision, and I have to fight to keep sight of her.

We throw down the anchor line, and the woman finally notices us. It's like she was in a dream, standing pummelled by the storm on that abandoned rock. Her boat is being dashed to pieces. She looks up at *Saltswept* as if the ship were an illusion. I suppose we both doubt each other's existence as I stretch out my hand and indicate the anchor line. The ship bucks and roils like an unwieldy pack animal rejecting another rider.

'Can you climb up?' I ask, cupping my hands around my mouth to yell.

The figure wipes water from her face and squints hard at me. She half staggers towards the edge of the rock and reaches for the swinging rope. I gasp as she loses her footing. She catches herself at the last minute. Her feet are bare. A sodden shawl and billowy dress add to the ghoulish look of her face, wan and gaunt, pale tendrils of hair whipping around her. What ordeal has this poor wretch been through? It's only then I notice the baby. It's strapped to her chest in a rudimentary sling, and it looks only a few months old: small and pale and worse for wear. I shudder to think how cold the poor babe must be. They crave the warmth of the womb, and you must try to recreate it for them. That was one of the last pieces of advice my fathers gave me, although they never lived to meet Biba.

The woman grasps and slides up the rope, snake-like. Her progress is painfully slow, and I doubt the strength of her arms.

'I have to help her!' I tell Finlyr, rushing down below deck. I open the hatch and nearly throw myself out of the window to secure her. She grips my hand, her fingers sharp and cold as ice.

'Give me the baby,' I yell.

She holds the infant close with her free arm, her face haunted.

'We're trying to help you,' I insist. 'You need free hands.' What has she been through?

She braces against me and makes it upwards, where the others are waiting to help her clamber overboard.

The captain's quarters are closest, and she stumbles to the room, collapsing in a heap as soon as her body finds soft furnishings. Her limbs are stiff and unyielding as I take the child from her arms. I empty a drawer and make a crib as best I can with piles of clothes and dry the child, rubbing some life back into her as she cries.

'She needs to eat,' I observe as the child reaches for me suckling empty air.

'I can't,' the woman moans.

She shivers so violently, the talisman at her neck jolts up and down. It's a dark stone with a strange swirling forest green pattern within. I peel the soaked shawl and dark dress and chemise from her.

Her arms are covered in faded cuts and lacerations, particularly her wrists and hands. The scars are white and raised in the cold. At the top of her left thigh, a deeper scar, livid and angry.

I bundle her in thick blankets. She eases a little, her shivers coming in less pronounced waves. I wrap my arms around her, trying to still my own shivers as my body warmth merges into her. It's like the core of her is ice. Her lips tremble, turning vein-blue to ghastly white and then finally to a pinkish tan. Despite the streaks of silver in her dark hair, I see how young her face is when it's not contorted in distress. When she seems to drift into sleep, I creak up, knees clicking. At the disturbance, she clutches at my arm, fingers still ice cold.

'Please don't leave me,' she implores, voice as sharp and clear as glass. 'I'm so cold.'

'I won't leave you,' I say instinctively.

I rub her hands and blow on her fingers, and she whimpers as they come back to life and warm up.

'Where am I?' she asks, eyes turning wildly in her head.

'Our vessel is called *Saltswept*. You're safe now.'

'Who are you?'

'My name's Ris,' I say gently, leaving a long pause for her to introduce herself. I show her the blue ribbon tucked in my hair and make the gesture for she. At first I think her hands are too stiff, but she looks at me agog.

'Hanan,' she finally says.

She looks less bedraggled and brought back from the brink. I look at the chemise, hanging and steaming as it warms and dries. It is dark and simple, of good strong material. The quality looks to be another Spring Isle farmstead, but there are no flourishes or embellishments. Her voice is cut glass in a way only native to nobility. I try to imagine her in a fine gown, a golden halo of thread woven through her hair.

'Why were you out there in the middle of the ocean?'

She pauses, biting her lip. 'I . . . angered the queen.'

I tense. So my instincts were right: she is a noble. No wonder she has no ribbon and was confused by my self-identifying gesture.

'What happened?'

I remember the way she grasped for my hand in the dark.

'I had to . . . leave.'

I stare at Hanan and then the baby, who is still looking peaky. 'I can't believe she would leave you and your daughter to die,' I say quietly.

She seems uneasy and unwilling to say more. I'll have to tease this tale out of her slowly, for she's clearly been through much. I can fully believe the Bastion treated her poorly, but I need to know if she still has love for the monarch.

She casts her eyes down. 'Her will is divine.'

There's something in her tone that makes me wonder, but I can't pull at that thread too quickly.

'What is your child's name?'

She smiles. 'She's called Raina.'

I follow her cue, despite the fact that us common-folk don't decide identifiers for others. 'And her father?'

She shakes her head and turns her face away.

I squeeze her hand. 'I'm sorry. That's like my Biba.'

She looks at me curiously. 'You have a child?'

I nod. 'There's a couple of kids on board actually, although none as young as your Raina. She doesn't look well. I think you should try to feed her.'

She stiffens and shrinks away. 'I can't do that.'

I sigh, getting up from the bed. 'I can see you're not in good shape. With a little food and rest, I'm sure it will all be right again.'

She stares distantly in Raina's direction, but I can tell she isn't truly seeing the child.

'Why are you helping me?' she asks. 'I'm nobody to you.'

I try to smooth the distraught expression that she must read on my face and sit back on the bed. 'You were in trouble. Why wouldn't we try to help?'

Tears begin to trickle down her face, but her expression remains impassive. 'You are good people.'

It shatters me to see her gratitude for an act that should be an instinct. I wipe her tears and adjust the blankets. 'We're all just doing our best. Now you get some rest, and I'll bring some tea and stew, all right?'

She lies down, almost childlike in her vulnerability. I tuck the blankets around her and stroke her hair. She nestles into it and breathes like it's the first time she has been able to unspool. I bend down and kiss her forehead. Her face is already warmer against my lips.

CHAPTER FIFTY-ONE

FINLYR

'Who are they?' Isagani asks through a mouthful of hard biscuit. They lean against the wall, hair pulled back into a slick bun. 'We don't know yet,' I say. 'Ris has taken charge.'

'Well?' I ask.

'She'll be all right, I think. The baby needs food, but she's too weak right now. Fetch the sampinit berry tea.'

I elbow Isagani, who rolls their eyes and hurries to the galley.

'Any water in the lungs?' I ask.

Ris shakes her head and then leans against me, stretching her neck with a crack. After a moment, I have to ask.

'What's the deal with us?'

'Deal?' She echoes, pulling away so she can look at me. 'Aren't you having fun?'

'Fun,' I echo, nodding. 'Is that what this is? Sneaking around and having a secret.'

She stares at me. 'You're angry with me, aren't you?'

I say nothing, letting her sit with my body language, my expression.

'I'm sorry about the silphium. I should have asked you.'

'Do you trust me?'

'Of course I do. It's not about that, and I know we're being careful. Everything's just so—' She cuts herself off, bringing her hands up and letting them drop.

'Complicated?' I offer.

'Delicate,' she says, holding my gaze. 'We're already holding so much. I just wanted something for us without the burden of consequences.'

I try to let her words wash over me. I am used to being inconsequential. I accepted I could never bet on tomorrow a long time ago. I don't know what I'd hoped for with Ris. Maybe that we could buy ourselves a bit more time before we got here. The unspoken 'if we live, what happens next?' hangs over us, but this dalliance, whatever it is, feels like the most trivial and also the most important thing in this whole voyage right now.

I clear my throat and stand straighter. 'You know a Lassairian remedy for resurrecting a drowning person is to blow smoke up their arse.'

She laughs low, the vibrations running through our bodies as they touch. 'Was that the carpenter's opening flirtation before they charged you a fortune for those taffrails?'

I tilt her face up to mine and steal a kiss. She sighs and melts against me again. We jump apart when we hear Isagani's footsteps round the corner. They're carefully carrying the tea kettle wrapped in a cloth, and Ris knocks on the door before pushing it open.

The woman is bundled in blankets and sheets, a length of seaweed tangled in her hair. The woman stirs, snuffling against the cushions. It's only then I spot the child in a drawer, wriggling its arms. Ris has dumped out half the contents onto the floor and is using my clothes as a nest for a baby.

Ris's voice is as gentle as a Summer Isle breeze. 'You'll have to sit up, my dear. Can you do that?'

The stranger opens her eyes with a pop and stares at us, her body going stiff and her hands bracing.

'Stand down,' Ris commands, holding the woman's hands. 'There's no need for that.'

The woman sits up, and Isagani slowly sets out the tea things, barely taking their eyes off her.

'Who are they?' she asks Ris. Her voice is like glass, a clipped lyrical lilt. She looks worse for wear right now, and her frame is lean, too gaunt.

'Some of the crew,' Ris says lightly, then addresses me. 'Do we have any of the jellyfish soup left?'

My hands sting with the memory of chopping up those things. 'A couple of servings, perhaps.'

Sinigang slinks into the room, soft wet fur dampening the ends of my trousers. Damnation, that otter-cat.

He watches as the woman cautiously takes the cup of tea she's offered. It's strange, as though I can see the warm glow of her reviving on her skin. For a moment she's anything but poised, greedy in her imbibing. I've looked at bottles and bodies that way myself after many a long journey. Then she wipes her mouth with the back of her hand and smiles. Sinigang looks at the baby, and twitches his nose.

The woman looks at Sinigang, cocking her head to the side. Eventually she reaches out a hand to stroke him, and he hisses.

'I'm not some common hybrid, madame.'

'Your otter-cat speaks?' she asks, retracting her hand in shock.

'Annoyingly, yes,' I chime in.

She stares at Sinigang, and he narrows his eyes at her. Sinigang's a snarky bastard, but he seems uneasy around Hanan. He swishes his tail, eyes furtively flicking from her to the baby and back again. Something washed up in that storm, but I'm not sure what manner of thing we've found.

Biba has followed the noise to the captain's quarters and stands in the doorway, staring at our new guest. She looks at each of us in turn and cautiously enters the room.

'This is my daughter, Biba,' Ris tells Hanan.

'A princess,' Biba whispers, eyes widening.

Ris laughs. 'She seems to think you're a princess.'

Biba furrows her eyebrows and stares at the baby.

'Careful, love. She's very small and not yet well again,' Ris says, gently guiding Biba away from the child.

Biba pulls away and touches the child, hands placed gently on either side of the baby's face. She wriggles and begins to burble, an unmistakably contented sound. Even at this distance I can see she is a more normal colour.

'What did you do?' Hanan asks, her voice full of wonder rather than reprimand.

Something strange happens. The lamp flickers bright and then snuffs out in an instant. The room fills with light smoke from the wick. Then in the gloom, there appears to be an afterglow. A soft halo of light that flares even when I close my eyes. The silhouettes of Hanan, Biba, the child, and Sinigang are outlined for just a moment.

I startle, edging forward to relight the lamp. 'What was that?'

Hanan and Biba share an incomprehensible look, and I search for Ris. Her face is inscrutable as she also tries to understand what has passed between them.

We go on with the ritual of niceties, letting Hanan eat and rest while we gather on the quarterdeck. The undead crew have everything under control, and the storm has settled as quickly as it came on, almost as if it was conjured and died with Hanan's arrival. A shudder runs down my spine. The touch of magic?

After a few hours, Hanan is strong enough to make her way onto deck and reluctantly leaves her daughter in the crib. She is fed and dressed and looks far better.

'Are you the captain of this vessel?' she asks, addressing me. I nod. 'This is no Seaguardian ship.'

I examine her body language. She's quite pretty, lean as a spear and all angles; not dainty or delicate, despite her fine speech. She looks us all in the eye, not like the stewards who look somewhere over our shoulders.

I lean back, arms crossed, and she's staring at my chest. I've accidentally pulled down the opening of my shirt, and she can see the brand.

Hanan's hand jerks towards her thigh. 'You're outlaws.'

'Not all of us,' Isagani protests.

'And what about your captain?' she asks, turning away from me.

'He's a good man,' Ris insists. 'Despite his body count.'

I start at that. I won't have my name besmirched in front of this stranger. 'Well, I've got a roving eye and a *lot* of energy—'

Ris gives me a dirty look. 'That's not what I meant.'

I lean casually on the helm and address Hanan. 'Yeah, well, I'm sure you've got some skeletons in your closet.'

Ris sighs loudly, and Hanan watches the exchange with intrigue. 'Where is the rest of the crew?'

Sinigang jumps out of Biba's lap. 'You're looking at them. At least the living ones.'

'The living ones?' she asks, stepping backwards until her spine is braced against the mizzenmast. It's as if she's noticed them for the first time and I watch her stare at the corpses.

'I know it's strange,' Ris is beginning, her voice a desperate justification.

'It is strange,' Hanan echoes. There's a horror there but also a morbid fascination. She approaches the undead, examining their bones and gristle. Her eyes rove over the yellow and brown spots of worn, exposed tibia; the eyeballs rotten in their skulls; the sinew poking through exposed flesh.

'Staring is ignoble – didn't they teach you that at the Bastion?' Sinigang whips his tail, fur bristling.

Isagani tugs on my sleeves. 'I don't like this,' they whisper. 'She's hiding something.'

You don't have to be a trickster to realise that.

'I know, but we can't exactly throw her overboard,' I murmur back.

I examine Hanan as she observes the skeletons. She isn't lying about having a connection to the Bastion – that much is evident from her manner and speech. I could believe the queen banishing a fallen noble. But that strange phenomenon with Biba. Sinigang's unrest.

I approach Hanan, turning her to face me. 'What are you hiding?' She doesn't say anything for a time, eyes flitting between us all. 'Show me yours, and I'll show you mine.'

She smiles coldly. 'A ragtag crew of mainly undead, children, and a talking otter-cat. You're a disreputable lot.'

'We have our reasons,' Ris says, suddenly defensive.

'Are you working for the Bastion,' Hanan asks, expression hardening.

'Not fucking likely,' I retort.

'Then why are you sailing under the royal sigil?'

That infernal crest on *Saltswept* is like a beacon on the side of the ship. Of course she spotted it; she would have been eye level with it as we pulled her up.

'We're running a contract, but we've no love for the crown,' I tell her. 'Get that clear in your head right now.'

She says nothing, surveying me. Her silence makes me uneasy, as though she's measuring the situation and examining us all. I continue my line of interrogation, hoping to rile her: 'What's going on with you then? You just wash up here alone with a child.'

'She's touched by magic,' Sinigang cuts through.

Hanan pushes her silver strands behind her ear, jutting her chin out defiantly.

'She had great power,' Sinigang continues, 'But it's tainted now. Tainted and diminished.'

CHAPTER FIFTY-TWO

HANAN

They recoil as soon as the otter-cat outs me. I hadn't predicted the presence of magic aboard this vessel, but it did feel almost extraordinary how the blessed ship emerged like a dream from the storm. In truth, I thought speaking otter-cats were fanciful stories. His words hold weight with them, as though confirming a truth they already suspected.

Their faces are twisted in disgust. I can't blame them. Magic is misunderstood, ever feared.

'Is it true? Do you have power?' Ris asks.

'Yes, but you don't understand what happened,' I implore. 'They used me.'

'If you are magic, and you came from the Bastion, you must be . . .' Finlyr says, slowly putting the pieces together.

'The priestess,' I confirm.

Ris is struck by paralysis as she watches me, slack-jawed. 'Holy Aistra.'

Finlyr grabs her arm, and the crew moves close together, keeping an eye on me as they mutter. Where would I run? I have no desire to return to the ocean. I wouldn't leave Raina.

Children and a talking otter-cat. Are they a family? What are they doing out here? I stare again at the bodies, dead but animated, moving in repetitive rhythmic fashion. These were once people, their bodies marking the violence of their death and decay. Now they are husks, moving by rote, by distant memory. I haven't yet discerned what power impels them to move like this, but I want to know it. I feel the same strange, bright and burning energy that I did in the bowels of the Tree. Fresh anguish, like a wound reopened, at the emptiness of my power stilled within me.

'So the queen is after you?' Finlyr asks eventually, breaking from the group and pacing the deck. He's broad and tan in the same way as Ris; people of hard labour and hard lives. I would have been someone like that if I hadn't been touched by magic.

'She will be, eventually,' I say quietly.

'Paranish, that's just perfect,' he says, still pacing. 'Here we are trying to find this cursed treasure to placate that bitch. Meanwhile, we dredge up the number-one enemy to the crown. We may as well just throw ourselves into the Maelstrom now and die.'

I try to understand his babbling speech. 'Maelstrom.' I hold on to the word. It feels familiar, like a memory from a dream.

Finlyr continues to unravel. 'That's assuming we still make it there.'

'What is the Maelstrom?'

They all look at me. Isagani shakes their head.

I sigh. 'Look, they already hurt me and banished me,' I say, opening my hands in supplication. 'Who am I going to tell? What do I have to lose?'

Finlyr looks at his crew.

'Fine,' Sinigang says eventually.

'The Lahon Maelstrom,' Finlyr confesses.

'I know a little of it.'

'Well then you'll know nobody's made it back alive.' Finlyr glares.

'Apart from you,' Isagani says, tentatively hopeful.

'You've been there before?' I can't hide the surprise in my voice.

'At a distance was plenty,' he corrects.

'And what do you hope to find there?' I try to keep my voice level, curious but afraid.

Finlyr and Ris shrug, making non-committal noises.

'Do you know what's down there?' Biba asks, approaching me slowly.

A Maelstrom. Cursed treasure.

She was a trickster and a thief.
She was a traitor to the crown.
She was corrupt beyond belief.
Follow her way and you will drown.

I have nothing to lose and everything to gain. A seed is planted in my mind, a sprouting hope of power regained. I find myself smiling.

'I'm not sure,' I say, crouching down beside her.

She reaches out to touch my hair and seems surprised when I don't flinch away. She gently brushes it out of my face and in my periphery I can see a few locks, dark as they were before the binding.

'You had sunshine hair, but now it's back to midnight hair,' Biba says.

I remember the energy pulsing between us down in the captain's quarters.

'Your daughter is blessed, isn't she?' I ask, standing up.

Ris and Finlyr are poised like animals about to fight or flee.

'I was a priestess. I'm not afraid of her, and neither should you be.'

I don't need them to like me, just to trust me. For now.

'She is touched,' Ris says, and I can see she is ill at ease with the notion.

'It is a gift,' I reassure her.

'You were raised at the temple,' she says after a time.

I nod.

'What . . . what was it like there?'

Ris's question has a weight to it, as though my answer could shatter her. She is hanging on my every word; I feel Biba watching me. She is hungry for knowledge of a place where there are others like her. I'm conscious of my face, my mannerisms.

I try to smile at Biba. 'It taught me a great deal. It was the only home I ever knew.'

The half-truth feels like poison on my tongue, but Ris looks relieved. She brings her daughter into a tight embrace. There's a fierce protection there that eclipses the fear radiating off her. I shuffle the pieces in my mind, wondering what Biba's gift could have to do with their being on a contract for the Bastion.

Sinigang slinks up to me and settles by my feet. I catch him surreptitiously looking at me out of the corner of one half-lidded eye. I am tempted to put up the wall, to dance around the naked truth. I have given them morsels of truth, enough to trust me. I shield my face with my shroud of hair, a dark reminder of who I used to be. It's as though their realisation of what I am has released a dam built against acknowledging my crimes, and now my chest is being crushed by the weight of water. I have survived by ignoring the shadow in the corner of my mind.

'The undead crew all have names, you know,' Sinigang says casually.

I turn to stare at him.

'Not what they were called in life,' he continues, 'but the children hold a great affection for them.'

'That's . . . macabre.'

'Any more macabre than what you did?'

I think of Pocket and the future I had imagined for him when I freed him from his cage in the Bastion library. It had given me solace to think of him unbound, untamed, free to make anywhere his home and owned by no one.

'What can you feel?' Sinigang asks, his intense expression making my skin prickle. His words are so gentle that they are a death by a thousand cuts, and I'm caught in a reverie. I am compelled to answer him truthfully, as though he is weaving a truth spell with his look.

'Nothing,' I confess.

'You were no petty witch. You were a priestess. I don't think you would accept that fate.'

'I should be dead. I'd rather be dead.'

Soft as a gentle breeze, he admits, 'You still reek of magic. It's faint but it's there.'

I close my eyes and feel for any ember of magic. His energy is in the distance, so close and yet out of reach. It's the rumble of thunder and lightning striking, an approaching storm. I feel him underneath my hand, his wet fur on my fingers. He's letting me touch him. I can feel his heartbeat, slow like crashing waves upon a beach. I yearn for it, so much I want to push my hand through his flesh and bone until I can touch it. The fact I can feel him, even faintly, is torture. My desire to take from him if I could terrifies me.

I snatch my hand back. 'I'm sorry. I would never—'

Sinigang looks at me, less afraid than curious, as if he's reading my mind, 'You would if you could. Power calls to power. Energy cannot be created nor destroyed, only transferred.'

'What do you mean?'

The boat lurches, and my hand slides across the wood, catching a splinter. I stagger back, clutching my hand. I wait for the moment the skin will begin to stitch itself together. It doesn't come. It never will. Sinigang looks to the wound and then back at me.

'With time, you can find the sweet in the salt.'

I have nothing to say to that. Expelled from the only places I've known, and having my power stilled within me. A bird whose wings have been clipped. The others are ungifted, or more like unburdened, by magic. They catch glimpses of what they think it is: the delicate power Biba possesses, something wild and untamed, creating out of love and joy. It isn't the hardened branches tied down and trained to grow only higher, reaching for the sun, never out to each other. Crown-shy.

CHAPTER FIFTY-THREE

FINLYR

To my naked eyes as I stand on the forecastle deck, it is a blot on the horizon. We've been on this journey for weeks, and yet I almost didn't believe the moment would come. I hold up the spyglass and watch the sea spray from the Maelstrom, catching the sunlight and creating a rainbow of colours. I shouldn't be this close to the bowsprit, but I want to see it first. Above the pit, the spiralling tendrils and branches of a tree. It seems impossible, a tree above a pit in the middle of the ocean. It stretches out, yawning over the chasm, bark streaked with vivid colours, new branches shooting from the skin of the old. The wood is gnarled and knotted at the base, livid growth of fungi and lichen splattering its surface. I thought I was fungi-fevered the first time I saw it. It comes upon you impossibly, the great mass churning, a white and clean foam disappearing into the endless void. My heart lurches, and I try to keep my hands steady. Even from this distance I can feel the standing waves forming from the upswelling surge. Soon they will be crashing against the bow stem. The jib sail pulls taut in the wind.

'What is that?' Hanan asks.

'What we came for,' I say, grimly.

'No, the tree,' she says, mesmerised.

'Impossible, isn't it?'

'It reminds me . . .' She trails off, going into that frustrating dreamlike reverie again. 'It's like the Tree of Life at Aistra.'

I feel the shudder pass through each of us.

'What do you mean?' Ris asks, steadying the helm.

'There must be a source of great power beneath the Maelstrom,' Hanan says, her voice distant. She's staring fiercely at the tree, wind whipping her streaked silver and black hair. 'Take root where the sea meets the sky.' Her eyes light up. 'It's here! Paranish, I think it's really here!'

We don't have time to question her riddles. Everything is drawn to the Maelstrom, the water churning, to the dark glass heart of the vortex. Not many sailors get to look at the Lahon Maelstrom and survive. I'm the only one who's dared to look twice. And to make it to the other side? Unheard of. I try to push away the memory of the previous voyage, of Larkin. I reach for Ris, needing to feel her solidity. She squeezes my hand as if she knows what I'm thinking.

'We're doing this together,' she says.

'I've got you,' I reassure her.

The deep whirling pit is a blue hole, a deep chasm that looks like the end of the world. I stare into the jaws of it, my entire being wanting to fall into it. There's an unearthliness about it, something unreal. By turns it undulates and seethes, a drawing in and exhalation like breathing or sometimes screaming.

'How is it possible?' Isagani asks, leaning over the balustrade.

We are caught in the strange softness as we stand aloft. Everything on course, smooth sailing, wind at our backs, a peaceful bliss as birds pass through the skies overhead. Nothing to indicate we would be on the edge of our destiny. Currents gently but firmly wrap around the ship.

'Do you think we can navigate past those roots?' Ris asks, ever the pragmatist.

We had discussed the steps so many times, but now that we're here, I think we're fucked. I know a smuggler's reputation doesn't mean much, but I hope I can keep it together.

'It's an ancient strangler; those branches are thick beasts,' Hanan observes.

'We stick to the plan we discussed,' I say, addressing them all. 'Follow the Maelstrom, don't try to fight it. It will drag us in and we need to ride it round so we minimise damage to the ship. We'll keep using the bilge pump religiously to stop us taking on too much water. Anyone not needed above gets to the living quarters in the berth deck.'

'Fine,' Ris says, with a nod. The ship is creaking now, trying to stay on course while being seduced towards the centre of the Maelstrom.

Resistance is futile. We are being lulled on the gentle waves into that great pit. I scramble up to meet Ris at the helm, and we try to keep her steady. The others are frantically tying down loose necessaries and throwing everything else into the hold. Even though this is what we came for, it feels as though we've been snapped from a reverie, and all is chaos.

'Steady, crew!' I shout over the sound of the rushing waters, growing ever louder. 'We're going to approach side on and try to meet the whirlpool of the Maelstrom and glide through. We're not trying to fight the current here. It's going to be rough going, but I trust this ship, and I trust all of you.'

They're all listening now, but their eyes stray to the Lahon Maelstrom. The waters foam and bubble, marine life shunted into the twists of the vortex. Fish flail and jump up, only to disappear in a helpless gulp. A creature swallowing everything from below.

The whirlpool pulls us closer to its dark heart, and we stare into the abyss.

'We have nothing to lose now except our lives.'

Sinigang claws into the deck to steady himself. 'Well, some of us have been blessed with more than one.'

We all brace on the starboard side as the Maelstrom sweeps us up, leaning into the curve of the swirl. The world tilts and spirals. Like being in bed after too much palm wine. Stomach in knots and arms numb with exhaustion at the helm. Ris's strong hands over mine.

Screaming. Wait, not from us. Wild yawning. Deep. Something long dormant finally awakening. Hanan waves her arms at me. I turn and the tree is moving. I blink away the salt spray. No, it really is moving. The branches creak, and it shivers itself awake, vines snaking and looping around itself. It rustles its leaves: forest greens, autumn golds, and blush reds. Its colours dazzle and sparkle, stunning and warding us off. The tree groans. The ship vibrates. Wood calling to wood. Holy Aistra, it's like rowing up to someone on a boat of bones. No wonder the tree almost seems angry at our presence.

We can't take our eyes off it. It rises up, engulfing the skies and blotting out the sun. Stretching. She's a beauty. Almost kraken-like with its tendrils that curl and dance endlessly. It smashes against the water, brutal blows that ricochet and rock the ship. The branches attack us with such ferocity, we're deafened by it.

The ship pitches hard, and Ris is tossed from my side, landing with a sickening crunch against the mast. I yell for her, trying desperately to reach her, but the ship is still unstable. I turn my attention to the helm, where the undead Askew and Pearl were bodying. They're nowhere to be found, and in their place a pile of bones and viscera rolls around the deck. Their remains are joined by their fellow former crewmates and I recognise Big Red's crimson britches, still hanging on to a pelvis. The skeletons rattle around the deck, knocking everything loose and acting as perfect obstacles for us remaining crew as we try to stay steady on our feet.

Hanan grasps Raina close, back in her trusty sling. Sinigang peeks from the opening of Isagani's top as the poor thing grips Biba's hand.

Fuck. It's time to fly or die.

I scream as we go down into the abyss. I'll confess I also piss myself. The water is a shock to the system. It clenches my heart and my throat and Paranish, I don't even know if we can all swim. *Saltswept* goes under slowly, like dropping a pebble in a lake. It's so smooth, a gentle caress after the noise and chaos.

Air. I have to have air. I don't even see the others. I'm flailing, swimming, treading water frantically. I have to slow down. You know where's the worst place to have a panic attack? Underwater. At least the cold soothes my anxiety, cooling me down. I kick and pump my arms. But which way is up? I follow the light, which is usually a good shout. Unless it's a trick, false light reflected in a cave. I'll take my chances. Either I'll find the surface, or I won't. If there even is a surface down here.

It is a light, but not sunlight. It pulses, and I startle back. Last thing I need is to get stung by a jelly. My body itches and swells just thinking about it. The light pulses again, radiant. Then I see *Saltswept*. Oh, my love, you were a treasure. She's dashed to bits, no good but for scuttling. She's already disappearing from view, silt and debris obscuring my last look at her. Fool. Forget the ship, where in brine are your family?

The light fizzles out, just for a moment. Then it sighs awake again, and I follow it, a man on his last lungful of air. I've trained my lungs but they're burning, involuntarily trying to choke down water. I reach out and feel flesh. It's Hanan, hair around her like a halo. She pulls me closer and – kisses me. Wait, it's more explosive. She pushes air insistently into my mouth. Paranish, is she helping me breathe? Now that I have something in the keg, I see she's holding Biba and Raina, although the kids look passed out. Are they breathing? Fuck, we have to get them breathing. I try to prise them away, but Hanan shakes her head. She is holding Biba's hand, and their palms are glowing. Raina's face shines like bioluminescence. It's like they are clutching the sun between them. My lungs are still burning, but it's a dull ache. As if the pain is distant, nothing to do with me. Then I see Biba is asleep. There's something happening here I don't understand. A powerful magic beyond anything I've seen. I won't question it. Just get us out of here.

I try to speak and get salt water for my trouble. But Hanan understands me. *Where are the others?*

She drags us, an awkward bundle of limbs floating together. I see Isagani and Sinigang struggling with Ris's unmoving body. The otter-cat yowls fiercely at us. How can he do that underwater? He swims quickly over, and we haul together. Hanan isn't using her eyes, but something else to guide us. She moves us with purpose and Sinigang follows confidently.

I gasp monstrously into the air pocket. Breathing here for the first time feels like being reborn, like I'm being eaten from the inside out. Everything hurts, and I think I'm dying. We flop onto the hard surface. It could be rock, or the queen's own bed for all I know. All I care is that there is oxygen, and my limbs feel like the weight of Paranish is crushing them. Eventually I crawl towards the other wet bodies, feeling and counting with my hands before my eyes. Wet matted fur. Lean strong leg. Soft doughy arms. Slender bony wrist. Cold smooth face. My crew. I scramble to my knees, dragging myself over to her.

'Ris, can you hear me?'

Her lips are the colour of the ocean. She isn't breathing. Her heart flutters, barely there. I pinch her nose and breathe air into her lungs.

'You need to compress her chest, like this,' Hanan says, moving to my side. She demonstrates, interweaving her fingers and miming pushing down on her chest. It's deeper than I expected.

'Continuous motions, like this.'

'What if I break a rib?'

'She's already beat up from that fall,' Isagani says quietly, voice so raspy I don't recognise it for a moment.

'What if you save her life?' Hanan says, looking into my eyes.

We all sit panting, no one daring to move or look away. I push down hard on Ris's chest. Three short sharp compressions and a silent hope, over and over again. Please don't leave. Please don't leave. Please don't leave.

CHAPTER FIFTY-FOUR

RIS

I JOLT AWAKE AND CLEAR my airways all over Finlyr's breeches. I'm coughing and spluttering, but he doesn't care. He holds me close, squeezing me so tight I think he might shatter me. I start to cry, even though it hurts and my breath comes out ragged.

'My ribs,' I wheeze, pushing Finlyr away, my breathing shallow and laboured. 'I can't breathe.'

'Oh fuck,' Hanan says, and the air stills around us. I think it's the first time I've heard the priestess swear.

Hanan pushes the rest of them out of the way, with more force than I thought possible. She's at my side, hands on my chest. I start to prise her hands away, and then I realise she's feeling under the flesh for the bones. Feeling for the breaks in my ribcage.

'Breathe slowly, look at me,' she instructs, and I stare at her, trying to stop her image from swimming. 'Biba, would you come here please?'

Biba looks surprised to be addressed and makes her way to my side.

'You can help,' Hanan insists.

I still can't speak but I reach out a hand to touch Biba's cheek, to let her know it's all right.

'Think of a tree branch split in the middle,' Hanan instructs. 'Do you see the crack, Biba?'

Biba focuses on Hanan and then nods, placing her hands with Hanan's guidance on my ribs as well.

'Imagine the tree is clay. Can you do that?' Hanan continues.

Biba scrunches her face and nods again.

'Now you are patching the split, smoothing the clay so it fits back together.'

Biba and Hanan move their hands, fingers pinching and moulding the invisible branch.

'It's not completely the same. It will be closer in time. But for now, it will hold. The sharp edges are smoothed, and the branch is strong enough.'

'Grow, grow,' Biba wishes quietly, almost to herself.

There's something in Hanan's voice, like a spell that guides us all. We relax, our bodies unclenching, limbs going limp. All in a rush, I feel so weak.

I can breathe then, the pain lingering but the sharpness is dulled. While my body becomes mush, there's nothing to do but take in our surroundings at last. We're in a cave, full dark, little light save the otherworldly glow that still emanates from Hanan, Biba, and Raina. The golden threads of this glowing reach out, like tendrils of a plant towards the rest of us. Only Sinigang is not sprawled on the floor. He sits upright, staring at the healing, tail swishing back and forth, keeping time.

I lie on my back and rest my head on the rock bed. At first I mistake it for the night's sky, stars above me. Then I recognise them as spiky stalactites threatening to drop on our heads, with glowwormslike pinpricks of stars on the cave's ceiling.

'Thank you,' I croak out.

'You're welcome. But it wasn't me. There's a power down here. I helped Biba and Raina channel it to fix your ribs.'

'A power? What kind of power?'

'I don't know exactly, but it's stronger than anything I've felt before.'

'What in Paranish was that?' I hear Finlyr ask, his voice barely recognisable in the echo.

A shuddering in the distance, and the rock begins to shake beneath our feet. Overhead, the stalactites wobble and crack.

'Move!' I shout, grabbing Biba. I shield her with my body, making us as small as possible against a rock. Silt in our lungs. There's grit in my eyes. A cloud of dust. A fearsome splash as the rocks hit the water. Desperate, incoherent screaming and imploring. When we stir, the air is thick and indistinct. A pile of rocks has fallen in on itself, an immovable solid wall in the narrowing of the cave.

I get up tentatively, my body tender. It takes a moment for my limbs to come together, like grasping for boots under my bed.

The cave hums around us. Hanan stills, standing slowly, like she's trying not to disturb a slumbering creature.

Once the dust settles, I realise what's happened. We assess the damage, speaking in close quiet whispers, reaching for each other through the filth. The cave seems to hum, strange echoes and our voices ricocheting off the walls. The air is rotten and close, clinging to the sides of my throat. I kneel to a gap in the rockfall and try to see through to the other side. It's incoherent gloom.

'Ris?' Finlyr's voice is distant, like when you're both underwater. It's indistinct, muffled, strange.

'Are you hurt?' It's Isagani, their voice reedy and wavering.

'We're here,' I shout back and then cringe as the stones shake again with fury. Biba clutches at my arm. 'Is Sini with you?'

'One life down perhaps, but I'm here.'

Hanan wipes the dust from her face and hair. She checks baby Raina, who is miraculously unhurt. 'We've got Biba and Raina; they're all right.'

'We can't stay here,' Hanan says, slowly. 'We're going to run out of air, and I don't know if I can move the obstruction.'

My heartbeat is thundering in my ears, going faster than seems possible. It's drumming a boisterous jig in my chest. I feel like I've swallowed a bird and it's beating against the cage of my sore ribs. I breathe short, sharp gulps of air and Hanan grips my arms.

'What's happening?'

'I can't breathe.'

'Look at me,' she says, holding my face in her hands. I focus on her touch, and it calms me. 'We fixed your ribs but there's only so much we can do. It needs time, and healing is painful.'

'What should I do?' I ask, plaintive. I try to breathe slow and deep.

'Imagine cool water washing over you,' she guides me, voice low. 'Sink into it. It touches your wrists, your neck, your cheeks. You float, weightless, in a lake.'

Her hands are on the insides of my wrists now, my palms, drawing circles with her fingers. They are cold, almost a shock at first, but then it feels wonderful on my skin. We listen to my breathing. It's almost regular and slow. I look at her face as she listens to my breathing. Her eyes are feline, focused, and her lips are parted slightly.

'I hear a bird.'

We turn and see Biba standing in the entrance of a tunnel. It's so small, we hadn't noticed it before. It's just above the height of her and she's crouched, looking deeper underground.

'No, Biba, wait!'

It's too late. 'The birdy shows the way. There's light here; I can see it!'

Her voice echoes out as we run towards the tunnel, trying to grab at her dress as it disappears into the gloom.

CHAPTER FIFTY-FIVE

FINLYR

'ISAGANI,' I SAY, reaching for them in the darkness. They find my hand, and we breathe together, and I try not to cough through the foulness.

I listen as the rocks finally settle, muffled voices on the other side of the wall.

'Wait, where did they go?' Isagani asks, scrabbling at the rock.

'They must be looking for another way out,' I insist, hauling us to our feet. I scrutinise Isagani, checking their scratches and bruises. 'Are you hurt?'

Isagani shakes their head, wiping the dirt from their eyes. 'Let's look around.'

Sinigang scours the walls, limping. 'There's no telling where any of these passages lead, if they lead anywhere.'

'Will you be all right?' I ask Sinigang, gently taking his paw in my hand. I brush away the fur to see his skin better, although that's futile in this lack of light. There's a gloaming light under the dust, but the darkness flattens everything, distance impossible to tell without touch.

The otter-cat closes his eyes slowly, more weary than in pain. After a moment he raises his head, ears flicking.

'Do you hear that?' he asks, walking away and following something we can't sense.

I get low and follow. I can't hear what he hears, but the air is less foul. It's almost bittersweet, something I can't quite place. It's fresher, a memory of something warm, something alive.

'What do you hear?' Isagani asks quietly.

'A song,' Sinigang says. His pupils are dilated, and he straightens up, walking with purpose, limp entirely gone. He pads over to the edge of the pool.

'Please don't tell me you're proposing going back in there?' I ask, staring into the dark abyss. Some of the fallen stalactites float on the surface. 'That cave almost cost us our lives.'

'You forget, I'm part otter,' Sinigang says calmly.

'Yes, but you don't have gills,' I snap back.

'I can hold my breath four times longer than you humans.'

'That's very helpful for us,' Isagani mutters.

'If you ask nicely I'll share my air,' Sinigang grins.

'Can you stop fucking around?' I say through gritted teeth.

'I'm not,' Sinigang says, his eyes glinting in the half-light. 'We can't help the others. We have to try and find our own way out of here. This is the only way I can sense.'

'It's black as night down there,' I insist. 'Full dark, freezing cold. Kick up silt and you're dead.'

'What do we follow then?' Isagani asks, worrying the inside of their cheek. 'We could swim in circles in the dark until we run out of air.'

Sinigang stills his swishing tail and nods. 'Hold our breath and follow the song. I'll lead and help as best I can.'

I sigh, and the sound echoes a little, showing me how small our space — and therefore air supply — truly is.

'What do you want to do, Isagani?'

Isagani kneels by the pool, looking at their hazy reflection in the water. Bioluminescent creatures swim in the water, and glow worms make their homes in the rock holes.

'We can't stay here forever,' they say with a decided tone. 'When I said I wanted an adventure, I didn't think I would live long enough for the terror to set in.'

We take the plunge, Sinigang leading down into the gloaming. I open my eyes to salt water and brace, squinting to follow the otter-cat, lithe in the water, a dark mound of undulating fur and bubbles. Isagani and I hold hands, despite how awkward it is while swimming. I won't lose that kid. I won't lose any of them.

The seabed is littered with giant clams. I try not to stray too close as they open their jaws, exposing their fleshy insides, supremely yonic in their look.

Then I spot it. Within the clam, large milky ridged spheres. Pearls. I see Isagani, mesmerised. We drift towards it, the clam's stream of bubbles enveloping us. We could trade these for comfort, protection. A soft and easy life. Isagani reaches out their hand, not with the feather touch of a fingersmith, but of a curious child, who will only be placated by just a little touch. The clam's jaws snap shut, and Isagani startles back. I drag them away and Sinigang is waiting, irritated. He blows an air bubble into the water, and it grows, enveloping our heads. We gasp in lungfuls of air. It's stale and fishy but I'll take anything.

'I had no idea otter-cats could do that,' Isagani says.

'We keep our secrets close. Careful, it will only last a short while,' Sinigang warns.

As we dive further, I start to make out the sound Sinigang caught on the surface. It's a chittering punctuated by humming and an ethereal whisper. It pulses, sending ripples through water. My muscles spasm, and my bones vibrate with the sound. It's not wholly unpleasant, my body tingling like my lips after a spicy broth. It's as though bees are in my head, and I follow it down, through the maw of caverns and blue holes. The resonance frequency feels as though it's crushing my ribs down onto my lungs. It may be the underwater pressure, but my muscles are enlivened and abused by it, pulses sharp and bright in my whole being.

Large dark shapes move in the water below us – flying, writhing masses. They hum, deep throbbing sounds that rattle my bones.

I kick desperately upwards, trying to find the water's surface. Wet mulch, slippery to the touch. It's in my eyes and mouth. Like hot wax sinking into my face. There's a milky froth, like dirty sea foam. I push, feeling the squelch of something giving way. Then we emerge into an air bubble, and I'm gasping and hacking mulch. I grab for the floating mass beside me.

'Don't touch it,' Sinigang warns, paddling to my side.

I let go of the mass and it floats away.

'What is that?' Isagani asks, treading water close by.

'The drowned dead can weigh you down,' Sinigang warns. 'Don't join their multitude.'

We haul ourselves out onto a narrow ledge nearby, collapsing with the effort of it, the glow worms our only company. I think about our undead crew, only bones now, and how easily we could become one of the dead. I slow my breathing, thinking of the limited air supply, even here, everywhere in these caves. Sinigang might be able to help us in the water, but it is a reusing of an existing supply.

'What were all those dark shapes down there?' Isagani eventually asks.

Sinigang shudders. 'Understand this: the ocean is a bath full of monsters.'

Isagani grunts, then raises their head. 'What did we follow? Will it lead us to the treasure?'

I'm in too much pain to hope. Life itself feels like a treasure at this point. My only hope is that we can find the others and get out of here.

I lie on my back for a moment longer. Ice shards threaten overhead. No, not ice — crystals, precious and sharp as daggers. I shudder to think of the stalactites and the cave collapse. That was a narrow escape. The song gets louder now we're out of the water. It takes on a melody, dissonant and melancholic. It's haunting, lapping over itself, repeating, echoing and harmonising. My limbs are heavy, and I'm rooted to the spot. There's a spasm in my heart, a tugging at the muscle, like a cramp or a seizure. I cry out, the sound cutting through the song.

The singing stops, and Isagani and I slowly crawl up onto our knees. Sinigang drags us up by the damp clothing sticking to our skin. He gives us a, perhaps deliberate, nip to check we still have life in our limbs.

Sinigang's ears perk up, fur standing on end as he arches his back.

I follow his gaze to something in the middle of the cavern. It opens its arms, no, its wingspan, feathers fluttering in the movement. Gold and reds, and colours I can't name, couldn't see before. The beast is as tall as the cavern, as though it has grown to fill the space. Its eyes are huge and terrified, the pupils darting between each of us in turn.

'What is that thing?' I ask, unable to tear my eyes away.

It opens its throat, and the wailing song pours out. It's the sound of my heart tugging at my breastbone, a thousand hurts and hopes tangled like a ball of wool. The song pulls each out slowly, dragging me forwards towards the creature. The bird wraps its mighty wings around an egg in the centre of collected detritus. It turns its face away from us and sings to the egg, now a gentle and soporific tune. No, not an egg. Something curled into a ball, fast asleep in its feathers. A small girl in a tattered dress and one shoe, dark hair strewn over its talons: Biba.

CHAPTER FIFTY-SIX

HANAN

Ris holds the empty air, as if willing Biba back into her grasp. She pauses, still as stone for a moment, and I scour the dark maw of the cave. In the distance we hear Biba's laugh, uncanny and distorted. It's followed by a song: not the bright rhymes of a child but a plaintive, otherworldly tune. It reminds me of the chants and recitations we would offer in the Temple of Aistra.

When she hears it, Ris drops to her belly and worms her way into the tunnel on her elbows. I grab her ankles and haul her out.

Her face is caked with mud, eyes ablaze. 'Biba's gone down there. I'm not leaving her.'

'You'll get trapped. You're not as small as she is.'

'I'm not leaving her,' she repeats stubbornly.

'Then let's find another tunnel. One big enough for all of us.' I look pointedly down at Raina. She is suckling quietly on my dress. My breasts are sore and heavy, and I feel something leaking from my nipples. My body feels stronger down here, how I feel on a good day when my muscles aren't screaming at me. I'll need to feed Raina at some point soon, and I think I can this time.

'Paranish, we brought three children down here to die,' Ris says, slumping against the wall with horror in her eyes.

'No one's dying today,' I say, with more faith in my voice than in my heart. 'I've destroyed enough lives.'

I take her hand and guide her away from the tunnel. We move into another passage, seeing with our hands and feet, wary of sudden drops and false tunnels. I try to breathe slow and steady, if nothing but to set a good example. I want everyone calm. I can't have her panicking as she did in the collapse. That would spell ruin for us all. And if I panic, Raina might panic.

'What happened to you?' Ris says after a time.

'The worst thing that can happen to someone like me. They bound me.'

'What does that mean?' she asks tentatively. There's a curiosity there, and a dread. We can't see each other, using touch as our only guide, and there's something about the darkness that makes us both more bold.

'It locks your power within you,' I say. 'You can't use your gift. You're an ordinary mortal with no protection from illness or injury. You can't channel life force.'

I can feel Ris stiffen with shock and then squeeze my hand.

'But what you did to fix my ribs, wasn't that magic?'

'Not my magic. There's an energy down here.'

I lead, inching forward painfully slowly. We scrape our skin and bruise our knees on the sharp, unforgiving rocks in a tight crevice. The air coming in is foul, and I swallow down the bile, hot and acid and in my throat. *Breathe. You must breathe.* I think of bad air. There's nowhere else to go. We wriggle through to the next passage and come out into a bigger chamber. There's more air, but it's as acrid as before. How long has it been trapped down here? Ris emerges next to me, clearing her eyes and gasping. There's more light here, a gloomy kind to see by, but being able to see her again is reassuring.

'Are you hurt?' I ask. She's scratched and banged up but doesn't look too bad considering she's broader and taller than I am.

'No. You?'

I bite down pain radiating from my arm. She notices my wince. 'Your arm, what's wrong?'

'I contorted my wrist going through the tunnel,' I say, examining the awkward angle of my hand.

'Oh Paranish, what should we do?'

I try to keep my voice level. 'We must keep going.'

'Can you make it?'

I ignore her question as I unwrap the sling and give Raina some fresh water from the pouch around my waist. She spits it up. Oh, my girl, I've taken all the softness from your life.

'I need to feed her,' I tell Ris.

Ris lets out a frustrated noise but stops when she hears her own breathlessness.

'We need to conserve air and move deliberately, as well as quickly,' I say.

'All right, we can rest for a moment,' she concedes.

When I don't move, she asks, 'What's wrong?'

'I . . . need you to see this,' I take Raina and cradle her in my arms.

Ris looks at me warily as I unlace my gown and bring Raina to my breast. For a moment I doubt the energy I've felt in the cave. Perhaps I'm wrong, and I can't feed her anymore. My mind begins to reel. Biba was able to placate Raina for a time, but without her here now, I don't know how long she'll survive without nutrients.

Raina latches on and feeds deeply, even more greedy than back at the Bastion, before I was bound. It feels different, too. Perhaps she's taking from this energy source in the same way. Those teeth are just as sharp, and I wince. When the princess is sated, she pulls away, her lips painted by that same dark mixture of crimson and green.

'What is that?' Ris asks, wide-eyed and pushing away from me.

'She needs to feed, or she'll die. They all do.'

'Who? What are you talking about?'

'The royals,' I say, trying to keep my voice even. I look down at Raina, stroking the peach fuzz of her soft cheek. 'I saved her. She's more mine now than theirs.'

'What do you mean? Isn't Raina your daughter?'

'She's the queen's,' I confess, wiping blood and mulch from the child's mouth.

Ris looks down at the baby. 'That's the princess?'

I nod.

Ris's face contorts in a flash of anger, then hurt. 'What else have you been lying about?'

'I only did it to protect us. You're on a quest for the queen, sailing under the royal sigil. I didn't know if I could trust you,' I insist. 'Wouldn't you do anything to protect your child?'

Ris stares at Raina as though she is an abomination. 'Is that what they teach you at the temple? To suckle monsters?'

I close my eyes slowly. 'The priestess is at the mercy of the Bastion, to be used any way they see fit.'

'Did the queen do that to you?' Ris asks, indicating my arms, the scars barely visible even as our eyes adjust to the darkness of the cave.

'No, I did,' I admit.

'Why?' she asks, horrified.

'I wanted to practise healing,' I say, placidly.

She looks appalled. 'And this too?'

She points to the royal brand on my thigh, visible through a rip in my dress. The outline of the brand is glowing as though it is white-hot.

'It hasn't looked like that since the day she marked me. It happened the first time the queen fed from me.'

'That's disgusting.'

'I'm a possession to her – that's all,' I say.

The song penetrates through the cave again, the strange plaintive chanting Biba followed. It feels much closer as we stare into the murk. My heart constricts, and my muscles tense and weaken under my skin. It pulls me forward, like an invisible thread I can't help but follow. Raina moves her head towards the sound too and burbles, as though she also wants it.

'Where do we go now?' Ris asks as I secure Raina back around my body.

'Biba followed the song. Our best chance of finding her is to do the same. It's closer now.'

'What do you think is singing?' Ris asks.

'I think we're getting closer to the source of energy.'

We stare hard into the space in front of us. This place is a labyrinth, and we only have the song to guide us. The cave is eerily still as we listen to the strange melody and trace it into the darkness.

I listen to the rise and fall of Ris's chest, wondering how her ribs feel, if they're healing well. My hands are shaking. We lean against the wall, trying to keep as still as possible. The glow from my mark emanates around the cave now, pulsing brighter in time with my frantic heartbeat.

'Is that a ledge?' Ris asks, so close to me I can feel the heat of her breath as she approaches.

'I think so,' I say, feeling the jutting rock.

'Do you think you can get up, with your arm?'

'No,' I say, examining my injury.

'All right. I think I can get some purchase; help me up?'

Ris pushes off my shoulder with her hands to grip the ledge. Her legs flail for footholds, and I shove her behind, giving her a final boost. She heaves herself up and over.

'Hand me Raina,' she says, leaning over the side of the ledge.

The princess wails in confusion as I hand the sling up to Ris. My body rebels as I try to pull myself onto the rock ledge, the method awkward as I try to protect my hurt arm. Holy Aistra, I'm transported for a moment back to that desperate time in the ocean after my expulsion.

'Help me,' I call to Ris, and she grips my arms. I cry out as she pulls on my sore wrist.

'Find a foothold,' she grunts, trying to haul me up. 'Or I'll dislocate your shoulder.'

I lean into the wall and balance on the ridges of the rock with my toes.

'That's it.' She heaves, scraping me up the side of the wall until I can crawl.

My body feels like one open wound, every movement a hurt. It is a pain that comes fast and fresh, stinging and then subsiding. We pant as we feel around for the way to go next. Voices in the distance. It's the song, but mixed with something else – human, familiar.

Ris stops and listens. 'It's them!'

She takes off urgently in the direction of the sound, disappearing into the darkness ahead.

'Ris, wait! Be careful!' My words are futile as I try to follow, my good hand tracing the whorls of the royal brand that glows like a torch. I have no choice but to be guided to whatever lies beyond.

CHAPTER FIFTY-SEVEN

FINLYR

Biba wakes gently, slowly stretching from her bed in the middle of the nest. She turns sleepily to me, her skin covered in a pale sheen, like polish.

'Fin,' Biba says. 'Adarna says we should stay here, together.'

I try to stay still, to keep my body language calm, while I eye the bird. It's watching us, wings fluttering nervously. 'Everything's going to be all right, Biba.'

I look around, desperate to find a way to her. There are strange statues in the chamber. Like Seaguardians, all dressed in white. They are posed dynamically: some cowering, curled over in a ball, others with their arms up, ready to strike. I blink rapidly, trying to capture their faces. A sculptor of great talent, to render their horror and terror so accurately.

Fool, fool. I slap my face hard, trying to stay awake. I look again. *Those are not statues – you know what they truly are. Look again. See your predecessors. The ones who forged the trail. Who disappeared in pursuit of their heart's desire. Thieves. Liars. Desperate outcasts. They were once like you. Everything dies. But to die like this, preserved in that final moment, looking upon your beast, your hope, your treasure. To have your voice ripped from your throat, stolen to lure in the next victims.*

I look back at Biba. That pale sheen, as if covered in clay, which might crack at any moment. She's becoming like them, turning to stone slowly. She looks dreamy, as if in a reverie, her eyelids and limbs heavy.

'Fin, what are you doing? Get back!' Isagani yells at me, hiding behind one of the stone victims.

Adarna rises up, beating its wings. The nest is disturbed, feathers and bone and dust in a whirlwind. Biba covers her eyes. I put my head to the cavern floor. Adarna shrieks, the song intensifying in my head. The creature is at its full height now, blocking the shards of light that filter through from the roof of the cave. I dare to look. Its eyes are wild and frenzied as they meet mine, its voice penetrating my brain. It's an unholy medley of human voices, a mass of prey. I bash the side of my skull with my hand, trying to shake it off. It's like trying to fight the waves. It's pulling myself out of a mudslide. All I want to do is succumb. My limbs are stiffening, unyielding despite the force pulling me closer, closer. I move awkwardly and then I'm on my knees. My hand tries for my dagger. Of course it's gone, long ago. With the wreck of *Saltswept* and all our worldly possessions. At least I have my body. I try to raise my arms, to prepare my hands for fists. The fingers curl reluctantly, and I wonder if I can hear the bones crack.

Sinigang hisses close to my ear, and I feel the otter-cat sink his claws into my arm. I scream, and the pain is a welcome reminder that I'm still made of flesh, not quite yet dead. Adarna's spell is weakened for a moment, and I feel in control of myself.

'Don't listen to it, Fin,' Sinigang says, dragging me behind one of the statues. 'The others are close, I can smell them. We have to hold on.'

Fin, where did you go?

I can't resist snatching a glance at Biba, but she's falling asleep again, swaying with the rhythm of the song. The voice is coming from the bird, and it splits straight into my skull.

Look at me!

The voice isn't Biba's now but Larkin's. His voice is thick, crying out for me.

Fin! Please, help me!

I close my eyes and dig my palms into the stone of the statue, willing the voice to disappear. How does Adarna know what he said?

It's like I feel the salt spray on me again, but it's a cold sweat on my neck and back. My stomach roils as if remembering him falling overboard, the desperate clawing at the rope. The rest of the crew acted more quickly than I did. I was frozen in shock until the protocol set in: turn the boat and slowly approach. I went as close as we could, anchoring into nothing as the Maelstrom tried to pull us into its orbit. He had the rope, I could see the relief on his face. And then he was gone, and we were hauling in empty.

'Captain, what should we do?' one of the other crew members asked, eyes wild with fear.

We were reaching the abort point, and everything in my body rebelled from the eye of the Maelstrom.

'He's gone, man. We're changing course!'

My priority had to be getting out of there. The ship was already beginning to be ripped apart by the wind. We needed to get downwind. Anything to escape the vortex before us.

You let me die. You took everything from me, but you can never replace me. She would never choose you.

The piercing voice of Adarna mocking Larkin comes back afresh, crushing my skull like a vice. I feel sick to my stomach, the remembrance of Ris's touch on my skin. The earthy smell of her against me, the feel of her fingers in my hair. Her laugh, low and warm.

You can't make me hate myself any more, I tell Adarna. I focus on the thought, like a prayer. I think of everyone I've ever hurt and let the guilt and shame get swept away by the current. I keep my eyes closed and reach out for Isagani, and they grip my hand. Sinigang is in my lap, saying something. But all I feel is the warmth of him. I hold on to the heat of them, forcing my breathing to slow, flexing my muscles to remind myself that my body is still mine.

CHAPTER FIFTY-EIGHT

RIS

I CRAWL OUT INTO an open cavern, and it's like I know what breathing feels like again. The light filters through here, illuminating a huge nest in the centre of the cave. A massive bird sits on the mound of rags and bones, spreading its colourful wings. The feathers catch the light from an opening in the cavern vault, dancing and making me dizzy. It has the bulk and heft of a bird of prey, and its large curved beak is stained with old blood. By its talons in the middle of the nest is Biba, so small and sound asleep.

'Ris, where are you?' Hanan says in a panic as she emerges from the crevice.

'I told you they were close,' comes Sinigang's melted-butter voice, and I see him detach himself from the darkness. 'Get behind this.'

'That thing has Biba!' I whisper through gritted teeth.

'We're going to get her, I promise,' Finlyr insists, emerging from behind a rocky pillar.

'I thought you were gone,' Isagani cries.

I pull them close until I think we might all meld together.

Finlyr smells of sweat, salt water, and fear. I reach for his hand but it's cold and stiff, and I see tiny teeth marks on his arms. 'What happened?'

'I'm sorry Ris. I tried to get to her, but—' Finlyr says, eyes meeting mine.

'We'll rescue her, Fin,' I tell him surveying the approach to Biba in the bird's nest.

'Did Adarna do that?' Hanan asks, pointing at Finlyr's strange skin.

'Who?' I ask, turning to Hanan, who hovers awkwardly at the edge of the group.

'The bird, Adarna. Her Majesty's Desire.' We all look at her and her face becomes strained. 'Holy Aistra, this is what you came for.'

Hanan winces in pain and clutches her thigh. She leans against the rock pillar and pulls up her skirt. She meets my eye. 'It burns, Ris.'

I examine her mark gently. 'What should we do?'

'Don't let her have it. If she wants Adarna, it's dangerous. She'll use any power she can get,' Hanan insists. She pulls me close to her. 'She wants to use the dead.'

The mark burns brighter, like embers in a fire, and illuminates the cave around us. I notice the stone we're crouching behind. There's something unnatural about it, like it's sculpted.

'What is that?' I ask, standing up and examining the rock.

'What are you doing? Adarna will see you,' Sinigang hisses, clawing at my clothes.

It's not a stone carved by nature. It's a statue of a human figure. I look at its hands, held up in surrender. I focus on its face, to find some hope of peace, of finality, as I crawl towards the same fate. It feels familiar. There's such fear and loneliness there. I look closely, trying to breathe colour and life into the figure.

Oh, my love. It can't be.

'Not statues,' I whisper. 'Sailors.'

It's him. Larkin.

I touch his face. Or the sign and semblance of it. I move close, as close as I can, putting my body against him. He's so cold, it's disgusting when I feel him on my skin, but I won't flinch. I've wanted this for so long. I've had dreams of him returning to me, crawling out of the sea and straight into my arms. Made of shell, of seaweed, barnacles, and driftwood. He would become human again as we touched, and when I kissed him, he would pour out the salt water. It would leave his body, and his mouth would be clear for him to say my name.

'He didn't drown,' Finlyr says quietly. 'I'm sorry, Ris. I had no idea he'd made it down here.'

When Larkin left for that last voyage, he sang an old sailor ditty, rocking baby Biba in his arms:

> 'Come, little one, it's time to part
> The waves lull you asleep
> Behold the beating of my heart
> Forever yours to keep'

He placed a kiss on her forehead as he lay her down. There is a moment when every guardian will put down a child and perhaps never hold them again. We didn't know that was the last time.

'It's not your fault, Fin,' I tell him, turning away from Larkin. I cup Finlyr's face in my hands and kiss him. His lips are cold and unmoving.

Adarna begins to sing again: a cacophony that vibrates around the cave. I can feel myself slipping under. I have my answers, a cold comfort. I fall to my knees, the pain of the rocks cutting through my skin a welcome relief.

'Ris, stay with me,' Finlyr says distantly. He's beside me, trying to keep me upright, supporting my weight. He says my name over and over again, and I can barely feel the tears sliding down my cheek.

I think about Biba, so close, and yet it feels like she could be back in Paranish. I can't close the distance, no matter how much I will my limbs to move, to make their way to her. I have failed her again, as

I have done so many times since she came into this world. I regret every moment I couldn't protect her, especially from my own fear. It's no use though. I slip away, limbs tightening, will bending to that of the bird's song: *Wouldn't it be sweeter to sleep?*

I watch the skin of my arms take on a strange sheen, pale and smooth and unyielding. It's cold to the touch, and I feel no sensation. There's Larkin's stone form; shock and despondency etched on his face. To be reunited simply to atrophy from the outside to our cores. I can't believe we've made it this far only to fail now. It's so close I can almost taste freedom. All my schemes and sacrifices to keep Biba safe were for nothing.

CHAPTER FIFTY-NINE

HANAN

PRIESTESS SINAYA'S SQUANDERED GIFT. The queen's heart's desire. I suspected as much when I saw the tree above the Maelstrom, and now I'm certain. I stare at the bird – *Adarna* it tells me in my head, voice piercing behind my eyes.

A creature that can turn flesh to stone has so much potential for chaos. I look to the bird as it sings its death chant, luring us to give up, to give in. It's a voice that tells us that succumbing is the easiest. It would be so sweet to close our eyes, to let our minds smooth and melt to a puddle. It would be as peaceful as slipping into sleep. One moment, flesh. The next, stone.

When I can finally pull my gaze away from the bird, my body resists movement. The others are stiffening, flesh turning to stone faster than before. Ris leans against me as we stagger for protection behind the rock figure. From their conversation I deduced this had been someone important to her once, and to Finlyr also. Biba's father, if I had to guess. There will be time to mourn the dead, but we must move if we hope to stay among the living.

'Fin,' Ris whispers as I examine her, measuring the extent of the turning.

Finlyr is worst of all. His arms are marble-veined, meeting from hand and shoulder at a point around the bicep with four small bleeding holes.

'What is that?' I ask, turning his arm carefully.

'That is my doing,' Sinigang admits.

Adarna shrieks, and Biba slowly opens her eyes and stretches. The bird scoops up Biba with its wings, and the girl grips hard onto its feathered breast. It beats its wings, and we duck as nest debris comes flying towards us. Feathers and swords and glass bottles. Detritus collected from its victims over the years.

We throw ourselves behind the statues, our bodies rebelling against the movements. A bottle smashes against one of them, glass raining down on us. There's a huge gash on my leg. I examine the cut: it's an angry red, deep and bloody. Everything's stopped. There's silence. Blissful blessed silence. The pain of the cut, the smell of the blood. Just like practising healing at Aistra. I grab another shard of glass and slice my skin.

Sinigang watches me. 'What are you doing?'

'Pain helps,' I gasp out through cuts.

Sinigang nods and then lunges for Finlyr. He yells and jerks back as the otter-cat sinks his teeth into the skin and releases. Blood seeps into the ragged torn shoulder of his shirt. He can't take his eyes off the wound, pulsating rhythmically.

'Why the fuck did you do that?' he shouts.

'You have to bleed,' Sinigang insists, extending his claws.

'Drown out the song,' I say, showing him the gash on my leg. 'Pain reminds you you're alive.'

'You never heard of cat-scratch fever?' he demurs. 'Get Ris, we need to get Biba back!'

The pain has quietened the song, and I can finally hear myself think. Adarna can turn flesh to stone, draining the life out of us. It feeds on our energy, just like the queen and Raina when they fed on me. I understand why she wants the bird home. A priestess is a conduit for the energy across all Paranishian life forms; a private feast for the royals. Adarna would be even more powerful and wouldn't burn out like the priestesses. The ultimate power over Life and Death. It would be the ruin of us all. I can't let her have it.

'You must hurt yourself; that's the only way we survive this,' I insist, as Ris stares at me helplessly. She's too rigid to move. I crawl over to her, the brand on my thigh burning, the flesh outlined like a rash. Like Finlyr's shoulder where Sinigang bit him. I have an idea, and instead of bringing the blade to her skin, I press the brand against her, my thigh against hers. A scorching, searing pain radiates across my body, and I hear a muffled cry from Ris. Then the stone is receding, flesh warm and soft beneath mine. I hold us together as the cold rock leaves her body enough so she can move. I'm only holding back the tide, but if I can buy us more time we might have a chance.

'We have to get Biba,' she says as soon as she can.

'I've got an idea,' I tell her. 'We need to get to the bird, all right?'

She nods, grabbing at the others who are being corralled by Sinigang.

I think back to the times the queen drained me. To the powerlessness I felt in those moments. Life slowly ebbing away, flowing down into the void. I picture a waterfall, and I flip it in my mind. I reverse the flow of the life force, a trickle but there, nonetheless. My power is just out of reach, but I can latch on to Adarna's. I touch Raina's cheek, joining her to the energy chain.

'Follow me,' I yell as I charge towards the bird and jump. I latch on to its feathers, trying to find purchase as I yank some of them out.

'Hanan,' Ris shrieks, following in my wake.

She helps me onto the bird's mantle. Once I have my legs either side of it, I grab at the tufts by its nape for purchase.

Adarna bucks and screams, but it's no good. I tug back the power it drained. I focus my mind on its throat, imagining I could place my hands down its gullet and still its voice.

'We don't have much time. Get up here!' I command, and the others grab hold, Finlyr wrestling Biba from Adarna's loosening grip. Remnants of us atrophying from the outside in. The song has stopped finally, and I just have to hope the effects will reverse quicker than it can kill us. We pull them bodily onto the bird in a graceless tussle fought by sheer will.

'Punch a hole to the sky,' I command it.

Adarna sways its head to and fro, trying to resist. It flies around the cavern, smashing into rocks, sending its past victims toppling one after another. Soon there is nothing but fragments and dust clouds.

'No!' I hear Ris screaming beside me.

I grab her and hold her tight.

'You're mine,' I insist. 'Adarna, fly.'

Finally, Adarna shoots up to the roof of the cavern and doesn't stop. We yell, clutching on to the bird as it takes to the air. We're going so fast, the water doesn't have time to catch up with us. We blast right through, breaking the surface and breaching like a whale. We gasp, grit and sand and water sloughing off us. It shakes its feathers and beats its wings, shrieking into the daylight. It flicks water from its ears. I've never seen a bird's ear before. It's a strange little thing, a fleshy layered orifice. Adarna's voice echoes across the expanse of the water as it struggles to maintain height, a shrill chattering squawk.

My ears pop from the change in pressure. My blood feels like it's fizzing. The layers of stone crack and break, slipping off my skin and into the water. The Maelstrom churns beneath us, and the daylight is golden and blue, wisps of cloud moving gently across the sky. I didn't expect to survive this. My stomach roils as Adarna finds its course, and we hold on for dear life.

'Where are we going?' Ris yells.

Adarna dances deadly in swirls and acrobatics through the air, and we hold on, feathers fluttering in the breeze. It feels like the brief moment I inhabited the insect back at the Bastion library, being one with the mind of a creature that could take wing. The freedom to slough off my human form, floating weightless in the air propelled only by instinct.

Adarna's heart beats steadily as it flies with determination, and I can feel it pulse along my body. The others are just a thought in the back of my mind as I try to maintain a course, wind whipping my hair and face. It takes everything in my will to keep Adarna from bucking us off.

'Where is it going?' Finlyr asks.

The expanse of water that took weeks to traverse is visible below us, whipping by faster than I can see it. Paranish comes into view in the distance. I understand now the tales they tell children about the great otter-cat whose paw print marked our land: the pad and four digits of our isles. The hill, which houses the Bastion on the mainland. And then the four seasonal isles, with their distinct colours. "The winter storm; golds and reds of autumn; the clear blue waters of summer; and the verdant green of spring."

As we get closer, the bird dives lower, and we shriek to hold on.

Adarna descends rapidly through the clouds, and I shiver, the skin on my arms gooseflesh. We emerge through the cold current onto Aistra, and I only have a few moments to survey the temple before the bird lands, sending dirt and snowfall flying. The smell of scorched bark lingers in the air, and I hold back my nausea as my feet hit the ground. I run to the Tree, heedless of everyone and everything else.

The bark is blackened and burned, cracked through the centre like lightning has struck it. The earth where I lay is still disturbed, showing the remnants of my escape.

'What are you doing here?'

I turn and find Salvacion leaning against an archway. Her face is bruised and swollen, so much so that I recognise her initially by her Seaguardian uniform, which is torn and dishevelled.

'Salvacion?' I ask, approaching her. 'What happened?'

Her eyes are molten as she staggers towards me. 'How dare you return!'

I turn my body to shield Raina. Then Ris is between us, and Salvacion backs down, light and recognition flooding across her face, and she pulls Ris into an embrace.

'I never thought I'd see you again,' she says, then draws away with a groan, clutching her side. 'What in Aistra is that thing?' She indicates Adarna, eyeing it warily.

'A powerful weapon,' I say.

'You're hurt. What happened to you?' Ris asks, supporting Salvacion's weight.

'Why don't you ask the priestess?' Salvacion asks derisively.

'You two know each other?' I ask, bewildered.

'What does she mean, Hanan?' Ris stares at me, confused and afraid.

I look around at the scorched Tree, and the blood smeared on the stones of the temple. 'I don't know,' I say quietly. 'I don't know what happened after I left.'

'You weren't here to face her wrath,' Salvacion says, closing her eyes in pain.

'What did she do?' I ask, my voice brittle.

'She tried to burn the Tree. And when that didn't work, she demanded the Temple Mothers destroy it.'

'But they couldn't,' I whisper.

'It was like what happened with you and that Temple Sister.'

'Malostra.' Her name slips out before I'm conscious of it.

Salvacion nods. 'She . . . she had to feed.'

'Holy Aistra.' I clap my hand to my mouth and try to swallow the bile rising in my throat.

'Feed? What does she mean feed?' Finlyr asks, but his voice is distant and cold.

'She nearly killed so many of them, Hanan.' Salvacion's voice wavers. 'She took more back to the Bastion. I had to stop it. I tried to stop the Seaguardians but . . .'

'Her will is divine,' I say, the words ash on my tongue.

'There was a kid, not much older than Biba, on that last boat,' Salvacion says, holding my gaze.

At Biba's name, Ris looks towards her daughter. It breaks the spell the three of us have been under and I look around for the first time in an age, acknowledging the others.

Ris drops to her knees and beckons Biba. 'This is your aunt Salvacion.'

Biba approaches reluctantly. 'Aunt?'

'Your father was my brother,' Salvacion says, clearing her throat and extending a hand towards the kid.

'Is it only you left?' I ask.

'No, a few Temple Sisters remain and Mother Joca. They have been cloistered in prayer for days.'

'Take me to them.'

'Hanan, she needs a healer, look at her,' Ris insists.

'What happened?' Biba asks, cocking her head to the side to look at Salvacion closely.

Salvacion smiles weakly. 'I'm not sure. I got beaten pretty bad.'

'We'll get you patched up,' Finlyr says. 'There's got to be something here, right, Hanan?'

'Yes, there's a herb garden and apothecary supplies. I don't know how much remains intact.'

Adarna has taken an interest in the rookery, and I hear the squawking and chittering of the birds inside. Some terrible chaos has taken place in my absence, but Adarna seems soothed by the noise. It's feeding off the fear, its own type of dark energy. Sinigang prowls around Adarna, hissing. At first I start, thinking they are fighting to hunt in the rookery. But then I realise Sinigang is protecting the rookery. As the two creatures stare at each other, Adarna seems to relent slightly, tucking its wings under itself and lying down on the ground.

As the others disperse in pursuit of remedies for Salvacion, I make my way into the temple. The halls are eerily quiet, and with no lamps burning I make my way in the gloom by memory and touch more than sight. There is no open horror, but the unsettling sensation of things upturned, of nothing in its rightful place.

I find the acolytes in the heart of the temple, the inner sanctum where we prayed daily. Back when I believed miracles could only be something beautiful, in service of something divine. The stained-glass Bastion is shattered, with the shards swept clumsily to one side. The Sisters kneel in their triangles, with Mother Joca in the centre. My presence disrupts the energy, and they break.

'I told you not to disturb—' Mother Joca breaks off when she sees me, the colour draining from her face. 'By all the powers, it can't be!'

The anxiety flutters through the small group, and they clutch each other, as though I am some nightmare creature.

'Is that the princess?' Mother Joca begins, eyes wide and brow furrowed.

'She is under my care now,' I insist. 'If anyone tries to take her from me, I won't hesitate to kill them.'

'We don't mean her harm. It is a great relief to see she is alive and well.'

'I am sorry for the pain she inflicted because of me. I know you're scared. But now you've seen what the queen can do now, what she means to do with everyone.'

'She has taken what she needs,' Mother Joca says. 'She will leave us be.'

I stare at her. 'You think she will ever be satisfied? How many more people have to die by her hands?'

'That is the way of things: the royals have always had a priestess.'

'You think you are safe here cowering in the temple?'

There is a deathly silence.

'What are you talking about?' Nusi snaps, not even trying to disguise her disgust.

'I know you have no reason to listen to me after everything. But this will be everyone's terror eventually. She will burn through those girls she has taken because none of them are strong enough to give her what she needs.'

'And you are?' Mother Joca bristles.

'I helped her. She will take not only from the living but also from the dead.'

CHAPTER SIXTY

RIS

I NEVER THOUGHT I would be tending Salvacion's wounds, applying salve to her busted lip and a cold compress to her black eye. There's no revelling in her pain like I thought there might be. I survey the tinctures on the counter and Biba, Finlyr, and Isagani raiding the remaining unopened cupboards, unstoppering bottles and sniffing their contents.

'Ryla, Kopiro, and Vullis did this for me after the last time we spoke.'

Salvacion looks at me and winces, only half from the pain. 'You know I didn't like to do it.'

'Let me see your side,' I insist and we labour to lift her uniform jacket, to examine the skin. It's bruised an angry red and deep plum, but there is no wound. 'I can't see an injury, but you may be bleeding internally.'

She runs her free hand through her short hair, grown shaggy in the months since I last saw her.

'So you rode the bird?' Salvacion asks, face incredulous.

'Adarna,' Isagani says. 'It was in the cave in the Maelstrom.'

'The queen, that's what she wanted recovered?'

I nod grimly.

Biba puts down the tonic she's been identifying. 'Let me try to see.' She places her hand on Salvacion's side and looks pensive, eyebrows furrowing and mouth pursing. 'You have thick blood. It's good for now.'

Salvacion brushes Biba's hair from her face. My daughter looks uncertain for a moment and examines Salvacion, studying her features.

'You look so much like him,' Salvacion says. Her voice is thin and her eyes begin to water. 'Fuck!' she yells, jumping back. Biba startles in alarm. 'Sorry, it stings to cry.'

I watch her laughing through the tears, smiling at her niece, trying to reassure her that it will be all right. She deserves to know.

'Salvacion, I saw him,' I say slowly. She looks up, and her face drops. 'I saw Larkin. He made it into the Maelstrom.'

She begins to stand. 'What do you mean? He's alive?'

I shake my head and place a hand on her shoulder. 'No, it . . . changed him.'

'What changed him? What happened?'

'It takes from you, kills you slowly,' Finlyr says, looking grim. 'Turns your flesh to stone.'

Hanan appears in the doorway, looking gaunt and pale. 'How are you, Salvacion?' she asks.

'Holding up.' She shrugs. 'Did you speak to them?'

Hanan nods, stepping reluctantly into the kitchen. 'Some of them understand the magnitude of what could happen. The ruin any more power in the queen's hands could bring.'

'But not all?' Salvacion asks, her voice resigned.

'No. They will pray for us and try to mend the Tree, but none of them will commit regicide.'

'Oh yes, regicide! Nice to have a new crime on my blotter,' Finlyr says, exasperated.

'She's going through those Temple Sisters fast, Hanan,' Salvacion interrupts. 'I've seen what it was like with you. This is different.'

'The queen is weak, vulnerable,' Hanan says. 'She's killing them fast, but then she will have nothing to sustain her. This is the best time to strike.'

'This is akin to a death sentence – you realise that?' Finlyr retorts, pacing the kitchen.

'If you have a better future lined up for yourself, feel free to take it,' Hanan cuts back.

I watch them arguing. What future had I imagined for us? I wanted to believe fulfilling the queen's quest might curry favour, buy us time. But that would just be for Biba. I look at the Temple of Aistra, a ruin of its former glory. A pile of rocks and scared girls.

I had been prepared to be selfish as long as it wasn't my child. But now I've seen the object of the queen's desires. It's a weapon. If what Hanan says is true, then becoming a fugitive forever is a drop in the ocean of horrors awaiting us. If I don't try to stop the queen from harnessing this, I'm complicit in the destruction she will cause. If I don't have a future, so be it. But I won't condemn anyone else to that fate.

'I won't take Biba there. It's too dangerous.'

The others turn and look at me. Biba recoils from my words and stands up. 'I want to go.'

'No, Biba. I'd be bringing you straight to the queen. She wants your gift.' I turn to Salvacion. 'Take her to the Spring Isle. It's the safest option. Find Kopiro, Vullis, and Ryla at my farm.'

'I'll take her,' Salvacion confirms.

'What about you, kid?' Finlyr turns to Isagani, who has been quietly observant since we arrived at Aistra.

'What do you mean?' Isagani returns.

'Well, you wanted to get off Paranish and I ended up bringing you right back. If you want out, this is the time.'

'Why do you keep trying to get rid of me?' Isagani asks, trying and failing to hide their pain under levity.

'I'm not,' Finlyr protests. 'I just want what's best for you. You're my responsibility.'

I'm not sure if it's Isagani or Finlyr who begins to cry first. The two are hugging and slapping each other on the back.

'What about Raina?' Biba says, looking over at Hanan with her sling.

'Raina stays with me,' she insists.

I pause, examining Hanan's face. 'Would it be better if she stayed with the Temple Sisters?'

'No,' she snaps. 'She has to stay with me.'

I catch Hanan's expression, a caged bird frantically beating its wings.

'You mean to use her as bait,' I say, unable to hide the revulsion in my voice.

'The princess is the queen's weakness,' Hanan says calmly. 'We have to exploit it.'

'What is your plan, Hanan?' I ask, folding my arms.

'Lure the queen. Kill the queen.'

'As simple as that?' Salvacion asks, laughing mirthlessly. 'Even without me she'll have the rest of the royal Seaguardians surrounding her. She's weak, yes, but she's paranoid now.'

'We'll have the three things she wants most desperately in the world,' Hanan says, patting Raina. She stares out of the window at Adarna, who is lying on the ground, staring at Sinigang.

'What if it doesn't work?' I ask her.

She turns back from the window, her eyes clear and focused. 'Then we cause as much chaos and destruction as we can on the way down.'

'How long do we have?'

'A few hours to rest. We'll have to rotate watch on Adarna. I think Sinigang's got it in some kind of trance, but who knows how long that will last. I'm sure the bird attracted some attention. We don't want to wait too long. Salvacion and Biba should leave now.'

I look to Biba, and she gives me a reassuring smile. 'It's all right, Mama.'

I hold her tight. 'You are not the parent, Biba. I'm supposed to take care of you.'

'When I lost you in the cave, I thought I was falling,' she says, voice quavering.

'Aunt Salvacion will be here for you. She'll take you home now.'

'You promise you'll come back?' she asks, light glinting in her eyes.

I can't lie to her. My throat is stopped with tears. I kiss her fluttering eyelids and then Salvacion takes her. I go with them to the dock and watch them board, rowing one of the boats away through the aqueduct.

There are many empty chambers in the temple, and we have our pick. I find a hairbrush when I pull back the sheets and break down in tears. Finlyr appears in the doorway and knocks gently on the open door.

'Can I come in?'

I nod silently, smoothing the sheets.

'How are you holding up?' he asks tentatively.

I say nothing but walk up to him and nuzzle his shoulder. He wraps his arms around me and strokes my hair.

SALTSWEPT

'What do you need from me right now? How can I help?'
'Just stay with me,' I say, crying straight into him.
He begins to sing, half-whispering:

'Remember as you cry for me
One with the earth evermore
Your waves will always reach my shore
As the moon loves the sea.'

Part Four

What Now?

CHAPTER SIXTY-ONE

FINLYR

EVERY OUTLAW KNOWS THE element of surprise is a blessed gift. Dirty tactics, but battle isn't honourable; even the Seaguardians will tell you that. It's about the only thing we do have on our side.

The dawn is breaking over the horizon as we leave the Winter Isle. I've never been great at goodbyes, preferring to slip away unnoticed.

So I focus on the feel of Adarna's feathers under my hand as Hanan connects with it, laying her forehead on the bird's as we mount. We fly swiftly, and as Adarna takes wing, my stomach drops out from under me. We hover above the Bastion, the patchwork towers and battlements, the keep. It looks so small, so insignificant. It's a child's toy from this height, and the bricks shake and dust whirls as the bird beats its great wings. Adarna's claws could do serious damage to the stonework with the right landing. She wouldn't see us coming. She carries her skirts, making her way across the flagstones. I've never laid eyes upon her, but I know it must be the queen from the bitter taste in my mouth. Based on the stories, I'd conjured up an idea of what she'd look like. My mother was never posted at the Bastion, but she saw her at a feast day once when she was patrolling the Umasan ports. Ethereal, she had said. I'm sure the queen bleeds like the rest of us.

She's dressed in a midnight blue I've never seen captured in cloth. She dazzles in the sunlight, gems and gold attached to the dress. The bird descends into the courtyard, landing in the centre of the sun mosaic, its extraordinary wings whipping up dust. The dozens of Seaguardians circle the queen, shielding her as her hair and clothes dance in the wind.

'You've brought my Adarna,' the queen says, looking at the bird hungrily.

Then she notices the rest of us clinging on Adarna's back. Hanan whispers into the bird's ears, and I feel Adarna shudder. I long to know what she's telling it. Hanan looks to all of us and we palm our weapons. Then Adarna begins to sing, an ethereal, enchanting sound that echoes and harmonises with itself. I keep my blade nicking my skin, out of sight, letting the streams of blood soak into my clothes. We keep ourselves present through pain as the Seaguardians begin to waver and then fall into a stupor. The queen resists Adarna's lure, staring instead at Hanan and moving towards us.

Raina begins to cry, writhing in her sling. The queen starts forward and Hanan puts a protective arm around the baby.

'Don't hurt her,' the queen says, reaching her hands out, voice anguished.

She never really looked much like Hanan to me, but I don't know much about babies.

Hanan soothes Raina, and Ris braces for a fight, shaking herself awake from the song.

Eventually the queen speaks, her voice thick and hoarse. 'What do you want?'

'Abdicate the crown to the princess,' Hanan says without hesitation.

She speaks so confidently, with a familiar intimacy that is uncomfortable to behold. What did Hanan say about her former life? She was bound and expelled. And this was the woman responsible. I don't know if I could look at the source of such pain with the defiance she does.

'She needs me to survive. The princess needs me more than she needs you. I want protection for me and my friends.'

The queen baulks at the suggestion and raises her hand towards the Seaguardians.

'If you hurt me, she'll die,' Hanan says.

The two women stare each other down, and the air hums with expectation. I think of Hanan's mark glowing in the cavern.

'Will you yield?' Hanan asks.

The queen falters, stopping in her tracks.

'I will consider your terms,' the queen says eventually, and we all hear the defeat in her voice.

Hanan holds Raina gently again, kissing the top of her head. 'Consider my terms? You're unfit to rule.' She turns to the Seaguardians, some of whom still have their weapons raised. 'Do you know what she has done? She has violated the Tree of Life. The holy sacrament of the dead. She has defiled the souls of the dead to feed her bloodlust. She feasts on your ancestors. Will you let this continue?'

The queen lunges for Raina, grabbing her out of the other woman's arms. We topple from Adarna's back, and there's a tangle of bodies as we all drop to the ground. The Seaguardians try to close rank, to maintain control. I swipe my blade, desperate to find the queen's flesh. We are all armed, and there is no glory in this killing. It is a case of who can get to her first. I grab her by the hair and gleaming pins scatter to the ground like embers.

'Mercy! For my daughter's sake!'

There is nothing divine about a woman crying and gasping for breath, putting herself between her child and my blade. Perhaps that's what puts my guard down. A sliver of humanity, some sign of a beating heart under that cold exterior. And then she grabs the edge of my blade, bloody-palmed, and thrusts the hilt into my stomach, winding me. As I'm doubled over, I hear her retreating in the distance, screaming: 'Seize the bird! Attack the traitors!'

The Seaguardians are rallied by her command. They swarm, and we're buffeted by the force of them. I'm underfoot, only the bite of metal, rust of blood and teeth to spit out. I yell, taking down Seaguardians and using their bodies as means, to find air in the chaos. I bite earlobes, punch soft bellies, break noses. Not much difference between animal bodies. Sinigang must be in the crowd somewhere, causing havoc. I wouldn't like to see what that otter-cat can do when let loose.

I wipe the blood from my eyes and push through the throng towards Hanan. She has the queen locked in some wild embrace, clinging on to her, nuzzling her. They hold hands together on Adarna, clutching at the bird's feathery breast, keeping it grounded. It must be compelled somehow, for it stays completely still at their touch. From their point of contact come streaks of blue. Pools of cerulean and turquoise spill onto the flagstones.

My knees give out, and I slump to the ground. In my periphery I see the same thing happen around me. We're all on our knees, begging, in supplication. I watch a leaf where I kneel turn crisp and golden. It shrivels and decays, changing to dust.

It feels like someone is trying to pull my insides out through my belly button. My organs are shutting down, ready to melt inside me. I collapse into myself, no longer in control of my body. Thoughts are all that's left to me. I can't see Isagani or Ris. I don't want them to be alone right now. In truth, *I* don't want to be alone right now.

Larkin. The image of those statues, an army of silent, unmoving vessels. Frozen in their agony and dying in fear and isolation. Only one thing in life is guaranteed: we're all going to die someday. All you can hope for is release from the pain, the sweetness of sleep. But the queen won't even give us that peace. The dead are an infinite source of energy. And that's too delicious for her to resist. The royals have been gorging on Paranish, feeding on every living thing like a parasite. I try to focus on Hanan, now struggling with the queen. At least I can die knowing I almost had the courage to strike.

CHAPTER SIXTY-TWO

HANAN

I WAS A FOOL to believe we could destroy the queen. She pushes our hands onto Adarna's feathers, and locks me in place, wrapping her arms tightly around me. She nuzzles hard into my neck, pushing the stone talisman out of the way. Then she bites, sucking hard. I scream, trying desperately to tear myself away from her. The times she fed on me before were games, little tests building my stamina, my tolerance for pain. But this is something else. This is finally real. She's a predator, teeth sunk into prey. She pushes Adarna's energy into my hand and then takes everything through me, through my blood. I don't know how much more I can take. I collapse into her, and she moans into my ear.

'You are nothing, Hanan.'

I understand it now. She takes pleasure not only in the feed, but in the kill. Slaying me will slake her bloodlust, for now. Punishment for disobeying her, for daring to live when she sentenced me to death, for stealing Raina and claiming her as mine.

Adarna bucks and shifts under our touch. I focus on the bird's energy, trying to dip my hand back into its mind's waters. Adarna looks at me with ferocious eyes. I had been so focused on the idea of the queen harnessing its power I hadn't considered the bird's unbridled hunger. We have shown it the world beyond the Maelstrom. An entire nation of energy for the feeding. It is a wild and untameable thing. Priestess Sinaya learned that, hiding herself in the cave to keep it from falling into the wrong hands. Among those bones and rags, I could feel hers.

'I will devour the world,' the queen says.

Adarna takes flight, shedding feathers and blood in its wake. The queen finally lets me go, staring after Adarna.

'I demand you return!'

Adarna looks down, and its body wrestles in the air, as though the spark of its will is trying to break through the imprint of the queen's touch.

'Bring it down!' she commands her Seaguardians. 'Don't hurt the beast, simply bring it aground. I want it captured. Ready those ropes!'

I strain and see several Seaguardians on the Bastion wall, levelling weapons at Adarna that are similar to the crossbows Finlyr had on *Saltswept*. They aim with difficulty as Adarna flies higher.

I scramble to my feet and away from the queen. She's forgotten I'm even there, eyes fixed on the sky. I push through the confused mass of people, all collapsed to their knees. We writhe and crawl forward as though moving through mud. Have we all been drained?

Eventually I make it to the wall, grabbing a weapon from one of the Seaguardians. They protest weakly, falling down as though their bones have softened. What havoc has Adarna wreaked on Paranish already?

I remember how I used my cane to disrupt the protective circle when I stole Raina. Like annihilates like. I wrench the quiver from the fallen Seaguardian and take an arrow. I loose the stone talisman of the bird from my neck. It's covered in blood and slips as I try to tie it around the arrowhead. My hands are cut up and I wipe them against my dress, desperately trying to notch the arrow against the string. I mimic the Seaguardians. Paranish, it takes a sturdy back to hoist this thing.

I let myself breathe for one moment, grieving the version of myself that remains buried within the Tree of Life. I kept a small flame of hope alive that the existence of Adarna could help me retrieve some of my powers. But we've all had to sacrifice our own little hopes for the greater good.

The bow quivers in my grip, and I pull back the string, everything taut. Adarna moves frantically, but I catch it in my line of sight. Aistra can't help me now. I can only pray this works. What comes next is up to fate.

'Everything must die,' I whisper, loosing the arrow.

The arrow moves faster than I thought was possible. The bow ricochets from the force, string snapping. I feel an excruciating pain, sharp and bright, emanating from my wrist. I stare at my hand, and my fingers are cut to ribbons. My body gives out, collapsing from the wall.

I'm on the flagstones, bones and flesh and skin, jagged scratching tearing. My vision is blurry, something drips from my eye. Cheekbone sore and swollen. I think I've been punched in the face by a Seaguardian. The sting feels sweet, takes me back to my days in the temple. It feels more real, more raw, knowing it will heal slowly, possibly never to be the same again.

Screaming from the other side of the courtyard. I'm drowning in bodies. I find a break in the crowd of Seaguardians, a window of blue sky, and try to breathe. Adarna gives a death cry, and I know the arrow found its mark.

The bird claws at the arrow and stone embedded in its flesh, feathers turning pale. I stare as Adarna goes rigid, turning deathly white from the site of the wound. When it reaches its eyes, I know there's no reversing this. Flesh becomes stone and shatters into pieces, huge boulders colliding with the side of the Bastion. Other stones break off and roll down the hillside, likely flattening half of Umasa in their wake. I shelter my head from the shower of rocks and riot of feathers that rain down on us.

'Hanan.'

A small voice calls to me from nearby rubble. I catch a shimmer of midnight blue and metal. The queen is trapped under the rubble and blanket of feathers, stone and bone pinning her arm.

The queen cries out in pain. She is mortal now, desperate to live. She tries to sit up and screams as she realises what's happened. She tries to unpin her arm, and I hear the flesh tear, see the white flash of bone beneath the blood and sinew. My legs jerk forward. Could I move that rock, repair her arm?

I can see the sling poking out from the rubble. The arm pinned under the stone was protecting, shielding. I know her as I would in any world, in any time. How could I not, after she took from me and I took from her? Something tears inside me, rupturing like an inflamed and infected wound. I recover my princess from the rubble and hold her close.

And then the queen says the princess's name. The name *she* gave her. I slowly back away, clutching Raina. I can't let the queen take her back. She's mine. After everything, she is mine. I cling on to Raina, cold sweat against my skin. I turn and flee, not looking back. If I look back, I'm damned.

Raina's heart beats beneath her small ribs. Heart's desire. I can almost hear it beating to the rhythm of those words as we run.

'I have regrets,' I tell Raina. 'I won't let you be one of them.'

'Hanan. You won't leave me.'

I turn, and the queen's eyes are barely open, looking at me retreating.

'You won't take her again. She's my daughter.'

'You are no mother. I saved her life, brought her back from the dead. She's more mine than yours.'

'I am your queen,' she says, reaching for me with her free hand.

'Enjoy your empire of dust.'

CHAPTER SIXTY-THREE

RIS

ANYONE IN WHITE is a target. I stab and slash wildly, slamming into bodies, walls. It feels like riding waves trying to get to the queen. My heart slows as I see Finlyr has her. Now, strike now. But he doesn't, and then he's doubled over, and the queen is escaping.

I pursue, grabbing at the hem of her dress and twisting it round her ankle. She goes down hard, slamming her shoulder onto the flagstones. She writhes under my grip as I try to cut her, slashing wildly at anything within my reach. I slither my way closer to her, possessed by some fury I can't describe. I swipe across the back of the ankle, and she screams in anguish. The blood flows thick and fast. Just like mine. She is mortal after all.

She kicks me hard in the chest, sending me sprawling. By the time I recover, she's out of sight. I try to follow her blood trail, but a deafening crack fills the air around me. I look up, and the sky is falling. At first that's what it feels like. It's raining stone, great chunks of rock smashing into the ground and colliding with the Bastion. Buildings begin to topple and explode around us, and there's dust in my eyes and my nose. It's like breathing sand, and I gasp in the chaos.

I try to find Finlyr and Hanan in the chaos, but the dust is thick in the air, making everything shadows. The confusion, deafening roar of hundreds of mouths, grasping hands, panicked eyes. Only Isagani is close to me, and I grab at their tunic, wrenching them close to me.

'Isagani, stay with me.'

'Is that your blood?' they ask, wiping dirt from their face.

I shake my head. 'It's the queen's.'

'We did it?' they ask, brightening.

'No, but she's badly hurt. We have to get out of here.'

The destruction has spilled downhill from the Bastion, and we move with determination through the remains of Umasa, following the mass of bodies pushing and pressing.

The streets are a confusion, half the buildings destroyed, and others threatening to collapse. There are people everywhere, clutching their possessions and loved ones, shouting and screaming. Some of them are running; others are standing in the town square paralysed with fear and overwhelm. I'm sure there are many others hunkered down in basements, hoping to wait out the devastation. Bodies impaled on smashed wooden walls. Homes aflame as smoke chokes and blinds. Blood and salt and water make rivers in the streets. I think of Narra, Morna, and Ligaya. Are they together? Did anyone have enough time? The chaos hit so quickly, I doubt it.

'Follow the shore,' I insist, and we start running towards the dock. 'We have to get off the mainland.'

'What about the others?' Isagani protests, stopping so suddenly they almost pull my arm.

I put one hand on their shoulder and meet their eye. 'Look around, kid. We have to go; it's not safe here. The others have to fend for themselves.'

'We can't leave them.'

'We have to get to the Spring Isle, all right?'

Isagani nods and reluctantly follows. The dock is quickly filling with desperation. Anyone with their own vessel is on the water.

Others who are setting off have either blades to protect their spot or goods to offer in exchange for one.

We make our way to the ferry, the largest boat, which already has a crowd roaring and beseeching.

'The ferry will return,' the captain says evenly. 'Now I won't let anyone on if you don't form an orderly line.'

'An orderly line? We need to shove off now!'

I barge my way to the front to see what's happening, dragging Isagani by the hand.

'We have to get on this boat,' I whisper to them. 'There may not be another.' My instinct to run is not quite quenched, fire licking at my heels. All I know is we must get home.

'I'll get as many of you on as I can, but we don't want to capsize.'

There are angry protests and accusations of injustice from the dock.

'Let's find a private vessel,' the agitated passenger insists, taking their partner by the arm and moving away.

The captain finally allows us to board, and I'm buffeted by bodies. I lose Isagani's hand as I get swept up, pushed hard against the railings of the boarding plank. They must be right behind me, but I can't see them. I try to avoid the clutching at my clothes and the livid stares. Some people are overladen with bags, hitting others with them to ensure they get priority. The captain is shouting at the top of their voice, and the eager crew try to maintain order, to no avail. We are cramped, and those on board are reluctant to move down.

'There's room on the aft side, move down.'

A surly-faced passenger holds their bags closer to them.

The captain looks frantic, trying to count the passengers, to estimate our combined weight. Paranish, I hope we don't sink.

'Isagani!' I try to call for them, to push through the throng and find them.

Everyone is shouting for someone or at someone else. It is a cesspool of fear and anger.

The captain shakes their head, as though they've given up, and has to force back overzealous passengers who are half-boarded. They wrestle with the crowd for the boarding plank, pushing back the land dwellers.

'We'll come back!' the captain insists, although the promises sound empty and desperate. 'The quicker you let go, the quicker we'll return!'

The captain begins to cast off, and the crowd undulates back and forward, eventually relinquishing the plank. One of the front row who was holding on is thrown forward by the impact, landing in the water. Some of the others rush to help retrieve them, hands and rope offered as a line. The captain looks torn as the plank is hauled onto the boat by the crew and we set sail.

I catch a glimpse between the press of bodies around me. At the front of the crowd, helping the person who fell off the dock, is a scrawny figure I recognise. A small pale face and large dark eyes.

'Isagani!' I yell, waving frantically. 'Isagani!'

I don't know if they can see or hear me, but they look up at the ferry and then around the dock, searching for me.

'Please, I need to go back for them!' I push my way towards one of the crew, my voice hoarse from yelling.

'There's no going back. They can get the next ferry.'

'There is no next ferry, you fucks, and you know it.'

The crew member looks at me aghast, and I break down in tears.

'Will you go back?' I ask over and over again, staring at Umasa's dock retreating in the distance. 'Go back.'

The nearby passengers lower their gaze and turn towards the sea.

'Your kid will be all right,' a young man tries to reassure me.

My kid. Isagani was my responsibility.

'I abandoned them,' I cry.

'No, it was an accident. You're not to blame,' the man says, trying for conviction in his voice.

We are all scattered to the wind. I look towards the Spring Isle in the distance and can only hope Salvacion and Biba made it safely there. We know we are the lucky ones.

CHAPTER SIXTY-FOUR

FINLYR

THE SLOW DEATH GRIP of Adarna suddenly loosens. I'm on my hands and knees, but my joints feel looser, warmth spreading across my skin. When I can look up, I see massive bits of stone falling from the sky and the echo of Adarna's shriek.

I roll to avoid the falling debris, crawling away across bodies mangled by stone. Seaguardians and stewards emerge from the ruin of the Bastion. I scramble down the hill, frantic among the chaos. Umasa is a wreck. Families scream as they try to shift the rubble.

The streets are alight with confusion. There's a feral energy to the town that sits uneasily with me. This is a pyre ready to catch. My instincts to run or hide have never been stronger.

Everyone else has had the same idea, and a head start on getting to the docks. Folks have their possessions with them; others have nothing but the clothes on their back. Children left crying and pissing in the streets. Ruins of houses plundered for everything they're worth. It never ceases to amaze how thin the fabric of Paranish truly is. We're all fucked, either way.

I move towards the dock, people parting when they feel my hand on their shoulder and see the bulky mass it's attached to.

'Where's the ferry?' I ask.

'Gone. They're all gone,' an older woman reluctantly admits.

'When are they coming back?'

A young man shrugs. 'Who knows.'

'There must be another way, other vessels,' I insist.

The young man laughs bitterly. 'No chance unless you got anything worth parting with.'

I bare my teeth and try to shake off the wallowing and wailing. It's then I spot a familiar gait, peeling off from the crowd.

'Isagani?' I call.

They turn and by Paranish, I can't believe it.

'Holy Aistra,' they shout, running through the crowd to meet me.

'Are you all right?' I ask, examining them. Isagani's face and hair is covered in ash and dust, save two tear streaks down their cheeks.

'I'm fine,' they say, shaking me off.

'Where are the others?'

Isagani turns to the sea, pointing to the ferry, just visible on the horizon.

'What do you mean? What happened?'

Isagani begins to cry, burying their face in my chest. 'She left me. Ris left me.'

I squeeze them harder, trying to process what they're saying. Ris adores them as fiercely as I do. Why would she leave them? As I shield Isagani, I understand what kind of ugly desperation seeps out of us during tragedy.

'I've got you, kid. I won't let go, I promise.'

Insects swarming – that's how it feels trying to push through Umasa. The ferries have left port; everyone is restless and terrified. I can't blame them. The dock is useless to us, and we head back towards Umasa town square, ducking and weaving through the throng. Paranish, they're good at being a shadow. Thunder roars in the distance.

'Storm's coming,' Isagani says, watching the sky darken.

I narrow my eyes and watch the overcast sky. Smoke and embers mix with clouds of stone and ash. 'This feels strange. We should get inside.'

Isagani leads us down winding, dingy closes, and we crawl and scuttle down stairways and through alleys to reach Narra's inn. We can't think of anywhere else to go. It's the closest thing that feels like home.

I bang on the door of the inn until my knuckles are bloody. Eventually a large brown eye appears at the peephole.

'Narra? Oh, thank Aistra. Please, you have to help us.'

'Look what the otter-cat dragged in.' Her voice is wary, and the eye roves over us both. 'Speaking of, where is Sinigang?'

'I don't know, I'm sorry, Narra. We all got separated,' Isagani says.

'Let us in, I beg you,' I insist. 'You can check we mean no harm.'

Eventually the door opens a crack, and I could cry. We squeeze through and it's barred tight against the outside world.

'What manner of chaos have you brought down on us?' Narra asks, patting us down. Her fingers crackle with a spark, and my skin tingles as she searches. She grunts in reluctant assent. 'You're both clean of mischief. But grief lies heavy on your shoulders.'

'Are the others here?' I ask hopefully.

Ligaya and Morna appear in the hallway. Their faces are blanched, and they clutch each other as if the fate of the world depended on the touch. I try to disguise my disappointment that Ris, Hanan, and the others aren't here.

'A nip of palm wine and a stew is what's needed.' Ligaya smiles weakly.

It's eerily quiet in here, the chaos of the town distant outside.

'Where are the guests?' I ask.

'The few we had fled to the docks at the first sign of trouble,' Narra says. 'They could smell mischief in the air.'

'I cast a protective circle around the inn,' Ligaya says quietly. 'It will hold for a time, and keep out anyone – or anything – unwanted, but our magic isn't strong enough.'

'What do you mean?' Isagani asks nervously.

Ligaya looks to Morna. 'We barely made it here from the shop. It's chaos out there; it doesn't feel safe.'

'Safe?' I repeat, incredulous. 'If magic was good for something, we wouldn't be in this mess.'

Ligaya cuts me a look. 'We don't have anything else to give.'

'What happened to you two?' Morna asks, biting her lip.

Isagani sits mute and hollow-eyed. There are some things that can't be told, but I try my best to put our ordeal into words. I look at the dark circles under their eyes and their hair matted with sweat. Holy Aistra, what we've put our children through.

'Then Paranish will be aligned now, right?' Ligaya asks, once my tale is concluded. 'Everything should return to balance now the royals are dead.'

'I don't know for sure they're dead.'

Narra sighs. 'Even if the royals are dead, that doesn't mean something good will take their place,' she says, chewing her lip in consternation. 'And the land remembers our abuse. The world won't return to harmony in an instant. It feels like a shift, an awakening of something.'

Morna gets up from her chair abruptly, looking uncomfortable. 'We're going to need more tea,' she says.

Ligaya and Narra look furtively at each other.

'What's going on?' I ask. Their disturbance is more personal, something unspoken. 'What happened?'

Morna pauses at the doorway. 'It's my fault,' she admits, turning. 'I was an informant for the Bastion.'

I start up from my seat. 'What the actual fuck?'

'It's all right,' Ligaya insists, trying to coax me down. 'She told us everything. And she's agreed to a binding spell.'

'Ris found me out and insisted I tell Ligaya and Narra.'

'Which she did,' Narra admitted. 'It's been a hard few months for us all.'

Isagani looks terrified. I stare at them and then back at Narra. 'Are we . . . safe here? Can we even trust them?'

'You have no threat from me, I swear,' Morna says. 'I didn't fully understand what I was doing. It was just an exchange of information.'

'What did they give you?' I ask, swallowing hard.

'It seems so trivial now. Books, maps, copies of documents.'

'You've never seen the queen, have you?' Isagani asks suddenly, their pupils blown.

Morna shakes her head.

'I have,' they say. 'I've seen what she can do. Not just to the gifted, but to everyone.'

'She means to consume the dead,' I whisper.

Ligaya gasps and makes the sign of the circle around her.

'You knew she was taking children from their families,' Isagani shouts. 'And you helped her. You pointed them out for her.'

Morna is sobbing, shoulders heaving, breaths coming in shallow gasps. Ligaya tries to comfort her.

'Breathe, my love. Breathe with me.'

I go over to Isagani and try to hold them. They are angry, resisting me for a moment. 'You're right to be angry,' I say, gently.

'We've forgiven her,' Narra says, finally. 'You can choose to do so or not, in time. She can't change the past, but she can make amends. I intend to make sure of that.'

Eventually Morna has no more tears, and the anger seeps out of Isagani. We are all too exhausted to fight anymore. I settle into the soft furnishings and turn to look at my kid. Isagani's fallen asleep sitting up. Tomorrow we will try to figure out what this means for all of us. Perhaps for a time we can breathe, come up for air before we dive back into the murky waters of our future.

CHAPTER SIXTY-FIVE

RIS

THE CAPTAIN BRINGS US into port at the Spring Isle, and the vessel is barely secured before passengers are scrambling over each other and scattering across the land. Where do they hope to go? There are inns and rooms, but not enough for this swell of people. Any roof will do, it seems.

I gather myself for the journey back to the farmstead.

'Thank you.' I meet the captain's eye, and he gives me a stiff nod. 'We're heading back now. Hopefully we can find your friend.'

I swallow the bile at the back of my throat, remembering Isagani's imploring eyes. 'Thank Aistra for folk like you,' I say, looking back across the water to the mainland.

Thunder booms in the distance and we watch forks of lightning illuminate the sky.

'Is it a storm?' I ask.

The captain stares at the distant sky and shakes his head, eyes glassy. 'We can't go back in this now.'

'I'm sorry!' I call back as I scramble up the hill, already slick with mud from travellers' boots. I'm running away again. I'm good at that. The farm comes into view, the land sparse and empty. The animals are in the shelter, and there is a small light on in the cottage. I stumble across the muddy grass, openly weeping. I lean against the rickety gate, which buckles under my weight, and I regain my balance.

I crash through the cottage door, and I'm met with a yell. Ryla bolts out of the bedroom, an axe in hand. They catch me as I stumble and collapse in their arms.

'Ris! Holy Aistra, am I glad to see you,' Ryla says, wide-eyed. 'What in Paranish is happening out there?'

'Where is Biba—' I start and wince at the sharp pressure on my chest. I try for shallow breaths, but then the world shrinks to a pinprick of light, and I have to let go.

When I wake, Ryla sits on the end of my bed, proffering a bowl. 'Here, eat this.'

I try to sit up and feel a sharp stab in my side.

'Easy,' they encourage, settling a hand on my shoulder. 'I set your bones while you were out cold. Your ribs were broken.'

'Hanan fixed them.'

'Not entirely,' Ryla disagrees. 'Who's Hanan?'

I shake my head. I can't, not yet. 'Is this medicine?' I ask, my voice dusty from lack of use.

They smile, mirthful but not unkind. 'Not quite. But it will make you feel better.'

I reluctantly take the steaming bowl from their hands. Small turquoise pearls float in a deep umami broth. They hand me a wooden spoon, and I take a tentative sip. The flavours dance on my tongue: an earthy base, nutty body, and tangy top notes. I scarf down the rest.

'Where's Biba? Where are the others?' I ask, wiping my mouth.

'Biba? Isn't she with you?'

I start, getting up. 'Salvacion isn't here yet?'

'What are you talking about? Why would that bitch be here?'

'Don't,' is all I can manage before my head starts swimming.

'Kopiro's with Vullis at the tap,' Ryla continues, filling the silence. 'He'll be so glad to see you. You gave me quite a fright,' they add slowly, examining my face. 'What's happening at the mainland? I saw the commotion from the ferry.'

They pause, and I can tell they're bursting with questions about my ordeal. We look out the window at the storm, coming down in earnest now.

'It's chaos out there,' I say quietly.

'It's all right,' Ryla says, and then I realise they aren't talking to me. Fetch has appeared in the doorway to the bedroom, making whining noises. 'Come here, boy.'

Fetch eventually goes over to Ryla and licks their hand. He sniffs me and then jumps up, wagging his tail in recognition.

'Didn't think I'd be seeing you again so soon,' I say, petting him enthusiastically.

A stream of light pours into the cottage, and I almost don't recognise Vullis in the doorway. It feels like years since I've seen my friends. A barrage of feet, and they're elbowing each other at the doorway. Vullis and Kopiro hold me, and Fetch ensures everything is covered in his slobber and moulting fur.

'Careful of her ribs,' Ryla insists.

'What in Paranish happened to you?' Vullis asks in wonder.

'How long have you got?' I smile weakly.

'It's wild out there. Nowhere we'd rather be,' Kopiro insists, kissing my cheek.

No one wants to break the silence after I've recounted our misfortunes.

'Do you think she's dead?' Vullis asks after a time.

Ryla grimaces. 'I don't know. Don't you think we'd . . . feel it?'

If prayers were good for something, as my mother used to say.

'Paranish will be thrown into calamity without a ruler,' Vullis says, visible fear on his face.

'Seaguardians will be crawling over the Spring Isle,' Ryla adds. 'Not to mention the desperate mainlanders.'

There is something to be afraid for, after all. We'll have to be smart about this. We can't go rushing out after the Seaguardians.

'How long do you propose we hide here?' I ask. 'I saw the chaos in Umasa. No one knows what to do.'

'Perhaps it's an opportunity for change, at last,' Kopiro suggests.

'That's a beautiful thought,' Ryla says, folding their arms. 'But what makes you think anything will change?'

A bash at the door, more a testing of the wood's give than a knock. We all look at each other. It's inevitable, like the tides. Fetch barks and growls at the intrusion. Ryla quiets him as best they can. I stand slowly, grabbing the metal fire poker as I open the door.

'Is this the kind of greeting I get?' Salvacion asks, barging into the cottage. She's rain-slick, her hair plastered to her face and trailing mud. I pull her into an embrace, heedless of the muck and grime I'm getting on myself.

'Mama!' Biba yells, and I can barely see her under the grit and dirt. I plant kisses all over her until she laughs, begging me to stop.

'I worried I wouldn't see you again,' I tell her, bringing them to the fire.

'Salvacion?' Ryla says, incredulous. They pick up the axe and brace, standing to their full height. 'You've got some nerve after what you did to Ris.'

'No, stop!' I insist, and Kopiro gently takes the axe from Ryla's grip. 'She helped bring Biba here. She's one of us now.'

'Is that true?' Vullis asks, rubbing his face.

Salvacion nods. 'We got caught in a riptide and nearly lost the whole skiff. The weather is almost as wild as the folk out there. She's right: I want no part of the Bastion. I couldn't in good faith continue to stand by her side once I truly understood what she was doing.'

Ryla sighs and settles back down in a chair. 'Well, don't just stand there getting the floorboards wet. Get yourself cleaned up.' Salvacion nods and lets a smile flicker on her face, heading into the other room to peel off her sodden layers. Biba is heedless to decorum, stripping off and mooning the fire.

'You need a bath,' I tell her, taking her by the hand to the bathroom for a scrub.

CHAPTER SIXTY-SIX

HANAN

THE SKY LIGHTS UP, forks of lightning cutting through the grey. It illuminates everything at ghastly angles, bathing it all in a strange light. The Bastion is jagged and dilapidated, damaged by Adarna's fall. Cracked flagstones where the bird pierced the ground. Debris scatters down the hill, obliterating parts of Umasa in its wake. Buried in the memories of my mistakes. Haunted by regret. I am poison, the ruination of everything I touch. I am running, Raina in her sling, back into the ruins of the Bastion. I use the shadows, hurrying around corners, avoiding the pockets of chaos I encounter. Survivors, embroiled in confusion or grief or anger. Seaguardians, nobles. None of them can be my ally. It's only me and Raina now.

I make my way through the tunnels. Some of them have caved in, but our exit is only partially blocked by debris. The aqueduct is holding, for now. There is a huge crack along the side of the wall, and the stones push inward towards us. There's only so much time that water pressure will be held back. I hurry into one of the boats and row through the aqueduct, feeling a strange sensation as I remember the last time I was here. I use the hydraulic screw to bring the boat to the ocean, and the sky is illuminated with lightning, like there are cracks in the clouds and they glitter. My skin tingles, and some force brings me up bodily, to my feet, and then into the air. I bring my arms around Raina, who cries out in alarm from her sling. I hover above the boat, waiting for the drop.

My breathing is ragged, and the sky fizzes with energy. I'm caught in the storm, watching the lightning crack in the distance. The thunder rolls in, its rumble coming from the distant waters. My body pulses with the sound, and it penetrates my eardrums so fully I wonder if I'll ever hear again.

I'm high up enough that I can see not only Umasa but all of Paranish. I watch the Winter Isle, where the clouds are darkest. I try to turn my body in the air. I see strange figures in the distance, suspended in the air like me. Some are screaming, thrashing. Others laugh and dance, more in control of their bodies. What in Aistra is happening? Then lightning strikes the Tree of Life. I smell sea salt, blood, the burned wood. A web of light emanates from the scorched Tree, connecting each of the suspended figures. When it hits me, my chest constricts, and I can't breathe. Something crushes my ribs, like squeezing my soul back into my body. The world falls out from under me, and I hurtle down, watching the ocean come towards me at full force. I shield Raina with my arms from the impact. The sky is full of screaming.

Something stops me within touching distance of the water. Energy flows into my body, like blood rushing to fill an open wound. My skin shimmers, full of potential. Every muscle throbs like I'm holding up the world. The force holding me up disappears, and I drop into the sea.

I tread water frantically, ignoring the shooting pain in my body. I try to keep as much of my torso out of the water as I can, the baby struggling for air. There is no one in the sky now. I grab the boat's mooring line and bring it to me slowly, feeling the slick rope under my hands. I feel the dirt under my fingernails and the water teeming all around me.

A jolt shoots up my arm, and I flinch, bracing it against my chest. I open my palm, and a small, fragile strand of seagrass begins to emerge from the lines in my skin. It winds its way down my wrist, wrapping it. The pain that has stayed with me since the cavern slowly ebbs away. I feel my flesh knitting, coral creeping over my bones to reset them. The fatigue that has dogged my steps feels distant now, not gone but smaller. Everything has changed. I've returned to myself. Broken but mending.

I pull myself onto the boat and check Raina. She's shimmering too, glowing with the incandescence dancing on my own skin. She burbles and reaches for me, freeing her arms from the sling. My dress is torn to bits and I move aside the fabric to bring her in contact with my skin. She latches on hungrily and feeds.

I marvel at my mending body, the slow resurrection of my power. I thought a binding was a permanent quelling of my ability, but the past few months have taught me that's not true. Not only could I harness the power of others, but now I am coming back to my old self. Adarna's death and the lightning striking my body has reawakened the magic in me. And not only me. I feel the energy of the others humming around me in the distance. Their confusion and curiosity. The gift used to show itself in its own time. But something changed when Adarna died. It meant to devour the world, but it opened it up. All those who were gifted have now been awakened, their potential fulfilled.

CHAPTER SIXTY-SEVEN

FINLYR

A DEEP SCRATCHING AT the door jolts me awake. I hadn't realised I'd fallen asleep in the armchair, and I have that horrible moment of not understanding where I am before I see Isagani in the chair next to me and feel deep relief. Narra gets up from her armchair, moving cautiously to the door.

'Who goes there?' she asks quietly.

A plaintive meow comes from the other side of the wood.

Ligaya cries out in relief. 'It's Sini.'

Narra cocks her head to one side, listening closely.

'What's wrong?' I ask, rising from my chair.

Narra says nothing but opens the door a sliver. The skinny black otter-cat slinks into the inn, dripping wet. He creates puddles on the wooden floor and shakes his fur until it stands on end.

'Looks like the storm's arrived,' Isagani says.

Sinigang pads into the room without a care in the world, leaving little wet paw prints in his wake. Narra chews her lip and watches as he brushes past her legs and into the parlour, beelining for the hearth. He tucks himself by the warm fire and begins to purr.

Isagani gets up from their chair and crouches by the otter-cat, making to pet him. He starts back, eyeing Isagani warily.

'What's wrong?' they ask. 'Is he hurt?'

'I don't know,' Ligaya says cautiously.

'Here,' Isagani proffers the half of the biscuit left on their saucer.

Sinigang approaches warily and sniffs the thing. Then he snatches it from Isagani's hand with his mouth and takes it back to the hearth, munching happily.

'Where's your sharp tongue?' I ask him, bending to stroke him.

The silence settles over all of us.

'Why isn't he saying anything?' Isagani asks, voice becoming more desperate.

'I don't think he can,' Ligaya says and then covers her mouth with her hand. 'I'm sorry,' she says, voice muffled.

'Is that true?' Isagani asks, their body deflating.

Narra sighs. 'Something has changed,' she says finally.

'He can't . . .' Isagani says, turning to Sinigang. They put their hand out and the otter-cat butts his head against it, trilling happily. Their voice trembles and they clear their throat. 'He can't be ordinary. He's magic; he'll always be magic.'

We look at Narra, begging her to say something. How do we answer? She looks so tired but gives Isagani a strained smile. Then her face becomes pained, and she clutches the armchair, doubling over. Ligaya is doing the same, having fallen to her knees. They are writhing in pain on the floor. And then they start to levitate, as if lifted by invisible strings, hair flowing and arms outstretched unnaturally. I fall out of my chair to see it. This is witchery gone wild. They press against the ceiling, as though something is pinning them in place. Their faces are blanched, and they scratch at their throats, turning a ghastly shade of purple.

'Fuck, what's happening to them?' I scramble up. 'They're dying!'

'What can we do?' Morna rushes up the stairs, desperately trying to grab at Ligaya's dress and bring her down.

The women let out a scream and gasp for air. They begin to glow, the same golden light that emanated from Hanan in the cave.

Actually glittering like the stars, glowing like the full moon. They shine from inside, gold and silver threads. I try to shield my eyes from it, when the wind is taken out of their sails and they drop like stones.

We all scream, rushing to break the fall. I roll onto my back, hoping I can cushion them with my bulk. They fall fast and then stop. Narra's face is inches from mine, and even she looks surprised. She drops the short distance, flopping onto my soft belly. The others are at the bottom of the stairs now, picking up Ligaya from the floor.

'Holy Aistra, what was that?'

Narra catches her breath, and then she makes haste into the kitchen. We all look at her quizzically. All apart from Ligaya.

When the hedge witch returns, she's carrying a potted plant. I recognise it as a propagated cutting of emerald vine. Ligaya's prized possession. It's withered and dried out, curling in on itself. A decaying world.

'Here,' she says, holding the pot out to Ligaya. The women hold the pot together, fingertips touching.

Slowly, painfully slowly, the plant comes back to life. It unbends, standing tall and proud. It's plump and green and verdant. The flowers bloom again, leaves no longer shrivelled, the fragrance filling the room.

'What in Paranish?' Morna whispers in awe. 'Is that the awakening you talked about, Narra?'

'It was a very rude awakening.' Ligaya smiles.

Sinigang meows, and we all turn to him. He makes a strange sound, like someone clearing their throat. And then he retches until a hairball comes out. He looks at it, disgusted, and then at me. There's something in his face, a knowing look, more like the old glint in his eye. He says nothing but pads away, seemingly unimpressed by the awakening that just took place before him.

CHAPTER SIXTY-EIGHT

RIS

I HAVE TO STOP myself from crying as we all sit by the fire, Biba and Salvacion wrapped in blankets.

'And he was so stubborn – as soon as he got an idea in his head, that was it.' Salvacion laughs.

I smile, my heart hurting from the memory but also from the squeal of laughter that comes from Biba.

'Bit of a family trait,' Kopiro says, affectionately, looking at me.

'I remember Larkin running frantically after Tricky,' Kopiro recalls. 'He'd accidentally let her out of the pen, and your father, Jon, was dying with laughter, watching him run around the farm.'

'He told me that's when he knew Larkin was family,' I say, and Kopiro squeezes my hand. 'My fathers were both already sick then. I think they wanted to know I'd have someone.'

'Mama.' Biba's wails cut through our conversation.

She's wheezing, choking sobs. They come on so suddenly I'm taken aback. I take her face in my hands and open her mouth, to see if there's something lodged there. She trembles, and then she's snatched out of my arms. We watch, stunned into silence, as she begins to float in mid-air. She looks confused and terrified, and I cannot reach her. We stand under her, watching her kick and suffocate.

'Why is she breathing like that?' I ask, desperately. We grasp each other, barely able to understand what we're seeing. We're all fixated on her. 'Biba, please, Biba!'

Her body is illuminated, and she thrashes and then falls. I scream, making to catch her. She stops abruptly in mid-air and then slowly floats into my arms. I squeeze her tight, holding her to my chest.

'Ris, you'll crush her,' Ryla says. 'Give her some air.'

They prise me away from Biba, and she breathes, ragged and deep. She sits up and stares at the hearth.

'Bright, bright,' she whispers.

The flames dance and flicker pale blue.

'What's she doing?' Salvacion asks, and I remember the fireplace at Narra's inn, the day we arrived. How Biba's confusion and fear had set the place ablaze for that one moment. I recall the strange afterglow surrounding Hanan, Sinigang, Biba, and Raina in the cavern.

'Magic,' I say quietly. 'Something's happening to her magic.'

A knock at the door. The door bulges on its hinges with the brute force. We all turn to each other.

'I'll handle this,' Salvacion says, shrugging on her tattered Seaguardian jacket and feeling for her weapon at her hip.

'Get under the bed and don't make a sound,' I whisper to Biba.

She's terrified, but she obeys. The others keep their weapons close by.

When I can no longer see her little feet sticking out under the bed, I give the signal.

Salvacion opens the door, and the Seaguardians come swarming in. 'What is the meaning of this?' she asks, sizing them up.

Fetch whines and scrambles to hide under the sofa.

The Seaguardians look at her dishevelled uniform and narrow their eyes. 'Did they do this to you?'

'No,' Salvacion insists. 'I was caught in the storm, and these fine folk took me in. They helped me.'

The leader of the Seaguardians sniffs. 'We have power of removal. All touched folk are to be taken at the queen's request.'

I start back. 'The queen? She's alive?'

The Seaguardian narrows his eyes at me, and I know I've fucked up.

'Thank Aistra. We heard there was an attempt on Our Majesty's life – horrible business,' Kopiro says, with a face that wouldn't melt butter. 'Have you found the culprits?'

He's the least intimidating of us, and he knows it, folding into himself to seem smaller, plastering on that winning smile.

'News travels fast, even in these backwaters,' the Seaguardian snorts. 'Your neighbours said they saw a shining light coming from this farmstead.'

Curse being in each other's pockets in a small community. Saving their own skin, happy to point the finger. They're doing what's best by them. But it takes a certain softness and shielding by privilege to think the Seaguardians have your best interests at heart.

'Shining light?' Salvacion asks. 'Perhaps they mistook the fire for something else?'

'I think we can tell the difference between firelight and something . . . unnatural,' one of the other Seaguardians spits.

'Look, if there is anything untoward happening here, I can deal with it,' Salvacion says, her tone commanding. She leans towards the Seaguardian who seems to be in charge. 'These are simple farming folk. Don't waste your time.'

The leading Seaguardian cocks his head, looking at the nest of blankets on the sofa and the Dodi doll. He raises an eyebrow.

'Now don't tell me this is yours.' He laughs, sneering at Salvacion.

His attention continues beyond to the other room. The door to the bedroom is ajar, and underneath pours out a light, too blue to be candlelight and pulsing strangely. We rush towards it, but we're powerless to stop the Seaguardians from entering the room and making towards the glow emanating from underneath the bed.

I throw myself in front of the lead Seaguardian, but he shoves me back onto the bed. He's on his knees, grabbing Biba forcefully by the ankle. She bucks and kicks and spits and bites like something rabid.

'Hold still, you witch,' he yells, defending himself from her attacks.

It's a free-for-all now. We try to waylay the other Seaguardians, to bring them down. We can't let them take Biba.

'Stop!' Biba yells, and a spark flies from her body to his. The Seaguardian seizes up, gripping his chest. He slackens, letting go, and tumbles to the floor.

'What in Paranish?' another Seaguardian rushes over to their leader, rolling him over. They listen for breathing and check his pulse. 'He's dead.'

We look at each other, and the air rushes out of the room. The Seaguardian lunges for Biba. 'She fucking killed him!'

The rest of them attack with fresh relish. They're no longer aiming to disarm us and take her. They are striking to kill.

We're a tangle of limbs. I grab flesh and wrench hard, careless of whether it's a friend or foe I'm hurting. All I know is I have to get to her. We're a sweaty tangle on the bed and floor. There's something wet seeping onto my stomach. I feel around for a wound, but it's not my blood.

Cutting through the chaos is an unsettling, eerie sound, repeated over and over.

'Vullis!' Hoarse and desperate wails.

Ryla's face is coated in grime and sweat. Their hands are shaking and there's blood on their tunic. They double over, a retch threatening their throat. Their expression shifts like a storm, whipping winds deciding their course.

Now I see him. Vullis's beard is matted with blood and his face is a pulp. It's a piece of fruit smashed against a rock. His body is bruised and broken, lying at horrible angles. Biba has her hands on his chest. Tiny fingers covered in blood and guts.

I grab a Seaguardian by the collar, lifting him bodily off the floor. I kick away the fireguard and throw him headfirst. He wails in pain, trying to crawl away. I have my boot on his back. He's going nowhere.

When he finally stops screaming, I see Ryla and Kopiro have taken care of the others. They've made less mess than I have, but it's been more personal, hands-on, throats choking the life out of them.

I rush over to Biba, who is still lying next to Vullis. She's wailing, streaks of blood in her hair and on her face.

The body stirs. It gasps and wheezes, bones cracking as its hands find purchase on the floor. Bruised knuckles, broken fingernails. It bends and crawls until it's on its knees. I look at Vullis, his blue eyes milky and unseeing. He's no longer my friend. This isn't Vullis, but the shell of him.

'Did it work?' Biba asks quietly, desperate hope on her lips. She stands next to him, reaching for his hand.

'Don't touch it – that's not Vullis!' I yell and she starts back.

Fetch emerges from under the sofa. He pads quietly over to the figure, sniffing curiously. He begins to whine.

'Fetch, come here, boy,' I say, trying to keep my voice steady.

The dog looks at me, confused, and cocks his head, ear flapping.

Vullis grabs Fetch by the scruff of his neck and raises the dog off the floor. We all start screaming, desperate to go to him but keeping a distance.

'Vullis!' Kopiro implores.

Those milky eyes again. They turn clear for a moment, back to Vullis's dark brown. There's warmth and life to his look. He opens his mouth to speak and then screams. Vullis falls to the floor with a sickening thud. No longer moving. Fetch lands on his feet with a yelp. I grab at the dog and check he's all right.

The corpse is on the floor, spurting blood from its belly. Everything is covered in dark viscera. I look at Biba.

'I couldn't do it,' she says. 'His soul wouldn't stay inside his body again.'

CHAPTER SIXTY-NINE

FINLYR

WE HAVE BEEN TALKING all night. More like arguing.

'We don't understand what any of it means. We don't know what's happening to you two.' Morna says. 'I think we need to let things blow over before we make any rash decisions.'

'I wish I'd taken more emerald vine before all this,' Ligaya frets. 'I didn't want to be greedy, but now it will all go to waste. Oh, that's a wicked thought, isn't it?'

'We have to find the others,' I insist. 'Hanan, Biba – they all had powers too.'

'Fuck the others,' Isagani says suddenly.

We all turn to them, our conversation dying down. Their face is red, angry blood vessels pulsing in their forehead.

'Why would you say that?' I ask, trying to quell my shock.

'We all need to look out for ourselves,' Isagani says, jutting out their chin.

'I know you're angry about what happened with Ris—'

'She said we were a family,' they interrupt, meeting my eyes. 'She's a liar!'

'What happened?' Ligaya asks, trying to comfort Isagani. They shrug her off.

'It's the same with everyone. They all leave or die.'

'Hey, don't talk like that,' I reprimand.

'Why not? It's true, isn't it?'

'We don't know what happened,' I say to Narra, Morna, and Ligaya. 'We all got separated in the chaos.'

Isagani digs their nails into the wooden arm of the chair, scratching. 'Hey!'

They look up at me, and I pull down my shirt, showing them the scar on my neck. 'You saved my life, I saved yours. We're keeping this score going, all right? We look out for each other.'

Ligaya nods, trying to smile, though her face is ashen with worry. 'In Lassren we have this saying, though I don't know how to say it perfectly in Nishian. But it's basically: tie your boat to mine, and altogether we will make a dock. Does that make sense?'

I nod, the old idiom coming back to me, letting the image wash over me. Then I stare at the kitchen witch. 'Boats.'

'Boats?' Ligaya asks, sipping her tea.

'You sailed from Lassair, right?'

'You know all this, Fin,' Morna says, exasperated.

'Do you still have the boat?'

'The boat?' Ligaya asks.

'Your boat, the one you sailed from Lassair.'

Ligaya nods. 'Yes. I haven't needed it since I realised the ferries would take me between the isles. But I still have it.'

'Where is it?' I stand up, rubbing my hands together.

'It's very small, a skiff really.'

'Yes, but where is it?'

'What are you planning on doing, Fin?' Narra takes me stiffly by the arm. 'First sign of trouble and you're making an escape plan, leaving us to pick up the pieces.'

'I'm not abandoning you,' I say firmly, looking Narra deep in the eyes. 'I swear on my honour.'

She gives me a withering stare.

'All right. I swear on the kid's honour.'

Isagani furrows their brow.

'The other lands don't know what's happening here,' Ligaya says slowly.

'We have to call for aid,' Morna adds.

'I'm asking you all to join me,' I say. 'No one gets left behind, not if I can help it.'

Isagani looks at me, worrying their bottom lip.

I turn to the kitchen witch and place my hands on her shoulders. 'Would you be willing to do this, Ligaya?'

'Do what?' she says, looking alarmed.

'Speak for us?'

'What do you mean?' she asks.

'Advocate. Be our ambassador.'

'Do you think they would listen to me?' She blanches. 'I'm nobody.'

'You're a witness,' Morna says. 'We all are.'

'But will the queen listen to the Lassairian council?' Narra asks, brooding. 'If there even is a queen.'

'I don't know, Fin,' Ligaya says slowly, backing away. The candlelight flickers, and the storm rages outside, threatening against the walls of the inn and Ligaya's protective circle. 'I'm just one person. What if they don't listen to me?'

'You're our best hope. You can speak to them, one Lassairian to another.'

'An alliance could be mutually beneficial,' Morna muses. 'It's not so wild. They might consider it.'

Narra paces the parlour, the floorboards creaking under our weight as we shift in our chairs. The rain bashes against the windows, heightening my anxiety as I try to turn it over in my mind. Sinigang slinks around my legs, having awoken from his nap. I scritch his chin and sigh.

'What do you think we should do?' I ask him.

He makes a noise. It sounds like something between a sneeze and the word 'leave'.

I cock my head to the side and stare at him. 'Did you—'

Isagani looks up, as though I've interrupted their thoughts. 'Are you talking to me?'

I look at Sinigang, then at the others, all embroiled in their own minds.

'Nothing,' I say, continuing to stroke the otter-cat.

'I don't want to leave Narra alone,' Ligaya says determinedly.

'Who said anything about leaving me alone?' Narra smiles.

Everyone looks at each other. 'Will you come with us?' I ask her.

'No such thing as a retired smuggler, right?' Narra smiles, a glint in her eye.

'Well, what are we waiting for?' I ask.

'Hold steady, Fin,' Narra urges. 'We have to ready ourselves and gather supplies. We'll need to figure out what's going on out there. Could be Seaguardians patrolling.'

'And we have to wait for the storm to die down,' Ligaya says. 'The cave will be flooded right now.'

'You're not talking about the spit, are you?'

Ligaya looks at Morna. 'I don't know. What is that?'

'There's a desolate spit of rock along the east. One of many caves I became acquainted with around the coast through my years as a smuggler.'

Ligaya shakes her head. 'I don't know; it could be.'

These secret places are sheltered by rocks, reachable only by those who know where to find them. There's always risk of them flooding or collapsing, eroded by the waves over the years. We have to hope the skiff was tied up with enough rope and that the sea level hasn't risen enough to smash it to bits against the roof of the cave.

'It feels like we're abandoning our home,' Morna says, glassy-eyed.

'No,' Isagani protests. 'We're not abandoning it.'

I sigh. 'We have to hope there's enough left of it to save when we return.'

CHAPTER SEVENTY

HANAN

As I row, I feel my wet clothing sticking to me, but I don't feel cold. The sun is high in the sky now, beating down on me. The light is like blades across my body – a startling, aching sensation. I listen to my breathing, fierce and confident. I take a break, dipping one of my hands into the water. It is teeming with life, everything connected to my own body. It's overwhelming, the energy of things long dormant moving beneath the surface. Creatures that lived in the darkness but now must come to the light to survive. I feel their confusion, their desperation, their hunger. I take my hand out and let the wind tickle my wet skin. The silence in the aftershock is glorious. It's empty and hollow and full of potential.

There's so much unknown. But I know what would have happened if I had succumbed. If I'd let the royals regain their control over Adarna. I had to make a choice, for all our sakes. No one is pure enough to wield such power. Perhaps we have been doomed for centuries, and this is nature's rebellion writ large. We're so small compared to it all, but we persist – hopeful fools trying to keep back the tide.

My theories and schemes come together as I row, relishing this time to reflect instead of the mindless panic of running. I remember Priestess Sinaya's sacrifice and wonder if she found peace. Whether part of her soul is trapped in that tome, or in the cave, or if any part of her found its way to the Tree of Life. Not that such a final resting place will remain that way for long, under the queen's plan. We have such small hopes for our lives, and even those get shattered by the fates.

I need help. I can't do this alone, and who knows where the others are, if they're still safe or even alive. I remember Sinaya saying she sought aid once she fled the Bastion. From those who practised necromancy, or the 'forbidden art' as she called it. I still know so little about the worlds outside Paranish, but I don't remember any place such as that. Not that they would freely admit to such practises necessarily.

My hand still stings, seawater getting into the wound where I cut myself on the arrow. Although my body is beginning to heal, it is a slow and painful process. I stare at the injury and think of the sharp force of the stone talisman. Like destroying like. I mourn for Adarna. The death of every living creature is always a loss for us all.

Then I look up, slow realisation dawning on me as I try to keep hold of the thread in my mind. Adarna's method of killing was through stone, and that was its own weakness. Perhaps there was some link between that and the aid Priestess Sinaya sought. I read an account in the Bastion library I considered apocryphal about the stone that built the Temple of Aistra. It supposedly came from a unique place. I reach around in my memory, trying to recall the name, to trace the map in my mind's eye. Orin. The place was called Orin.

I turn towards the Bastion for one last look. The great fortress has broken, slabs of stone crumbled and displaced, and the flag of the royal sigil is burning, smoke plumes drifting across Paranish. I had looked up at it from my knees at the Temple of Aistra and wondered what secrets it held. Now I know. It is built on the labour and lives of its people. The queen no longer has Adarna, her heart's desire. But she will drain every single life-giving force on Paranish if she can. There will be no peace, no balance in Life, no sanctity in Death while the Bastion exists.

I look at Raina, who stares at me while chewing on her bottom lip, and kiss her forehead. 'You're the lucky one, Princess. Let's see if I can't make something good out of you.'

Someone as young as Raina is clay, shaped by her memories and experiences, still flexible and yet to be kilned. Perhaps I can turn the salt to sweet.

Count every grain of your rice mountain, Your Grace, and watch it rot. We'll be coming back for Paranish. And when we do, I hope you see us coming from the prison of your own making.

Acknowledgements

Thanks to everyone who's ever taken the time to read my work, and especially you dear reader, if you've chosen to set sail with *Saltswept*. I had so much fun writing it and I hope you enjoy the ride. In this book I've stirred in my favourite things from fantasy I love as well as things I wanted to see when I was devouring novels as a child.

Thanks to my agent Robbie for encouraging this romp of a novel from its tempest of a first draft and for keeping me right on all things nautical and the stages of childhood development. To Calah, for her organisation, editorial vision, and unwavering support - this book really shines because of you. To Delayna, for being a wonderful editorial co-parent to this book and for fully letting me unleash my dark side.

To Natalie Chen and Jason Lyon for designing and illustrating the most beautiful cover, and Charis Loke for such thoughtful and evocative cartography - thank you for bringing Paranish to life with such spectacular visuals. And to the rest of the team at Hodderscape for being absolute stars every step of the way: Marketing and Audio editor - Robyn Bowler, Senior Audio editor - Carrie Hutchinson, Production Controller - Katy Aries, Publicist - George Biggs, Proofreader - Ruth Lilly, Copyeditor - Helena Newton, Desk editor - Katy Archer.

To the ultimate hype team: Hannah, Lyndsey, Annabel, and River, for understanding me completely and believing in this book from the very beginning. To Eris Young, Authenticity Editor extraordinaire! To the Witchual: Bex, Kirstyn, and Jack for deep sea horror chats, movie nights, and being absolutely feral together. To everyone in the Scream Team and Funghouls for sharing frustrations and celebrations so transparently and gracefully. To all my lovely pals over the years, for all your support, words of encouragement, and spaces to vent. Particularly the non-writers in my life who keep me grounded.

For everyone in the industry who has been so generous with their time, words of support, and gems of advice, particularly Rita, Alice, Nadine, Heather, and El. Thank you to everyone who has said a kind word about this novel, particularly the authors who made time to read early versions and provide blurb quotes. Also to the folks involved in festivals, publishers, bookshops, magazines and more who have supported my work and created opportunities including: AIR Literature Writing Residency at Konstkollektivet for the enthusiasm, time, and space to edit; Scottish BPOC Writers Network for all the amazing work you do and creators you nourish; Cymera Festival for creating and platforming such a vibrant SFFH community. To ESFF and the entire Scottish literary community: what a joy to be part of such a supportive space.

To my parents and in-laws for always championing and reading my work, even when it's super weird and NSFW. For my ancestors who were sharp-tongued island-dwellers, I wish I could have known all your stories.

And finally to Craig, for everything. The anchor to my wild ship. Someone who will spend hours on the phone unraveling plot knots with you, and enthusiastically pitch your books at dance parties and cycle meet-ups. No one else I'd rather do laundry and taxes with.

ABOUT THE AUTHOR

Katalina Watt is an Edinburgh-based author of speculative fiction. They were selected for a 2025 Literature Matters Award from Royal Society of Literature, AIR Literature UNESCO 2024 Gothenburg Writer in Residence, and 2023 Hugo Award Finalist for Best Semiprozine as founding Audio Director for khōréō. *Saltswept* is their debut novel.

HODDERSCAPE

WANT MORE HODDERSCAPE? JOIN US!

Sign up to our mailing list to get exclusive early sneak peeks and offers:

Follow us on our social channels:
@hodderscape

Buy our books, find out more, and discover exclusive content:
www.hodderscape.co.uk